Don't Tell Zina

Cover Art: Giovanni Pitrolo Gentile

Audrey & Paul

To my family
And future family

PART 1

He who leaves succeeds. Achieving my dream of a better life requires forward-moving action, as well as leaving behind the past. The trouble is, the past is always one step behind, stalking like a shadow.

~Domenico Brex (or Bregas or Brechisci or Brecese)

~ENTRY #1~

9/2/1929: Labor Day

How does a girl start something like this? I've been staring at you for the past ten minutes – both of us blank.

I guess I'll just write whatever is on my mind. Unfortunately for you, you're held captive as my audience. Unfortunately for me, you can't communicate back. Hopefully, the idea that you might be listening will be enough for me. And no, I don't always have conversations with inanimate objects.

Of course, Duey is excluded. He is very animated. But being a kitten does hamper his ability to provide me with some answers. (He does what he can, so I forgive his meager vocabulary.)

Meet Duey. He just set his paw here to shake your hand, but you don't have hands so never mind.

Ah! I wish I could just talk to you – and you could answer. I hate that I never have someone to talk with when I really need to.

Have you ever been up at night with some soul-searching,

spirit-wrenching thoughts, but there's nobody around to talk to, and of course you can't possibly leave your house because it's so late? I know you haven't. You are a book, I realize that.

And don't even suggest that I could pick up the phone to call Nan, or Gracie, or even Frank because – first and foremost – it will ring. Our parents don't appreciate any calls after 7pm, and when it's a call for one of us 'kids,' privacy is meaningless. Which brings me to the second point about using the phone, that we never really know who might be listening. Nan and I had that issue once with her little sister, and we've been much more cautious ever since.

Are you wondering what is weighing so heavily on my mind? I am getting to it. It's funny, just writing to you is making me feel a little bit better.

I hope I don't sound down and depressed. I'm not, I am just torn. On the one hand, I'm grateful for you, but on the other hand, I received you because I am off to be on my own and even more lonely in the days to come. I'm sorry, when I am reminded of that, I struggle to see the bright side of this whole unfair situation. But you are such a thoughtful gift, and you deserve better attention, so I will attempt to adjust my mindset and try some gratitude instead.

Nan is so generous. I can't believe she saved enough money to buy you for me. She knows I'm a little more practical than she is, so a journal really is a perfect gift; not to mention how sweet she is to want to still be there for me, especially since we won't be seeing each other as much this school year.

She said, 'Here Zina, you can confide in this book like a dear friend until we can talk again.'

So that's what I will call you! My dear friend. You are not quite a diary, and you are more than a journal. You are a confidant. Oh, it does make me feel better to know that I have you, my dear friend.

Ok, moving on then. We now know who you are and why I am grateful to have you. So here are some facts about me since I just started babbling and didn't properly introduce myself.

My name is Vincenza Rose Sagone. I was named Vincenza for my father's mother, Vincenzia, and Rose for my mother. My cousins call me Zina. I've been told that Frank gave me that name. His mother, my aunt Maria, said that when we were very little, he called me Vincenza and it just came out Zia. That was silly, since zia means "aunt" in Sicilian. Zina just came to be after that. I secretly like to think that at two years old Frank planned for us to be married someday and if I were Vincenza Vincenti I might not like it. So, he was smart to re-name me early in life so it would stick. He is always thinking ahead, not that we could really marry, but we can talk about that another time; it's complicated.

What else? I'm an only child, but I have lots of cousins. I don't see them as often as I'd sometimes like.

Here is a sketch that might help you, my dear friend, since you don't know everyone as well as I do – well not yet!

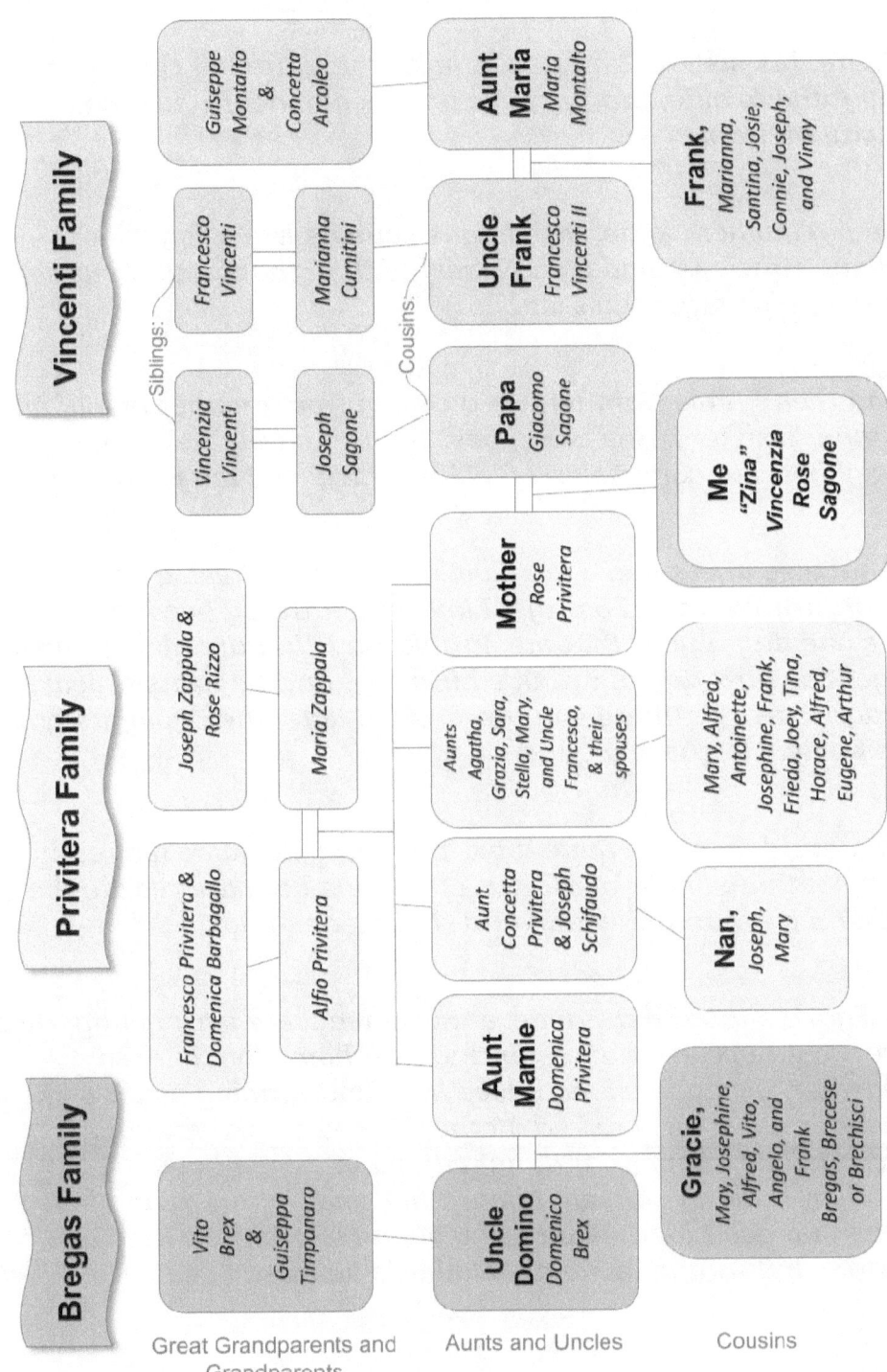

Vincenti Family

Guiseppe Montalto & Concetta Arcoleo

Francesco Vincenti

Marianna Cumitini

Siblings:

Vincenzia Vincenti

Joseph Sagone

Cousins:

Aunt Maria *Maria Montalto*

Uncle Frank *Francesco Vincenti II*

Papa *Giacomo Sagone*

Frank, *Marianna, Santina, Josie, Connie, Joseph, and Vinny*

Me "Zina" Vincenzia Rose Sagone

Privitera Family

Joseph Zappala & Rose Rizzo

Maria Zappala

Francesco Privitera & Domenica Barbagallo

Alfio Privitera

Mother *Rose Privitera*

Aunts Agatha, Grazia, Sara, Stella, Mary, and Uncle Francesco, & their spouses

Aunt Concetta Privitera & Joseph Schifaudo

Aunt Mamie *Domenica Privitera*

Mary, Alfred, Antoinette, Josephine, Frank, Frieda, Joey, Tina, Horace, Alfred, Eugene, Arthur

Nan, *Joseph, Mary*

Bregas Family

Vito Brex & Guiseppa Timpanaro

Uncle Domino *Domenico Brex*

Gracie, *May, Josephine, Alfred, Vito, Angelo, and Frank Bregas, Brecese or Brechisci*

Great Grandparents and Grandparents

Aunts and Uncles

Cousins

Frank, his sisters, and two little brothers are my cousins on my father's side, but they live in Mineola, nearly two hours away by train.

On my mother's side, my Bregas cousins live a few blocks away. Gracie is who I am closest with in that family, but she is a little younger than me.

And then I have Nan, who is a cousin from another one of my mother's sisters. She is my best friend and my next-door neighbor; but sometimes I feel like she is still too far away.

What else about me? I am eleven; I will turn twelve on February 24th, in 175 days. I love my birthday because it is the one day a year that me, Frank, and Nan are all the same age. The next day is Frank's birthday, and he turns a year older. Nan's birthday is in April, so at least the two of us have some time to share an age.

Nan and I do share quite a bit. It's funny because we really are not that similar at all, but I think we both appreciate the other's view and honesty, and that means a lot.

We have shared a dream ever since we were very young, that we would become nurses and open a home for children together, because we both love kids and nursing sounds like a wonderful career. I asked Mother if I could take first aid classes last summer and, as with most things I ask my mother, it didn't go well. I heard her and Papa arguing how it wasn't a good idea – that I wasn't cut out for that kind of work – but that was mostly Mother's opinion.

And now, (I am convinced) as the result of that discussion, I'm starting tomorrow in the eighth grade at – oh, this new all-girls school. The Brooklyn Girls' Continuation School.

Now comes a stomachache. Again. The whole situation is unfair. I enjoyed going to David A. Boody Junior High School with my cousins, and it is just a few blocks away, instead of an hour away by train! I wish I could decide for myself what to study and set the direction for my own life. But Mother made me change schools so I can be an interpreter instead of having dreams with Nan.

Why Mother thinks being an interpreter is more important than being a nurse I have no idea. And why would I need to study Italian anyway? Everyone I know speaks an Italian and Sicilian mix; my parents and aunts and uncles lived in Sicily and will only speak Sicilian, even though we live in New York.

Does that make sense to you, my dear friend? Right, I knew you would agree, it doesn't. I must sit through boring lessons in Italian, even though I am fluent. Now, if we traveled often, I could see this as a useful skill, but we don't. I've never even been to Sicily. It had to be a great place; it's all they ever talk about. The old world, new world; the old ways and new ways. Their opinion is that everything old is gold and everything new is tarnished. I wonder why they left if they loved it so much.

I'm going to imagine that I'm traveling to Sicily tomorrow instead of to Schermerhorn Street. Such a non-Italian street name for where I will learn to "interpret" Italian, don't you think so too?

And if I need to study Italian, why can't my parents learn English? And they've been here for almost thirty years and still won't learn? They are just so set in their ways. Sometimes I wish I could go back in time. I would talk to my parents, and even my aunts and uncles, and tell them to learn English if they go to America. If not, just stay in Sicily!

I think this is the root of most of my problems, my dear friend, and you have helped me to see it. I am caught somewhere in the middle of old Sicily and young New York. My family brought with them their old ways and habits, packed tightly in whatever tiny suitcase they carried with them off the ship; and I was born into wide-open possibilities with new ideas and dreams of living in a much different world. Only they don't seem to recognize that what they brought is worn and ragged now, metaphorically speaking of course. If we were really talking about fashion, Nan would have a fit! Could you imagine if they wore those...

Oh! I'm sorry, I was interrupted. Papa told me I had a phone call, and would you believe it, it was Frank! He is so thoughtful to call and wish me well tomorrow. He said all I need to do is smile, be myself, and the girls will befriend me; isn't he sweet? I don't think he knows just how much that was exactly what I needed to hear, but he should have just ended on that note. Instead, he awkwardly changed the subject and lost me a little, but that's typical of Frank.

I haven't told you that much about him yet, so here's one quick trait: he has a very unique way of looking at things, so he is always coming up with topics nobody else thinks about. So, on the phone call, he told me another one of his little mind puzzles (that's what Nan and I call them. Frank is good at them. But let me clarify, it's not a real puzzle, but it does *effectively distract me while I try to figure it out.)*

So, after I said, 'I don't know why I have to study Italian anyway, I am Sicilian.' He started talking about trees. Trees! Right, I didn't see a connection either.

He said something that sounded like it was from some poetry or biology book, or a biology book written as poetry, if there is such a thing. He said, "A seed will never see the tree it is becoming while it is growing in the ground. Neither can see where it came from or what it will become, but they each just know the other existed because they themselves exist."

Yes, that's Frank! So, not helpful as far as advice goes – I'm not sure how "trees and seeds" will fit into my journey tomorrow but I'm sure I will see trees during the train ride. Maybe I will figure it out then.

Well, it's time I get some sleep, my dear friend. Thank you for listening, we can continue our "conversation" soon. I promise to write here often, and I hope you will promise to listen and help whenever you can. You might think I'm crazy, but I just might enjoy this. I like finally having someone to share my thoughts with. I look forward to our next discussion. Maybe we can "talk" more about Frank!

Wish me luck tomorrow,

~Zina

CHAPTER 1

Zina

Tuesday, September 3, 1929

Quietly stepping onto her front porch, Zina looked toward the house next door to see if her cousin was awake yet.

She was relieved when Nan greeted her, excitedly waving while almost losing her grip on the corners of the quilt she wrapped herself in to block the cool morning air. She appeared to have just left her bed, but Zina knew her cousin well enough to know she would be fully dressed and ready underneath.

"Good morning, world traveler!" Nan shouted.

Zina hid her smile, lowering her head and shaking it at the reference. It was impossible for Nan to know what she wrote last night about visiting Sicily, yet, somehow, Nan knew.

"Are you ready for your first big adventure?" Nan called out again from her porch, the mirror image of Zina's.

Zina couldn't find her voice, not yet. She felt a soft purr circling her white stockings and shiny black Mary Janes. She knelt to pick up her calico kitten and gave him a hug of gratitude for his thoughtfulness in knowing she needed a small hug. Wondering how he got out of the house, she turned and saw the outline of her mother peering through the cracked-open front door, silhouetted against the dim foyer light.

"I wish I didn't have to go, Duey." Zina whispered and hoped her mother heard her too.

Nan noticed Zina's less-than-enthusiastic mood and began to walk over. The girls often met each other halfway on the stepping stones laid between their houses. Being that they lived next door on Lloyd Court, they never had to go far to visit their best friend, neighbor, cousin; those lines were blurred in their world.

The girls greeted each other with a hug. Nan unwrapped her blanket to show Zina her first day of school outfit. She pointed out all the details: how the new tortoise hair combs Zina bought her coordinated with her hair scarf and a ribbon she pinned to her shirtwaist.

Zina knew Nan would like the combs she bought her and that she would be excited to show off her outfit. Nan prided herself in knowing just enough about the latest fashion to find pieces to polish off any ensemble. Spending money on new things was frivolous, both girls agreed, but Nan decided she could look as though she spends money, just by being creative. Their parents would bring home bags of scraps from their tailoring jobs that were perfect for remaking finishing touches. Zina just didn't see the point the way Nan did. Zina preferred a more practical style. Nan knew that, hence the gift of the book.

Zina cleared her throat to loosen its tightness before attempting any conversation. "Nan, you look lovely on this first day of school, even with your crazy quilt as a shawl." Zina teased with a small smile.

Nan began to reciprocate a review of Zina's outfit but paused slightly.

Feeling self-conscious, Zina ran her hands over the arms of her coat thinking it might be too shabby and removed a few stray Duey hairs. She second-guessed her decision to wear her pale blue dress which was beginning to feel much too unceremonious. She probably should have taken Nan's offer of fashion advice when she was planning what she'd wear, but she did not want to set a precedent she couldn't keep up with on her own.

"And you, my dear, always look lovely. Just be yourself and everyone will love you as I do." Nan smiled warmly and patted Zina's dark brown wool coat with a briefly released hand and gave her a kiss on the cheek.

Be myself, that is a very common sentiment, Zina thought. *First Frank, now Nan. Will people really like me for me?*

"Vincenza!" Zina's mother's voice interrupted the girls' fashion assessments.

Nan waved a quick goodbye and retreated to her own porch. She didn't have to leave for her school for another hour even though she was fully ready. Boody was just a few blocks away, but Zina's new school would take an hour by bus and train.

Zina turned toward her mother who was again peering through the slightly opened front door, and she headed up the steps. "Yes, Mother?"

"Vincenza, what are you doing with that coat on and holding that darn cat? Put him in your room with your door closed and come back down for this jacket. Your Aunt Mamie mended it for you."

Zina was excited about the prospect of any new-to-her garment, but a jacket! She settled Duey quickly and gladly handed her mother the dowdy wool coat in exchange for a light navy parka. Zina was all smiles, but her mother frowned.

"I only allowed it because it doesn't fit anyone else right now. In the spring, you'll have to give it back, I'm sure it will fit Gracie then."

"That's fine, Mother, I am happy to have it."

"And be sure to thank Aunt Mamie, she said she took a lot of care with this hem for you."

Zina started to twirl with appreciation but stopped short, deciding to save her enthusiasm for Nan and Gracie. Her mother scoffed while disappearing into the house once again, while at the same time, her papa exited.

He cleared his throat. "Hurry now, Zina dear. Oh, you look very nice." He smiled with adoration at his daughter. Her near-black wavy hair was smooth and shiny and done up neatly with a light blue ribbon. She looked at him with her light brown eyes and dark lashes, smiling back.

"Thank you, Papa."

"Now, it is a long train ride, your uncle Domenico is on his way."

"Uncle Domino? Wait, Papa, aren't you coming with me on the train?"

"No, I'm sorry Zina. Uncle *Do-men-ic-o* said he was already heading uptown this morning, so it made more sense for him to accompany you." He gently but deliberately corrected Zina's name for her uncle.

"Papa, why do I have to go with Uncle Domino? He doesn't like me. Can't you come with me?"

"Shush, no, it is decided. Your uncle is just a quiet man, and he is fond of you my dear, of course he is. He will go with you on the train on your first day and help you know where to go. Pay attention, and don't make him wait. I see him walking down the court now."

Zina settled her nerves by turning her attention back to the jacket. She smoothed it and adjusted the belt at her waist. She grabbed her book bag and readied herself.

"*Ciao*, Giacomo, Zina." Her uncle called as he approached, and she and her papa went to greet him. Her papa held out his hand to shake, then pulled her uncle in for hugging and shoulder slapping. "*Buon giorno* Domenico. She is ready now." Her papa turned to her. "*Ciao,* Zina, you will have a great first day."

Zina stood with her uncle as she watched her papa return to their house. The glow of Nan's bedroom window next door caught her eye, with a flicker that was Nan, twirling in front of her mirror and then disappearing, probably to revisit her closet to try other looks.

Zina sighed and walked with her uncle toward the bus stop. In the early morning light, she had the impression that they could be mistaken for two schoolchildren. He was short, close to her height. Zina snuck a glance at him, thinking, *the only thing that makes him look like a grown man is all that hair*.

Her uncle Domenico was the hairiest man she knew. He had hair on his neck, knuckles, and one arm – dark, thick, unruly hair. His other arm was bald with a white and pink scar – which she never thought to ask him about. The hair on his head was the only place where all that hair was thinning. He had straight-set eyebrows with only a small division of space between them and pale blue eyes. When you combined all that with his mustache, most of his face was concealed.

They walked the next few minutes to the bus stop in silence. Then they sat for the next fifteen minutes on the bus to the Kings Highway station in quiet, heavy thought. The silent twenty-five-minute transit ride to Atlantic Avenue station became torturous for Zina. They arrived at the train and Zina quietly moaned. The trip was not yet done.

Zina was not a stranger to loneliness; however, it was worse to be in the company of someone and still be lonely. And bored. Her mind wandered back to her new book, and she wished she had its companionship for the ride.

Maybe I'll have to bring it along tomorrow, she considered, as she remembered writing about old Sicily and young New York. That gave her an idea.

"Why did you come to America, Uncle Domino?" Zina decided to be bold, just ask. She even thought she'd make it easy on him and ask in Sicilian. *What was wrong with bringing it up? What is the worst he can do? Say nothing during the entire train ride? Well, that's likely anyway so there is no risk.*

"Why do you still call me Uncle Domino, you know how to say it. How old are you now?"

"I'm eleven, *Uncle Domino.*" Zina smiled at getting him to react. She liked the nickname; she liked being the only one who called him that. She really didn't mind his quiet nature; it was nice sometimes to fill in the blanks of his life with her imagination. But not today. She needed to replace her brimming anxiety about this new school with some distracting conversation.

"You changed the subject. I really want to know. What made you decide to leave Sicily and come to New York?"

"He who leaves, succeeds. See, we succeed in America." Her uncle stated with finality. His ending to Zina's conversation turned into more quiet minutes.

She thought about what she knew so far. Once she worked out the math in her head she decided to try again. "Papa said you were the first of our family to come to America. You lived here alone for two years before your brother came, and that was even nine years before the Priviteras came and you got married to Aunt Mamie. You must have been lonely, since you-"

"Zina. That was thirty years ago. Now, we have jobs, a nice house, and a nice life. Peace here, nice neighborhood, good families. We are very blessed. We came to New York for a better life, and we found paradise. There is no more to talk about."

"But you usually talk about Sicily like you miss it; everybody does. Why did all of you leave if you loved it there so much?"

"Oh, Sicily, we love our homeland, yes. The memory of the rich soil, beautiful landscape, delicious smelling foods, none of that is the same here, we miss that, yes. Do we miss the rest? No."

"What do you mean? The rest? The rest of what?"

"Ah, Zina, a young girl in this great country does not need to be concerned with hardships of the past; let's just leave it at that." He stared at her a few moments more, perhaps considering saying something else but changing his mind.

What did he mean by that? What hardships? She wondered.

They arrived at the train, found their seats and their own quiet solitude again, listening to the tracks and their own thoughts.

Zina looked out the slightly soot-covered window. As the train accelerated, she imagined all of the vibrantly colored trees slowly gaining speed to run ahead of them. Zina thought about what Frank said. *I wonder what he would say now about these "traveling" trees. Probably something like, "the seed doesn't see the tree, especially when it's moving so fast, heading somewhere new."* The idea that one couldn't see the other now made her sad and even more lonely.

Zina hoped her uncle would share something about himself, but he wouldn't open up. She needed to know how he handled coming to America without knowing anybody. *I know nobody at my new school. I'm just like Uncle Domino; but he was so brave. He probably never had second thoughts or anxiety like I feel now. He who leaves, succeeds? I wish I had his confidence.*

Her uncle stared out the window of the train watching the transition from trees to the city — a new landscape of people bustling and buildings looming.

Zina watched him. *I wonder what he thinks about when he sees New York and remembers Sicily. What would an Italian countryside look like?*

Only a few more minutes to the station, and they passed Prospect Park. It was open, natural, and multicolored like confetti as autumn was just getting started.

Would Sicily look like this? Zina wondered.

Her uncle finally spoke in a low whisper, but Zina couldn't make it out except for a few words. As if he were in a trance, he stared out the train window and mumbled something about Regalbuto and everything changing.

Zina imagined what he was seeing. *What is the difference between New York and, where did he say? Regalbuto? Does Uncle Domino wish he was being whisked away back to his hometown in Sicily right now?*

Zina hoped for one last hint at what he might be thinking about in the minutes before the train stopped. She needed all the strength of her imagination to distract herself from what was coming next: being a stranger in a new, strange place.

As she took a deep breath to calm her nerves, she didn't notice the small beads of sweat dampening her uncle's hairy forehead.

He who leaves succeeds.

CHAPTER 2

Domenico, 1895

May, Before Sunrise
Regalbuto, Sicily

*T*ry *not to look back.*

No, don't look back. Breathe.

He shook his head; refocused his thoughts.

Everything will change this morning. This is it. Finally, the day to leave. Take a deep breath and move forward. And move quickly. Head east toward Mount Etna. Once you pass her on the southern side, catch the train to head north to the port. Once on the mainland, head toward Napoli and get onboard a ship.

You must go, Domenico. His mother's voice, begging him to leave, echoed in his head. He imagined her stating it with more urgency now.

I must go. This will work. Don't look back.

He rushed down the path, refraining from swatting the catalpa seed pods and kicking the fallen chestnut burrs as he would habitually do on this route. Each morning when he went to his meager employment, this all-too-familiar walk reminded him of a reality he didn't choose – putting all his effort into working the land he loved but could no longer call his own.

The greens and browns of the landscape blurred gray in the dim morning light as he swiftly ducked and quietly weaved through the tall grasses. He turned off the road and headed downhill on the path, with the idea that staying off the border road may keep the neighbors and their dogs from noticing his presence. No longer able to fight the urge to look back, he glanced, anxiously. All was still, no sign of any followers.

Breathe.

He stopped where the bushes and trees were thick enough for him to stay hidden and caught his breath. He hoped it was a safe distance. He noticed he had reached the farthest point – where his father's claim to this property ended eight years ago.

As he was growing up, Domenico dreamed it would be his one day, but his father lost his grip on managing it before he lost his life. Domenico aspired to redeem the land but quickly found out just what he was up against. The reputation the townspeople gave his father was held onto with an iron grip. They still believed the terrible rumor that cursed his name and extended it to Domenico. The only one who didn't believe the curse was his mother's new husband, but probably because he brought his own brand of torment.

Domenico listened again for something and hoped not to hear it. He held his breath to quiet his heavy breathing. His thudding heart echoed in his ears, muffled by his already sweaty scarves and coat collars, all of which would likely make it hard to hear approaching footsteps. He thought he'd move faster without a bag but didn't consider the downside of wearing everything at once.

He exhaled, taking one last look at his family's home before he left it, forever. It looked so lonely up on the hill, silhouetted by the peeking sun. The missing terracotta tiles and sagging porch boards gazed back at him like a reflection. He lived in scarcity; downcast and despised, his father lost face in his hometown as easily as the rotten porch roof crumbled. He looked down the road at the homes closer to the town center and was reminded again – the contrast. The esteemed displayed their pride just a few minutes' walk from his house, with fresh paint and healthy planters. But he knew from recent experiences that impressions couldn't be trusted.

He turned the corner and climbed the overgrown slope up to the road. The dawn was still heavy, and the rest of Regalbuto was still asleep. He quietly made his way through the plaza, which in the low light was eerily still, like a body of water – where the lampposts were swamp trees, and the benches were logs intermittently breaking the surface.

He bounded up to the topmost step of the church he had known his whole life, Chiesa Madre di San Basilio. He promised his mother he would attend one last time before leaving, but he couldn't bring himself to. He put his hand on the heavily carved wood door, hoping through his touch he could absorb a blessing for the journey. He hoped it would be enough.

After that quick but reverent pause, he descended, retreating into the shadows and cutting through the town to the valley on the other side.

He who leaves succeeds. I must go. This will work.

ॐ

The dawning sun emerged enough for his route to be more easily visible, and he could see the dirt path lined by the tall grasses. To his left, a lemon grove, and to his right, an artichoke farm. The walk began to feel more like a normal errand, and Domenico relaxed a little now that he was past the town. He absentmindedly removed the flat, gray wool coppola that once belonged to his father and ran his fingers through his dark brown hair which was beginning to be too long. He had no time for a barber visit to improve his appearance: that would have caused a certain person to become suspicious. Remembering again that he could be followed spurred him to take a deep breath and refocus on his steps ahead.

The profile of the great Mount Etna in the far distance was visible: a beacon, a compass, a source of comfort and fear his whole life. Appearing now as an innocent mountain on the horizon partially camouflaged by clouds, her potential power was never truly hidden.

Mount Etna could be volatile, not unlike the life he was leaving. Within his home an unpredictable threat of destruction was always looming – and not just from the grumblings of the volcano.

He sighed, feeling overwhelmed. "How many days have I spent waiting to make this trek, staring at the volcano and thinking about what lies beyond it? And now, each step I take doesn't feel as though I'm getting any closer. Will I ever get past it?" The distance to the great mountain was only a tiny fraction of the entire journey.

A bright, ominous glow began to emerge at Etna's topmost tip. Domenico hesitated, then frowned. It was just the sun rising. He was used to the possibility of eruption threats, but he felt a pang of sadness that he wouldn't be around anymore to diminish Mother Etna's moods to reassure his eleven-year-old brother.

Angelo.

Domenico turned away quickly to look back home. For a second he forgot that his little brother wouldn't be tagging behind. Toward the west, all that accompanied him were smears on the dirt path from the shuffle of his boots. He blinked away the dust before it dampened around his eyes, refocused, and retrieved his bearings not only in physical location but in spirit. It was too soon to begin missing his brother.

ℰᘓᘔ

I must go. It will work. He who leaves succeeds.

He walked for about two hours, muttering a mixture of mantras that had a calming effect. He reached what he thought was the Fiume Simento and took the opportunity to drink and refresh his face.

But there, kneeling at the narrow river, Domenico was reminded of another small stream, the one back at home, when he was just three years old…

"No. No." He attempted to shake the memory, but it was too late. When water finds a crack, it doesn't take long for a flood to break through.

It was 1873 and he was three years old. His two older sisters took him to the stream out back to distract him with pebbles while their father consoled their mother at home. The new baby died, only a year old. Everyone was sad; that was all he understood then.

Like the water rushing by, the years flowed.

He was five, then six. Another baby sister gone, then a little brother who almost made it to his second birthday. Then, another new brother didn't last his first year.

He was nine and no longer happy about siblings arriving; they lost the next brother. He was twelve; they lost another. He was fourteen, and his mother was pregnant again.

Surrendering to the invading memories, Domenico sat down close to the stream and hoped the cool water would revive him.

What a celebration the family had when this new brother reached three years old – the first of six babies to do so. Domenico finally decided to call him by his name, Angelo. The family thought they were done with grieving.

But then, a few months later, his father died. Domenico was seventeen.

The last words he heard from his father were that he was sorry. Sorry that Domenico couldn't start planning his own life when he needed to be the man of the house. Domenico promised to take care of his mother and the three-year-old brother he was now responsible for.

"Was that eight years ago? It could have been last week; the memory still feels heavy on my shoulders – just like the now sweaty clothes that I should have bundled into a bag," He mumbled, exasperated. He splashed his face, wiped it with his sleeve, and continued walking.

ೋದ್ರ

The sun was directly overhead, and Domenico made it to the other side of the great valley. Feeling even more overheated, he spotted some shade trees in the distance and decided to follow the waterline that led to them instead of staying on the road, at least until it was no longer heading southeast.

"You, there," A man yelled to him from over the meager beginnings of a wall. He appeared to be gathering melon-sized stones from the waterway to strategically stack to form a perimeter around his property. "Are you looking for work? I can't pay but can give you two cooked meals a day. Are you interested?"

Domenico hoped he would find opportunities like this. There was no time or money to pack provisions, so he thought he would barter odd jobs for meals.

"Yes, sir, thank you for the kind offer. I can help you today and perhaps tomorrow, but I must be on my way after then."

The man nodded and offered his hand to set the deal. "What's your name, son?"

"Domenico Brex, sir."

The man withdrew his hand too quickly, his smile faded too abruptly.

Why did I tell him? I hoped I was far enough away from Regalbuto by now.

Domenico quickly made an excuse about forgetting about the errand he was on, and he regretfully declined the offer with a strained, yet polite, "good day, sir." He turned quickly to avoid the temptation to respond to the man's rude gestures which were typically used when chasing away a mangy stray.

It wasn't long after that frustration with his mind's replay of the scene set in, and Domenico found himself stepping heavily while pulling wildflowers off the stems as he brushed past them. He crumbled them and left them behind as he continued on the path.

"This must end today. I will keep walking until I double my distance; surely my last name could not have traveled farther than that. Right. Better days are ahead."

He stopped where the Fiume was making a turn – due south; not in the direction he needed to go, unfortunately. He sat on a log by the elbow of the stream and removed a few top layers of his heavy garments. He decided it was best to rest a bit under the trees while the sun was high.

He closed his eyes to calm himself and restore his strength, but the encounter on the road stirred up other recollections of the past. Closing his eyes did not stop more memories from overtaking him.

His father was dead.

The community walked to the cemetery monument in a customary funeral procession.

Domenico held his mother's wilted arm and Angelo's innocent hand, setting the pace for those who walked with them. His two older sisters and their husbands followed in the crowd, deferring to Domenico who was now the head of the family.

Comments from nameless, faceless men walking behind the group carried on the quiet wind. They whispered pity on the dead man's soul. Others wondered if the curse would die with him. Domenico was rattled by what he overheard.

Later that evening, back at their house, family members came to pay their respects. Domenico took three year old Angelo out back by the stream, to let him throw pebbles in the water. His father's most trusted cousin, best friend, and confidant, Cardaci, saw them and approached.

"Your father had a hard life, Domenico. All he wanted was for your life to be a little easier and..." He took a breath before revealing something Domenico already knew. Easier would be unfathomable.

He continued, "I'm so sorry. Nothing will be easy for you. I could take Angelo to stay with me."

Domenico had planned to be on his own, leave home, and make his own way; he was seventeen and ready. But he gave in to duty. "No, thank you, I will stay for Angelo's sake; he's only three years old, he doesn't deserve to lose both me and Father."

Cardaci patted Domenico's shoulder and gave it a squeeze.

"Wait, Cardaci." His father never referred to him by his first name, so Domenico never did either. "I heard others talking today – why are they saying my father was cursed? What is everyone keeping from me?" He looked for the answer in the older man's face. "Am I cursed too?"

Cardaci looked down and told him the story after gesturing the sign of the cross and asking the dead to rest in peace. Men in Domenico's family had violent natures. Their surname, Brex, was tainted by unexplained deaths and suicides, and blame was placed on those hot tempers. Their name was rarely trusted; likely, that was what made his father a target for blame when, yet another unexplainable event occurred. Domenico's father, Vito, strived to go against the grain. He was a good man who always felt there was a peaceful way to handle any situation, yet he couldn't escape this preconception.

"So, you see, the curse they speak of was just a terrible rumor, accusing your father of murder."

"A rumor? Murder? Who would say such a thing?"

"Well, it started with your father's uncle."

Startled awake, Domenico rose with confusion and shook his head in defeat.

31

"I don't understand why I have never heard of this uncle." Domenico groggily expected Cardaci to continue the conversation.

He shrugged, defeated; realizing he was talking to nobody, and he hoped he was still alone on the trail. He surveyed his surroundings and exhaled relief. He noticed the sun's position and started again. The plan was to go as far as possible on this first day and there was so much more ground to cover.

"Living under the curse on my father's name will soon be over," he said under his breath as he continued on the path. *I must go. He who leaves succeeds.*

₭₰

About mid-afternoon, he reached a town called Biancavilla. It was a pretty place with hills and valleys similar to Regalbuto, but this town felt larger. The people bustled around the decorated market carts in the streets with more air around them, they seemed lighter – as if having more space created weightlessness in the townspeople.

The bright colors of an elaborately painted wagon caught his eye a moment before the sweet scent of its cargo of lemons and strawberries reached his nose.

"You would like to buy, son?"

Domenico was pleasantly surprised by the friendly greeting. He didn't realize he was nearly salivating, craving the delicious fruits. "Um, I don't have much, but I am hungry and thirsty, and these look wonderful."

The vendor beamed at his produce and proudly said, "Yes, the ash from Mother Etna provides well for us this growing season." He nodded toward the door of the shop behind him. "If you need work, you can ask in there, they need men for the strawberry picking tomorrow, and they will provide a meal."

"Oh, thank you, but I am only passing through. I do not have time to work today." Domenico didn't want to refuse, but he was still sore from the last rejection.

The vendor shrugged, surprised at the snub, and suspiciously watched as Domenico turned to leave the cart. "Say, son, what did you say your name was?"

Domenico pretended he didn't hear and quickly left, avoiding another confrontation.

Obviously, I am still not far enough away from home. But distance will not just appear between where I am and where I want to be unless I move. I am still a few hours from reaching the base of Mount Etna.

Leaving the oasis-like town, he returned to the dirt path.

₧₧

Late evening arrived, and Domenico found a place to spend the night: Grotta d'Angelo. The name comforted him. Thankful now for his excessive layers, he used the garments to make the dry grass comfortable. He was happy to be off his feet. His aching legs and back felt some relief, even if his mind did not.

All thoughts and plans had led to this day for the last five years. Today, he finally started on a path to do something besides feeling frustrated every single day with direction his life was heading.

Cardaci agreed that Domenico's father would have wanted him to make this journey and escape the aggression that now occupied his home. His father always talked to Domenico about having calm, reasonable discussions about disputes, teaching his son that there was a better way to handle things than with fists. Unfortunately, Domenico's mother's new husband did not share the same thoughts about arguments. 'That Man' had a punishingly violent nature.

It's going to work, right? No, this is not the time for doubt, not again; the conversation with Mother last night must continue to reassure me.

> *"You must go, Domenico, it's your only chance to have a good life." She squeezed my hand with a strength she rarely had.*
>
> *"But Mother..."*
>
> *"You must." She was firm and I could no longer look at her. Tears were not allowed.*
>
> *"But what about Angelo? He's so young. And you, Mother? I can't leave you both alone with..."*
>
> *"Do not worry about us; family will protect. You go, make the money. Angelo will meet you in America when he is old enough. We will work it out here. This will work. You must. And secretly too, Domenico. 'That Man,' as you call him, cannot know or he will try to stop you."*

I must go. It will work. 'That Man' cannot know.

As his mother's words reassured him, thoughts of her new husband dragged him down.

Oh, that man; I hate to think of him, and I won't say his name. He deserves to be called many names – snake, weasel, fraud – but I won't, out of respect for Mother – who has to live with him, and Father – who would not approve of name calling.

In the first three years after his father's death, life was so difficult for all of them, especially his mother. Only a few close friends rejected the rumor. But then Domenico saw a change in her when 'That Man' began to visit. She was flattered by this handsome and wealthy man. She tried to convince Domenico to make room in their lives for him, that he could provide for them financially, and would make a suitable father figure for Angelo. Domenico couldn't and wouldn't accept him. He didn't understand his mother's blind trust, and he was constantly suspicious of 'That Man.'

"What kind of man throws away his youthful years to marry a barren and sad widow sixteen years older than he is? He is just nine years older than me; he could be a sibling. He's closer in age to me than Angelo is, how is that appropriate? And a father figure?" Questioning the grass did not produce an answer.

I wonder if Angelo considers me to be more of a father than a brother. Does Angelo feel lost now that I've left?

"No, shake off that doubt. It wouldn't be fair to him if he came with me now, he's too young to start working, and I can move faster, with less, when alone." Domenico startled a nearby bird that quickly flew away.

The past five years with 'That Man' in their house had only shown Domenico and his mother that first impressions don't last. 'That Man' became a drain on all of Domenico's father's assets and a violent aggressor who continually threatened their family to comply with his wishes. Domenico knew he needed to find a better situation for his mother and Angelo. America was the logical option.

In those years, he secretly skimmed wages from what 'That Man' demanded of him to contribute to the household, Domenico hoped it would be enough for this plan.

Once I get past the mountain, I will find work to barter for food. I have my passage money, about five American dollars, even if it might only get me a ticket in a cargo hold. I won't mind it. Any other hold is better than the grip of 'That Man' over our lives.

Looking up at the stars, Domenico thought of Angelo, again. It hurt that he didn't say goodbye this morning, but he couldn't face his little brother.

It was bad enough that I had to tell him months ago that I had plans for leaving. Bad enough that the little man tried to be strong and brave. But he will be fine in the few years it takes me to make enough money for his passage. Cardaci will check in on him and protect him. With me gone, I'm sure 'That Man' will continue to try to shape Angelo into the son he wants.

At least Angelo can let him believe that. The quieter our plans are, the better.

Angelo was a little confused why he had to lie about what was happening when Domenico told him the plan. He told him it was best to let 'That Man' believe Domenico would never come home, never try to take Angelo away. Angelo had to keep their plan of America a secret or else who knows what 'That Man' might do to Angelo, their mother, or even their older sisters and their families.

His body was getting heavy, but his mind was still too busy to sleep. The journey on this first day was a longer walk than he imagined, but he thought back to how far he had come. He began to get drowsy as he planned for tomorrow, to stop for some provisions in the next town of Pedara and perhaps find some work to do so he could eat.

Certainly, my name could not have traveled to the other side of the great mountain. Tonight, I do feel some peace, sleeping under the vast night sky. I haven't felt free like this in years, but if Angelo were with me, it would be much better.

"I will make this work, Angelo."

Drifting off, he imagined his whisper was carried by the fireflies to his little brother.

~ENTRY #2~

9/9/1929

My dear friend,

I can't believe it's been a week since we've "talked." I've been getting used to the way things are now, but time seems to drag on. I'm moving along, but I don't feel like I'm getting anywhere, does that make sense?

School is settling into a pattern. I leave early for the bus, then to the train, then walk the blocks to the school. I go alone now and it's boring. I would like to bring you along, my dear friend, but the ride is too jittery for writing, so I bring a small bag with a ball of yarn and a hook, and I crochet a little. Heading home it's the same thing in reverse. A tidy pattern I have memorized, like the stitches in my granny circles. The circles aren't making anything useful by themselves, so even my project isn't getting anywhere.

Anyway, after school today, I got to see my cousin, Gracie. I haven't seen her since school started! She met me at the Kings Highway bus stop to walk home with me, which was so sweet of her. She is two grades younger than me, so this year is her first at Boody Junior High. We share that small speck in a vast universe feeling, but she is doing very well making friends.

We have always gotten along the best of all my Bregas cousins. May is two years older than me but she seems older than that somehow. I guess I'm not yet as grown up as she is. Their oldest sister, Josephine, is treated as a grown up, and she reminds us of that often. Gracie and May have a brother between their ages, but he is always busy doing some odd job for someone; when the boys get older, they tend to work more and play less, unless it's a holiday or if they are still in school.

Well, except for Frank. He is an exception. He works at his father's barber shop, and he can still keep up with his studies. Frank's father, who is also named Frank, has a barber shop on Willis Avenue in Mineola that he opened four years ago in 1925. I still haven't told you much about Frank, I wouldn't know where to start, there's so much I can say. I probably can devote an entire separate journal trying to explain him!

So, back to walking home with Gracie. She asked how my day at the park was with Nan last weekend, and I felt bad. Nan wanted to talk about the boy she likes, Michael, so we didn't ask Gracie to come along – but to her credit, she didn't seem a bit jealous. Maybe because she has so many siblings, she doesn't know the feeling of being left out. I know I would have felt slighted to not be invited along, what about you? Probably in a houseful of brothers and sisters, if one doesn't want to spend time with you, there's always another. I don't have that luxury, I just have Duey, and you, my dear friend.

I sometimes wonder what it would be like if Gracie and I

switched places. Would I feel less lonely in their busy house? Does having so many siblings really shape who you are and what you think about life? Would I become a different person if I were in her shoes?

It's fun to sleep over from time to time, even at Nan's house, but I'm sure it's entirely different if that home life is your everyday reality. As a visitor, you are just that: visiting.

If it is really your life, I think there's a different sense of belonging and attachment that I feel like I miss out on because I am an only child. Does that make sense to you?

Maybe I should take you, my dear friend, over to their house so you can tell me what you think. Oh, I wish you could!

~Zina

CHAPTER 3

Zina

Sunday, September 15, 1929

As she was changing after church, Zina heard a faint tapping sound outside on the sidewalk. She looked out her bedroom window to see Nan and Gracie taking turns with a new jump rope. *Nan must've gotten it from Coney Island yesterday*, she thought, and quickly headed down the stairs, eager to meet up with her cousins and join in with the novelty.

Zina's mother called out after her. "Vincenza? Where are you going?"

"Just here, Mother." Zina responded, slightly pointing outside to the sidewalk.

Her mother followed Zina to the open front door to see for herself. "Oh, hello girls."

"Hello Aunt Rose, what a pretty apron." Gracie said, always being polite. Nan was concentrating too hard on jumping to also answer.

"Thank you, Gracie. Would you mind heading back home to pick up the wine your mother has for me?"

"Sure, Aunt Rose." Gracie frowned, thinking she'd miss her turn with the jump rope, but Zina suggested they all go. Rose began to object, but Zina rushed the girls off quickly, before she could stop them.

The girls took turns jumping and skipping down the sidewalk to 70th Street – only fifteen minutes away but they got there in ten.

Nan and Zina walked up the paver stones to the Bregas' porch while Gracie finished up her turn in front of her house.

Josephine, their oldest cousin, was sitting on the porch swing. She cleared her throat when the girls approached. "Oh, if it isn't the Bobbsey twins. Hey Zina, how's the interpretation going? Are you able to interpret *everything* people are saying now?"

Josephine was about twenty-three and a beauty. Sometimes she seemed to speak sarcastically but Zina usually couldn't decide when. Zina just ignored her.

Nan followed Zina inside the house, and Gracie hurried in after them, stopping for a second to give her older sister a smirk.

"Aunt Mamie, we're here." Zina called.

"Good! Zina honey! Come, Come." She yelled from deep in the house.

Zina was greeted at the kitchen entrance with a hug that was cut short. "Oh, I didn't know you were all coming. *Ciao* Nan. Gracie, can you take out the cookies to share, please. So, how are things at home, Zina honey? How is that ridiculous school? Oh, excuse me." She covered her mouth, not meaning to misspeak about Zina's parent's decision.

Zina didn't seem to notice the criticism. "Everything is fine, Aunt Mamie. Thank you. Thank you for the wine. We should go now."

Mamie had hoped for a longer visit but relented. She securely wrapped the wine bottle in a cloth and handed it to Zina with an attempt at another hug. She waved to Nan, then pointed to the jump rope and wiggled her finger side to side.

"Right, no jumping on the way home with the wine." Zina translated the gesture. "We will be careful, Aunt Mamie."

Zina held the bottle first while Nan retrieved the jump rope from Gracie, and the girls said their goodbyes.

Nan skipped the rope a few yards, stopped, and waited for Zina to catch up.

Mamie peered out the window at Zina and Nan and sighed. The girls reminded her about her own youth, living in Sicily, and running errands. "Ah, the days of carrying crates of fruit for Papa's liqueur making. Rose and I, we were about their ages when we dreamed about America and imagined what our futures could hold." She cleared a rising tightness in her throat. "Innocence was such a blessing."

The girls turned the corner, out of her view, but Mamie kept watching anyway.

CHAPTER 4

Mamie, 1895

May, Early Morning
Pedara, Sicily

Holding open the curtain, she looked from her second-story window down at the beauty filling her family's small corner of the world.

But Rose interrupted her with a nudge, and quickly passed her by to be the first one downstairs. "Time to get to work."

"Why are you such an early bird today?" Mamie mumbled, but remembered the newest American magazine was due to arrive so of course Rose would be in a hurry. Shaking her head, she turned her attention back to the view outside the bedroom she shared with her sister and sighed.

The early morning sun streaked through the spaces between the green leaves and wispy branches of the olive trees lining the edges of their courtyard. It was still a nice view, although she preferred waking up to see what Mother Etna looked like each morning.

Her northern view was recently obscured by the neighbor's new floor addition, which was built for their oldest, and newly married, daughter.

If we add a new floor to the top of our house could we see the volcano again over their house? she wondered. *I suppose new construction and improvement of my view is way off in the future. I have a few years until I am of age, and sadly, I still have yet to notice any good prospects. And to be noticed, well that's another story.*

Mamie, which was her family's nickname for Domenica, lived in Pedara all her twelve years, on lands that have been in her family for generations, from the Zappalas on her mother's side, to the Rapisardas on her father's great-great-grandmother's side.

They were the Priviteras, which means "Private Earth;" a suitable description of their sweet courtyard and the atmosphere of their home and store – a serene break from the rest of the world.

But the town around them was changing fast. Since their property was a short walk from their church, their papa built a store on their corner. Many others were also clamoring to build around them since it was a good location for business. Their perimeter began to shrink so they cut back on growing in town and used the neighboring lands in the family, such as the Barbagallos' farm. There were now more neighbors and activity than farmland and trees. It was great for business but not so much for privacy.

Mamie realized she had been dawdling, and it was time to get moving. She tied on her apron and headed downstairs. Once outside, those sun streaks felt as warm as they looked.

She reached for the handle of the straw broom propped against the porch wall. Every morning she swept away the endless debris nature deposited. It was the one daily task she didn't mind. She loved mornings like this: still winds and the dust dampened by the dew, although being alone with the birds singing would make it even more perfect, she thought. But there was Rose.

Her sister was noisily humming and clicking Mamie's handed-down brown leather laced-up Sunday boots in a sort of dance on the walkway. She choreographed her song and dance with the clipping of a few of the prettiest pink buds from their rose garden as the snip, snip of her shears became part of her performance, upstaging Mother Nature with her own cacophony and hacking Her blooming gifts to die miserably indoors.

Mamie tried not to let her thoughts become disrupted by Rose's noisy accompaniment, and observed the unique sounds of birds and cicadas and sweet scents of roses, olives, and figs. Every day new blends floated in the air, and Mamie appreciated them like whispered promises of something good to come.

Rose, on the other hand, thought of beauty as something to obtain. As she shook the early morning dew off her cut flowers, Mamie shook her head, now having to re-sweep the pollen and dead leaves that sprinkled off like a layer of confectioners' sugar on the grey lava stone walkway.

"Careful, Rose. I just swept there." She stated what she thought was obvious.

Rose just gave her a confused, questioning look, oblivious that her actions affected anyone else. She went on to hum a little louder as she brushed past Mamie into the house through the porch door, no doubt to find a vase – a final resting place for the beauties who suffered at her hand. "Come on, Mamie, let's hurry, I have to see that magazine!"

Mamie looked up in exasperation and her eye caught her own bedroom window and its curtain she forgot to close this morning.

The room next to hers seemed peacefully quiet and still as her mother and the little ones were sleeping just a few minutes longer, blissfully unaware of Rose's recital.

Their papa was already leaving their garden shed at the far corner of the yard and was heading to the shop, and Mamie and Rose were expected to follow suit, being the oldest two. Wake at dawn, tidy themselves and the courtyard, and head to the store to be presentable to customers: this was how their days began as shopkeepers.

Rose carried the vase and buds while Mamie continued with her broom. They would rather follow their papa and cut through the back rooms to head to the shop since their home and shop buildings are interconnected, but their papa liked the idea that they would clear the path the customers would walk out front. That sweeping fell to Mamie. Rose was still humming ahead of her sister when they entered the shop from the road and began to full-out sing when she saw that the newest fashion magazine had indeed arrived.

Their papa's booming voice cut through Rose's melody as he called out to his oldest daughter, "Mamie, at lunchtime could you please pick up the lemons from Barbagallos'? I see my supplies have arrived so I will be starting a new *limoncello* tonight. I think our shelves will need restocking for the next feast day." Their papa appeared from the back room after assessing that his order of wine and spirits was correct, and when he saw Mamie, gave her a wink.

She cringed as she moved behind the counter to stow the broom. *Every day he asks me to head to Barbagallo's farm for something or other, but why, on this day, is it with a wink?* she wondered.

Mamie was not looking forward to seeing their cousin Salvatore at the farm. Rose and Mamie have secretly called him "Foul Sal" for years. He was four years older than Mamie and had been particularly attentive when she came by to pick up produce. The girls thought he was crude, rough-mannered, scrawny, and bad-smelling – not unlike a sickly animal.

It was not long before they heard their mother and the little ones walking around upstairs, so Mamie and Rose finished getting organized to meet the first customer of the day.

∞⚬⚬∞

Around mid-morning, their mother prepared them all some cheese and bread. Rose and Mamie took turns staying in the shop while the other one ate. When they were done, their papa brought in a basket from the shed and instructed, "Mamie, better get going. And Rose, watch the counter while I head to the neighbor's for some supplies, and please, don't crinkle that new magazine, it still needs to be sellable."

"Yes, Papa." The girls responded together, but their tones clashed. Mamie was the only one to notice. *Rose sounds like a tweeting bird, the annoyingly happy kind. I hope I didn't sound as irritated as I feel about having to see Foul Sal,* she thought.

As Mamie reached the end of their walkway, Rose peeked out the back porch door, met Mamie's eyes, and gave her a smile and a small wave.

Mamie smiled warmly back, not able to help it. Her frustration was not with her younger sister, it's not her fault their chores were divided the way they were. Rose was just happy to be working at the shop now, promoted last week from 'Mama's helper' to 'counter girl.'

Mamie's new promotion to 'errand girl' just added to her sweeping duties, other shop duties, and being a helper to their mother. She sighed in frustration. *I suppose I should be glad for Rose, and at least my new task comes with a little freedom.*

She had been longing to have the opportunity to experience change and adventure. If it weren't for her foul cousin she wouldn't have minded the added chore.

ℰↃ◌ℛ

Their cousin's farm was a forty-minute walk to the next town over to the west, called Nicolosi. It was an uphill, dirt road lined with prickly pear cacti and chestnut trees, intermittently sunny and shaded since it was early afternoon.

On a positive note, I am in the shade, and this uphill trek is with an empty basket. Once I get the fruit, it's all downhill toward home. And it is such a beautiful day to be outdoors in the sunshine and fresh air.

Taking in the view around her, she sighed in awe, fully able to see Mount Etna now; stripes of black soil radiating outward like thick ribbons cascading down Her head.

Mamie recalled her papa talking about how much Mother Etna supplied. Volcanic ash takes years to change an area from barren to fertile, and they just happen to be lucky enough to have that fertile soil striping right through their town of Pedara. Mamie realized then that their 'luck' meant a hot molten lava stream flowed right through their beloved backyard, but she chose to not dwell on that fact.

She passed an old man and donkey heading towards her with a basket over its back and she shifted her own empty basket to her hip to see better where she was stepping.

Oh, a donkey would make things so much easier but just forget about it, Mamie. Obtaining our own donkey is not a luxury we can afford. I can still hear Papa, 'why get a donkey when I have you, Mamie?' Not amusing.

She kicked a chestnut with her next step, her old frustrations surfacing now, clouding her sunny intentions for this outing.

According to Mother, arduous work will build my character. But why do I need more work? Isn't growing up the oldest of a family of seven children at the base of this volcanic mountain enough to make me strong and tough? And why is this model the one I am being molded into, but Rose is being cast differently?

Mamie's heartbeat increased and her temperature rose.

Mother says I am at an age when young men will come courting, and Papa seems to think lifting baskets of fruit is something I need to do to learn to be a good wife and homemaker. But then, the rules for Rose involve her smiling and looking pretty. I know I can easily handle what Rose can't, but it doesn't change that it feels unfair.

A couple of shuffling kicks sent more chestnuts rolling back onto the grass.

She passed by a few travelers and yet another donkey. That donkey gave her a nod. Mamie looked disgusted that the only appreciation she was receiving was from a lowly beast.

The people all around me are oblivious to my presence, but the donkey nods. Ugh. Mother says a nice, young man will appreciate me being a strong, hard-working young woman. But ever since I started working in the shop a year ago, I've had my fill of hard work and no sign of any appreciation whatsoever. None. Rose has been working for a week now and all the young men are admiring the pretty Rose behind the counter. Not once has someone shown admiration for my crate hauling strength like my parents think will be the case. It certainly doesn't count that donkeys are impressed.

A few more chestnuts rolled.

Mamie took a deep breath to shake off her thoughts and tried again to just enjoy the walk on such a nice day. Barbagallo's farm was just around the bend, so she stopped for a moment, looking back toward home.

Our town really is a beautiful place, but the only place I've ever known or lived in, I wonder how it compares to other places.

Since they started the shop and others in the town began building, there were many more visitors than ever before – Mamie's only window to the world. People traveling up and down Mount Etna would stop in for something to eat or drink, excited about their next adventure. They would talk of beautiful places they'd been, and she would listen, always wondering if there might be somewhere else she would like better than Pedara, Sicily.

I remember that time Papa took us to where he grew up, Trecastagni, about forty kilometers east of here. I wish I wasn't too young to remember what it was like there. I guess because Mother is from Pedara, we live here, being that it is customary for the married couple to live and be a part of the wife's community when they marry. It is what it is. I suppose that means I will stay here forever, even if there was somewhere else I'd rather live. Mother's family of Zappalas and Barbagallos have been firmly planted in Pedara and our Church of Santa Caterina for probably the last 300 years, maybe

49

longer.

She followed the bend in the road and there were no more chestnuts, only dirt. She tried not to shuffle and get her boots dusty.

I wish I could be allowed to decide something about my future. Girls my age at church talk about betrothal and dream about finding true love, but we all know we will be doing what our fathers tell us. We listen to our fathers; what he says is best for our family. It's been that way for generations. Family is sacred, purposeful, and planned. Is that who Cousin Salvatore is? Is "Foul Sal" the plan Papa has for me?

If I could decide for myself, I'd rather have some intrigue, adventure. If I had my way, I'd live where I can try new things and meet new people, and have an opportunity to fall in love, for real. Not "grow in love" as Mother puts it; that feels as confining as a tree trying to grow in a shrinking courtyard.

ℴℴ

Mamie finally arrived about an hour later at Via Barbagallo in Nicolosi. It didn't usually take that long. She supposed she could have made better time if it wasn't for kicking chestnuts in frustration about her parent's philosophy for the direction of her life.

She walked through their shop door and stopped at the counter to wait for Cousin Salvatore to finish with another customer. When he saw her, he smiled widely.

Oh no.

"Um hello, Salvatore. I'm here for the lemons for my papa." *Best to keep things short and sweet, matter of fact. I realize I probably sound rude, but I really don't want to encourage him. How can Papa think Salvatore is a good match for me? Have they already talked, is that why Papa gave me a wink today?*

"Mamie? Is that you?" Aunt Agatha called out from behind Salvatore, and Mamie breathed a sigh of relief that maybe she wouldn't have to deal with her dreaded cousin.

"Come here, my girl, I have the lemons and a *pizelle* for you. How is your mama?" Aunt Agatha ushered her niece to the back storeroom. Mamie intended to say that she shouldn't stay to visit, but Aunt Agatha insisted she also have an *anarancina* she made with a little ham and mozzarella, with a cold glass of lemon water. She wrapped more of the cookies for Mamie to take home to share with the little ones.

As Mamie was leaving, Salvatore motioned for her to come to talk with him, but she shook her head and left quickly to head home.

The sun was no longer directly above, but she still stayed on the same treed side of the road to stay shaded, and, well, to avoid the side the donkeys take. With the basket in front of her she'd rather not have to watch where she stepped. Chestnuts were one thing; she thought she did a pretty good job in clearing those.

Donkeys kept passing, looking curiously at her still.

"*Heee hawww*," one said looking directly at her, with a face remarkably like Foul Sal's. She shook to regain her senses; surely the donkey did not just address her.

Mamie was about to turn the corner off Via Barbagallo toward home when she felt a tap on the back of her shoulder. "*Eh, mi scusi signorina.*"

She jumped at the voice, lost her balance with the basket and dropped it. The lemons tumbled out onto the road.

"Oh miss, I am so sorry, please, let me help you."

They were on hands and knees on the lava stones, rescuing, to her relief, all the lemons without casualty. Mamie stood and brushed her hands on her apron, and the deep-voiced boy stood and handed her the basket.

"Again, I am sorry. Perhaps I can carry this for you?" He offered, awkwardly.

"No, I was managing just fine until you snuck up on me. Whatever were you thinking, you..." She turned to scold the boy as she would her younger brother but realized he was much older. She stopped, deciding it was best if she just left. "Uh, no, *grazie. Ciao*," she said and turned to leave.

He held his hand out to her. "No, please wait, can you possibly help me? I'm looking for a place to spend the night. In the morning I wish to travel up Mount Etna," he said, sounding tired, but also somewhat satisfied with himself. "I've been walking since yesterday, and I just need a place to rest."

Mamie looked at him carefully now and realized he was not a boy at all but a young man with long disheveled hair, wearing rags and what looked like layers of shirts and a coat made of horse hair, holding a wool coppola.

Who is this young man? I've never seen him in town before, his appearance is a bit rough, but his manners are friendly enough. His eyes. His eyes are really blue. He has really nice blue eyes, she thought. "Oh, um, yes. You can inquire at Barbagallos over there, ask for Salvatore."

"*Grazie*, thank you miss." The young man said and looked in the direction she pointed.

She took that opportunity to leave him quickly before he could ask her any more questions. *I really don't like the idea of meeting an unfamiliar man on the street, especially one so oddly dressed. Even if he does have nice blue eyes, like the clearest sky. And right, I want to make it home before the evening meal.*

To her relief, the young man headed in Salvatore's direction. She glanced back and saw Salvatore standing out in the street, looking directly at her, waving for her to come back. The stranger thought the gesture was directed toward him, so he returned the wave to the shopkeeper, who now stopped looking toward Mamie.

"Small favors." Mamie whispered to herself as she hurried around the bend.

In the downhill home stretch, lugging the basket of fruit, she quickly passed her fellow donkeys along the way. She ignored them now that she felt she was late.

Just a little out of breath, she finally made it to their courtyard and placed the crate on a table under the porch overhang. Rose heard her and hurried over to inspect. "You were gone a long while, Mamie. Papa needed you."

"Oh, I know. Aunt Agatha was in one of her talking moods. She did give me cookies."

"Not now, hurry, let's get the lemons washed and cut before Papa comes looking for them."

The sisters stood silently by the well pump, Mamie washed each fruit in the barrel, then Rose began quartering them. Mamie noticed Rose's hands, white and thin. *And my hands, bulky and rough. How can two sisters contrast so much? Are we really so different?*

"So, it was Aunt Agatha who delayed you? You weren't spending time talking with Foul Sal?" Rose gave her a teasing smile.

"No, Rose! Ugh, why does Papa want me to be with Salvatore anyway? It's really not fair, he's so crude and lanky and, well, not handsome at all, and well, *pezzu di carni cu l'occhi.*" She just blurted it out.

"Wow, Mamie, an impressive insult. A piece of meat with eyes." Rose held up two lemons to her own eyes to illustrate.

Both girls giggled. "Yes, that sums up Foul Sal pretty well."

"But really, Mamie. He is a Barbagallo and the only son. You could live off all those acres of farmland and never lift a finger again in your life."

"Yes, Mother says, 'with a good farm, garden, and vineyard, all your problems will be cured.' I know, I know. But I would rather live a life of hard work and have love than despise my husband and lounge around." Mamie said determinedly.

"Well, you just may get your wish of hard work, but if you don't start lounging a little bit men will not like your rough manners. You'll never find one that will give you a second look."

"I am just being myself, Rose. I don't mind working, and I like being outdoors. Being dainty and delicate doesn't seem practical to me. I will just have to find a man that appreciates the things I'm good at." She hoped she sounded convincing.

"Sure, that's what you think now. I'm only saying to consider it."

"Would YOU marry Salvatore?"

"Well of course not, I have my mind set on a different sort of man."

"Oh really, who?"

"I haven't found him yet. But he will be a well-mannered, refined, and handsome gentleman, maybe blonde, like the one on the cover of the new magazine that came today – a *signore biondo* – and I will be just the woman he is looking for."

"How can you be so sure of that, Rose?"

"Well, I can BE sure because I will MAKE sure that it happens that way, that's how." Rose cut the final lemon and put the knife down to accentuate her point with a smile.

The girls took each quarter and began to separate the rind and pith from the flesh.

I wish I had her confidence. Carrying crates is not going to lead me where I'd like to go, which is certainly not into our cousin Salvatore's life. But is that what is in store for me? I just wish I had more to look forward to than working like a pack mule, or having a loveless marriage to an obnoxious man, even if he would inherit his family's farm. I wish for a handsome beau to walk into our shop and fall in love with me. Someone with a sense of adventure, someone to see the world with. Ah, what would that be like? We could travel to beautiful places...

Her papa's gruff voice startled her fantasy. "Mamie? Mamie where are you?" Mamie and Rose looked up at each other like they both just returned from deep thought, far away. *What could Rose have been thinking about?* She wondered.

"Oh, there you are. I've been calling for you, Mamie. Now stop your daydreaming. It is almost closing time, and our evening meal will be ready soon. Bring your mother the fruit and bring those peels out back to the shed, I want to start them soaking tonight. Rose, please finish helping our neighbor in the shop; he will be our last customer today, so tidy up."

"Yes, Papa," the girls responded in their off-tune unison yet again. Mamie headed to the shed with the lemon rinds but paused to watch Rose for a minute, as she was behaving oddly. Mamie saw her younger sister stop for a quick assessment – looking into the glass by the porch door like a mirror. She patted her hair and wet her lips before greeting the customer.

Mamie thought of her own hair. She thought about trying to smooth it, but her hands were full. She licked her lips, but they were dry and tasted dusty.

Am I really becoming as rough as Rose says I am?

Her papa yelled at her with his eyes, and she quickly brought him the rinds.

ଚ୨ଓଓ

That evening, Mamie had trouble falling asleep. Rose's words rolled around in her mind, 'I will BE sure because I will MAKE sure it happens that way.'

She is so sure that she will get what she wants in life just because she wants it. How does she do that, and can it work for me?

And then Mother's advice for me is to work hard and the right man will appreciate a strong woman. That is not Rose's idea of how to go about it; why are we so different?

Rose turned out their bedroom light and whispered, "Good night, Mamie."

"Good night, Rose."

I should say my prayers, but I might say too much tonight, God. There's so much to think about. But God, you don't mind, right? You know everything anyway.

Father, please bless my family.

Bless my sister, Rose, she is so assertive and confident, and I would like to be as well.

Father, please bless Concetta, and help her to enjoy the little ones. She is always reading and doesn't play when they ask her to.

And please help Grazia, she is probably the second most miserable with chores, next to me, as she has the diapering duties. That's about all I wish to say about that.

Perhaps I may ask you, Father, to bless the babies Agatha and Joseph with some calmness this week? I'm sure Grazia would appreciate that as well.

Oh, and I'm still not that tired! And there's Francesco, Father. Bless our brother, being the oldest boy smack in the middle of a family overrun by girls, he is learning a new trade as a barber to help him become more mature. I'd rather that he helped me with the lifting and hauling but Papa thinks otherwise, probably because he is always teasing us sisters.

Please continue to bless Papa with wisdom to guide our family. He says it's good business for our family to diversify our skills to help provide for the family. It's probably a smart thing, but I don't see the practicality of barbering for our family, as all of us girls tie up our long hair. Papa thinks grooming will be an important trade in the future. You, Father, and Papa, know best about this.

And then there's Mother. Please bless Mother, who takes care of all of us. She does the cooking and laundering, as much as she can with as pregnant as she is. It must be lovely to have a baby, all that cuddling and nursing and everyone else around you helps with the chores you used to do alone. You sit sweetly with this new little human who loves you best. It must be nice, until the nursing time is over. Then the babies are pushed to grasp independence more than cuddling. She must pine away for that closeness, so she decides to start a new baby. I've seen this cycle many times since I'm the oldest. Bless Mother and our new baby brother or sister, due anytime now.

Thank you, Father, for all our blessings and thank you for listening to me tonight. In your name, Amen.

I will try to sleep but I still feel anxious for my future life; when will it start? When the shop becomes more successful and father hires my replacement (doubtful), or when I marry and leave this place (unlikely), or when I fall dead from lifting baskets of lemons (hmm, or perhaps I can fake an injury?)

I don't know. I'll just wake up again tomorrow and do what I'm told. Despite all the routine, tomorrow always holds the potential of something new.

~ENTRY #3~

9/30/1929

My dear friend,

Good news! Mother said Aunt Maria will be coming over this weekend, oh I hope that means Frank will be visiting too!

So maybe it's time I tell you more about Frank. I know you have been wondering, am I right?

Here's what I like about him:

1) *He listens and actually hears me.*

2) *He supports the dreams I have and wants me to follow them.*

3) *He is fun to be with and he is someone I don't get tired of. (Oh, don't you think that I'm tired of you, my dear friend. I hope* <u>you</u> *are not tired of "listening.")*

I often wish that Frank and I weren't cousins. There I said it. The unfortunate thing is I can't change that fact just by wishing it. It's not like I can make it not true.

I know someday I will have to think more seriously about finding my soulmate, but why can't I imagine who that might be now?

Oh, if it weren't for this new school! If I could meet boys there it might be different, but an all-girls school? Highly unlikely. And I don't think it would be wise to meet someone on the bus or the train to school, Papa wouldn't like that much. Papa even calls the boys in our neighborhood "unsuitable," but what he means is "not Sicilian." I hate to admit that, but I think it is true.

Maybe if Nan didn't talk so much about her feelings toward the boy she likes, I wouldn't feel like I am lagging behind in the romance department.

And what also makes me feel like I am a late bloomer in some love schedule is that sometimes my mother and Frank's mother act as if one day Frank and I will be, well, a couple. They think it's cute and funny. Why do they keep teasing us? Do you think they think I will never find a boy to marry so I will have to settle for my cousin? I know the church makes special dispensations, but it is insulting if our mothers think that is my only option.

And all of this troubles me more because I do like Frank and that makes it even worse. No, I have to think of him as an <u>example </u>of someone to find. That's harmless, right?

I don't know what my future will hold, my dear friend.

There is just so much I feel excluded from in life sometimes. It's like the life I want only happens to other people. And the direction I want to go isn't up to me.

I hope he will visit this weekend, fingers crossed.

~Zina

CHAPTER 5

Zina

Sunday, October 6, 1929

T he bulk of that week, the fall weather delivered a streak of

unexpectedly warm days. Between school, the long train rides, and daylight shortening, Zina couldn't enjoy the sunshine during the week. Sunday was highly anticipated; this meant visiting 'Aunt Etna.'

She took her crocheting bag to the park to visit her favorite rock she, Nan, and Frank good-humoredly named for the volcano their parents often referred to. If there was a delay in the subway schedule, or if they had to walk home in the rain, they would say to each other, "well, at least Mount Etna isn't erupting." So, if they sought to think about or talk about something serious, they would visit 'Aunt Etna' to discover the bright side of a situation.

It was an odd feature of McDonald Park, a giant boulder left there after the glaciers melted throughout Long Island, or after the bulldozers combed through while building the neighborhoods; nobody really knew which, and it was probably a result of both. Having never been to Sicily or seen a volcano in their lives, 'Aunt Etna' was the most massive, permanent, and ancient presence they had access to. It was the perfect spot because, being a good five feet up from ground level, it added an elevated perspective to any discussion Zina had with Nan, or sometimes with Frank.

But being alone at your most favorite conversation place is not at all enlightening when the voice in your head is louder than the outside noise. Lately, home's silence seemed magnified, and she was tired of hearing herself think way too loudly.

I guess it's nice to be alone to think sometimes, but it might be nice if Frank happened to come by, she thought. *But it's because of his conversational skills, that's why I like having him around. Yes, that is better than, well, having other feelings.*

Zina quieted the voice in her head and began to crochet a new chain.

She thought about what a houseful of people might be like every day. Was it possible to be lonely in a full house? Would she still be able to hear the voices in her head? When she would go the Bregas' house, it would hold nonstop noise; thumping, talking, laughing, chewing, gossiping, laughing some more, loudly remarking from another room, taunting, on and on. *Were there other noisy noises*, she wondered.

The quiet noises she knew too well. Snoring. Breathing. Humming, whirring of the fan, buzzing of a fly, the drone of nothingness in your ears, the wind in the window, the curtain flapping. She was acutely familiar with these sounds. The solitude was lonely.

Her favorite boulder suddenly felt lonely too as the spirit of an imaginary 'Aunt Etna' left behind just a rock. She moved her hand over it, as if it too needed some consoling. As rocks go, it was comfortable. She liked the flat grittiness of the texture and preferred the coolness on the backs of her legs while the top was warm from the sunshine. She scooted to a new shaded spot and provided by the enormous dogwood tree. It was the biggest one in Brooklyn. Dogwoods don't typically get as big; this one had been there for many, many years. She looked up at the tree, the light through its branches and leaves created a dappled canopy over her.

Zina spotted Frank coming down the street to the park. Happily, she stuffed her hook and yarn back in her bag, smoothed out her play dress, and fixed her bobby socks. Her shoes had a small scuff and she rubbed it away when she saw Frank running toward the rock now that he had caught a glimpse of her.

I shouldn't be so excited to see him. She shook her head hoping to stop thinking of him like that. She pretended there was a fly buzzing near her ear.

"Hi, Zina," Frank said, breathless. He then cleared his throat, remembering to play it cool. He recently overheard his mother on the phone talking about Zina and it changed everything. He decided on the way over that she needed to hear this and he was going to tell her, but he wasn't sure how to just yet.

"Hi, Frank." she responded with a smile.

He almost forgot that was his name. "Hi. Um, your mother – she and my mother are done laying out the new dress pattern and they told me to come tell you that we will have dinner in about an hour."

"Oh." Zina said, waving her hand around her head at some invisible pesky fly.

Seeing her now, he realized he couldn't tell her. The timing didn't feel right.

He leaned up against the boulder and asked, "how is school going?"

Zina said it was okay, but she didn't sound convincing.

"Do...do you like...your school?" He looked down at his shoes, now at a loss for conversation.

"What did you say? Did you just ask if I like it? Not really, I don't like being around so many odd people on the train and I haven't made any friends in classes yet, my books are heavy, and…" Zina rubbed her neck as if mentioning it brought about its soreness.

Frank looked up and just stared at her. Her slight movements and touches distracted him; he didn't hear anything else she said then.

"I guess I can see why my mother insists I attend that school to become an Italian interpreter, it can be a very important job for my family as well as the community. We certainly need more people that can understand English to help all those who came from Sicily and Italy without any schooling. Don't you agree, Frank?"

Frank had to shake his head to recall what she just said. His thoughts were elsewhere: her neck, her chin, the small lines of frustration that appeared in the corners of her mouth when she was speaking. She looked different, sitting on top of the rock: her black hair shielded her face, backlit by the sun flickering between the leaves of the tree. She could be an angel sitting up there…

"But it's not what I want!" Zina spurted; the exclamation caused her to begin coughing. She slapped her hands down at her sides in frustration.

Frank was fully at attention now.

Her throat cleared.

"The language comes easy to me, but I don't think I like the idea of always reflecting someone else's words. Spending my life expressing someone else's thoughts and ideas? What about my own? To be an interpreter I would have to be like a mirror, where people look at me, speak their words, and I am the reverse image speaking back. Who would care about me or my thoughts; they want to hear their own said a different way. Does that make sense, Frank?"

She didn't even pause for him to answer. "Where will I be but invisible? I really want to make a difference, really help people. I want to be seen and appreciated for who I am and what I think. Not just merely interpreting." When she said it, she made a face like the words tasted bad.

Frank considered all of this. He had a feeling something like this bothered her. Zina was quiet but she had so many ideas. She saw things others didn't see about how people looked and reacted. She had a great imagination and a great heart.

He decided to climb up the rock and sit beside her, and in this moment he had an overwhelming feeling to console her, contradict her, even comfort her. He wanted her to see herself as someone with more worth and more potential – the way he saw her.

"Zina, you could never be a mere mirror," he started. "You are an original, unique. A creation like no other." Zina hid her eyes and he thought he must have struck a chord with her. He took a breath to get bolder, but instead, he blundered. "Sort of like that blanket you are crocheting." He spurted, pointing to her bag.

"What?"

Frank looked uncomfortable. He had an idea of a great analogy in his head, one that would tell her how special she was, but "blanket" is what came out. "Uh, um. I mean...yes, instead of being a mirror you want to be a blanket." He recovered.

Zina looked at him incredulously. "What in the world are you talking about now, Frank?"

"You know, when I see you crocheting those little circles of yarn – what do you call them? Granny circles? Do you want to know what I think?"

Zina looked confused about why he wanted to talk about yarn, they were talking about school, her plans, her dreams. Not yarn.

"Yarn is a long strand of fibers all twisted around so that it is sturdy and continuous. Of course, the quality of that yarn varies, but..." He got back on track. "The point is the yarn continues in a long line until something new happens to it: you. You come along with a tool, your crochet hook, and bend and shape the yarn into something new. The yarn is like the days of your life." He sneaked a glance at her to see her expression, and she seemed interested, so he continued.

"Sometimes you make a granny circle, right? But sometimes you make a row of stitches, and it makes a blanket. Sometimes you take all those granny circles individually and stitch them together to make the overall afghan or some clothing creation. You design how you want it to be stitched, and if you don't like it, you back up, pull out the stitches, and rework it, right?"

Zina looked at him then, and he thought maybe she understood where he was going with this.

He looked at her. "But you keep going along that line of yarn, working and looping until you step back and say, I made that. And it is beautiful." He hoped she understood.

Zina just stared at Frank now.

After a pause, at the same time, they both became uncomfortable. He looked away to stare at the kids on the swings, intently, as if they were all that mattered.

She fumbled with her stuff to leave.

"You know what else?" He wished he could salvage the moment.

"No, what, Frank?" she asked, breathless.

But he couldn't say it, not now, she was not ready to hear it. Seeing her expectant look drove all the confidence from him. Oh, but how he wanted her to know. He stumbled to find anything to say, but his mind was blank. He ran his hand through his hair and finally thought of something: work.

She sighed and listened to him discuss the difficulties with sharpening the barber's shears at his father's shop as they left 'Aunt Etna' and the park to head to Zina's home for dinner.

~<u>ENTRY #4</u>~

11/24/1929

My dear friend,

Thanksgiving will be here this Thursday, and Frank will be coming over to celebrate with us over the weekend. I hate to admit this to you, but now I'm having mixed feelings about that.

Let me try to explain. Ever since a few Sundays ago when he met me at the park, I sensed a different tone from him. He seemed happy to see me and anticipating something, and I wasn't sure what I was supposed to do or say. And then he kept looking at me funny, the kind of look that you give someone when they have something on their face, but you don't know how to tell them, do you know what I mean? Maybe you do but I realize as a book you can't tell them anyway, but that is beside the point.

Why do you think he was acting that way? Do you think maybe he likes me too? It's all so confusing! If we are cousins and can't be sweethearts, why do I feel so conflicted?

~Zina

CHAPTER 6

Zina

Sunday, December 1, 1929

Dinners spanned over a few days when the families got together for the holidays. Thursday's Thanksgiving festivities continued until late Sunday evening.

This year, Zina's family hosted Mamie and Domenico, with some of their younger children, as well as Frank's family, who always spent the holidays with Zina's family because Frank's father and Zina's papa were cousins and the only family Zina's papa had in America.

Zina's house was small, but the living room, when combined with the dining room area, accommodated everyone nicely.

After dinner, Zina's aunt Mamie asked her to share what she has learned in her interpretation classes. Zina was not in a mood to think about school. Besides, she knew the adults were comfortable with the little English they knew to get by. She thought the adults were just grasping for some entertainment, so she was relieved when she heard giggles getting louder at the other end of the room and noticed Frank was making everyone laugh playing a hand-piling game with his littlest sister.

Zina sighed. *He can be so charming. Do all boys have this natural knack for making people smile?*

Frank put his hand down flat on the table and motioned for his sister to put hers on top. Then he put his other hand on top of hers. She then copied him. Then he removed his bottom hand and put it on top of the pile. She then did the same.

The pile never went any higher, since it was made of only four hands, but they pretended it did, building on top of air now instead of the table.

Frank liked the infinite nature of this game and used it to illustrate to everyone his dream for the future. Zina watched the scene and knew the story of "Frank's Dream" was coming next. She and Nan had heard it before, and now she waited to see how the others would react.

"As sure as I am Frank the third, someday..." he said, placing one hand on the table, "I will have a son named Frank." He put his other hand on top of his little sister's. "And then my son Frank will have a son named Frank."

His little sister focused her concentration on their hands.

"And then his son will have a son named Frank." He pulled out his bottom hand and placed it on the top. "And he will have a Frank, and then he will have a Frank." He sped up until his little sister got confused and they wound up just slapping each other's hands instead of piling them.

"Oh Frank, that will take two hundred years!" His little sister giggled. Everyone was laughing now, marveling at Frank's imagination for the future and their silly game.

"And also," Frank turned to his father — the second 'Frank' because *his* father was *also* Frank — and he became very serious. "Father, I plan to continue to run the barber shop you started."

"OHH." Now everyone applauded, chattered, and then dispersed, eventually turning their attention to their desserts or other conversations.

"Oh Zina, why don't you go sit by Frank?" Aunt Maria called out to her.

Zina pretended not to hear and moved from her spot after taking her empty dish to the sink. She sat down next to her uncle who was in the only quiet corner. "Frank is charming the room again, Uncle Domino." Zina said, trying to get him to talk, again.

He surprised her with a question, "Do you feel lonely being an only child, Zina?"

Zina wasn't sure how to answer that. "Sometimes yes, because it is quiet." She paused. "But other times no, because it is quiet." Zina replied with a smile, hoping he would smile too.

She saw her mother standing across the room, giving them both a stern look, which Zina chose to ignore. She still wanted to know something and maybe her uncle felt like talking today.

"Why?" Zina asked, "is that how you felt when you first came to America: lonely?"

He sighed, realizing he was cornered into Zina's line of thinking, and said, "Ah yes, you did ask me that before, and yes, it was lonely being here, the first to come to America." He paused. "And it is lonely now when family is all around me, but they are not really related to me. So much talk about legacy. I do miss my brother Angelo. I hope to see him again soon."

Domenico's brother Angelo married one of Zina's aunts, whom she never met. She died the year Zina was born. She did, however, know her daughter, they were once very close but now she only got to see her once a year on Easter since Angelo remarried. His new wife at least allowed that

71

much.

Zina thought about how it was possible for him to feel lonely with family all around. She understood. There feels like something is missing. You know that you belong, but you feel like you are on the outside looking in.

As if on cue, her uncle Domenico got up from the table and went out the back door with his wine. Frank saw that Zina was no longer occupied and called her over.

While outside, Domenico whispered to the night sky, "Legacy. It's what you wanted desperately for me, Father. Now, I have a wife, many sons and daughters, a happy home, and good work. Yes, I have done well by leaving Sicily, I just wish you were alive to see it." He shivered, realizing something new. "But I suppose if you hadn't died and Mother hadn't remarried 'That Man,' I may never have left Sicily."

He took another sip of wine and wondered what kind of life he and Angelo would have had with the curse of their name looming over them if they stayed in Sicily.

"At least here in America, I've been able to sever my sons from the association; protect them. Their names only sound like 'Brex' if you say it right, otherwise the spellings are all different. The Brex name is just a memory now, no path can lead to all of us. I hope that knowledge brings you peace, Father." He finished off his wine, placed the glass on the porch table, and left – melancholy and sad.

"He who leaves succeeds." He mumbled and walked home.

Achieving my dream of a better life requires forward-moving action,

as well as leaving behind the past.

CHAPTER 7

Domenico, 1895

*A Few Days Later
On the Road to Pedara*

The first night of his journey was spent dreaming of his brother and fireflies in the Grotta d'Angelo. The second night, he thought of the crate-carrying girl and the shopkeeper at Barbagallo's who directed him to sleep in a field of grass in Nicolosi. It was pleasantly secluded even though it was full of biting insects. That night he was tormented by an itch as well as the fact that his father's uncle, whom he never knew, ruined their lives with a terrible rumor.

The next morning, Domenico reminded himself of one of the treasured sayings of his father's – to not carry one day's burdens to the next day.

For how long has closing my eyes at night made no difference. Sometimes the only clue that time passes is when the darkness fades into morning. For the last five years I have felt life would always be that way for me – one endless day. No, no more complaints. Look around. I can make a difference today.

Today, he would take a slight detour from his route. Cardaci suggested, if he felt inclined to, that he take a day to travel the mountain trail to the craters of Mount Etna to pay homage before he left Sicily. Since Domenico was closer to the volcano than he had ever been in his life, he thought it was time to venture higher.

The idea was, from Mount Etna, he would be able to see his town of Regalbuto and gain a new perspective. "See the mountain from home yesterday; see home from the mountain today. Then I can move on, toward my new home in America," he reflected aloud.

He trekked as far as he could go, and by midday, he felt overwhelmed by the barren landscape. The ash and dust emitted a feeling of cleansed purgatory, which gave him an idea.

Let Mount Etna absorb all that I am leaving behind, even if it is just symbolically. Let the volcano deal with it once and for all.

The weight of the grief because his father left them too soon and the pain it brought was left among the lava rocks.

The burden of the knowledge of how his father's uncle's rumor changed all of their lives, he deposited in a crater.

His own heated anger toward his mother's weakness in bringing 'That Man' into their lives with his brand of authoritative violence Domenico released with the erupting air pockets from a nearby fissure.

He left all of his frustrations there for the volcano to consume and eradicate from his life.

"In a few months I will be in America. I have to stay focused on where I'm heading and leave the rest behind. I have to trust. Cardaci will help Angelo in my place. Cardaci will keep an eye on Angelo until we are reunited in America."

That night, he returned from the mountain trail to sleep again in the same field of grass.

The fourth morning he woke feeling differently. He remembered the crate-carrying girl. He smiled and shook his head. *The look on her face. It was refreshing to be seen as a stranger. It was still a look of suspicion, but she didn't have a recognition that related to my name or the curse. I was merely what a young girl would consider an ordinary beggaring threat.*

He chuckled. "If I happen to see that look again on someone's face, I will consider it absolution. Perhaps the volcano will truly turn my burdens to dust. Perhaps today the curse will finally be over."

Heading past Nicolosi to Pedara, he followed the route that Cardaci suggested as it was the straightest, with the most opportunity for food and shelter.

He said I will see a sign at the storefront near the Church of Santa Caterina: Privitera's Shop.

CHAPTER 8

Mamie, 1895

Pedara, Sicily

Sweeping and other chores done for the day, Mamie decided to take a short walk toward the church and piazza and see if anything interesting was going on, and then head back to work. It was mid-afternoon, so she told Rose and her papa she wouldn't be away for too long in case she was needed, but she knew they would manage.

It was a very slow day; haze hung heavy in the streets, partially due to Mother Etna blowing off some steam earlier that morning, and partially due to the springtime humidity. For Mamie, it felt like a blanket of boredom set in all around her.

She happened to spot a figure down the road approaching from the west. After her initial shock of seeing someone else on the street, she assumed the figure must be a tourist leaving Nicolosi on foot to head to the Mount Etna trail near her corner of town. But the figure moved slowly, hunched like someone downtrodden, not like a hiker embarking on an adventure.

She quickly walked back to the security of her family's shop. Moments later, the bulky, hairy figure stood in their doorway. He was hunched over a bit and seemed to have to reach across his face to grab the doorknob, he was uncommonly short.

He stomped his feet and brushed his shoes on the mat before stepping in. Rose glanced at the man disapprovingly. She whispered to Mamie, "Do I have to assist *orso bruno* now?"

"Rose, don't be silly, that is not a brown bear." Mamie shushed her younger sister. Her earlier fear of this stranger approaching now changed to surprise, she reached up to cover her astonished mouth. *Could this be the same man I mistook as a boy the other day near Barbagallo's? If not, it would certainly be strange if we were having a wave of very short, hairy men traveling in the area.*

"Good afternoon, I'd like a sandwich, please." The traveler asked in their general direction. Mamie ran back through the door behind the counter to hide her amusement and to find her papa. She knocked into him as he walked toward her.

"Hello there, what can I get for you, son?" Her papa asked after he said 'umph' and rubbed his chest where Mamie's head smacked.

Mamie shifted to stand close behind her papa and not draw attention to herself, but she was so curious she couldn't help but peek over his shoulder at this odd customer. Her papa waved his hand by his ear at her to say "shoo" so Mamie would give him more space.

"Yes, I'd like a sandwich to carry with me to the train." The request was repeated.

"Oh? Leaving for America, are you?"

"Yes, sir. I suppose that's obvious," the traveler said and immediately looked down at his shoes.

Mamie looked down there too, wondering why he did. She saw ordinary looking worn-out boots, probably a size or two too big or else his feet were very disproportionate to his height.

She inspected him more closely without the threat of him looking directly at her, and she noticed that he was not at all a vagabond or a bear, just a regular young man.

Well, at least his clothes are mended and neat, even though they are old and dirty. I feel like he could just be any other boy in town, but a little older, and definitely not rich, but not really poor - just simple, lacking. I guess that's how we are all doing these days - lacking in the things we'd really like to have, settling for what we do have, and making the most of it. Ha, he certainly isn't lacking in the hair department - but in height, well, hm. I might be slightly taller, and I am twelve.

"Apparently all the young men are leaving. Pretty soon there will not be an eligible man around when my daughters are of age," their papa said while he prepared a hunk of his wife's fresh bread.

Mamie heard Rose gasp and shushed her again. They never heard their papa talk openly of their being married before, especially with a stranger.

"Perhaps you should consider America as well, sir." The young man said, a little too firmly. He shifted his gaze, hoping his comment wouldn't be taken in offense, and he focused on the sandwich being built for him.

"Perhaps I should," the older man said, mostly to the salami, "yes, son, perhaps."

Rose looked at Mamie with eyes open as large as they get when the newest fashion magazine arrives. Mamie turned away from Rose to hide her own eye roll. Mamie was more interested in why this young man thought America was a good idea, not why Rose did.

"You are planning on working, and then you will return to Sicily?"

"No, I do not plan on returning, sadly. I plan on working and sending for my brother, Angelo, in a few years. My mother, well, she..." He trailed off and looked down again.

To his credit, their papa did not pry. Mamie wondered what this young man's story was though, so she kept listening for clues. "What town are you from, son?" her papa asked, changing the subject while cutting a slice of cheese.

"Regalbuto, sir." The young man looked up, cautiously, wondering what kind of reaction this admittance would stir in *this* shopkeeper.

"Oh, Regalbuto is far, no? Nine hours to walk?"

Mamie noticed a familiar look on her papa's face. This was one of his ways of probing if a customer had enough money for transportation prior to buying lunch. She's seen how he reacts to those who have a donkey outside or a carriage as opposed to those on foot. He would leave off the onions or tomatoes for the sandwich to not embarrass the people who can't pay for them. Her papa may not have made a lot of money this way, but he thought having customers with their pride intact was a better business model than gouging them with expenses they really couldn't afford. For the ones he thought could afford it, he would make many suggestions for additional meats and cheeses.

What is it about this young man? He looks filthy, but he has very nice manners. Papa seems to like him, at least he treats him not like the beggars that come around, but like the friends.

"Yes, sir. At a brisk pace, yes. Nine hours in two days." The young man exhaled. He looked tired just saying the words. "Then yesterday up and down Mount Etna."

"That is some quest in three days."

"Yes, well, I've been saving up my strength for this journey for a long time," he sort of mumbled to himself.

This has to be the same man that bumped into me two days ago. The one I told to see Salvatore for lodging, Mamie concluded.

"And Regalbuto, it is a wonderful place, yes? I have considered doing business there." The shopkeeper changed the subject again and handed the young man the completed sandwich, wrapped for travel.

"Oh, well, if you shall wish to inquire about business, you must speak with Cardaci. He is well connected and can help you out with any request. Guiseppe Cardaci."

"Thank you I shall remember his name."

"Tell him I recommended him to you; my name is Domenico."

Mamie inhaled sharply. *His name, so much like my own. Domenico, Domenica – not uncommon names, but it is curious to see my name embodied in this short, hairy young man.*

Rose snickered from the other end of the counter, and Mamie shushed her teasing sister again, a little too loudly this time. That was a mistake; she realized she was no longer inconspicuous.

"Hello again, miss," he said to her, softly.

His eyes. Blue, like he tucked some of the bright, warm sky in between his bushy brows and long lashes. I feel warm as the afterimage of his eyes thaws me.

Mamie looked at the others, hoping they did not hear him greet her, and began to blush. She escaped to the back room before it showed.

Rose was confused about Mamie's abrupt and rude exit, and her papa questioned where she was going. Mamie sneaked a last peek at the young man from her hiding place in the storeroom.

Domenico cleared his throat to conclude his transaction, but the shopkeeper was still looking towards Mamie, bewildered at her behavior.

Domenico attempted to get his attention again with a loud farewell. "Thank you for your hospitality, sir. I am going to America to make a new start and leave a legacy. *Chi esce riesce.*"

He who leaves succeeds.

"Be sure you seek me out in America when you arrive." Domenico concluded.

The older man shook his head and chuckled at this young man's confidence and determination. Mamie knew that meant her papa liked the young man; he liked those traits in the men he did business with.

Her papa often remarked with customers that so many townspeople were losing that light of hope in their eyes. Sure, the neighbors may build rooms on top of their homes, but out of necessity instead of choice. The dream of building a legacy for generations was dwindling in the current political and economic climate. Her papa had an energy while talking to this stranger that Mamie hadn't seen in him in a long while, as if his faith in the human spirit had been renewed.

Papa is actually smiling. With teeth showing. A rare sight, Mamie thought.

After Domenico left, Rose appeared ready to burst. Mamie joined her again behind the counter.

Rose whispered loudly before the young man even got both feet out the door. "HE'S going to America?" She was surprisingly indignant. "I didn't think America would let his lot in. Oh Papa, could *we* ever go to America? I've seen pictures of the shops and the theatres and the dresses and..." She sobered a little when their papa groaned, but then continued, trying to hold his attention as he walked away into the back room, "...and of course, there's opportunity and profits to be made. Would we really go? Could we?"

Oh, there's the Rose I know, she wisely caught herself and switched tactics, realizing that the case of American finery is not going to be the winning argument with Papa. She has learned one thing working in the shop now and that is that 'business rules.' If she can argue how something could be good for business, it could be considered, like all her silly frosting on the cannoli.

In the back storeroom, their papa was installing a new shelf earlier that day, so he returned to his task. Rose tried a new angle on her persuading, clearing her throat first. "Papa, what I mean is, he does have a point about the good men. In my class alone there has been a shortage of boys – one for every four girls; and if all those hard-working boys leave for America…" Her voice trailed away since their papa brushed right by her, walking out the door and heading to the shed.

"Rose, maybe now's not the time." Mamie suggested.

⁊)α

Even throughout the next day Rose was fixated on the idea. "Can you imagine America, Mamie? All the possibilities we would have, we can have any future we want!" She twirled and hummed a new song and dance. Their papa walked in after spending some time rummaging in the shed for tools he needed.

He held the hammer and nails and mumbled about nailing Rose's dress to the floor so she would sit at the counter. He passed the girls and returned to the storeroom to continue on the shelf that turned into a long two-day project due to constant distraction.

Rose stopped suddenly, deflated at the threat and returned behind the counter. She sat heavily on the stool, partly pouting, partly dreaming of America. Mamie glanced at her, and although Rose was sitting calmly now, she could see on her sister's face that her imagination was still twirling. Their papa resumed hammering and wouldn't have any discussion, no matter how many times Rose attempted.

"Papa, I only meant…" Rose tried a quiet apology but stopped when a man entered the shop; a man that would understandably make anyone stop mid-sentence.

83

Wearing a pressed wool tweed suit and gleaming leather shoes, the fair-colored gentleman was well groomed, combed, and coiffed. His cleanly shaven face highlighted his crisp bone structure and clear brown eyes; he clutched his hat in his soft and smooth hand as he held open the shop door. A more handsome man did not exist on the pages of Rose's fashion magazines. And he was tall; he had to slightly bend to not brush his neatly styled hair on the top of the door jamb. Rose looked astonished, and he noticed her immediately.

Rose breathed a sigh and whispered in awe, "A *signore biondo*." She recovered slightly, gave him her sweetest smile, and asked how she could assist this handsome, blonde gentleman. She draped herself over the counter, playing with her hair.

Mamie peered peripherally at her sister's behavior but paid more attention to the attraction she noticed on the beautiful man's face toward her sister. *It's interesting, his expression, I've never quite seen that look before when I speak to customers.*

Their papa stuck his head in the shop, asking Mamie to come back in the storeroom to help him when he noticed the customer. His eyes flipped to suspicion after seeing the interaction between his daughter and this man.

"Can I help you, sir?" He set his hammer down on the shop counter with a thud. Mamie noticed that their papa typically used "sir" when a man was dressed nicely, and "son" if they looked like the rest of them, like Domenico.

"Yes." The gentleman seemed to be trying to find the words, stumbling a bit. "Uh, yes, you can help me. Has there been a man through here, ragged, short, with lots of dark hair? From Regalbuto?" He said, now impatiently.

I wonder why he is asking that. He doesn't look like any kind of official, just a well-dressed man.

"Who? Oh, a nice young man from Regalbuto? I might have seen him. Would you like to see our cannoli today?"

"Oh, you've seen him, hmm?" The gentleman mumbled something under his breath then realized the shopkeeper was staring, expecting an answer. Completely ignoring the offer of pastry, the gentleman turned away and continued to talk to himself, mostly. "Wandering around, traveling by foot I suppose" he remarked, with a condescending chuckle. Mamie looked outside to see how he was traveling, and of course, there was a beautiful carriage with horses outside the shop door.

Even though his adornments were impressive, Mamie didn't like his tone and attitude; he seemed to be looking down his nose at the shopkeepers that were bereft of his fineries. Rose didn't seem to mind, but Mamie couldn't stand his smugness.

"No, sir, for your information, he was heading to America." She offered. The gentleman looked at Mamie, incredulous that she would speak to him. He smiled snidely and looked her up and down; his stare penetrated her insides.

She felt uneasy. *Why I would try to have the last word, I don't know. But how dare he come into our shop and treat us like this? I wanted to say that the visitor from Regalbuto was more welcome than he was, money or no money.*

The gentleman looked away from Mamie and dismissed her altogether, brushing the whole discussion off with a wave, as if by doing so, he could make anything disappear. He was now more at ease, satisfied with his assertion of status, but he again appeared to be looking for something, his eyes darting around, uneasily.

His gaze found Rose again and his countenance shifted like he remembered his lines for a performance on stage. "So, I was told I could find a, uh, bottle of fine wine here?" The gentleman said, with his eyes still on Rose, emphasizing the word "fine" with a slight eyebrow raise. Mamie looked at him with further disapproval.

"Oh, uh, yes sir, let me show you to the shelves." Their papa didn't notice the man's lewdness toward his younger daughter as he showed the

85

gentleman to the shelves where his homemade wine variety was displayed with pride.

The gentleman made his way to the back of the store with their papa with his nose turned up at the other wares he passed, purposefully ignoring the varied assortment. Their store was known to stock many goods for every class of worker and homemaker, but this man appeared to be overly conscious and disgusted by the class clashes.

Mamie watched them together and remembered how differently her papa reacted to the young hairy man who was dirty and smelled odd, and how he was now treating this well-kept handsome blonde gentleman. She was surprised her papa didn't seem to trust *this* man.

The men exchanged a few words in hushed whispers and finally the gentleman put his hat back on his head and gave it a flick toward the shopkeeper before turning to leave without purchasing any wine or even bidding good afternoon. Rose blushed and hid her smile as the gentleman walked past her.

Mamie frowned. *I wonder what kind of encouraging or appreciative look he gave her. Heaven knows I have no idea what that look looks like.*

When the man exited, the door nearly blew open. Mamie told her papa that it looked like a storm was coming and he responded that they would close early. She rushed to move the shop sign to "closed" and looked questioningly at her papa. She wasn't sure if his handwringing and eyebrow furrowing was due to his discussion with their recent customer or the weather.

Inside, the mood was somber and hesitant; outside, the light was fading fast, and the wind was swirling around the small debris. *Could the wind cause there to be less to sweep tomorrow?* Mamie sighed at that fleeting thought.

Her papa grabbed the hammer and went back to the shelf, pounding it louder and with more nails than it likely needed, echoing the thunder that started to shake the shop.

CHAPTER 9

Mamie, 1895

Pedara, Sicily

T he next morning, Mamie woke extra early because her papa needed her to help repair the damage the storm did to their shed overnight.

Mamie tried her best to hold up the broken board as high as he wanted her to, but she couldn't hold it – or hold back her tears.

"Papa, I am not of any help to you." She set her end of the board down in frustration. "I'm so sorry. I am trying, but I can't do this kind of lifting. Carrying crates of fruit is hard enough."

"Mamie don't be sorry. I do rely on you my girl, but it is ok to know your limitations. Please don't cry, we will get help."

Mamie felt relieved but ashamed at the same time.

"Go wake Rose so she can make preparations in the shop, and wake Francesco so he can at least begin cleaning up the yard. Then go ask Cousin Salvatore if he can spare a worker for a few days to help us with the shed."

Cringing at the thought of seeing him again so soon, she resigned. She wasn't in the mood to engage with Foul Sal's personality today, but it was the best option.

She headed down Via LaRosa until she came to Via Barbagallo and entered Salvatore's shop on the corner. Announcing her papa's request, she was told there was not a spare man as many others were tending to damage as well. Mamie noticed the strain in his response. He was short with her, instead of his typically over-attentive manner. Mamie looked confused at the change.

A voice addressed her from a dark corner of the shop.

"Ah, the Privitera shopkeeper's daughter."

Salvatore looked into the shadow then looked right at Mamie, motioning as if presenting the man as her solution and left through the door behind the counter.

Alone now, her senses sharpened. She shivered at being recognized and thought of yesterday's seemingly handsome "*signore biondo*" with his snide remarks and rude attitude. He didn't like that she challenged him about his questions about Domenico and America. She didn't like how her father didn't seem to trust him. She headed out the door quickly, nervously.

Once outside, she walked faster. The man followed her out of the store and stopped her on the road. "Please wait, I just want to ask you about your inquiry. What kind of work does your papa need help with?"

Mamie stopped and turned to face the voice. In the sunlight now she realized it was Domenico, not the rude, blonde man, and she exhaled a sigh of relief.

"Oh, it's you. Wait, why are you even here? This isn't the way to the train…" She stopped. *What if Domenico can't be trusted either? He said he was going to America, but here he is, backtracking in the exact opposite direction.* She quickly turned to leave.

After a few steps, she remembered her errand and stopped. *I can't go home and tell Papa he won't have any help, and I can't be the one who helps. I must find someone, and Domenico seems to be the only one available. Papa did seem to like him when they met. Should I take a chance? If Papa wants to refuse him, he can; he just asked me to find someone.*

She turned back to the young man to reply and found him staring at her. Caught off guard, her eyes locked with his. *His blue eyes are like calm waters. I feel like I am floating on an ocean far, far away.*

He started to say that he underestimated the money he needed for the train at the same time Mamie began to explain, "I... I think Papa is repairing the shed, and I cannot hold the boards."

She sobered a little, cleared her throat, and continued, "I can of course, hold them, but not over my head for lengths of time, that is, of course, for him to nail and repair them, the boards. But I can lift them, you know, they are not too heavy for me."

What is wrong with me? Why am I trying to lead him to believe I am strong? Right, Mother's words remind me. Oh, but he is not the sort of man I wish to gain the appreciation of. I wouldn't want to end up with him in my life. Not at all.

She shook her head "no" to correspond with her thoughts.

The young man just looked at her, obviously confused. "So no, they are not heavy, or no, you don't need help?"

"No. I mean yes, we need help. Please, Papa could use your help." She finally blurted it out just as Salvatore appeared in the doorway of the shop, looking interested in their conversation and a little bit defeated.

Maybe Domenico can continue to fix Foul Sal's interest in me, along with the shed.

"Follow me." Mamie turned and led Domenico down the road to her family's shop. After a few feet, Domenico looked over his shoulder back at

Barbagallo's.

"Is there something wrong?" Mamie asked and looked where he was looking.

"Oh, no, I just wondered if that shop boy was still watching us leave."

Why is he wanting to make sure Salvatore is watching us? Or maybe he wants to make sure that nobody is watching us. Maybe this is a bad idea. "Why were you wondering that?" she asked, nervously.

"Is he interested in you? He kept giving me the *mal'occhio*, like he had a claim on you. I just wanted to be sure he wasn't going to jump me from behind to defend your honor."

Mamie had to laugh. *An evil-eyed donkey jumping on the back of a bear.* "Who, Salvatore? We call him Foul Sal. He is interested in me, but I am definitely not interested in him."

"I see."

"Is that why you wear that coral horn? To ward off the evil eye? I've heard of that, but my mother does not believe it, so she forbids us to."

He realized the long orange pendant he wore was now exposed, so he safely tucked it back under his shirt. "Yes, this *cornicello* is to protect me from *mal'occhio*; it is from my mother."

Mamie thought it was sweet that his mother would want to protect her grown son, probably because he was making such a journey.

"May I ask your name, miss?"

"I am Domenica Privitera, but my family calls me Mamie."

"It is nice to officially meet you, and nice to see you again. I would be honored to be of assistance to your father."

Mamie could feel herself blushing, so she was thankful that he began a conversation to put her more at ease. He started with a string of questions like, what did she like best about their town? Does she still go to school? How many siblings does she have? He seemed genuinely interested in being friendly. Her suspicions subsided.

Their questions and answers began to just flow, naturally.

This is nice. He is so easy to talk to. I forget how much older he is than me, I forget his hairiness and crude look. He has nice eyes and a nice smile. He is kind and well-mannered. I know he wasn't actually a wild animal to start with, but now I feel as though during our walk and talk, he has been transformed into a domesticated, yet still hairy, nice person.

She was still smiling when they arrived at her courtyard and headed toward her papa, who was impatiently awaiting help with the shed.

Surprisingly, they were received with a frown. "Ah, Mamie, you brought the traveler from Regalbuto. Back from America so soon?" Her papa glared at them with his arms crossed.

Mamie looked at her papa and laughed nervously at the awkwardness.

Domenico was confused about the older man's cold greeting and quickly explained. "Sir, I found out from other travelers that the money I had for the trip was not going to be enough to get to America, only enough for a train to the Port of Messina, unless I'd want to walk another seven days." He took a breath and sighed. "Five years of saving and I don't even have enough to leave Sicily for the mainland of Italy, much less get to the port of Napoli where the boats for America depart. I backtracked to Nicolosi since I remembered seeing shops when I passed on my way here, and then, by a stroke of luck, I saw your daughter at Barbagallo's again, looking for a worker. Sir, I need a wage for a few days if you are looking to hire someone to help." He finally finished, breathless and hopeful that the older man would understand and consider his situation.

Mamie looked at her papa hoping he was unaware that this man had seen

91

her at Barbagallo's more than once. She was relieved that she wouldn't have to explain that she dropped the lemons the other day.

"But one condition." Her papa paused first to weigh the decision to give Domenico a warning. "No one is to know you are here. You work a few days, and once the job is done you are done and you leave, yes?"

Domenico seemed confused by this cool arrangement but agreed. "Yes, I shall be discreet and then depart. No problems from me, sir."

"I can pay you a fair sum for up to four days to help me with the shed, and I will provide you with one meal a day. You can sleep in the part of the shed that is not damaged, and then save your earnings."

"Oh, yes, that is a deal."

Mamie's papa nodded and returned to a friendlier mood towards Domenico. Perhaps he was just grateful to have anyone help that whatever apprehension he had when Domenico reappeared now dissipated.

They shook hands on it and Domenico took off his coat and his first layer of shirts. He placed them under the nearest olive tree so he could start working immediately. As the pile of discarded garments grew, the young man shrunk. His hair was matted with sweat which made him look dirtier than he was; the dust just clinging to the dampness. He was much thinner and neater looking without wearing his luggage; the bear man was just a young man.

Mamie looked at both men with satisfaction. They both had something they needed help with, and she brought them together. She smiled to herself knowing she wouldn't have to be the one helping, and she looked forward to perhaps having more conversations with Domenico in the coming days. But then she remembered the men's arrangement and wasn't sure if she should be more cautious.

I wonder why Papa didn't want Domenico to let anyone know that he is here to help us. We aren't used to having visitors staying, and we've had our fill of interesting encounters these last few days, but why the secrecy?

ℬↃℭℛ

During the next few days, their hired worker slept, ate, and worked near the Privitera's shop and family. They kept him inconspicuous like her papa wanted, whatever his reason was for why seemed to no longer be important.

The men sounded like they got along well. Mamie was called outside to fetch things as the men worked, and she welcomed the chance to listen to their conversations. They had many things in common, and they discussed topics Mamie never heard her papa talk about before: growing new types of grapes, distilling wine from peaches, towns on the other side of Mount Etna, cities her papa's family was from, the exporting business, and America. Mamie found she couldn't stay away; she kept finding reasons to linger and listen.

"Mamie, come here, away from that tree, what are you doing there? Please take our friend Domenico over to the pump to wash up before dinner. Mama has been making her sauce all day, it's calling my name so we will end work for today."

"Papa," she began, but it sounded like a whine so instead she asked quietly, "why do I have to escort him to wash his hands? Didn't he do that all by himself yesterday?" She looked at her father with that question and he understood. He leaned in to whisper an explanation.

"Mamie, Domenico is a nice young man. I misunderstood his intentions when he came back, looking for work. Remember that well-dressed gentleman who came to our shop? He whispered something to me, something I did not want to have to tell you girls."

"What, Papa?" Mamie had wondered what that was all about and why he seemed so secretive.

"He told me to be on the lookout for his stepson, who he said was an untrustworthy young man from Regalbuto on the run from his family and

93

his responsibilities. I suspected it could be Domenico because he too is from Regalbuto, he didn't leave for America like he said he planned to, and because he showed up here again."

He put his hand on his daughter's arm to reassure her. "But after talking with Domenico, he is clearly not the person that gentleman was looking for. Domenico is a nice young man." Her papa said that part again with emphasis. His eyes had a smiling quality, a knowing look, and he nodded his head at his daughter that everything was alright. She understood this as his approval.

So, Mamie obeyed and motioned for Domenico to follow her to the well.

ഇൗൽ

"How much longer is that bear going to be staying here?" Rose whined.

"What do you have against Domenico? Papa is happy with him and I'm glad he can help so I don't have to. He seems nice enough."

Rose looked at Mamie questioningly and wondered why she was standing up for him.

"I only mean to say we should be grateful for his help, not call him names, Rose."

"He is staying on our property and sharing our food, Mamie. I can call him what I want. He is dirty and hairy, and he looks like a bear. I've been having nightmares about bears ever since he showed up!" Rose stated, dramatically. She got up from her bed and declared, "Let's just finish the chores this morning, Mamie, and stop all this talk. *La Festa Patronale* is tomorrow!" Rose had been looking forward to this for months: the Feast Day of Saint Rita, the Saint of Lost Causes.

The girls headed down to breakfast before the shop opened and saw that everyone in their family was wide awake today. Their mother was cooking some eggs, Concetta was looking for Joseph, and Francesco was fixing

Agatha's hair, trying to tie it up out of her eyes and laughing about how she kept getting food in it.

"Francesco is just about the same age and height as my brother, Angelo." Domenico said to nobody. He looked at Francesco and then down, with that sad mumble to himself.

Mamie was surprised to see that their guest was at her place at their table.

Grazia was the most intrigued by this guest. It was mutual, as Domenico looked impressed by everything she did, a small girl of six, full of little girl precociousness.

Concetta sat a wriggling Joseph at the table and retreated to a corner of the room, not participating in any conversation. She put her nose in a book and stayed by herself. The rest of the group ignored her too.

Mamie thought Domenico's attention would be absorbed with the cuteness of the babies, Agatha and Joseph, but he seemed to ignore the little ones completely. She supposed he felt awkward around the small children's neediness and behaviors. Domenico seemed interested in Grazia and Francesco the most.

After breakfast, Mamie headed out with her basket again, and Domenico surprised her by asking if he could walk with her. He needed to go to Nicolosi to get a few more boards that her papa asked for, and she could have company on her walk to get more fruit.

Mamie looked back to her papa who was standing on the porch. He gave her a wave, looking satisfied with himself.

She didn't object to Domenico's request, and they began what felt to her to be a very long, quiet walk. *What will I talk to him about now? We used up all the basic conversation topics the other day, and I can't let on that I've been eavesdropping on his conversations with Papa.*

"So, your brother Angelo is the same age as my brother, Francesco, is that

95

right?" Mamie asked, already knowing the answer.

"Yes."

They walked a few more minutes in silence.

I guess I didn't do a good job starting a conversation, she thought, so she tried again. "It must be hard for you to leave your brother. I know it would be hard for me to live even a few towns away from my family. How someone can live a whole continent away, I can't comprehend."

"Yes, but I have a plan, he will not stay in Sicily. I will bring him to America with me, where he will be safe."

"Safe? What do you mean?" She asked.

He turned away, quiet again.

Oh, I know I'm trying too hard. I just want to know a little more about this man who has been sharing our table and helping us all these days. This man that Papa seems to like and might like for me.

"Family is really important to me too; I would do anything for my family." Mamie related to him that they shared common ground. "I would never want to hurt them or do something that puts them in harm's way. We are safe here in Pedara; is Regalbuto a safe place?"

He quickly changed the subject and made an unexpected remark about how happy and healthy Mamie's two baby siblings appeared to be.

She looked at him. *He hardly paid any attention to the little ones. Why would he be surprised they were healthy?*

Mamie tried something else. "What does your family call you? Do you have a nickname?"

"Oh, well, no, I'm just Domenico." He said, and slowly added; quietly, "My little brother, Angelo, is the only one that calls me Dom."

Domenico. Dom.

"I like it." She hoped he didn't hear her. *I'd like to call him Dom too, but I am sensing that any reminder of Angelo pains him. I have a feeling the nickname is special to only the two of them and I would be intruding; I'm not quite special enough to use it and I'm not sure why I want to. What is his story? He seems lonely, this unkempt and rough young man who looks sad about leaving behind his younger brother. Why would they not travel together?*

She moved to another topic, something that he might like to talk about. "Can you tell me more about your plans when you get to America?"

He told her about the Scalabrinians and their mission. She asked questions about what that was. He talked about how his church in Regalbuto has been working with this group whose purpose is to assist Sicilians immigrating to America. He knew of some people who do work with a sister church in New York City, so both sides of the voyage cooperate. This group helped with the language translation, bookings of passage, even with wiring money to family.

"Cardaci has recommended them to me, he supports them, and he helps in the mission too."

Mamie found herself trying to commit the names to memory just in case she would ever go to America too. *I suppose I can dream.*

"So, do you have plans to marry in America?" Mamie said and quickly wished she didn't. Blushing, she ran ahead of him to try to escape the awkwardness, hoping he didn't even hear her.

Why did I ask that? It just slipped out and I don't even know where the question came from. Now there is nowhere to hide; no way to take it back. I'll just ignore it, pretend that I ever asked him about his marriage plans; it really is none of my business.

Domenico caught up to her and said nothing more about it.

She wanted to catch a glimpse of his expression, to decide what to say next. But instead, she found him staring straight at her. This time his blue eyes were as cold as the top of Mount Etna in March, where the snow meets the sky. Mamie shivered.

"You should be spending time with boys your own age, Domenica."

Oh no, he did hear me.

"You must've learned some etiquette regarding talking to elders somewhere, from your parents, or schoolmates?" He questioned.

Rules? Elders? Etiquette? Is he reprimanding me? Oh, Mamie, you ruined everything.

She fumbled to explain; the heat rising in her cheeks. "I stopped going to school when I was ten, the year I started in the shop. We didn't talk much about boys there if that's what you mean. Well, after church the girls talked about boys, but nobody talks about *how* to talk to them."

I am not sure what to say, I'm not even sure why I'm trying to explain anything. I am rambling like I want him to see me as innocent. Which of course I am. Why is it so wrong that I am interested in talking with him?

"Well, let me just give you one small piece of advice if I may. Men will always want to get to know you better. You must be the one to decide when and how that occurs. Patience is always the best choice, Domenica."

She just put her head down to hide her embarrassment and vowed to herself that she would not speak again until she said goodbye to him tomorrow.

Or maybe I won't even say goodbye. I don't owe him anything. I didn't ask for his advice. What on earth does he mean? Patience, for what? For getting to know someone? For asking questions? For how long? I don't want to be patient; I think that is it. It's condescending, like I am a small child he brushed aside. I want to be ready for when the perfect man comes along. I can't help it. I want to know. Mother's advice never covers what to say, only how to be a hard worker. How do you live with a husband until you die but not know how to talk to him? The only good thing here is, Domenico will be gone soon, and I'll never have to see him again.

But why does that thought give me a weird feeling?

☙❧

The barn shed was finished the next morning, everyone was satisfied with the job, and it was time for Domenico to move on. Mamie felt edgy, thinking about his upcoming departure. She had originally hoped he would have at least stayed until the feast day picnic later, but now she can understand his need to be away from her as quickly as he could go.

Oh, why did I mess things up? Putting aside the hints that Papa thought he might be a match for me, I feel as though I am losing a new friend, and this makes me sad.

I can't help dreaming, wondering about what could have been with Dom (I am secretly calling him that in my mind.) Not only has he been the only man besides family that I have ever talked to at length – actual conversations, but he is also so different in how he talks, and how he views my family.

He's been my glimpse as to what a young man should be, who I should look for and what traits to seek out. Like Rose, I'm forming my idea of the perfect man; for me it would be one that talks and thinks like Dom and looks and dresses like a man in an American magazine.

Whatever Dom means by patience, I will just ignore. I will try to still be friendly and wish him well when we say goodbye today.

And as far as finding my perfect man, I'm planning on...what? I have no idea what should happen next. Maybe that is what I am impatient for, knowing what comes next. I suppose I can demonstrate my various lifting and carrying capabilities. Ugh.

Maybe I am doomed since there are so few boys my age here in Pedara, and

I certainly do not want to be available for Foul Sal.

But then, there is America. I can dream. I can imagine who I might meet there, and maybe there will be plenty of good-looking men to choose from.

One of them will look at me and see that I am his perfect mate. We will get married, have a big family, and make lots of money; be in love and be happy.

Or maybe someone will cross my path at the feast day picnic later. Yes, that is more realistic than an encounter in America, and I wouldn't have to wait so long either.

Oh, Dear Saint Rita, hear my prayer. Help my love life to not be a lost cause. Amen.

~ENTRY #5~

12/24/1929

My dear friend,

Oh, Christmas Eve! Tomorrow I can finally give everyone their presents! I'm excited to give Nan the light pink handkerchief I crocheted white lace roses on; and Gracie and May will each get new crocheted slippers. I made Mother a pot scrubber and Papa a short wool scarf. Frank will get a longer scarf since I started his first. For his sisters and Aunt Maria I made small lace flowers they can use as hair pins or sew on a dress or collar. And for you, my dear friend, I braided these ribbons for you as a bookmark! Do you like it? I hope everyone will like what I've made for them.

I'm so excited! Mother has been cooking all day; I wish I could describe delicious aromas that fill the house when she makes her homemade sauce. If I could translate smell into text for you, my dear friend, I would.

In the morning, we will take the subway to Mineola to Frank's house on Willis Avenue. It's a fun house to visit, they have so many doors and stairwells. They live in one of the two apartments above their barbershop. Frank's grandmother, Mrs. Arcoleo, lives in the other with her husband, Frank Curti.

They've been married for about fifteen years, and they are very demonstrative of their affection for each other. Aunt Maria has asked them on more than one occasion to stop acting like newlyweds as they tend to make everyone uncomfortable. I will just say that much.

Well. Now that I've said that much, I can't stop thinking about it! Yuck. I never see my parents act that way, but they seem to love each other too. So how do people really act when they are in love?

If I had a boyfriend, and I'm not saying it would be Frank, but someone like Frank, would I even want to hold hands and kiss? What would that be like? And another thing, do all boys smell of shaving tonic like Frank does? Would they all have little stubbles on their chin? Would every boy's hair be shiny with grease, and would that be soft or sticky if I touched it?

Oh, I can't believe I'm letting my thoughts wander like this. If I had an older sister or cousin maybe she could tell me what boys are like. Gracie's older sister, Josephine, is my only possibility, but she never tells me anything. I guess I'll just rely on my imagination.

Now, time to un-imagine these things, especially about Frank. I have to see him tomorrow! What if he knew I was thinking about how he smelled? So embarrassing! I better get to sleep before I think of something else. Goodnight,

~Zina

CHAPTER 10

Zina

Wednesday, December 25, 1929

"**M**erry Christmas, Frank." Zina said shyly and looked away. She greeted everyone else first when she arrived at the Vincenti's house, but somehow in addressing Frank she felt like she was speaking for the first time. Thankfully, eight-year-old Connie ran up to give Zina a hug hello, which gave her a way to hide her blushing face.

"Zina, come help us in the kitchen." Josie called, impatiently, then took Zina's hand and led her to the room where the ladies were bustling with preparations for the family feast. Josie was a year younger than Frank and the same age as Zina. Frank's oldest sisters, Santina and Marianna, were already layering the rice, homemade tomato sauce, the mozzarella and parmesan, and the homemade meatballs prepared just that morning into large pans for Baked Rice, or *Riso al Forno,* a family tradition tracing back to the days of their great grandparents in Caltagirone, Sicily. The girls gave Zina smiles, partial waves, and Merry Christmas greetings and concentrated back on the ratios and placement of the layers, being sure to avoid clumps or light spots. They had this recipe memorized and Zina watched, mesmerized. One day she would like to learn to make this dish too, because it is so delicious.

"Zina, put on an apron and come help me with the cookies." Maria waved her over, gave her a kiss on both cheeks and a pat on the back, and set Zina up in front of the flour and dough to roll. By help, she meant to 'stand in this place and take care of this task'.

"Aunt Maria, why don't you shape these as the letter "V" for Vincenti? When my mother make this recipe, we shape them as the letter "S" for Sagone." Zina asked.

"Yes, Zina, how clever. Ah, but someday, when you make these cookies, perhaps you will shape them as a "V," too, yes?" Maria winked.

Zina looked away, embarrassed. *I wish she wouldn't do that,* she thought.

"The "S" is for Sicily, Zina." Santina leaned over and whispered, giving her a wink too. Zina blushed even more if that were possible.

Maria continued to orchestrate the preparations. "Connie, get the table set, I've already laid out the dishes and glasses. When I come back from talking with Rose, we will eat."

Connie slightly rolled her eyes so her mother wouldn't see. Zina realized this meant she was being asked to not only handle the silverware, napkins, and trivets but also juggle her little brothers. Joseph, at age four, usually followed her directions well, but baby Vinny was not yet two. She would have to carry him around on her hip unless she could find a place to deposit him with the men in the other small room.

The Vincenti's house was different than Zina's. There were only a few rooms in their apartment above the barber shop, and being on the second floor, it was not as easy to spread out when entertaining. Most of the furniture typically in the living and dining rooms was moved into the girls' bedroom to make space for only the furniture one could comfortably sit at to eat.

Rose waited in Maria's bedroom since arriving, wanting to get a few minutes alone with Maria. She paced back and forth until Maria finally entered.

"Rose, what has gotten you so wound up? Come on, it's Christmas."

"Maria, she is at it again, now its every week. What am I going to do?"

"First, take a deep breath. Now, let us enjoy our meal and not think about it, we can talk more after."

After their delicious Christmas dinner, the women cleared the table for the men to play cards and went to the kitchen to clean up after the preparations. The younger kids went to play on the couch now found in the girls' room, and some of the older girls went to sit on the stairs in the hall outside of the apartment door.

Zina was sitting with Josie and Marianna when Santina peeked her head in the stairwell. She said she had something for Zina. "Not really a gift, but sort of a gift."

"Ooh, a hand-me-down?" Zina guessed and clapped.

Fifteen-year-old Santina just laughed. "You're the only one who loves them that much, Zina."

"It's because it is so rare to me. Thank you." Zina said and cleared a tickle forming in her throat.

Santina deposited her too-small roller skates by Zina's feet. Normally she would hand them down to her sisters but, miraculously, Zina's feet were smaller than Connie's. Zina gave her a hug carefully after securing the skates so they would not roll down the stairs.

Santina told her it was just a little thing, smiled, and went down the stairs to deliver "S" cookies to their neighbors.

The other girls left to either investigate what the little kids were doing in their room or make a phone call. Zina sat alone on the stairs admiring her new skates when she overheard her mother and her aunt Maria whispering in the kitchen.

"She is being unreasonable. What's done is done, it is final."

Who is Mother saying is unreasonable? What is final? She listened some more.

"And, why on earth is she doing this now? She is nearly twelve years old. Yes, I know she has started this a few times in the past, yes, and she forgets about it in a few weeks, but now, no, she has no right! She has to realize that."

Oh no, what did I do? Is this about me not liking the new school? And I have no right? I don't understand.

Maria said calmly, "She cannot do anything about it, remember? You are letting your imagination run away with you. It will all blow over."

"I hope so, her whims have made my life miserable far too many times. She has always played the victim, even when she was younger, and she expects everyone around her to make restitutions. She has to stop."

Just then Zina felt a tap on her shoulder and jumped. "Oh Joseph! Thank you." Her young cousin shyly gave her a cookie and ran away.

She cringed when she saw Frank standing behind his little brother.

Feeling caught, Zina stood up quickly and brushed off her skirt. Frank thankfully didn't seem to notice she was eavesdropping. He was gathering everyone to open presents before dessert, so she followed.

She didn't feel like opening gifts now. That conversation caused her to feel like she was just given some sort of Pandora's box; a trunk of disruption that should've remained closed.

The mothers' conversation continued out of Zina's earshot.

"Calm down, Rose, she can't undo this."

~ENTRY #6~

12/26/1929

My dear friend,

Christmas at the Vincenti's was lovely, of course; the visit was nice, the food was delicious, and the gifts were gracious and generous. Everyone loved what I made them, too.

But even with all the goodness around me, I got a funny feeling that isn't going away. Like there is something underneath the pretty packaging that is not a sentiment that would make me smile.

It's not just what I overheard Mother and Aunt Maria say last night, others have been acting oddly too, when I really start to think about it.

Josephine continues to ask if I'm able to "interpret" everything people say now. I get the feeling there's some kind of joke behind it, why is she being sarcastic about what I'm learning at school?

Then Aunt Mamie said a few weeks ago that she thought my school was ridiculous. Then she stopped herself like she shouldn't say more. Do I complain that much about school?

And now, whatever my mother and Aunt Maria were talking about yesterday is mixed in. Am I really making my mother miserable? That I think the world should cater to me?

I'm so confused. Is there something that everyone wants to tell me, but they don't know how to say it? Is there something wrong with me, with how I act or talk? I'm sure you would be open with me, my dear friend, if you could be. I'm afraid that sometimes I can imagine something out of nothing, but do you see it? Do you think everyone is acting strangely?

At least Aunt Mamie made an effort to talk to me earlier this morning when she came over to help Mother start the dinner we are all having tonight. Mother never talks to me about anything, but Aunt Mamie loves to talk. Aunt Mamie and Mother are so different; it's amazing to me sometimes that they are sisters.

So, when Mother went to answer a phone call from Aunt Maria, Aunt Mamie had me help her start the lasagna. While we worked, she told me about her life in Sicily when she was twelve like I am (almost.) She shared how her father was the one to determine who she should marry and other traditions that dictated where she would live; she talked about how she felt so controlled and not in control of her own life.

I feel like that sometimes too, and I told her. My parents want me to go to this school to be an interpreter, and I want to be a nurse. Aunt Mamie looked so surprised when I said that. She said my mother did too. That made me a little sad and she asked why. I couldn't really say that I didn't feel close to my mother, that she never told me about wanting to be a nurse herself. So, I just said I wished my mother would talk to me more.

She looked like she would start to cry and asked me what I would want to talk to her about. I told her I am not happy at my school, and I am frustrated. That I wish I could decide for myself what to study and I don't understand why I can't. When they all came to America, they got to decide to do that – change their life. Why can't they understand that I might want to do that too?

She really didn't have anything to say in response, she just turned her focus back to the lasagna preparation. Her lips were tightened as if she was forcing herself to keep them closed. Do you think she was afraid to tell me how much I am complaining? Does everyone think that of me?

Then she took the pan out to begin assembling the lasagna. She pointed to the empty pan and asked me what I thought.

I said it will be delicious, and she said, 'thank you but no, that's not what I mean.' Then she asked me another unexpected question, 'do you want to know what lasagna has taught me?' and I just shrugged.

She said, 'patience.' She said, 'your uncle Domenico told me years ago to have patience and I was upset about that. I wanted to see how things would turn out and get through it quickly.'

I understood. I want to know why I am being put on the path of being an interpreter, why I am teased about Frank, and if I am really complaining too much.

So, she says, 'do you know that once I made a lasagna quickly, and it turned out terribly? It was scorched and raw at the same time. Zina, each layer has its own timing. Rushing things turns everything bad. Lasagna is like life; each layer takes time.'

I suppose, my dear friend, that I am in a rush to know how everything will turn out. Is this what Frank was talking about when he said that the growing seed cannot see the tree it will become? Oh, and now lasagna. Everyone I know talks in word pictures. You know, it's funny that this is a type of interpretation I'm learning too, and it is more difficult than any other language.

So, back to the feelings I've been having. Maybe I shouldn't jump to conclusions. Maybe Josephine is just teasing and has no reason. Maybe I misheard my mother. I suppose I will just wait and see; let the layers melt. Maybe if I'm patient, all will be revealed.

I just hope it's soon!!

Good night for now,

~Zina

CHAPTER 11

Zina

Thursday, December 26, 1929

It was late afternoon, nearly time for the rest of the Bregas family to arrive for lasagna and other Christmas day leftovers. Zina's mother was completing the preparations and called Zina to come downstairs.

She made sure Duey was safely in her room with the door closed before she went to greet the family. Zina knew that with so many people in the house he would love some attention, but her mother never permitted him as an extra guest.

Just as she entered the warm kitchen, she began to cough uncontrollably.

"Vincenza! How long has that been going on?" Her mother asked.

Zina's throat had a tickle since she started school. She popped a lemon candy in her mouth and said, "It's nothing." She didn't think her mother would hear her anyway.

The cool air outside also helped to soothe her cough when she answered the door, and she put on a big smile, excited to see her cousins.

Josephine brushed past her and went to say hello to the mothers and other grown-ups, as did Zina's older boy cousins, Vito and Alfred. Zina led the girls, Gracie and May, up to her room right away. She hoped to have a little time with them to hear all about their Christmas before they were all needed to help set the table.

The two youngest, Angelo and Frankie, followed, and kept knocking on Zina's closed door to play with the girls.

"They can't come in Zina; they will mess up your room." May reminded her.

Zina said, "Oh, let them, who else will mess it?"

May was dumbfounded. "You're so lucky Zina, to have all this to yourself. Gracie and I have to share with Josephine, and she always lets us know how she isn't too happy about that."

"Well, she is twenty-three. She will be married sometime soon, May, then we will have more space," said Gracie, always trying to keep the peace.

"The boys have the attic room for the four of them and I don't know how they manage. But again, like you point out, Gracie, Vito is twenty-one and Alfred is twenty, so they ought to be on their own soon too. Oh, won't it be wonderful to only have four of us kids at home instead of seven of us to share everything?" May looked away with an exaggeratedly hopeful smile.

"Well," Zina said, "it is sometimes nice to not have to share. But it's also pretty lonely. Sometimes you want to share, right?"

Gracie and May looked at each other and laughed. "No, we don't ever like to share. If I could keep all my stuff away from *her* I would." May pointed, and Gracie feigned offense.

"You are the lucky one, Zina. Nobody comes in to borrow something without asking, and nobody comes in and messes something you just put away. Nobody comes in, period. It must be so nice." Gracie said, eyeballing May.

Zina knew they wouldn't understand. *Being lonely is more than my things not being disrupted.*

"Lonely is feeling secluded and excluded: not a *part* of something. It would feel nice to be more connected with something I belong to. Sure, I'm a part of my little family trio, and that is a blessing too, but to be a part of a group of peers, others around my own age, is different. I'm lonely at home. I'm lonely at school. I don't even fit in with my love life." Zina didn't pay much attention to what she was saying, and now she realized she shared too much.

The girls were shocked. "Oh Zina, we had no idea you felt that way." Gracie said and put her hand on Zina's arm, consolingly.

By now the boys were quiet outside of the door. The girls forgot they were there until eight-year-old Frankie shouted, "what love life?" and the girls giggled.

"What are you boys doing outside Zina's door?" Mamie apparently had been looking for them. "Both of you, downstairs. Find something else to do." She gave Zina's door a quick knock and opened it. "Girls, why don't you start setting the table now?"

Zina and the girls went into the small kitchen to gather the dishes and glasses, but they were more successful in bumping elbows.

After the family ate, the girls returned to their same positions in the kitchen, now avoiding being sprayed with someone's damp towel. The younger boys played outside, and Josephine and the older boys stayed at the table, sipping their *limoncellos* and talking about grownup stuff with the men. The mothers went upstairs.

Standing closest to one of the kitchen doors, Zina overheard her papa say that her uncle Frank, Frank's father, was glad to have bought his barber shop in 1925, paying cash for it after making some money in the stock market – back when things finally got better after the war ended twelve years ago.

"So, he may have no debt, but also no money in the bank," Domenico said in response.

Zina's papa countered that by pointing out Frank's money was, instead, in his building, his business, and his mattress. The men chuckled.

She was interested in their conversations. She heard next how President Hoover said the effects from the stock market crash will be over "in the next sixty days" and that was almost a year ago now. The men didn't think things had gotten better. One of them said they think it will get worse – way worse – before it actually got better.

Zina heard them name friends who had already lost their jobs. She hoped her Papa would not. It was as if he knew Zina's worry since she heard him remark that there will always be some work to do and someone who will pay to have it done, so he didn't seem concerned in the least.

She heard her uncle Domenico ask where her aunt Mamie was, he was ready to leave. "He who leaves succeeds," he said as she heard the door open. "If only, one of these days, I could succeed in leaving with my family in a timely manner..." He and Zina's papa laughed.

Zina looked out the window over the kitchen sink. Her uncle was waiting there, looking at the garden. She wondered again if he was thinking about how he left Sicily for this new life. Maybe he never imagined America could still have its own share of problems: there was wartime right before she was born and now the Depression that the men were talking about.

Zina asked the girls what they thought as she hung up her dishtowel. They each just shrugged, not having paid attention, so she left to find her aunt to let her know that her uncle was ready to leave.

Upstairs, she found her mother's bedroom door closed. The ladies often relaxed away from the rest of the family after cooking all day, but Zina heard them arguing.

"Mamie, please understand, nothing can change."

"Rose, it is you who needs to understand. Maybe things should be different now that she is older."

"Can you stop bringing this up? Stop telling me I am wrong because I won't allow things to change from my original plan? Can this be over, finally?"

The sisters were disturbed by Zina's quiet knock. "Um, sorry to interrupt Mother, but Aunt Mamie, you are wanted."

The door flew open, and Mamie looked surprised to see Zina standing there. She brushed quickly past, hiding her face.

"I'm sorry, Mother, Uncle Domenico was ready to leave. I was only letting you both know."

Her mother responded with a fierce stare. Zina shivered and quickly went to her room.

The trouble is, the past is always one step behind,

stalking like a shadow.

CHAPTER 12

Domenico, 1895

From Pedara to the Port of Messina, Sicily

H e was leaving again and leaving something behind. Now, it was the repaired shed, the little children, the hospitality, and the brown-eyed Domenica. Mamie.

Why do my thoughts keep returning to the girl who was sneaking glances through her long lashes? Right, she's a girl – a very young girl. I regret that I had to dissuade her like I did, she was so embarrassed. I suppose it's better than her thinking we'll have any continued connection.

"But why is that better?" he asked himself.

And why is she so intriguing? She isn't interested in frills or silly things like Rose, and she is not bookish like the other sister, Concetta. She is not afraid of working hard and is a pretty good conversationalist – at least she was trying, clumsily, in a sweet way. She is not concerned with her looks, or with dainty, impractical, or wasteful things.

"Yes, those are the traits I'd like to find in a woman in America. One who is witty, sweet, and loyal, yet companionable, hard-working – a mate for

life. I'm sure there will be plenty of women like this to choose from."
Domenico felt the loneliness of the journey setting in. Instinctively, he
spoke aloud, and found that his own voice was a comfort, so he continued.

"But how can a mere twelve-year-old girl's attributes cement in my mind
the direction for my future bride? Surely, she doesn't have that much power;
that she controls the shape of my destiny? No. He who leaves succeeds."

He reached the trail that would lead to town, then the train for Messina. The
sun was rising higher, and his many layers nagged him once more that this
was not a good way to pack. He wiped his face, blinked, and tried to focus.

Why can't I wipe Mamie from my mind? She keeps creeping back in.

*There is no solution that includes her in my life. It's not like I can wait years
for her to be of a more suitable marrying age, and her papa did not indicate
they'd actually ever leave for America. Could I marry her sooner? Maybe,
but I'm not sure her family would want her to leave them sooner. She might
be a good worker, but I don't have enough money to support a wife.*

*In three years, I hope to have enough money to rescue Angelo, so could I
wait until after that? Would she wait that long? No, it wouldn't be fair to
her. I don't even know that she or her papa would be open to the idea. She
seems eager and attentive, but it could be a child's curiosity, not real
interest.*

"I must think of what lies ahead and not be tethered to all I'm leaving
behind. Conserve my health, work odd jobs for a meal, progress at a steady
pace. I just hope that there will be someone like her where I am heading.
Try to just think forward, the next stop, the next town, the next mode of
transportation."

He reached the path to the train. His plan was to leave Sicily by ferryboat
from the port of Messina to the mainland and Napoli. Then board one of the
large ships to America.

Still days and miles away; no idea how long. Perhaps a few weeks? A month or two? Traveling on foot is slow; and money for food will go as fast as eating.

Thankfully, I've gained a few days wages in Pedara. The shed, the request for help. Oh, I must stop thinking of her, I will never make any progress forward if I keep my eyes backwards.

He who leaves succeeds. I must go. It will work.

'The journey would be the worst of it. But just get there Domenico. Then, work will be plentiful, a fortune can be made, all the opportunity you ever dreamed of awaits.' Cardaci's confidence reminds me.

Oh, but what would you think of me right now, Cardaci? I feel my faith weakening. But yes, I trust you and God. You both are looking after Angelo and Mother. You will keep 'That Man' in his place until Angelo is safe with me again. You, with your connections, your "ways," you always reassure me, and it always works out. God will help us and protect us. I must stop wavering in my faith and in this plan. He who leaves succeeds. It's what my father would have wanted: his sons to succeed.

"Oh Father, you wanted more for us. Did I ever truly appreciate you? I understand you much better now. You lived outside the political causes, never engaging, and you were always purposefully seeking peace. Worrying about Angelo, now I can relate. You wanted a future for us sons. The girls are married and cared for but how would we boys start our own families with such poverty? What women would want our lives to share? Well, Father, I am on a path now. Leaving the curse you struggled to remedy but ran out of time."

Domenico felt a fire in his stomach, he didn't want to be stuck here.

"I hope, Father, that you could forgive Mother for marrying 'That Man', and only three years after you died." His words began to stick in his throat as he still struggled to forgive his mother himself. "It is because of that marriage that I'm on this journey – this path that Cardaci helped me strategize."

He continued his walk, trying to keep his mind occupied, and strengthening his resolve by coming to terms with all his feelings of the past. His memory was like a companion for him to share his thoughts with as he moved along.

He remembered the first night he talked with Angelo and conspired with Cardaci to plan for them both to get away. Why it was best, why it was what his father would have wanted – the shortened version for his little brother's ears. He was only six, so Domenico didn't tell him much.

Their mother overheard, and surprisingly did not try to talk them out of it. Domenico expressed his guilt about leaving her behind, but she said that was exactly what she wanted him to do. She didn't want to go to America, her life was in Sicily, and she would die there too. Domenico had to make a new life for himself and for Angelo.

While Domenico worked toward the plan, she kept 'That Man' in the dark, especially when his true nature became more apparent. All his feigned finery disappeared. Domenico's mother finally saw him for who he truly was.

They were careful, knowing that if he found out they were scheming to leave Sicily, he would be furious and keep them from leaving, somehow. He wanted the boys, well at least Angelo; he thought they would be his sons.

Domenico's three-hour walk began to move faster than he thought it would; his thoughts fueled his feet.

Finally, he saw a sign for the AciReale train station and bought his ticket for Messina. He reviewed his meager funds and resolved to find work when he arrived at the port so he could finally have something to eat as well as continue on his trip.

He sat at the front of the train car, the first one aboard. Passengers filled the seats from behind him, the train blew its whistle, and they left the station. He was so physically exhausted that he didn't bother to remove any of his layers.

He watched the blur of the trees and was amazed at the pace, having never been on a train before. The air hummed; the tracks shook. Domenico found that the motion was calming his nerves, but he couldn't keep his mind quiet. He reviewed his plans again – a habit formed in the last few years that was hard to break.

After this train, next, I will board a ferryboat to cross from Messina to the port of Napoli, then board a steamship from Napoli to America. Cardaci travels back and forth so easily; I can certainly do this.

I will work in America and send Angelo the money through the churches and their immigrant aid mission. I will save enough to head back here to get him. Bring him with me to America. I will avoid 'That Man', somehow, when I do. The plan will work. It must.

He felt assured enough now to rest, and he closed his eyes.

"Ha, ha, yeah," A loud, deep and scratchy voice assaulted Domenico's attempt to relax. Somewhere behind him, a man boasted, "the chubby daughter is the one who told me, that silly girl. She must've thought she was defending his honor or something."

"Won't he be surprised if you catch him before he leaves for America?" A second man joined in with a cackling laugh, obnoxiously.

"Right. We have the element of surprise. He doesn't know that we've been following him. Even though we've lost sight of him a few days ago, at least we know where he's heading."

Domenico's calm quickly vanished, and all the heat of his body dissipated.

"Ticket, please, sir."

His eyes flashed open upon hearing this impatient request right by his ear. Domenico fumbled, nodded, and handed over the paper. The collector continued toward the back of the train, and Domenico's eyes covertly followed him, glancing carefully in the direction of the voices.

A very well-dressed gentleman sat next to an unkempt one. Domenico considered for a moment that he mistook the identity of the one man; the way he was dressed confused him. But then he realized it was indeed 'That Man,' peculiarly dressed in finery that Domenico knew he didn't own.

He quickly faced forward again, hoping to avoid attracting any attention. Sweating now, he realized the true blessing of his own garments. The added thickness changed his silhouette, he might be harder to recognize.

"Tickets, gentlemen." The voices continued a few rows behind him.

He knows I left. He is looking for me.

Sit still. As long as the men are talking, I will know they are distracted. They said the daughter told him. Chubby daughter. Could they mean Mamie? What would she have said and why?

Oh, I can't blame that family, they couldn't have known anything. But then, they wanted me to stay a secret. They didn't want anyone to know I was there, in their shed. Did they know? Were they looking to turn me in? No, that doesn't make sense. If Mr. Privitera planned to hand me over, why would he let me speak with Mamie so often? Eat dinner with the family? No, they must be innocent.

Maybe they thought they were being helpful; if someone asks about me, they help. Yes, that sounds more like them. But now what? I can't go to America now, 'That Man' is following me. He will stop me and that can't happen.

I must change my plans, somehow.

My stop is ahead, I will lose the men between the station and the dock before boarding the ferryboat.

Okay, here goes. Step off the train, casually.

Move with the crowd.

I still see them. They may spot me, I'm still too exposed.

Duck and hide. Slightly glance behind, act natural, keep them in sight.

Cargo boxes. Walk casually behind them as concealment. Now, wait.

The men were getting their tickets at the window for the ferryboat – the same window and the same boat Domenico needed to be on.

They board. I will wait. But for what? I cannot travel along with them, but what would happen if I let them out of my sight? I need to be rid of them. But how?

The way 'That Man' is dressed gives me an idea – pretend he is someone else. I'll report him to the authorities. But I can't be the one – I don't have time for their suspicions of me. I need someone who can inform them...

A pretty, young woman with some expensive luggage walked toward the ferryboat. Domenico walked alongside her, talking loudly to nobody so she would think she was overhearing a conversation.

"A man on this ship is a murderer. Vito Brex, from Nissoria. And he is travelling with a thief." He spoke the lie others told about his father, adding the "thief" part for the companion.

It worked. The woman covered her mouth and fearfully ran to the carabinieri standing nearby.

The uniformed men boarded the ferryboat to pursue the woman's accused. They just said "Vito Brex" to every passenger until they got to 'That Man.' His countenance noticeably changed, and his eyes flashed hatred. The authorities saw this as admittance, acknowledgement. The well-dressed fraud started an uproar. The authorities took him and his loud scruffy friend away, both were furious.

I wasn't sure it would work. Breathe.

Sneak on the ferryboat, get out of Sicily.

Breathe.

All I know is he is not here; he cannot continue to follow me today.

℘℘℘

Domenico found a quiet place away from any passengers and sat, his head heavy in his hands. He needed rest but feared letting his guard down again. Since he didn't have time to get his ticket, he needed to be cautious and alert to remain hidden.

Once we land in Napoli, I will have to be quick. This might have been the last ferryboat of the day, but what if they find another way? I don't know how long they will be detained.

He replayed the encounter in his mind. Having to use the lie about his father pained him, but it worked.

The story that has hurt me all these years is the exact story I needed to help me. My father's own uncle started the rumor in 1860. The curse. This uncle's son was the guilty one, but he made my father the scapegoat. Told everyone that it was Vito Brex, my father, who participated in the massacre that terrible night, not Vincenzo Brex, his son. He protected his son but ruined our lives. Well today, that story might have just saved mine.

Domenico exhaled, exhausted. He reassured himself he was safe.

I am not being followed; I am moving toward Napoli and closer to America.

CHAPTER 13

Domenico, 1895

August
New York City, New York

Vaguely remembering the ferryboat journey from Messina to Napoli, he was always watching the passengers, avoiding them. Hiding in steerage class on a ship called The Werra, he crossed the ocean for two weeks.

Waiting in line with so many others at Ellis Island, the clothes on his back and a dollar left, he complied with all the authorities and papers.

After the first inquiry, he found that by feigning illiteracy, his name could be obscured.

Ah, let them spell it wrong, not a bad idea, 'That Man' would have a harder time tracking me that way.

Time was a blur. Days, maybe weeks passed before rest produced enough clarity for realization to finally break through his consciousness.

Where am I now? A wood floor, someone's room. An unfamiliar blanket. My clothes are in a pile.

Wait, what?

I am in America. Can it be true?

I remember. It was Monday, July 22. I was lost. Alone. Thankfully alone. No sign of anyone following me.

Ah yes, I remember being nervous, seasick, and hungry. What does it matter anymore, I am here. I should go out to see where 'here' is.

He bounded down the stairs to the street, his energy surging. Happily, he smiled at the first person he saw, a lovely lady.

She looked at him with disgust, and she hurried away.

What is wrong? Maybe I forgot to wash, whatever do I look like?

He spotted a barber pole, walked up to the door, and reviewed his reflection in the glass front window. His hair wasn't combed but his eyes looked well-rested; his coat was a bit ragged, but the lady only saw his face. He thought he might benefit from a shave, so he went in.

A young man greeted him in Italian, and Domenico wondered aloud if he was really in America, and both men laughed.

He had his hair cut and his face shaved and left with a nice, handsome mustache, with slight curls on the ends, just the way the other men in the shop were being groomed.

Domenico felt like a gentleman now, except for his clothes. "Can you tell me where I might find a tailor? My coat needs improvement."

"Oh, you can pay much for a tailor to mend your coat. But if you need a new one, you can go to Montgomery Ward a few blocks away, they have readymade ones."

"America! Amazing! *Grazie*, oh um thank you, sir, yes, a new coat would be nice." Domenico left the barber who was chuckling at the newcomer's enthusiasm.

So many people, so many fineries. The wares in the shops were as diverse and individual as each new face he saw. New York was certainly not limited to the Sicilian, there were tones and colors and shapes so unique, Domenico realized he was certainly not a man of the world. But here, in New York, he could see a glimpse of the earth's population smiling, laughing, and full of life around him.

He felt caught up and pulled in. The allure of the new and exciting swept him away with the masses, caught him up in all the hustle, but he did not really have any sense of direction. *What to do first? What to do next?* He wished Angelo could see all this too.

Angelo.

"What am I doing?" He stopped, walkers behind him stumbled and grumbled that he was now in the way. "How will I save enough to get Angelo here quickly if I keep on like this?" He said to nobody in particular. "I almost spent good money on a coat I don't need. One that pleases others, fits in with the others." A passerby nodded. Domenico continued walking and talking aloud, "No, my brother comes first. I need to forget about any luxuries. I need to find work."

Looking around, he quickly became distracted by another pretty lady.

Are they all this pretty in New York? Fine details, adornments, perfumes. I feel dizzy. How does one meet a woman to marry among so many? No, must stay focused on the plan. No thoughts of finding a woman until Angelo is here, safe.

He spotted a steeple on the horizon of the streetscape. *Perhaps I need to pray for strength and guidance in my wait to marry.*

And patience.

Oh, the conversation with Mamie. I understand why she seemed so confused. Patience, what does that even mean? What do we do when we are patient? Wait? So, if it means to sit and wait, how does anything ever happen? I prefer action. Oh, Mamie, her brown eyes; wide, questioning, wanting more answers – but there was something else, something else they revealed. Something deeper: a longing, a sense of adventure maybe? I'm not sure. Well, so much for forgetting about her.

He shook his head to clear it and then looked up.

Ah, blue, soft clouds. The sky does not change from one continent to the other. It is the same.

He closed his eyes and thought of Regalbuto's wide-open expanses over the horizon where he'd look up and dream of finding a new life, a better life. He remembered why he was here now in America, and he opened his eyes again.

He walked until he found himself face to face with a stone sign etched into the side wall of the church he spotted from blocks away: Our Lady of Pompeii. This was the place Cardaci told him to find. The name reminded him of his homeland and beloved Mount Etna, so he walked in the open door.

It was not an ornate church, but was simple, like a hardworking man. Domenico immediately liked it.

"Can I help you, son?"

He heard the voice and turned around. A man in a cassock appeared from some unknown corner to greet him. Domenico appeared confused so the man asked again in Italian. Domenico understood what was said and reviewed the taller man who was holding his hand out to shake his. Domenico replied in his native Sicilian, and both men smiled, relieved to find a common bond to easily continue a conversation.

"Yes, sir, I have just arrived in America, and I am looking for work. I must raise money to bring my brother here, and very soon. Can you tell me if there is work nearby?"

The man laughed and Domenico looked embarrassed. "Work? Look around you, this city, opportunity is everywhere. Workers are plentiful too. But ones who are trustworthy and hardworking with a strong purpose to help the church are harder to find. Many want to make money quickly and move on, is this your plan as well, son?"

This was an unsettling question. It was his plan, but now he felt himself second-guessing, and his eyes began to mist.

For the last five years I had been trying to leave, never thinking about how to stay somewhere. Now finally, after all the planning, can I give myself permission to slow down to take stock of myself, my life, and what I want to do?

"Father," he began, "I have been lost. I have focused so much on leaving my situation that I have not allowed myself to find another purpose in life. So, yes, I am such a man who wants to make money quickly, rescue my brother, and bring him here. I have no idea what to do next beyond that. Find a wife and start a family? Yes, perhaps. Find a church like San Basilica in Regalbuto? Perhaps." He trailed off, feeling a pang of homesickness.

The older clergyman touched his elbow and met the young man's eyes. "Son, you are the man I have been looking for. I asked God just minutes before you walked in the door to send me a hard-working, dedicated man who could help me with my vision for our church's mission. And you are from Regalbuto, yes? Even better!"

Father Domo introduced himself and invited Domenico back to his office to explain. First, he planned to turn the church basement into a meeting room, then expand some programs. Domenico felt a sense of camaraderie he hadn't known for years, especially with a clergyman, and he finally felt at peace in his arrival to New York.

The men discussed their connections in Regalbuto and how the Scalabrinian order was helping others with their travels to America. Father Domo's vision included welcoming and assisting those immigrating from Italy, so that more wouldn't feel lost, like Domenico did when he arrived.

Father Domo offered him a place to stay in the rectory and wages for some handyman work as well as for assisting in the mission: escorting Italian Immigrants arriving in NY and helping them to get settled. The mission also helped families bring other loved ones over.

Domenico accepted the job and lodgings gladly, thinking it was a perfect situation – good, honest work, and he could be sure his money would go directly to Angelo safely. *And it certainly doesn't hurt to live in a church – with its spiritual support – while trying to abstain from women until my goal is met.*

Domenico arrived back at the rooming house to retrieve his meager belongings. He scanned the room with a feeling of gratitude and thought about those others from his community in Regalbuto who were told to find this same rooming house when they leave the docks in New York. "Find Broome Street, Number 526," they were all told when they left Sicily. It was a good landing place; he wondered who might use this room next.

He thought back to his conversation with Father Domo. Yes, helping immigrants was something he was already trying to do. He smiled and sighed with a sense of pride that he will now have more resources to help more people.

Truly, fate has led me here. I am confident that I will be able to get Angelo here much faster, and if God put me on this path – practically leading me into Father Domo's office Himself – there must be something important in my future.

He gathered his bundle and closed the door behind him. He descended the stairs from the second story room two at a time with eager excitement.

Another guest in the rooming house was heading up, rounding the corner of the double back steps, and Domenico clumsily bumped into him. "Oh, excuse, um, sir, um, sorry," he tried in his weak English phrases while he helped to smooth the man's coat with apology.

"You are sorry, eh, son?" A familiar sounding Sicilian response startled Domenico. The tone started off stern, annoyed, but then ended with a playful lilt as the accosted man was the first to acknowledge the recognition.

Domenico was confused by the way the old man grabbed both of Domenico's elbows but finally, recognition hit him. "Cardaci!"

Both men laughed and hugged with a mix of happiness and shock at this serendipitous meeting. They began with a flurry of questions and answers, each eager to both hear and explain their stories of how they both arrived at the same landing in the same building at the same time.

The men walked down the steps together; Domenico invited Cardaci to visit Father Domo, and he told his cousin about his journey from Regalbuto along the way.

"Cardaci, 'That Man' was following me, I saw him on the train. He knows I was heading to America."

Cardaci looked only mildly concerned.

"He and his friend were arrested though. I had to use the story of the Brex curse to my advantage." Domenico looked away, guiltily.

"You did what you had to. Don't worry, Domenico, my connections at the port said they were detained. 'That Man' will not be going anywhere for a while."

"I just need to get Angelo away from there as soon as possible. I can work and send him money now, but I don't know if I will have enough money fast enough for my own passage as well, to escort him back here. He is still just a boy; I can't have him travel alone. I don't think I can face 'That Man' again if I saw him, I don't know what he would do."

Cardaci thought about this and suggested a plan. "I will need to make the round trip again for business soon. That gives you some time to raise the cost of Angelo's passage, and then I will escort your brother back here to you. This will save you from buying yourself a ticket and you won't have to chance running into 'That Man' in Regalbuto."

"But what if *you* run into him? He will be furious if you remove Angelo from Mother. He thinks he has a claim on him since he is married to her."

"Don't worry about that, I will handle him." Cardaci replied. Domenico knew better than to ask any more questions.

PART 2

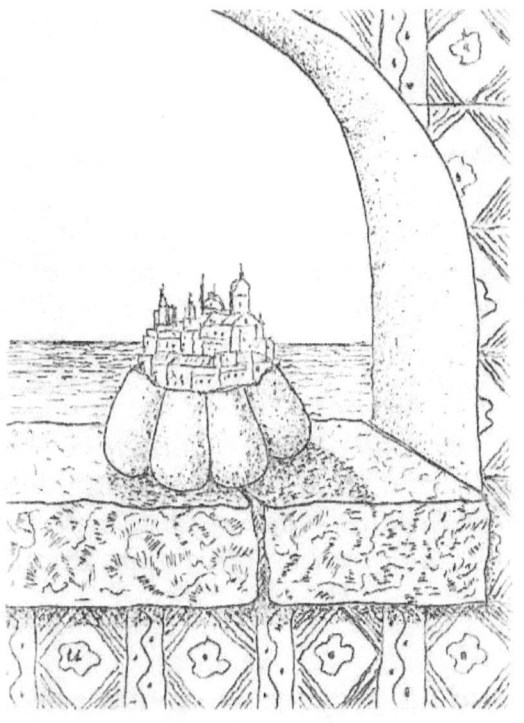

Effectively asserting myself has always been my downfall.
When I push, the world just pushes harder.

~Domenica (Mamie) Privitera

~ENTRY #7~

1/4/1930

My dear friend,

I know I said I will try to be patient, give the layers time – like the lasagna. Well now there's a new ingredient added to the mix, and I don't know what to make of this either!

So, remember when Mother allowed me to use Gracie's too-big parka on my first day of school in September? Well, the time came for me to return it to Gracie. When I pulled it out of my closet, Duey immediately began playing with a loose string dangling from the hem, and wouldn't you know it, he pulled out the stitches.

I examined it, ready to make repairs, and I found the oddest thing. In the hem there was this small bag, only about the size of the first digit of my thumb. That's right, it was hidden in the hem! The bag was made of a piece of beige muslin scrap and had tiny hand stitches closing all the edges. It didn't have a scent, so it wasn't a sachet, but it had a little weight to it, but not as heavy as a curtain weight. Such a mystery, right? I was curious, so I pulled out all the stitches of the little bag. When I saw what was inside, I ran next door to show Nan.

She knew right away that it was an evil eye amulet. You're probably also thinking, what in the world? Am I right, my dear friend?

What was something like that doing in the hem of this jacket? So, when Gracie came to pick it up, I made sure I told her what I found and that I would repair the hem.

Mother overheard me and was furious! She grabbed the little amulet from me, told Gracie to go straight home, and she followed behind her to talk to Aunt Mamie.

Gracie told me later that they yelled a lot, but did she hear that it was put there for protection against the mal'occhio. Her mother believes that stuff and mine does not. She said her mother forgot it was there, she put it in the coat a long time ago. Gracie said my mother didn't believe her and then their yelling turned into whispering. She didn't know what else they said.

Why would Mother not believe her? Why would Aunt Mamie lie about such a thing? My family is acting so strangely: whispering sometimes and yelling other times. And it always seems to have to do with me.

My dear friend, I wish everyone would just be open and honest and just tell me what is going on.

~Zina

CHAPTER 14

Zina

Sunday, January 5, 1930

The holiday gatherings wound down after Christmas ended, and the new year started. In the past two weeks, Zina spent as much time as she could with her Bregas cousins and with Nan since their schools were closed in observance of the holiday season. She didn't have as much opportunity to see Frank, so she was excited when she overheard her mother say she and her aunt Mamie were going to Mineola for a visit with her aunt Maria.

Zina wondered why her mother didn't look happy about the visit, and she was a little confused why her aunt Mamie was coming along, but she decided not to dwell on the tension she felt in their company. She was so looking forward to seeing Frank.

When they arrived at the Vincenti's, Maria greeted the ladies with a questioning look, and they all stared at Zina.

Zina just waved and looked around her aunt Maria for her cousins.

Maria finally spoke. "Zina, why not go downstairs and help Frank in the shop? There isn't much for you to do here, nobody else is home."

"Yes, Aunt Maria." Zina felt the strange sensation that she wasn't invited and wondered what was going on. She took her time as she went down the stairs, lingering to catch the ladies conversation.

"Please sit down, have some cookies." The ladies sat at the small table in Maria's kitchen with some of the leftover holiday desserts and started some small talk.

"Zina is becoming quite the young lady, Rose." Maria complimented, while eating one of the last "S" cookies.

Mamie immediately grabbed the salt shaker from next to the stove, shook some out into her hand, and threw the crystals onto the floor.

"Mamie, must you do that?"

Rose's tone caused Maria to sense that their whispering was going to get louder and more serious, so she got up and out of the way of the sisters. She turned on the faucet to wash some of the glasses and drown out their voices.

Zina strained to hear them, as she took one step down at a time, but couldn't make anything out.

"Why do you do that, Mamie? Maria doesn't wish any evil, and she is certainly not jealous; since when have you become so superstitious? Maria, did you know that she put an amulet in Zina's coat?"

"I'm just doing what I can to protect my family." Mamie said, "you can't be in control of everything that happens to Zina, Rose."

Rose slapped the table and emphatically waved the back of her hand at her sister. "Once again, Mamie, you are overstepping."

"What? I can't care for her?"

"Ladies, shh. I wanted you two to come here so you can work this out and finally be open and honest with each other. You are being too careless and reckless in your conversations, and *someone* is going to get hurt."

"I'm sorry, Maria, what could I say to Zina? She wanted to come along when she found out that we were planning on visiting."

"Well, Rose, maybe if she found out *more* we wouldn't have to..."

Rose stood abruptly from her chair, about to charge at her sister. Maria quickly grabbed her arm to settle her back down.

"Ladies, calm down. Let's just have a polite conversation." Maria hinted with her expression that sound traveled easily in her house. "Let's have some tea. Who wants another cookie?"

"Mamie, I can't take it – your seemingly innocent requests. Please, we have talked about this. I am not changing my mind." Rose responded, slapping her hand on the table again.

"Rose, please. Mamie, you did make a promise. You must keep your thoughts and feelings contained and respect Rose's wishes. I know it won't be easy – for either of you. But this is what you both agreed to. So please, be civilized."

In her slow descent, Zina didn't hear much more than a word here and there, water running, chairs scraping, and a few dull thuds.

When she reached the door to the barbershop, she opened it slowly, peeking to see what Frank was doing and wanting to watch him do it.

From inside the shop, the door to the stairway that led to up their apartment was small and narrow, its outline concealed by the lines of the oak paneling. Frank's father couldn't have the customers thinking it was an exit, and he made sure the family never used it during business hours. To the customers, the door looked just like part of the wall.

"Argh, when will this be over," Frank quietly muttered while Zina covertly watched. He turned his broom to attack some stubborn stray hairs in a corner while his thoughts also strayed. "How. Much. Longer?" he wondered aloud, and Zina thought the question had to do with the chore. Frank was noisily knocking the broom's head against the corner baseboards, hammering out his frustrations at the cruelness of the charade he was caught in. What he really wondered was how much longer he would have to masquerade his feelings for a certain black-haired young lady.

He propped the broom against the nearest barber chair and proceeded to swat the glossy mahogany vinyl vigorously with a white towel to scatter any hair from sight. Zina chuckled to herself at the irony when Frank said "I give up! Why can't I speak my mind?" while waving the white towel around.

Zina felt increasingly guilty for observing him from her hiding place. Afraid she might start coughing and be found out, she decided to make a bunch of noise as if she just arrived at the door. She knocked and opened it in a grand gesture, "Frank, hello, where are you? Your mother said I should come to help."

His arm outstretched; he held the towel as if during the last swipe he became frozen.

Zina smiled. "Oh, hello Frank. What were you doing?"

He quickly composed himself. "Just cleaning up, dusting, that sort of thing. After being closed for the holidays, the dust just settles." He put the towel down and grabbed the broom again. "You were sent down here to help me?"

"Well, that's what she told me to do. If you don't want my help, I can go."
"No, that's not what I meant. It's just that, well, with so many sisters that could help, you are the first, well, girl, who has been sent to see what you can do to help me in the shop. I am just surprised by it, that's all."

Zina paused. She had an idea why she was sent. "Frank, do you sometimes feel like our mothers like to see us together?" She needed to ask even though it was painfully embarrassing.

"Yes! I do!" Frank shouted. "I thought it was just my imagination, but you see it too?" Frank stopped and realized he seemed a bit too excited, and noticed that Zina looked annoyed, so he toned it back.

"I wish they would stop teasing, don't you? Can you ask your mother, and she can tell my mother?" Zina timidly asked.

He was dejected. He didn't want her to give up on him just yet. He wished she could know how he felt right now; it would change everything between them, but he promised himself he wouldn't say anything yet. Afraid he might slip up, he attempted to change the subject and the mood. "Ah, hm. Hello miss, welcome to my barber shop. Please have a seat."

Zina looked at him with a surprised, hesitant smile.

Over-dramatically, he moved the broom aside then waved Zina to the chair with one hand, fluttered the white towel with the other, and ended this performance with a slight bow.

Zina laughed. "Frank, you don't cut girls' hair, do you?" She cleared her throat and decided to play along. Speaking in a theatrically deep voice, she sat down. "I'd like a little off the top and trim the sideburns please."

"Ah, yes, exactly what I was thinking, sir. Then, perhaps a shave?" Frank mimed some scissors trimming and some soap lathering.

"Frank, do you think I need a shave? Shame on you!" Zina laughed and they smiled at each other in the mirror.

The bell dinged at the door, and they both turned around. An elderly gentleman appeared with a tweed hat and mismatched tweed coat as was the typical fashion in this Mineola neighborhood. He stopped, dumbfounded to notice the barber was a young boy and the customer was a girl. He scoffed and harumphed and was so perplexed that he nearly tripped while backtracking to leave. He walked back out, the door's bell rattling with complaints of this man's one too many attempts to push the heavy door closed in his haste.

Frank and Zina laughed uncontrollably when the man left. "I suppose I shouldn't have put the open sign in the window just yet," Frank confessed, fixed the sign, locked the door, and they laughed some more.

Upstairs, the ladies exhausted their conversation, polished off their tea and cookies, and descended the steps to the shop. At the door, Rose and Maria heard the pair getting along so well and exchanged smiles. They were reluctant to have to interrupt.

"Sounds like somebody is having fun instead of working." Maria teasingly scolded her son as she and Rose finally entered the barbershop.

Mamie was only a few steps behind the women when those words caused her to freeze halfway down the stairs.

"Frank, unlock the door again please, so our guests can just exit from here."

Rose told Zina that it was time for them to leave, and they both said their goodbyes. Rose and Maria looked around for Mamie, but she was still standing on the stairs.

"Mamie, are you feeling alright?" Maria remarked.

Rose assessed Mamie and recognized a familiar, haunted look in her older sister's eyes. "She'll be fine. Do you need some air, Mamie?" She guided her sister the rest of the way down the stairs and to the exit, Zina already skipped ahead to the subway stop.

Mamie shivered when the bell at the door faintly rang, and she walked out quickly. She felt cold and sweaty, remembering a day, long ago, in another shop – theirs in Pedara.

Effectively asserting myself has always been my downfall.

CHAPTER 15

Mamie, 1897

February 20,
Pedara, Sicily

W*as it just two years ago that I first met Dom? That sounds like such*

a short time frame. If I didn't think about him daily the days might have felt short too. The antidote for wanting something you can't have is NOT to have patience for it to come in its own timing. I am convinced now that Dom's advice was misguided and hypocritical. If you can't have it, you can't. Patience doesn't change it. Oh, why do I think about him so much? He doesn't even live in Sicily anymore. He is in America, probably married, successful, with one child and maybe even another on the way.

Mamie woke that morning with a lot on her mind. Her thoughts accompanied her to the wash basin, then while she was getting dressed, and then as she stood at the shop counter. She went through the motions with her customers while her mind was restless, like most mornings these days. And each day, she hoped something would change and her future would start.

So now, I can only imagine the type of man I'd like to meet. Someone easy *to talk to, like Dom, who Papa likes too. But there hasn't been another young man like him coming by the shop in these last two years. Where are all the good men? I'm beginning to think it's a lost cause. Oh, that's right, it was almost Saint Rita's feast day when he left, and now the festival will be coming up again and I am <u>still</u> looking for love, two years later.*

It's probably just as we thought: all the young men have left for America. Maybe I have to just face it, Papa will never decide to just uproot and move our family and I might be stuck here forever with Foul Sal, or worse.

It would be so freeing to be in charge of my own life, but I'm barely fourteen, and options for a girl are limited. It's just the way of the world, and I must accept that. I doubt the man for me will just walk right into the shop, like Dom did all those long days ago. I need to get out of here, that is what I need. I need to be able to meet a nice young man who will help me toward my destiny.

Mamie was startled by Rose charging in the shop door, talking too loudly for the early morning, authoritatively announcing instructions to Mamie while gathering some medicinal items and other supplies.

"Mamie, I must go with Mama. Don't just stand there, help me."

"What's going on, Rose?" Mamie asked, confused about the sudden urgency and flurry of activity that interrupted her reverie.

"As I was saying," Rose started again, painfully slow this time. "I have to go with Mama, we must move her to the midwife's house so she can be looked after around the clock." She kept gathering and packing, only partially talking to Mamie. "Why anyone would want to go through all this trouble to have a baby is a mystery to me. Anyway, the children will go to the Zappalas'. You will need to be here by yourself the rest of today, Papa says he expects to be back late tonight."

Rose left without any sort of goodbye or apology; she didn't even make sure Mamie understood or heard everything.

Mamie didn't know why she expected anything more and just rolled her eyes.

How ironic. Of course, I was just dreaming about getting out of this store, and now I am stuck. But then, I feel bad that Mother is so ill, especially when the baby is due anytime now. All I can do is hope she gets rest and quiet, for her sake, and for the sake of the baby to come.

A short time later, Mamie watched as her uncle, Santo Zappala, came by with a cart to help transport her mother. Rose helped her climb in, then piled blankets around her, adjusting them for some comfort. Mamie sighed, knowing her mother was in good hands. Rose has shown herself to have natural instincts about caretaking, so they didn't usually call on a doctor, unless Rose was sick too. Rose walked alongside the cart, holding hands with the littlest ones, and the group slowly left.

Well, I'm alone now. I've been alone in the shop before, lots of times. Just never for the entire day, but I can handle it. Papa couldn't have known the midwife would be so concerned about Mama, she seemed fine when he left yesterday to get more supplies in Catania. I will show Papa that the shop is in good hands with me. Maybe then he will trust me to make other important decisions for my life.

Business was slow after the family left; she hadn't seen a customer for over an hour. To help pass the time, Mamie decided to rearrange some of the jars on the shelves, dust them off, and create a new display. She thought she would surprise her papa with a fresh look.

Excited about the idea, she hummed while she engrossed herself in the project. She didn't hear when the door opened.

"Ss-sounds like ss-somebody is having fun instead of working." A man's voice startled her, and she dropped a jar of orange marmalade. Thankfully for the jar, it didn't break as her foot cushioned its impact on the way down, but the fate of her toes was now questionable.

"Sorry to ss-startle you miss-ss, are you alright?" The man asked, amused.

Mamie tried to stand and reply to the voice, but her big toe throbbed too much, so instead, she grimaced and groaned.

He held her arm to support her as she hopped to the counter. Even though she was ashamed that anyone would see her in pain, she took the man's offered assistance. She was shocked at the effortless way he lifted her to the countertop to allow for the examination of the injured foot.

She pushed her hair, all a mess, out of her face. An image of how Rose would act in this situation, being rescued by a man, must have crossed her mind, or maybe she was still imagining romantic scenarios of the man of her dreams making an appearance. Either way, she was secretly pleased that she had just been whisked off her feet.

Now embarrassed, she composed herself quickly. "Thank you, I'm alright now. I am sorry sir. I didn't hear the bell at the door when you walked in. What can I help you with today?" She looked at him more closely, he looked vaguely familiar.

She gave him a smile like she imagined Rose would.

He gave Mamie a strained smile back. "What were you doing miss-ss?" he asked, still holding her at the counter.

He looked somewhat like that blonde gentleman that came in their shop two years ago. He was all Rose talked about for months afterwards. Mamie only remembered him since he might have been the last handsome and well-dressed man to come by.

She began to feel slightly uncomfortable, now remembering how he looked at Rose back then and how rude he was.

"Oh, I was just rearranging some shelves, you know, shop stuff," she said, nonchalantly. She looked around while waving her hand as if to encircle the enormity of the work.

It was then that she noticed a figure standing in the shadow by the closed shop door. The bell kept faintly ringing as he impatiently shifted his weight, bumping his back against the door.

"Vince, we don't have time for this." The shadowed man mumbled.

That reminder agitated the man called Vince, and he abruptly grabbed Mamie's chin, turning her to face him again. "Why don't you let the other workers do that? Or your pretty ss-sister, where is she today? I had hoped to see *her* again," he said, looking straight into her eyes. "Or are you the only one here, *ragazza paffuta*?"

Mamie gasped at the insult and began to shake. "No, my family... my family is here, we live upstairs, I can just shout to them, and they will come, eager to assist me in any way I need." She knew her voice was not helping her lie sound convincing, and she saw in his face that he heard it too.

"Don't be silly, we saw everyone leave earlier. You are alone, aren't you, *chubby girl*." The shadowed man by the door chuckled, exhaling puffs of cigarette smoke.

Mamie held down her panic and thought of what she could do. She looked to the floor where the fallen jar lay and thought about her options for something to hold on to or grab for protection; these men made her feel threatened and all she could find were jellies and jams.

Vince's one hand moved from her jaw to her neck. The other squeezed the top part of her thigh as he leaned in to breathe by her ear, "Not so talkative now, are you?"

This *signore biondo* that her sister fancied turned vile. His breath was hot and stale, a mix of a little tobacco and a lot of liquor. He laughed with a deep nightmarish sound.

Vince confirmed with his cohort, "She is the girl you ss-saw him with, right?"

"Yeah, boss, that's the one. He was carrying boards and she had some basket. They were laughing and smiling together, all friendly-like."

"You're ss-sure? It was two years ago, you are ss-sure?"

"Yeah Vince, it was her."

"Well, too bad it wasn't the pretty one."

Mamie struggled to shake her head. She uttered, "no..." but she heard no sound.

His hands gripped tighter, and his stale breath moved closer. "Tell me again what he ss-said before he left, where he was *really* going."

"Who? Please, you are hurting me, I don't know who you are talking about." She attempted to wiggle free, but his hold was unyielding.

"You do know, I know you do. I've been trying to find him for two years. Two. Years." Through clenched teeth, he groaned and squeezed her leg harder with frustration. "You. You were the one who told me he went to America. I've been ss-ent on a chase, haven't I?"

"Please, please stop. I don't know...I don't know who you are talking about."

"Vince, come on. If we can't get what we came for, we might as well make this worth our while, right boss?" He turned to peek out the door of the shop and gave Vince the sign that the coast was clear.

A frustrated grunt was the reply, followed by another menacing laugh.

Mamie's eyes widened when a hand shot up and blurred across her face with a hot sting. She fell off the counter and slipped into darkness.

"What did you do that for? How are we supposed to find him if we can't ask the girl?"

"Just ss-shut up, she is lighter than she looks. Hurry, get what you can."

The shadowed man hurdled over the counter to the till, and swiftly began to empty the contents, a cigarette dangling from his sinister smile.

"Vince, now what? Are you just going to leave her there? You do realize she will be able to identify us when she comes to."

"You mean *if*." Without much thought, Vince removed the cigarette from the lip of his accomplice and flicked it into the crate of Mamie's father's liquor making supplies. "*If* she comes to."

ᔓᑏᘒ

An eerie light flickered. Thuds echoed off the floor and through her bones. An agonizing heat rose from somewhere near her as she laid there, unable to move, waiting for the darkness to return.

ᔓᑏᘒ

She heard smashing at the shop door, someone shouting for help to come. *Papa is that you?* Her mind floated back to where it was dark and quiet and still, while her body was lifted and pulled somewhere.

ᔓᑏᘒ

Soft bed beneath me, mine? Where? How did I get here?

Orange light. Curtains opening. Too bright. Eyes hurt to open.

ᔓᑏᘒ

"Mamie? Oh my, no, no, what happened, are you ok? Mamie answer me."

She couldn't answer.

ᔓᑏᘒ

Head throbbing. The air is so loud. Is Rose humming...a church hymn?

Cool and damp rag. Drips on my cheek. A sharp ache over my eyes. My head: it feels as though I'm trying to move a boulder.

Thinking hurts. Drift away. Please darkness, come again.

ঞ০ঞ

When Mamie awakened hours later, the room was dim, and the smell of antiseptic wafted from somewhere down the hospital corridor.

She heard a whimper at the corner of her bed and realized it came from Rose, who quickly got up from a chair and went to Mamie's side, relieved.

Rose wiped a cool, wet rag on her sister's forehead and whispered to her quietly, trying to ask what happened, but Mamie was too confused. Her answers were garbled and incoherent.

Rose admitted it was still too soon to talk. "Hush, take a sip of broth." She lifted Mamie's chin and put the cup to her sister's lips. Most of it didn't make it down, as if her throat forgot how to swallow. Rose looked sympathetically at the red and purple welts on her sister's neck.

Mamie closed her eyes and Rose put the cup on the bedside table mumbling that maybe it was too soon to drink too.

Rose placed another cool rag gently on Mamie's neck and wiped her forehead again. Traces of soot still remained near the roots of her hairline and in her eyebrows. She went back to watch over her sister from the chair and allowed her patient to fall back asleep, but that was only for a few moments.

A man's voice. Who is this man? Why is he here?

What is he doing to me, that hurts, you are hurting me! Stop!

His hands are on my throat. Scream, but the sound doesn't come.

153

Mamie woke in a fright, looking for the man. Rose approached her carefully, "Shh, it was just a nightmare." She laid a gentle hand on her sister's arm.

Mamie slowly touched her sister's hand. She looked around, confused. She spotted a strange man in the doorway behind Rose and panicked.

"Mamie, my hand, you are squeezing too hard." Rose turned to look where Mamie stared with wide eyes. "Mamie, this is the doctor."

Rose introduced the voice that Mamie confused with the one in her nightmare.

"Domenica, I am Doctor diPrima. You have suffered a severe blow to your forehead, as well as bruising to your throat and windpipe. You also inhaled a lot of smoke. Perhaps your sister can leave now, and let you rest."

Don't leave me. Shake my head 'no.' Oh, that was a mistake, my brain – rattling around, banging at the insides of my skull. Lights flashing behind my eyelids, the room spinning.

"Are you sure you would like your sister here? Where are your parents?" The doctor asked Mamie.

Mamie answered him by slightly holding up Rose's hand clasped in hers since it hurt too much to move her head or talk. Rose answered him with a trite, "Our mother is indisposed, having just given birth, and our father is dealing with a great deal of fire damage. She has me. Would you give us a few minutes, Doctor?" Rose dismissed him and turned to her sister.

"Mamie, the authorities want to know what happened." She started, gently. "Someone in town said they saw two men running out the gate of our courtyard. Do you remember the men? Do you remember what they did? Anything you can remember will help them find who did this, this terrible…" Rose held back the tears threatening to fall.

Mamie gave Rose a questioning look and felt a surge of panic to see such seriousness in her sister's face.

Trying to speak hurts so much, and it hurts to touch my neck.

"Yes, Mamie, your neck is going to be sore. The doctor believes one of the men held your throat to stop you from screaming out and struck you around your chin, then you fell, hit your head, and were knocked unconscious. Somehow a fire got started. It is lucky that Papa returned home early to pull you out."

Papa? Is Papa okay? The pain, along with the explanation was making it hard for her to breathe. Mamie looked at Rose in terror, forming the question, "Papa?" with her lips.

"Papa is fine, Mamie. He is with Mama now; they are so worried about you. Everyone else is fine, even our new baby sister. It was a blessing that nobody was home when..." Rose looked away, guiltily. "And a blessing that you are going to be alright, Mamie."

A fire? The shop? Who would do this?

Mamie winced and closed her eyes. The pain intensified when she tried to remember what happened.

Rose saw the agony on her sister's face and told her to rest again.

‍‍‍

One week after the incident the family returned to their home above the shop to survey the damages, the acrid smoke odor still lingered. They gathered the few items that looked salvageable and were relieved when heirlooms that were tucked away securely in boxes or drawers were safe. They couldn't stay, the rooms were uninhabitable. Mamie was saddened to leave the only home she'd ever known, never to return.

The children continued to stay at the Zappalas' with their mother, and Mamie, Rose and their papa went to stay with Aunt Agatha.

Mamie was able to speak a few words but mostly wrote down her responses or requests. She was comfortable enough in her aunt's guest room with her sister, but she was still afraid to be alone. If Rose was busy, Aunt Agatha came to sit with her.

In week two, Mamie's throat was slowly improving, but her sensitivity to light and sound lingered. Foul Sal, along with some of his other workers, went to help clean the shop, but it quickly became apparent that it was beyond repair. Mamie's papa salvaged as many of the dry goods as he could, but unfortunately, the smoke damaged labels were illegible. In his attempt to recuperate some funds, he held a sale on the walkway outside of the store. Most passersby would say "tsk," shake their heads at the misfortune with an apology, and then leave quickly after their curiosity was satisfied – without purchasing anything. Perhaps they thought the family was cursed now, and they didn't want any part of it, especially that the authorities still had not yet caught the men responsible.

The third week, they sold the last of the remaining inventory, and even some household items. Mamie gathered the nerve to walk through the shop again, but after only a few steps she began sobbing. Seeing the charred and sooty mess that was once their beloved business and livelihood was too distressing.

Their mother continued to be bedridden, so Rose helped with the newborn baby, Stella, who was as healthy as can be. The birth was so difficult for their mother – she battled an illness, the news of the store, and her worry about Mamie – that the midwife said she may not be able to have any more children. Since then, she had been different, not wanting to care for anyone, not even herself.

Rose was different too, as if she had been promoted to "Nurse and Deputized Mother." Mamie felt demoted to "The One Who Caused All This Pain."

The girls and their Aunt Agatha visited the Zappalas' to lend their mother a hand when they could. During one such visit, Mamie overheard Rose confide in their aunt the opinion the midwife gave their mother. Aunt

Agatha sympathetically said, "Ah, your father can eventually recover financially, but if your mother can no longer have children, what will she do with her life now?"

Rose was surprised. "She can still raise the children she does have. Really, just because she might not be able to have more kids does not mean she is worthless."

Mamie was shocked at how Rose stood up to Aunt Agatha to defend their mother. *Perhaps her change in role lately is providing her with a new perspective for what holds value in life. It's not all about fancy fashions.*

Mamie sensed that the entire experience had Rose reviewing what she wanted from life. And, if she knew her sister, she knew that anytime Rose wanted something, she could *be sure* she would get it because she would *make sure* it happened.

She smiled weakly at that little reminder of better days in the past. All Mamie wanted now was for things to become normal again.

CHAPTER 16

Mamie, 1897

Midday, March 19,
Pedara

Spring was on its way; even though the air held onto a chill from the snowcaps on the volcano, Mamie didn't mind. It was a month after the fire, and her fourteenth birthday. She wasn't sure if she should dare to hope for something good to come on her special day.

If I imagined my life now, turning fourteen, back when I was still twelve, our business would be thriving, and I would have found a nice young man. But now, nothing. I know I ruined everything. I wish I knew what I did to cause those men to do what they did. I wish I could remember what happened.

She took a deep breath and looked around the empty store. Last week, her papa started asking her to meet him in the shop, it was his way of helping her face her fear and prompt her memory. But today was her birthday, so she hoped there was more than rehabilitation in store for her.

While waiting, she wiped the portion of the counter that survived. It was already as clean as it was going to get, but she needed to be doing something. The store was so bare and barren, cleaned of the debris but still covered in soot. Only a portion of the first four walls that were there before their business started remained, and it gave her chills. It was hard to notice their business had been there at all.

Her papa walked in with a serious and somber look on his face. "Mamie, we should talk," he said. *He never says this,* she thought, concerned, and she stopped mid-swipe.

She put the rag down, realizing he did not ask her here about her birthday, and she was overcome with guilt. *Of course, why would I think I deserve something for my birthday, look what I've put everyone through.*

Mamie began sobbing. Tears dripped to the counter, and she wiped them away too. "The entire future of this family is ruined because of me."

Her papa was caught off guard and moved around like he was trying to leave the room, uncomfortable. "No Mamie, you are not at fault. It happened *to you*; you were the victim. You did nothing to cause this." He was adamant. Mamie sobbed harder, so he softened his tone, "Mamie, we are family. The family will protect and provide. We will just chart a new course, a new destiny." He faced her directly. "Mamie, it is you who is irreplaceable. I am glad you are alright; I am the one who is sorry you were put in that situation. Will you ever forgive me?" Now her papa looked as if he would cry.

Mamie sniffled and put her hand on his. "Yes, of course. Thank you, Papa, I was feeling like it was my fault."

"I don't want you to think about it anymore, okay? The men were caught yesterday and are likely in jail now. We can move on."

"Really?" She held her breath.

"Yes, I've been told that the neighbor who saw them run out of our courtyard saw where they went. They were tracked down and identified but it took some time for the authorities to catch them."

Mamie exhaled, wanting to feel more relieved than she did. "Who were they? What were they even after? Why did they come here, of all places?"

"Let's just let the authorities do their job. You don't remember anything from that day, right?"

She shook her head.

"It's okay, it's probably best not to relive it, let's just put it behind us, okay? They can't hurt us anymore."

Mamie ached to tell him how the men still tormented her: how she caught flashes of their faces in her nightmares. She wished she could put it behind her, just like her papa wanted her to, she just wasn't sure she'd ever be able to.

Her papa looked around the shop. "Can I tell you something?" He really wanted to say how angry he was, but he didn't want to scare his young daughter, who had already been through so much. So, he began to tell Mamie some of the financial details he didn't usually discuss with her, but she understood the basic ideas: the shop had a debt for the products they lost, and the shop had a business loan – no products, no business and no business, no way to pay the debt. The restitution payment would only cover a portion. "All I can think of is to move and start over. If we can live simply while we work, in a few years we can save enough money for a new life. I have made a connection with a man named Guiseppe Cardaci."

"Haven't I heard that name before?" Mamie asked.

"Yes, he is the cousin of that young man from Regalbuto: Domenico. You do remember him, right Mamie? That we met him years ago must have been fate. It seemed everyone I knew in Pedara was losing hope with how the economy was turning, but not him. He had a plan. He recommended I talk with Cardaci."

Dom. Papa remembers him too. "So, did you? Talk to that Cardaci?" Mamie hoped she might hear more about what Domenico was up to.

"Well, do you remember how Domenico talked about America? I am seriously considering our new start to be in America."

Mamie was shocked to actually hear the words. "Really, Papa?" She held her breath to hear what he would say next. She was tempted to pinch herself to test if this conversation was even real.

"Would you be upset if we left Sicily? We won't have anything to come back to, so when we leave, it would be for good." He looked a little sad and hung his head. "All I ever wanted was to provide a secure and safe future for you and all the others. I feel like that is in extreme jeopardy right now. But, because you are the oldest, if you were alright with such a change, I would feel better."

"What does Mother think?"

"I think this news might cheer her up. I think the best thing for her is a change in direction, a change in purpose. She would do well in a new environment, one that doesn't remind her of pain or sickness, and one that is all about beginnings."

"Why would you think I would not be okay with this Papa? I have actually thought about America for years now, but I never thought we'd go. I, too, remember the day Domenico came to the shop and then stayed to help you with the shed. He was the first person to really make me think about it. It makes a lot of sense to start over there." Mamie hoped she sounded businesslike and not overemotional.

He didn't notice and continued, "I know Rose will be alright with it, she never stops talking about the riches and fineries. I was mostly concerned with you, Mamie. You are always rolling your eyes when Rose talks about America."

"No, Papa, I'm sorry, her dreaming exhausts me sometimes. I would not be against going to America." She quietly confessed, feeling guilty that those expressions were noticed.

"Well then it's settled, let's go."

Mamie was startled. "Wait, what? When Papa?"

"Let me rephrase that. We are settled in the discussion that we will now work toward a plan to get to America. Of course, we do not have the finances now. First, we need to move from Pedara."

Mamie took a few minutes to process that fact. She looked again around the shop, a ghost of its former self. *Move from Pedara? The only place I've ever lived? My twelve year old self was always wondering if there might be somewhere else I'd like better than here. I hoped for a chance to try new things and meet new people, and have an opportunity to fall in love, for real. Will I have that chance now?*

"Right. So then, when do we plan? I am ready to get to work on our future!" Mamie couldn't help but smile. "Thank you, Papa, this has turned out to be the best birthday."

And, for the second time in her life, she saw her papa smile too. With teeth showing.

CHAPTER 17

Mamie, 1897

June
The Move to Regalbuto

"**M**amie, Mamie wake up!"

She felt something hit her legs before the words hit her ears.

Have I been dreaming? I am in my bed: sweaty, my heart racing. What is Rose's pillow doing next to me?

"You are having another nightmare! What is going on with you? You never had nightmares before, but ever since the fire…" Her tone shifted. "Oh. Mamie, are you ok?" Rose was whispering more gently now. "Let's go, it's time to move."

She is pitying me again. It's too dark and still to be morning, I'm going to lay here a bit longer…

Wait. But I can't. It's moving day!

The girls quickly got ready. They tidied up the guest room so that they would leave it in the same condition as it was when they arrived, as a courtesy for the hospitality they received the past four months.

Since that discussion on Mamie's birthday three months ago about a master plan to go to America, they sold their land and whatever undamaged house contents someone would buy. Items that came clean enough to be used they packed up, but for a family of ten, it only amounted to a couple of trunks worth.

With the restitution money, their papa was able to pay some of the debt back, but he figured it would take them three years to pay the rest, as well as save for passage and travel to America.

By that time baby Stella will be older for traveling more easily. I can wait three years, then I will be nearly eighteen years old, and be in a better position to marry and work. And it will be 1900. What better way to start a new century than to be in America!

As it became sunnier with the dawn, Mamie thought she understood things more clearly. Their first step of moving to Regalbuto was not a move of desperation, or the beginning of the end. It was a stepping stone toward a new life, potential, a future for their entire family. In Regalbuto, they can work hard, save money, and plan. They can then get to America and design their futures. For Mamie, the day felt even brighter than it had for months.

Mamie and Rose gathered her small bags and left to find their papa. They were getting ready to begin their trip on foot, traveling from Aunt Agatha's house to the Zappalas' to meet up with the others.

Outside, the girls and their papa said their goodbyes to Aunt Agatha, and even to Foul Sal. Salvatore looked a little upset that they were leaving, but Mamie certainly didn't encourage him to visit them in Regalbuto or in America. She hugged Aunt Agatha goodbye, heeding her warning to stay safe.

Once at the Zappalas', Mamie and their papa said goodbye to Rose. She was going to stay the night with their mother and the smaller ones and planned to ride in the borrowed carriage the next morning. Francesco would manage the horses and Rose would help with the little ones. The carriage couldn't hold everyone, and a second carriage was out of the question. Mamie insisted she felt up to the journey on foot with her papa.

Once the pair left, Mamie's papa said he hoped to head up the mountain on the way, so that they could bid farewell to the volcano that had been nothing but good to them. Mamie asked why now, since they would still be nearby in Regalbuto for a few more years, but he remarked that the soil in Regalbuto would not be from Etna, it would not be the same.

They started up the mountain trail, but unfortunately, the uphill trek was too much for her papa so he decided that they would find lodging earlier than they anticipated. They stayed at an inn called the Sapienza Boarding Rooms. Her papa said his great, great, great grandfather married a woman with the surname Sapienza, so they were probably family.

₧)ℛ

The next day, again, her papa's plan for how much walking he could complete in one day was underestimated, so they stopped somewhere near Adrano, a halfway stop. They would have to finish the following day, and, unfortunately, the family and the carriage would now arrive at Regalbuto before they did.

When they finally reached their destination on their third day of traveling, her papa inquired at a local shop, one he said he had been to before, when he was trying to find buyers for the slightly damaged goods after the fire.

He spoke with a man whom Mamie assumed was Giuseppe Cardaci, a middle-aged man like her papa.

"So, you know my cousin's son, Domenico, you say?" The man said to her papa, apparently not recognizing that they have already met a few months ago. He then leaned in to ask, suspiciously, "What is his last name?"

Her papa looked confused by this questioning process, and Mamie wondered if maybe they had the wrong Guiseppe Cardaci. "Um, I don't remember exactly, was it Bregas? Brechisci?"

"Hm, did he say anything else that I may know if we speak of the same man?" The man asked.

Her papa attempted to recall a past conversation, feeling now very foolish for not getting more information from Domenico back then. "Ah, we talked, yes, he helped with the shed, oh, wait, he kept saying '*he who leaves succeeds.*'"

This was helpful. The man's defenses lowered, and he welcomed Mamie's papa over. "I am sorry, sir, for so many questions, one can never be too careful when dealing with business or connections." They shook hands. "Yes, yes, that is a favorite saying of Domenico's."

Mamie's cheeks warmed at the mention of his name.

"Ah! I will help you. I just saw him in America. He is doing well. I will be seeing him again in about a year when I travel to New York next."

Mamie searched the man's face for more information but dared not ask. *Oh, I wish he would say more. How is he doing? Is he married?*

Mamie's papa's eyes opened wide. This man, Cardaci, impressively traveled to and from America as easily as to a nearby town.

"I am grateful for your help, Mr. Cardaci. Have my wife and children arrived in a carriage yesterday or today?"

Cardaci assured him the family was safe, and he pointed up the road to where they were staying. He walked with Mamie and her papa to settle details of their arrangements.

Cardaci explained that his dear relation, Guiseppa Timpanaro, had been in constant worry for her sons, and this had caused her to become ill. After her first husband, the children's father, died a few years ago, she remarried. Her new husband left angrily and hasn't been back since her oldest, Domenico, left for America. With only a young son at home, she could use some help.

Mamie's papa suggested to Cardaci that Mamie could help with the vineyard and other chores, and Rose could help nurse Mrs. Timpanaro back to health. Concetta, Francesco, and Grazia could work with her son, Angelo, being they are all about the same age.

It sounded like a good plan to Mamie. *We will have work, a small income, and a place to live nearby in one of Cardaci's lodgings. Perhaps Mother can find a friend in Mrs. Timpanaro, and they can keep each other company. Maybe I can find out news about Dom too.*

It was an arrangement that benefited everyone. All that was left to discuss was work for her papa. "Will you farm?" Cardaci asked.

"I will do anything."

Mamie noticed it took her papa a minute to swallow his pride first, he was always a self-reliant man.

"Yes, well, I lost my best farm hand to America last week. You will have to know how to tend to the vineyards. Will you plan to stay long in Regalbuto? I keep losing men to America."

"I will do it, and yes, we plan to be here at least three years."

"Good, then are we settled?"

Mamie looked at her papa, remembering back to when he took a chance on Domenico, they both needed something, and they arranged to help each other. "Yes, I accept your offer." He told him. "How will I ever thank you, Mr. Cardaci?"

"Just Cardaci, please. And if my cousin gave my name to you, it means to me that you have helped him. When you help my family, I help you. No thanks needed."

The men parted. Mamie and her papa went to reunite with the family and access their new situation.

Cardaci watched as they left, shaking his head at this poor family's situation. Even with all of his connections, he couldn't possibly have known they'd be caught in the middle like this. All he could do now was help them make a comfortable life while keeping 'That Man' out of the picture for as long as he could, legally, of course.

CHAPTER 18

Domenico, 1898

May
New York

Three years ago, he left Sicily on faith that everything would work out.

Since arriving in NY, all he could do each day was focus on what was directly in front of him and the things he could control: working, hoping, and praying. Now the final moment was approaching, he just didn't know exactly which day. He had to trust that Cardaci would help his brother travel to America, and he prayed often for their safe journey.

Finally, the day arrived.

Miss Canali, the young housekeeper's apprentice, timidly knocked on the door of his room at the rectory. "Excuse me, Mr. Domenico, you have visitors in the front vestibule."

The poor girl was shocked and surprised when he threw the door open and grabbed her by the shoulders.

"Yes, thank you. It must be my brother and Cardaci!" Domenico released her, realizing how awkward his excitement was, and steadied himself. "Oh, please do excuse me. I hope it is them. Did they give names?"

"No, sir, but it is indeed two men: one young, one older."

Feigning composure, he thanked her again before running through the church to the lobby like a rambunctious teenager. He saw the visitors at the bottom of the staircase.

"Angelo! At long last! Oh, my brother, you are here! He landed at the bottom of the stairs, hugged the young boy, and looked him over, not believing his eyes. "How you've grown to be a young man now, what thirteen?"

He turned to the other man. "Ah, Cardaci, I can never thank you enough. 'Thanks' is not even a big enough word. I am forever grateful." Domenico bowed his head, gave the older man a hug, but couldn't contain his emotions any longer. He began to cry tears of relief and joy; all his pent-up anxiety, fear, and apprehension was released with the realization that they'd made it. Angelo was here. He and his brother were finally safe.

"Oh, the happy reunion. Tears of joy, no?" Father Domo came down the stairs after hearing the commotion in the lobby. "Miss Canali has made us some cold lemonade in the kitchen of the rectory. Shall we?"

Domenico couldn't wait for the group to be settled. "Oh Angelo, America is all that we've dreamed of and in the next few weeks I will show you around. And you'll have to tell me about home, how is Mother?"

Angelo cut right to what was on his mind. "We can never go back to Sicily, Dom."

"Why speak of travel, you just got here!" Father Domo interjected with a chuckle, but the young boy had been holding in his thoughts for much too long. The priest sobered, recognizing the look of a person needing to get something off his chest.

"No, I'm serious. Dom, we can never. Mother knows this. She was quiet and sad when I left, but she knows. Our sisters know this. They are happy that you are going to look after me here in America and that I will have a better life away from 'That Man'."

Angelo grew more pained. "He threatened you Dom, he threatened all of us. When you left, 'That Man' said if you ever contact Mother, or our sisters, or showed up in town again, he would come after you. You can't ever go back. He cursed your life. He was serious and furious. I was scared for Mother, but she told me he would never hurt her, and he never has, just as he never hurt me. He thought I would be his son. He said if you ever came for me, he threatened to come and take *your* sons in the future."

The men just stared at him, stunned, processing the serious story coming from this stranger of a young man, a not-so-little brother. "All I can say is it was nice when he wasn't around, things were quiet for a while. Although he was acting peculiarly when he left." Angelo sat at the table and took a sip of lemonade.

"What do you mean?" Cardaci asked.

"I don't know, when you left, he left, saying how he had a way to find you. Then he came back wearing some new hat and jacket, and he had a suitcase. I don't know where he got the money for such things. Then he left again."

Domenico told them 'That Man' was behind him on the train when he was trying to leave Sicily, and how he was oddly dressed then. He shared with Angelo and Cardaci how he gave him and his companion the slip.

"I suppose he thought he'd have more credibility disguised as a gentleman. I'm glad it didn't work." Angelo remarked. "I'm glad he got caught, and not you."

Domenico looked away, not wanting to share with his little brother the details of the story he told: the lie about their father. He hoped he'd never have to.

171

"Yes, well, the men spent some time in questioning at the Port of Messina and were released. They then left for America, probably two months later." Cardaci concluded.

"Oh, but thankfully they did not find me here. A church is a wonderful place to live and work – and lay low." Domenico said and looked with appreciation to Father Domo. Father patted Domenico's shoulder and took his leave, excusing himself from the conversation to get back to his daily schedule.

Domenico leaned in to his younger brother. "Wait, Angelo, you said it was quiet – for a while. Did 'That Man' return to Regalbuto?"

Angelo and Cardaci looked at each other.

"Domenico. I must ask you something." Cardaci interjected. "You met a family in Pedara, yes? You must've told them at some point that if they were to need anything, to ask for me, correct?"

"Do you mean the Priviteras? Yes, I told them that." Domenico answered, nervously.

"Domenico, how well did you know that family?"

"Why? What do you mean? They were nice people. They trusted me, I helped them with some work."

"Did you meet the daughter, the oldest one? Domenica?"

"Mamie? I mean..." He cleared his throat. "Why yes, what happened?"

"Sit down." Cardaci's tone was suddenly serious. "So, 'That Man' didn't return to Regalbuto, but he went to Pedara. He returned to their shop after not finding you in America. He must have retraced your steps from when you left, two years earlier. He heard you were sleeping in their shed then. He thought the family was keeping secrets for you and that they sent him on a wild chase. He got angry. Domenica was there, alone."

Domenico paced around the room, not sure what to do. "What happened, is she ok?"

"She was assaulted and injured; she recovered but the store suffered badly. There was a fire. The family had to move."

"Oh, no. That's terrible." Domenico sat down to process what he was hearing. "But they are ok? Did they come to America?"

"Oh, no. They didn't have enough money to do that. They moved to Regalbuto."

Angelo talked about how he worked with Mamie, Rose, and Francesco, and how Grazia and Concetta were closest to his age. He mentioned that their mother and the Privitera's mother became good friends. The family lived very close by.

Domenico asked, "and how are they now?" The suspense for a report on their well-being was making him impatient.

"They are well. They send their regards." Angelo looked at his brother with a question on his mind but wasn't sure if he should ask.

"What is it, Angelo?"

"Well, Dom. Um, Domenica asked if you would write, only if you weren't already married when I saw you."

Domenico laughed, but sobered quickly when he realized something. "Wait, but where is 'That Man'? Does he know the Priviteras are now in Regalbuto?"

"The authorities caught him and his friend after the assault and fire. They are in jail right now." Cardaci reassured him.

"Well, what happens when they get out? What about the family's safety then? He won't have to look far to find them this time. He already set out to

173

harm them once and succeeded." Domenico hung his head. "This is all my fault."

"Don't worry Domenico, now that Angelo is with you, I will continue with the other business I have here in the city. I will return to Sicily again next month and I will check in on the family." Cardaci hoped to calm Domenico's concerns.

"You must, Cardaci, please. It is my fault they are in this situation now; I never meant any harm to come to them, they only helped me. Please, do, please make sure they are safe."

"I will do what I can."

Domenico trusted Cardaci, but he wanted to do more. He remembered the *cornicello* that his mother gave him before he came to America. "Wait, can you give Mamie...um, Domenica something for me when you return to Sicily?" He thought she could use some protection from any curse that could be following her now.

Ignoring Cardaci's questioning look, he headed up the stairs, calling back, "I will be just a few minutes, getting it from my room. Perhaps you two can discuss what Angelo would like to do first in America!"

₭₩‑

Gathering the long coral horn, he wrapped it in a handkerchief.

Not sure if Mamie would even know what to do with it since it wasn't something they had ever discussed, he wrote a quick note to accompany the charm.

I feel responsible. I should apologize for putting her in harm's way. At least that will be the reason for the letter. Any other feelings I have – well, I will just have to wait and see.

July 1898

Dear Mamie,

How long it has been since the day I bumped into your basket of lemons on the road to your cousin's farm? Now, I am in America and so is Angelo. He says you have met, and that you live near our home in Regalbuto. I am sorry to hear what happened to you and to your family's home in Pedara. Please, be cautious. Cardaci will help you. He is a faithful cousin and has promised me he would.

Angelo told me that you and your papa plan to come to America in 1900, I wish you safe travels. When I came to America, my mother gave me this amulet. I would like you to have it. Just keep it concealed and it will protect you from evil thoughts of others during your journey. You may not believe these things, but I would still like you to have it.

Angelo says you see my mother often, please give her my love and let her know her sons are safe and well.

Kind regards, Domenico

Hoping the gesture would be looked at as friendly – and nothing inappropriate, he enclosed the long coral horn in the folds of his letter and tied it securely with a string.

Writing the note helped dissipate some of his guilt, and gifting the charm helped calm his nerves about Mamie's safety. But, he sighed, the feelings he kept at bay for so long were resurfacing again now that Angelo arrived.

Now what? He wondered.

All his efforts these last few years were channeled into helping Angelo travel to America, so he put his own needs and future aside.

Now that Angelo is safe, is it safe to think about my own future now? Should I look for a woman to marry in America? Or should I wait for Mamie to arrive in a few years, and be patient?

But what if I wait and she isn't interested in me when she finally comes to America? I am quite a bit older than she is, and she deserves a handsome young gentleman, not a rough working man.

Let her come to America. If we find each other here and it works out, then I will be a happy man.

If it doesn't work out between us, then at least I can wish her to be happy. In my heart that is what will make me happy, to know that she is.

He returned to the men and the plans for sight-seeing.

When I push, the world just pushes harder.

CHAPTER 19

Mamie, 1900

July
Regalbuto, Sicily

*A*s she looked forward to the 1800s ending, Mamie anticipated that celebrations and fanfare would last indefinitely. The entire world would reset, and she wondered what new beginnings were in store. But after the first month of 1900, the novelty was gone, and the waiting had begun again. This was the year they would move to America, and it couldn't happen quick enough.

They carried out their three year plan in Regalbuto and saved enough for Mamie and her papa to leave by the end of September of this year. They couldn't save enough for the entire family to leave together, so they made a new three year plan to get everyone to America.

In this plan, Mamie and her papa first would make the trip this year, then they would both work in America and send money home. Then in year two, Francesco, Rose and Concetta would travel. They all would work and combine their wages for another year to help bring the rest of the family at the end of year three.

With every passing minute she felt impatient. When she felt impatient she was always reminded of Domenico. And then she *really* felt impatient.

Ever since Cardaci returned from New York bringing her the note and gift from Domenico, she held onto a small hope that they might correspond often. She sent him a thank you note with many questions about his life in New York, but he never responded.

She reached into her apron pocket to touch the token he sent. Snugly wrapped in a few layers of muslin, she gave it a gentle squeeze of appreciation. It was a sweet gift, and although she didn't understand the protection it was meant to provide, she treasured the idea that Domenico thought enough of her to send it. She also liked its reminder that a trip to America would be in her future. She closed her eyes and took a deep breath, gathering strength to be patient once again; her trip was just two long months away now.

"You are deep in thought today," Mrs. Timpanaro interrupted.

Mamie looked up from the silk flower petals she was wiring together the way Mrs. Timpanaro instructed. Domenico's mother was teaching her this craft so that Mamie could make and sell these flowers in America. Mamie spent many hours with her between learning new skills, helping her with Cardaci's farm and vineyard, and listening to her stories.

Mamie wished she would talk more about what Domenico was like as a young boy and how he would entertain his baby brother, Angelo. She felt the older woman was lonely, having no children at home anymore, and her husband never being around, but Mamie didn't mind her company. She felt the time was worth it whenever she'd hear something new about Domenico.

"Would you do an errand for me? Cardaci went to Caltagirone on business, and I promised him that someone would check on the grapes. My old joints are acting up again today. Can you do it?"

"Certainly, Mrs. Timpanaro." Mamie welcomed the chance to be out in the fresh air and sunshine, just like her errand girl days back in Pedara.

As she walked, she took her time, noticing new things about Regalbuto's rolling hills that were different from the places she had been before. There were vistas along the road where you could stand as if you were on a fourth-floor balcony, seeing for miles. Mamie loved this on-top-of-the-world feeling.

One such roadway had a perfect view of Mount Etna in the distance, and Mamie was mesmerized, thinking about how much power lay under the calm and quiet surface. She didn't notice when someone climbed up from the side of the hill toward her.

"You, there."

Mamie was startled out of her contemplation.

"What are you ddd-doing on my land?"

She didn't think the road was part of private property. She looked around, confused, not sure if this man was even talking to her.

"Yes, you. You are ss-standing on my pp-property." The haggard man swayed toward her, and she nervously backed away. She turned to walk quickly back the way she came.

The man walked faster and caught up.

Surprised, Mamie stumbled and fell.

He offered his hand to help her up. "Oh, I am sorry to ss-startle you, miss." He mocked a polite tone.

The sound of his voice had an eerie familiarity to it. She didn't trust it. She just sat on the ground, stunned.

He clumsily grabbed her forearm and pulled her to her feet. Mamie brushed off her dress with her free hand and looked at his hand on her other arm. He didn't let it go.

She looked directly at his face and gasped.

Something registered on his face too.

Recognition.

"Ah, miss-ss." He hissed, more sober but spiteful. "You, again. Do you know what trouble you have caused me? Two years on the chase you ss-sent me, looking for him in America. Then two years-ss in jail because I needed you to help me find that scum, that ss-stepson, and you had to go and be difficult. What luck that I got out early, and hah, here you are, in my yard." As he raved, he squeezed Mamie's arm tighter.

Mamie struggled to break free but only swayed and stumbled.

"All that wasted time, and now how will I ever find him? Even worse, he came back and took my ss-son." He spat.

The shaking caused Mamie to see pinpricks of flashing light, and she now remembered everything: the man – blonde, pretending to be a gentleman, his accomplice – sneering and smoking, her throat – the pain, and the guilt – everything her family lost because of her. She couldn't stop this man before; she did not have a chance to fight back.

Her heartbeat thumped in her ears, her eyes, and her throat. She found a second of courage and screamed at him, "*Lassami in paci!* Leave me alone!" This was not a good plan, she soon realized. This was not a way for her to get out of this situation unharmed, unscathed. She knew it, but in this moment nothing else mattered but standing up for herself. She refused to be a victim again. She couldn't stop her battle cry once it escaped, she couldn't stop her fist from meeting his jaw, or her foot from reaching his shins. But it was a futile effort.

His eyes shot fire into hers. He grabbed her swinging fist and got a handful of her apron instead.

She heard a faint snap. She knew in that moment that whatever curse

181

Domenico hoped to help her ward off, was fully upon her. She was in trouble.

ഔരദ

In the weeks later, Mamie still couldn't remember what happened next. At night, her subconscious shifted to reveal information from that day that she couldn't accept. The nightmares she suffered after the assault and fire years earlier have intensified, with a clearer face in them: a haunting, angry face that despised and blamed her.

In her nightmares, the same man from the fire trapped her on the hill of Regalbuto as lava flowed from Mount Etna toward her. She was roughly pushed down in the tall grass. She fought to stand up, fearing for her life, covering her ears so she wouldn't hear his angry voice anymore, writhing her body to avoid the flames slowing burning toward her.

"This is your fault, filthy girl." He blamed her with a mix of heinous laughter and threats of harming her family if she told anyone she saw him.

She was stuck. Heat rose over her, a stench filled her senses, and fire seared through her body. The lava consumed her, and her insides burned. He laughed again as he left her, sickeningly satisfied. She was still trapped, her body solidifying into black rock like the lava stones on a common path.

She would wake up with Rose at her side, looking sympathetically at her but also somewhat frustrated. Mamie wished she could feel rested and energetic again, she wished she could talk to someone but feared the man's threat. She thought by distancing herself from her family, she could protect them. She thought by keeping her thoughts contained, she could avoid reality.

About a month later, in addition to struggling with the demon in her sleep, her body began to fight the nightmare in the daytime too. Scratches and bruises surfaced that were a constant physical reminder that something terrible happened: white scars striped across her arms and legs. She began every morning feeling sweaty and disoriented. Now, Mamie was feeling nauseous and dizzy, vomiting daily.

She feebly hoped she would be well enough to travel. They were to leave for America in a week.

℘℃℃

Mamie's mother and Mrs. Timpanaro were sitting in the garden one afternoon, it was their last chance to relax before the upcoming trip. Many things would change without Mamie and her papa being around to help.

They spotted Mamie walking past and asked her to bring them some lemonades.

The mothers looked at her longingly, realizing they would miss her. These emotions became more sentimental; paralleling feelings they have had in the past when other children have left them.

Mrs. Timpanaro confided to Mamie's mother how she had lost many babies.

Mamie overheard them but stayed out of sight. Her mother then confessed a miscarriage she herself had almost two years ago. Mamie didn't even know about it, so she listened. Her mother told Mrs. Timpanaro that the pregnancy was a surprise. She talked about the unnerving nausea and cramping on and off for months due to the stress from the move to this new town. Then, there was the terrible day in October when the baby came too soon. Too fast. So much blood. So tiny. Her mother said she named the lifeless baby Alfia. She was spiteful, she blamed Mamie's papa. The women touched hands and exchanged sympathies.

Mamie knew she should walk away, but she couldn't help but listen. Babies were born so frequently, but she never heard anyone actually talking about how the mother feels when she is pregnant or how she feels when she loses a baby. Those things were not discussed, especially not with a mother and daughter. And not with Mamie's mother. She never said much to Mamie.

Mamie listened some more. Mrs. Timpanaro told of the six babies she lost between Domenico and Angelo. She began to say that her new husband wanted her to have his children and she did not. Even if she could, she wouldn't.

"Then why did you marry him?" Mamie's mother asked her.

Mrs. Timpanaro began to weep, she said she met him after three years of mourning her husband and she knew Domenico yearned to leave the house and have a family of his own. She didn't want to be alone with only her young son. It was nice to have this man's attention. She made so many mistakes and now she would be alone anyway, she said; her children despised her for the choice she made.

She tensed her jaw and leaned in to tell Mamie's mother, "I once thought him to be very handsome, and he treated me well. But something happened shortly after we were married. He started drinking. He fought with Domenico. He was cruel and violent to women in town. He came back a few weeks ago after being in jail for two years for some crime he committed. He was drunk and filthy; he walked in and fell asleep on the floor for hours. When he woke up, he couldn't remember where he was or how he got back home. He just mumbled something about some *ragazza paffuta* wasting his time again and he had to give her what she deserved. From what I have heard in town, I knew what that meant. Then he left again, thankfully, and I haven't seen him since. He drinks so much; I fear what he might do." She grew quieter. "Oh, I wish I never married that Vince, 'That Man' has brought my family nothing but trouble."

Mamie cringed when she heard the insult again. Her stomach flipped at the man's name. *Vince? Was this the same man?*

The realization hit her with a wave of nausea.

He is Mrs. Timpanaro's husband?

Domenico and Angelo's stepfather?

Rose's "signore biondo?"

The man in the shop, the drunk from the road.

The man in my nightmare.

The fire…The…the lava.

A noise: a whimper or groan escaped from somewhere inside Mamie, but it sounded far away. All the blood in her head roared in her ears and she heard nothing else.

The women stood quickly when they heard the tray of lemonades crash onto the terracotta tiles, along with a thud.

They cradled the young girl and checked if she was injured. As they revived her, they noticed peculiar month-old scars on her forearms. As they helped her stand, they felt her extra fullness in her midsection and bosom. The two wise women perceived Mamie's condition with shock, staring at each other with wide eyes.

They whispered to each other that this changed everything.

CHAPTER 20

Mamie, 1903

July
Regalbuto, Sicily

T he plans for America were no longer. Mamie knew, deep down, that she was the reason, yet again. The year 1900 came and went.

Mamie was racked with guilt – starting six years ago when they left Pedara and compounding in the past three. She was tormented by fragmented nightmares – events and injuries that awakened full force at night, reminding her, scolding her, blaming her.

Her body was a shell she didn't recognize; changes and scars emerged that she didn't remember developing. No pain, no happiness. Just numb. The reason was in a fog that was so thick during the day, the only time her memory broke through was when she slept. The last three years were lost, locked in her mind.

Rose sat next to her, again, it was a regular thing each morning. Mamie would wake up startled, sweating, day after day.

"Why Rose? I can't bear it any longer, why can't this just stop?" The recurring shame she felt was so persistent, but in the moments she would first wake up, she would sometimes catch a glimpse of the contrast between the Mamie she used to be and the Mamie she was now. In those moments of clarity, there was hope: a reason to escape from her tormentor because she knew it wasn't always like this.

Rose got up gently from the edge of her sister's bed and brought her a handkerchief. She offered a sip of water from the glass on the nightstand.

"Sometimes life can't be explained." Rose began to rationalize, trying to be consoling without allowing her own disappointment to show. "Sure, we have had a few setbacks in our plans for America, but Papa thinks the timing is better. He is right now securing the passage! Isn't that happy news? We have worked so hard for this for so long. And now, after all this time, you will go with Papa to start your fresh, new life in America."

"What, really?" Mamie searched her thoughts to recollect if she should have known about this. She had trouble processing this news but didn't want to alarm Rose, she just felt confused.

"Yes, really, Mamie. Aren't you happy? Papa said we will be back on track – just a few years later than the original plan." Rose looked away. "But maybe this is better; the little ones will be older, and baby Mary will be easier to travel with for Mama when it's their turn.

Mamie was struck by the mention of her newest sister. "How old is Baby Mary now, Rose?" *Baby Mary. Have I been numb for so long that I don't even know this sister?* She thought.

"Why, she is two, why do you ask?" Rose was concerned this lapse might be a new symptom rearing its head. "You do remember our baby sister, don't you? You spent so much time with her when she was first born; you were inseparable. Then when she turned three months old you just left her for Mama to care for like you never knew her." Rose chided, looked at her sister for a sign that this was registering, and said softly, mostly to herself, "It was such a change in your attitude with her. I don't understand your moods, Mamie. Sometimes you are barely present and sometimes you are far, far away. What is wrong with you?"

Mamie wished she could explain, but how? *The voice I hear yells that I am to blame; I cannot tell anyone what took place. What if there is a reason for that? What if I tell someone and more bad things happen?*

They heard the door open in the downstairs foyer, and someone entered. The pattern of the footsteps signaled to them that their papa had arrived.

Rose quietly headed downstairs to ask if he had gotten the tickets.

"Yes, Rose. Hurry to help Mamie pack her bags, and make sure you pack yours as well."

"Mine, Papa? Surely I'm not going *now*?"

"Yes, Mamie will need you during the voyage, with all that she has been through. With your nursing nature you will be a big help to me on the ship as well as when we get to America. I don't know how long before she will feel like finding work, but she will need you."

"Won't Mama need me with all the young ones?" She started to say but didn't wait for an answer. They would all do what was necessary if she wasn't there.

"AMERICA! I can hardly believe it!" Rose squealed. Overly excited, she headed back to their room and forgot about being quiet. "Mamie, did you hear?"

"Shh Rose, I'm sure the neighbors could hear." Their papa jokingly reprimanded.

Rose tried again to rouse her sister. "We are leaving in the morning for the port of Napoli! I've heard that the train ride will be at least two days with stops, so we can do our sleeping then. Come on, get up Mamie! Let us pack our cares and woes and leave them behind, we are off to begin our new lives!"

After hearing about so many of their papa's friends and family leaving Sicily and heading to New York, the move seemed so unattainable – something just for others, not them, not with their poor luck and circumstances. Some of those friends returned, but many have not, and perhaps would never. The ones who did, turned right back around and left again for America, with their wife and kids this time, or even with their elderly parents. They would describe America in one word: abundance – any kind of job you wanted; you can get. Money flowed there like nobody had ever seen before. So many people with so many needs to fill; so many people were needed. They've said it was amazing. Rose could not wait.

Rose helped Mamie up and took her outside for some fresh air. Mamie looked around the yard, the horizon spread across the landscape from east to west, with a few small hills and rows of overflowing grapevines. Rose began to think aloud, narrating what she thought Mamie was also thinking, "America's going to be so different. What will a city be like, all those people? Will we fit in? Will we find work? What does our future hold?"

Rose continued, running through all of the details she had heard about America in bits and pieces over the years. She gushed about the New York City life – full of excitement, movies, musical productions, restaurants, and more. "What will those things be like to experience? Perhaps I will meet a suitor in some fancy place. Maybe you will meet someone too, Mamie. We can have the life we've longed for since we were little girls."

They went back inside. Rose told Mamie to pack her small bag: only a few things she couldn't do without – a few small, surviving memories of growing up in Pedara. Mamie slowly picked up her comb and considered her patchwork pillow. She ran her fingers over the chain from their grandmother, whom they only vaguely knew, but being the oldest, Mamie was bestowed with this treasure. Rose received a less than glamorous hair locket which she wanted to trade for Mamie's gift years ago.

The items brought back memories of her youth and the dreams she had. *Can I have a new life in America, one where I can be dainty and feminine like Rose, where maybe I don't have to lift crates of fruit to impress a man? Maybe my hands can soften, my middle can slender…*

189

The shell she used to imprison a certain reality cracked just slightly, and a small truth trickled through to her consciousness even though she tried so hard to keep it locked up.

Flashes of violation, shame, secrecy, despair, ruin, then realization broke through. *Who am I kidding? Those days if innocence are behind me now because of that day on the road, whether I want to acknowledge it or not. What man will want me now?*

Rose rushed back to their room, set her embroidered apron on top of her bag, and then her many handkerchiefs. She was singing about all the possibilities, that whatever else she may need she will find in America, just do a little work, earn a few coins, and then get anything she wants. She paused to imagine what that could be and grabbed another bag to fill, just in case. She didn't want to leave *all* of the shopping choices in America to chance.

Mamie sat staring at her own bag and its emptiness. Silent tears fell, unbeknownst to Rose, but Mamie was finally fully aware of why. She thought of everything she would want to bring but never could. She remembered all that she would have to leave behind, forever, that would never be hers again. Overwhelmed now, she mumbled that she would go back to sleep.

Rose was oblivious to all but her own daydreams.

₧₨

The next morning, Rose said her goodbyes to her mother and the little ones. They would come on a future voyage; the family would be reunited soon enough.

"We will work hard and make money to pay for everyone's passage in another year or so. Maybe we will even find men and marry! Can you imagine me, married? Oh!" Rose was beyond containment.

Mamie slowly made her way downstairs to say her goodbyes as well. She hugged her sisters, the boys, and looked at her mother who reached out to hold Mamie's face in her hands. Mamie was surprised by the closest thing to a caress she had ever known from her mother.

"Begin your new life, Mamie. Leave the old one behind, this is my hope for you, my daughter."

Mamie walked out quickly before a dam of emotion burst.

Outside, Mrs. Timpanaro waited to have a word with Mamie. Seeing her now, Mamie thought of Domenico. She wondered how he was doing in America, and if she might see him there. She thought of how he became the model of a man she'd like to find but caught herself before that line of thinking went any farther. *That dream will never be the same*, she thought, *as I will never be the same.* Feeling yet another loss, Mamie couldn't stop the tears.

The older woman approached her, relentlessly begging for forgiveness, but Mamie and her parents knew she was not to blame. She couldn't be responsible for that man's actions, but she continued to feel guilty. Still, she constantly sought to make amends.

"Here, my dear, I want to give you this, please don't be upset." She took Mamie's hand. In it, she placed a small object on a string, and closed Mamie's fist around it. "This is important, please, even if you don't believe in it. Take this and wear it around your neck for your journey and new life in America."

Mamie knew what it was. She remembered how it didn't protect her before. She shook her head to refuse it, but Mrs. Timpanaro was adamant. The older woman said it was broken into pieces now, perhaps like Mamie felt her life was, but she performed a new ritual to remove any remaining bad luck. The charm had been made into something new, just like Mamie could be.

Rose urged Mamie to hurry, stopping her sister's flow of thoughts like a plug in a dam.

191

Mrs. Timpanaro watched Mamie leave with her father and sister. She nodded, relieved that the young girl accepted the amulet and would be protected. She was satisfied that she had now done all she could to mend a terrible situation. The charm was the last piece.

CHAPTER 21

Mamie, 1903

*August 12,
Arrival Day in New York*

"**M**amie, hurry up!" Rose grunted through clenched teeth, turning her head back to shout her impatience at her sister. She carried a large bag which seemed to make her irritable. Following her was their papa, carrying his own and Rose's extra baggage, without complaint. Mamie, with only her small satchel, was carefully walking only a few paces behind them as they made their way from the cabins to the gangplank.

Mamie was next in line to disembark. She stood, carefully, at the top of the rickety bridge, holding fast to the ship railing; her first step in America coming up. *That might not be the only thing coming up, my stomach is still so unsettled.*

She paused to look toward the horizon to get her bearings and caught her first glimpse of their new home. *It seems an awful lot like the pier in Napoli we left weeks ago, but here, the sky seems to shimmer,* she thought.

Mamie looked in awe of the crowned statue, a hundred feet high; and the buildings on the horizon were like a dense forest of illuminated trees.

She heard a man in the distance directing others on the dock, away from the crowds, calling out names. His booming voice was heard over the buzzing of all the people around her.

I wonder what my first glimpse of an American man will hold. She shook her head to remove that thought. *If I've learned anything about men, it's that the look of him does not tell you his character. It must be Rose's influence that made me forget that for a moment.*

The last two weeks were full of Mamie listening to Rose describing who she would meet, what he would look like, where he would take her to dine, how he would court her, and on and on. Occasionally, Rose would imagine a nice man for her sister, since Mamie had trouble imagining one for herself. Rose's descriptive conversations, along with the change in scenery and sea air, effectively transported her sister, and Mamie felt more and more like she used to.

Mamie attempted to see the boisterous man, wondering if Rose would consider him handsome or not. *It doesn't matter anymore. I have come to the decision that a handsome man is not to be trusted; so ordinary-looking would be fine with me. I just hope there's a man out there who will give me a second look with all that I have been through.*

Her eyes landed where the voice originated and laughed at herself that she thought she might see some new specimen of a man in America; from afar, he looked much the same as all the others in Sicily.

She looked from the pier to the sky, the bright blueness over the waters. The color reminded her of the eyes of a certain man years ago that were just as blue.

Months ago, Rose made the arrangements for a representative from Our Lady of Pompeii Church to be there to greet them when they arrived at the dock in New York and help them get to their boarding house destination of 13 Mulberry Street.

They were looking for this representative, scanning the docks but not knowing who they were looking for. Everything was hectic and confusing with hundreds of people looking so varied, there was so much to take in. Mamie strained to see everything, craning her neck and walking on her tip toes, but she wasn't seeing much more than the backs of hats and collars.

Rose looked around as well, with an air about her. Her mannerism was reminiscent of the poses portrayed in the many American magazines she used to flip through as a young girl in their shop in Pedara.

Mamie thought her sister was behaving strangely. *I know she is excited to be here, finally, but it's like she has every page, every image of a fashionable woman memorized, like a script of how to hold herself. Me, I don't really care how I look – a mess probably, but I'm sure that I will not be finding the man of my dreams the minute I step off the boat in America. Who am I to have that sort of luck? So, it doesn't matter how I look right now.*

Mamie heard a familiar sounding Sicilian accent that yelled out their last name, *Privitera*, but thought she was imagining it. She peered again over the heads to see if it was their escort searching for them. *Of course, I'm shorter than the wall of people around me so trying to see anything is futile.*

Their papa's loud voice bellowed in response to the call, which apparently was not in Mamie's head. He stopped and moved around so quickly, taking the bag straps off his shoulders and laughing, the bags landing on the paved walkway at his feet. Mamie bumped into him like she used to all those times behind the counter at the shop, when she would trail him to see what he was doing, and he would stop suddenly.

Mamie glimpsed the man who was yelling; the same loud man she spotted from the ship, now standing in front of them. He and her papa excitedly talked at all once in Sicilian and shook hands heartily. This man's face glowed with so much anticipation. Mamie was struck by his expression and greeting, as if everyone who disembarked was congratulated for entering the promise land.

His face was stocky and rough with small, white hints of some past pains hidden behind a massive amount of hair, which grew all over. His head, his eyebrows, his nose, his chin, his cheeks, the edges of his ears, the top of his chest; hair was coming out of the neck and sleeves of his shirt. Mamie felt an odd sense of familiarity; she was compelled by the look of pleasantness in his eyes, like a vast blue sky over a brown grassy prairie.

His eyes.

Could it be?

She stretched to look at the man over her papa's shoulder to figure out why they were *still* shaking hands, laughing as if sharing the most hilarious joke. The man's blue eyes met Mamie's, and she sharply took in a breath.

Mamie looked down right away, embarrassed, not sure what her face was revealing. *How is this possible? I haven't seen him in over eight years. We are one in a million people arriving and he is one in a million people in New York, how is it possible that we come across each other again? My first steps in America put me face to face with the only man I ever thought twice about, since I was twelve.*

She heard him inquire about her to her papa, "and you have arrived with your daughter?" *Did his voice crack a little with expectation?* She wasn't sure if she imagined it.

"Yes, yes, both oldest, you might remember Rose, and Domenica." Her papa turned to Mamie and reached to put his arm around her back, to present her to him as if to say, 'here she is, surprise!' but the people around them were crowding so much, Mamie ducked slightly out of the way of his arm; and couldn't move.

Rose was a few feet away, scanning the crowd and looking at the men's coats and women's hats as if she was shopping the styles and colors available in America. She completely ignored the man in front of her papa. His was not the look of the escort she imagined so she kept looking around, hoping that another would arrive.

Mamie was frozen, her head still down. She sensed the blue-eyed man was trying to catch her eye again, but she was afraid to look up. *His unforgettable eyes appear to not have forgotten me; will he see that I haven't forgotten him either? Will I see that he is married now, which is why he never wrote back? I am not the young girl I was when he met me: the young shop girl with so many questions. Maybe he will be disgusted with me now, who I've been forced to become, what I've been through. What will he see?*

Mamie immediately realized that she cared nothing for her appearance a few minutes ago. She pushed back her loose hair into its original bun created days before; and she wiped some of the dust and sea air grime from her face with the small, embroidered handkerchief she kept in her sleeve. She realized that smoothing her clothes was pointless; she was a crumpled mess.

She saw him with the edges of her eyes, he was still waiting for her to look at him, so she gathered some courage. *I am here, in America, finally. I am here to start my life over again and make a new future. I am presented in this very moment with an opportunity I never thought I would get and I'm investigating my boot laces?*

Mamie took a deep breath, trying to trust, and slowly looked up. Faintly, she heard Rose mumble, "However in this mess of people are we going to find our escort? Papa, what are you doing? Ugh, don't put my bag on this filthy ground!"

Mamie's attention was diverted to Rose's concerns, and then she heard her sister sharply inhale, and whisper, "Mamie, it's that bear man from my nightmares."

Rose directed her attention to the escort and protested with a disgusted expression, "Oh, it's you? *You* are our escort from Our Lady of Pompeii Church? I was assured a trustworthy Sicilian man, one that will know his way around, guide us in what we need to know, and help us in the English translations. You can't be that person."

He was not at all affected by her mouthiness; he was only watching Mamie.

197

"It is my pleasure, Mister Privitera, and Missus Privitera, to be the first to welcome you to America! I am privileged to show you to your sponsor's address." Domenico said in a well-practiced, gentleman's voice and tone, ignoring Rose's opposing one.

Seeing no other options, Rose quieted. Domenico offered to carry Rose's bag, the extra bag her papa carried for her, and Mamie's small bag. Her papa nodded appreciatively, putting his own bag back on his shoulder and went to link his arms with both his daughters, but Domenico was quicker; he held an arm out to Mamie.

Mamie looked at it dumbly, like she had never seen an arm before in her life. *I certainly never saw one with such hair, but it looks almost like a dark wool shirt, so I don't mind. Here is a man's arm; not to mention it is attached to a man. A man. Paying attention to me. Why am I hesitating?*

I am worthy to be on a man's arm. My life in America will have promise and happiness. I will have escorts and men who appreciate me. Or maybe it will be just this one man; and maybe it will be just today.

Regardless, I can be happy right at this moment that, for once, I have the appreciation of a man. Ha. And wouldn't Mother be surprised; I didn't have to carry a crate of fruit to get it, well, not today. I must've done something good to deserve this moment.

CHAPTER 22

Zina

Monday, January 6, 1930

E piphany Day was unfortunately not celebrated at Zina's new school,

so she was due back. Zina grumbled that it wasn't fair that she had to miss out on the last fun day of the holiday season with her cousins because she went to a different school, but her parents were not convinced by this argument.

She was already disappointed this morning as the Epiphany Witch did not bring her any presents overnight. She imagined her cousins all waking up today to a basket of small gifts and candies and playing all day in the snow.

She didn't like feeling left out but resigned. *Maybe I haven't been as well behaved as I should have been, so the good witch didn't come to reward me. If I've been making my mother's life miserable, this is confirmation. Maybe I need to change my ways. I will try to be extra well-behaved today and do as I am told.*

"See you later, Duey," She gave her kitten an extra hug and whispered, "please be good and not pull out any more hems from my clothes. And if *Befana* happens to show up today instead of last night, please let her know I am at school today instead of playing in the snow. Will you tell her that? Thank you."

Zina left for the walk to her first bus stop.

At school, Zina was so engrossed in overhearing some girls talking in the hallway that she was startled when her teacher approached her.

"Vincenza, I would like to congratulate you."

Zina's mood lifted when she was awarded a special medal for the first half of the term in Italian Interpretation Excellence. Her teacher even asked her to help grade papers, saying she was a natural.

Zina considered the medal as her special gift, whether *Befana the Epiphany Witch* had something to do with it or not, so she was glad she decided to have a better attitude.

ಬಿಂಕ

On the train ride home, Zina was inspecting her new golden medal when she heard someone ask, "Wow is that a purple heart?"

Zina turned, not sure at first who the voice was talking to. A boy was staring right at her, asking her about her medal. Zina had seen him before on the train but had never talked to him, they were both quiet and kept to themselves.

"Uh, no. It's a medal I got at school today."

"Oh, well, congratulations, then." He said.

"Thank you." Zina put the medal in her coat pocket and took out her crocheting. The boy went back to his attempt to see out the frosted windows.

Since Boody was closed today, Zina's cousins met her when she got off the bus from the train.

"Gracie, Nan, what are you girls doing here?"

"We've been waiting for you to come home from school to do something nice for Epiphany Day." Gracie said.

Zina beamed. It was the sweetest thing. *Another small gift for being well-behaved! Well, it was worth it. Even though I have not been happy about going to this school today, or any day really, I guess a good attitude is paying off.*

The snow was plowed and shoveled over the weekend, which resulted in the snow banks by the sidewalks being waist high. The girls used to love stomping on these and sinking to their knees but now the reality of drying out their leather lace-up boots outweighed the fun. The girls instead looked for icy patches to skate on.

"We should all go ice skating!" Nan suggested.

"Oh, but I only have roller skates, no ice skates." Zina said.

"You can borrow mine," said Gracie, her skates were just slightly larger than Zina's size. "We can take turns."

After skating in the park, the girls returned to their homes. The cool air and activity initiated a tickle in Zina's throat that she didn't notice until she entered the warmth of her house. After she took off her coat and boots, she had a full-on coughing fit.

"Zina, whatever is wrong?" Her papa appeared, tapping her back until the spasms subsided.

"Papa, its nothing. A tickle."

"You have had no cough these last few weeks and now a cough?"

"Let's all go into the kitchen, and I will make Vincenza a nice cup of lemon tea and honey." Her mother directed.

"It's not an illness, Papa, it is from the dust and dirt on the train, and then the cold air. I had a nice break from it over the holidays, and now that I have gone back to school, the cough is back. It's nothing to be concerned about." Zina hoped this slight complaint didn't negate her good behavior today.

As the trio stepped into the kitchen, her parents looked at each other. Coughs were never "nothing to be concerned about" in their generation who saw so many lung related illnesses. Zina's mother reminded them of the Spanish Flu epidemic the year Zina was born. "First a cough, then my poor sister..." Her mother covered her mouth with one hand and made the sign of the cross with the other.

Zina looked at her and looked down. The Spanish Flu was how Zina's aunt died, the aunt that married her uncle Domenico's brother Angelo, but whom she had never met.

"Rose, it is not the same, you heard her. Zina, you will tell us if your cough is worse, right? Or you feel feverish or ill in any way?"

"Yes Papa."

Zina's mother turned and started the teapot, deep in thought. Mamie's words at Maria's yesterday still haunted her. She wondered if she really was too controlling of Zina, if she was trying too hard, and if she might lose her anyway.

"I got a medal today for Italian interpretation excellence and teacher wants me to assist her with grading papers."

"That's wonderful, Zina." Her papa said.

"Oh, um, yes, congratulations." Her mother leaned over from the stove and gave her daughter a kiss on the cheek.

Zina was stunned. *What has gotten into Mother?*

"Well, as long as you still get home at the same time. Does your teacher realize how long of a ride you have from school?" Papa asked.

Her mother returned from her reverie and looked at her husband, not knowing what he just said. She looked at Zina again. "Vincenza, do you look thinner? Are you sure you are feeling ok? Here, drink your tea."

Zina wondered why it seemed as though her parents were seeing her for the first time in a long time. Especially her mother. *Yes, I have lost some weight, and no, I'm not feeling well all the time, but it's mostly because my books are so heavy, and I must carry them for almost a mile every day while walking the various routes to get to school.*

But she didn't say that, reminding herself again about being obedient about listening to her parent's wishes about school in honor of Epiphany Day.

They didn't seem convinced that their daughter was well. They sent her upstairs to her room to rest before having a late supper.

Once they heard her bedroom door close upstairs, her parents whispered to each other. "Giacomo, do you think going to that school is putting her in a position that does her more harm than good?"

"Rose, she is doing well, she earned a medal for her efforts."

"But that is not important if she loses her health in the process, Giacomo."

"Rose, don't worry, she is a strong girl. She is smart. She will let us know if something is wrong. Nothing bad is going to happen to her."

Rose didn't notice that her husband was pouring out their unfinished teas into the sink and went back to the teapot to pour more tea.

She wondered how he could know nothing bad would happen and was preoccupied, creating upsetting scenarios in her mind. The threat of losing Zina weighed heavily in her thoughts lately, and she struggled to see how she could keep life the way it is for much longer.

Giacomo got up and headed upstairs and left his wife alone with her thoughts.

"Protection." She said to herself. "Maybe I shouldn't have discounted that 'charm' Zina found in that coat hem. What if whatever protection it was meant for is now lost because I took it from her? What if, after all the ways I've been trying to make a good life for Zina, I become the cause of some kind of pain she is now destined to suffer?"

PART 3

The 'unexpected' is just evidence of poor planning and lack of vision. I can fashion the life I desire by applying enough focus and determination.
I certainly don't plan to leave my destiny to chance.

~Rose Privitera

~ENTRY #8~

1/13/1930

My dear friend,

The weather is threatening snowstorms, so I have to stay inside. I keep making up new games and sewing projects, but it is only causing me to feel lonelier. Nan hasn't been allowed out because her sister is sick, and now Gracie is sick too. Mother won't let me go to visit them because she is constantly suspicious of whenever I cough, thinking all week that it is getting worse when it's not. Just in case, she says, I am to rest and stay in my room as much as possible.

With all this time on my hands, I've been thinking that maybe I need to just take charge of what I want. Remember last time I wrote about wanting everyone to be open and honest? If I want them to be, maybe I should be too. Instead of wondering what other people are thinking, I will just change my attitude toward them and maybe things will work out, what do you think?

So here is my list of remedies.

    1. *Instead of pretending I like my school, I will ask my parents if we can talk about it. Maybe I can study*

something else.

2. *Instead of wondering why my Mother is being more attentive, I will just accept it. I have wished we could be closer, and maybe she is taking the first step, even though it is awkward.*

3. *Instead of feeling uncertain about Frank, I will stop thinking about him because he is my cousin. And come to think of it, I am not even sure Frank has been thinking of me in the same potential "courting" way at all. He has been friendly, doting, and kind-hearted, but has he been considering what it would be like to marry me someday like I have been thinking about him? Oh, this is embarrassing. No, of course he hasn't.*

4. *Instead of feeling sad and lonely about being an only child, I will talk to my mother. Maybe it's not too late for her to have another baby!*

Oh, my dear friend, I really do wish I had a sibling, especially a sister, so when I am cooped up like this there is someone else around. How is it that my parents can give me a kitten for company, but not a brother or sister?

Every other family I know has at least two children, five is more the average, and nobody "from the old country" is shocked at eight. The shock is that all eight would still be living, as so many babies died young in my parent's generation back in Sicily – I hear that all the time because they still aren't used to things being different in America – but I don't know anyone else that is an only child, especially at my age. It's puzzling, don't you think?

So why would it be unreasonable for Mother to have a baby now? Mother's sister, my Aunt Mary, is pregnant, due in a few months. They are probably around the same age, right?

I have to ask! Be right back!

I'm back. That did not go well.

I just made a terrible mistake. When Mother got off the phone, I asked if she would consider having a baby sister or even a brother for me and she gave me such an angry look. Her face turned a few shades of orangey red that matched the bottom of the copper pot on the stove she was standing next to, steam rising around her either from her head or the pot of milk, it was hard to tell.

I don't know why she got so mad about it, so I certainly will not mention it again. I guess I'll be a lonely, only child for the rest of my life. So much for taking charge of what I want.

~Zina

CHAPTER 23

Zina

Sunday, January 19, 1930

The storms passed and left an accumulation of snow. It was still lightly falling, but the sun was out, so Zina was permitted to go out and play when Frank and his mother came to visit.

She leaned her head back to catch the flakes in her mouth and Frank pretended to do the same. He kept sneaking glances at Zina with her face toward the sky; her eyes closed. Her rosy cheeks glowed and the melted snow on her nose glistened. He shook his head to come to his senses, wanting to think of something else besides how pretty Zina looked.

"Um, Zina, tomorrow is 1-20-30." Frank grasped for some topic but forgot in his momentary panic that he had already reminded her of this three times today.

"Thank you, yet again, Frank, I was almost certain that today is tomorrow's yesterday, but now you have set me straight." Zina smiled, happy that she decided Frank was just her friend now.

Frank laughed that she casually quipped one of his favorite lines back at him, relieved that she didn't notice his nervousness. He mimed throwing snow at her. Zina gasped in mock horror and ran to make a real snowball to retaliate.

Through the window in the dining room, their mothers watched. "How easily they laugh with each other. Oh Maria, they really do get along nicely." Zina's mother smiled and sipped her tea at the cozy dining table.

"Ah, but Rose, Frank asked me to talk to you about the teasing. He said Zina asked, and-" Maria leaned in and quietly added, "you don't want her to get suspicious, right, especially if you don't want to tell her anything yet," she suggested.

Rose was quiet, her mood shifted.

"...and he thinks you should tell her."

"Oh, is that so?" Rose stirred her tea, noisily, and began to get agitated.

Maria meant to diffuse the situation by winking and smiling. "So how about I put a stop to it all right now?" She joked and pretended to open the window to call out to Zina.

"No. Maria. Don't do that, please. You wouldn't do that, right?" Rose pleaded, panicked.

"Ah ha," said Maria with a smile.

"Now who is teasing?"

"Oh Rose, I'm sorry but don't be annoyed, look at our young loves talking, laughing, and smiling with each other; it's all we thought it would be. Remember that day?" Maria asked in a playful tone, recalling their favorite memory.

Rose relented with a smile and went along. "Yes, you came over about two weeks after Vincenza was born, with little one-year-old baby Frank."

"Yes, and I asked him, 'do you know where we are going, Frankie?' And he gave me a big smile and shook his head no. I said, 'we are going to your aunt's house because I have someone very special for you to see.'

"He stopped shaking his head mid-shake and put on a slightly puzzled look. 'See?' he asked, and I said, 'Yes my smart boy, we will see your aunt CeeCee." Remember when we called you that, Rose?"

"Oh yes, the cat Giacomo got right before Vincenza was born. But wait, you called *me* by the cat's name?" She never heard that part of the story.

"It was just easier for Frankie to relate to a cat than to remember who all the grownups were." Maria dismissed the interruption with a wave of her hand.

Rose laughed.

Maria continued, "So I told him, 'Aunt CeeCee has a brand-new baby. And I want you to meet her.' I used to love to show Frankie babies in baby buggies in the neighborhood, but I don't think he cared very much. He was more interested in seeing your cat, and in his little baby way he told me so. He asked me again, 'Cee-?' and I said, 'No, honey. A baby. You, my dear little son, are going to love *this* baby.'"

The ladies huddled their heads closer together for that last remark. They could no longer see Frank and Zina outside and assumed they went for a walk.

"Remember Rose, I said nothing when we first walked into your house, I wanted to see what Frankie would do when he saw your baby. I carried him into the foyer and set him down on his little feet. He had just started to walk a few days before, and he was determined to stand. He wobbled

211

and walked toward the moving pram in the living room. It was right over there." She pointed to the corner by the window where Giacomo's chair is now, next to Rose's writing desk.

"The pram was wiggling, and we could hear her little cries. Then, Rose, you picked up Frankie and leaned him over the pram to introduce him."

"Yes, I remember that." Rose interjected and continued. "I said, 'So, Frankie, what do you think? Frankie, meet Vincenza.' He took his little wet fingers from his mouth and leaned over to touch her, so I helped him get closer. When he touched Vincenza's small balled up fist, instantly her little cries quieted, and she opened her eyes wide. Only a week old, but she looked right at him."

Maria finished, "Frankie beamed a smile at your baby, then at me. Then he yelled 'MINE!'"

The mothers giggled like young schoolgirls.

"Remember how surprised we were. How he seemed to understand they belong together!" Maria laughed.

"Oh, that was a precious moment – the first time I felt like life in America was going to be alright, that all my dreams were *finally* going to come true." Rose said, putting her hand on Maria's.

Zina and Frank came in through the back door, cold and wet. They heard their mothers say their names, 'Frankie, meet Vincenza'. Zina and Frank looked at each other with a mutual agreement to be quiet, curious about what the mothers were saying about them.

They started to take off their coats and boots just outside the kitchen when someone yelled 'MINE' and the mothers both laughed.

Zina's heart raced with realization. "Please stop!" Zina barged in and impolitely scolded the mothers. "Why do you always tease, like we can be together someday?"

The women looked at each other and sobered.

"Oh Vincenza, you two were just so cute. We are not teasing; we are only remembering. You are being rude walking into our private conversation, not to mention tracking wet spots in the kitchen." Her mother admonished.

Zina looked down. "I am sorry, Mother. But please stop. It is more than just teasing, can't you see? You are talking like there was some promise made. But we know it can never happen. We are cousins, and cousins don't marry here in America. Maybe in Sicily years ago that was okay but not here. We are friends, that is all. We are not meant to be together and it's not polite to continue to talk as though we are when it will never happen."

Zina realized Frank was listening, standing just behind her. Mortified, she went up to her room and closed the door. She fell on her bed sobbing, not caring that the edges of her pants and sleeves were still icy wet.

Frank stood by the kitchen door and motioned to his mother so he could ask her something. He whispered so his aunt Rose wouldn't hear. "Why won't you tell Aunt Rose to tell her? You know she is suspicious of something going on, and you are both making it worse by excluding her from the truth that she has a right to know."

His mother quietly scolded him, "No, it is not our decision to make. Now get your things and head back outside while I say goodbye." They turned back to Zina's mother, who was looking at them, wondering what they were discussing.

"Rose, I am so sorry. We should be more discreet in the future. Frank and I will head home now, I'll call you tomorrow-"

"Wait, Maria. How did Frank even find out?"

"I'm sorry Rose, I will have to make sure nobody hears our phone conversations. But he was concerned-"

"He won't tell her, will he?"

"No, no, he promised, don't worry."

"What should I do, Maria? Should I go upstairs to talk to her? What would I say? She is right, but I cannot tell her that, and I cannot tell her more. I'm not ready to tell her, Maria. What do I do?"

"Get some rest, Rose, a talk can wait."

After Maria left, Zina's mother sat down heavily in the dining chair with her cold teacup in one hand and her head in the other and mumbled quietly, "A talk can wait." Emotions surrounding the full truth bubbled to the surface from years ago. "Does Maria think I *should* tell her? But I never wanted to tell her."

She remembered her younger self and the nervous new-mom happiness she felt when Vincenza was a baby. She remembered farther back to when she first got married and love held so much promise. She remembered even farther back when she first came to America, and the future was full of potential.

In those days, her certainty came from her confidence, she could *be* sure something went her way because she would *make* sure that it did.

She sighed, no longer feeling in control. "When did I change? Am I even the same person anymore?"

The 'unexpected' is just evidence of poor planning and lack of vision.

CHAPTER 24

Rose, 1903

August 12,
Arrival Day in New York

*A*merica has already begun to transform us. I see a big difference in

Mamie's countenance, and Papa is like a young man again. Me, I feel like a butterfly finally emerging!

We are literally on the other side of the world. As soon as we stepped off that stifling, stinking boat it was like my sister molted the skin of the old Mamie and threw it on the heaps of sacks piled on the bow where the flies fester on the rotting garbage. New Mamie walks off the gangplank with her head held so high; her eyes fixed with determination.

Truly, it has been my hope these last few years that she would finally decide to make herself a new life. I hope that's what she is thinking; that the future awaits. I have said it so many times, maybe it finally has sunk in. Ha, sunk. A bad pun for just getting off a ship.

And look at Papa; I can almost hear the gears turning in his head. All the opportunities. All the customers. Everyone buying something from

someone. Anything from anyone. Money just flows and swirls around in and out of pockets like the sludge and sewage flowing in and out of the street gutters.

Despite the surprising filth, I knew I would love it here. The sights, the people, a mix-up of every corner of the world jammed in one place.

I feel hope, I feel life, I feel potential. So many different people looking like odd-shaped bundles all tied up. And that's not just because of what they are carrying. Some have layers of clothes on as if they were headed for the Arctic (in August!) Some with such fine umbrellas and hats, and other less fortunate ones appearing to follow them with luggage on wheeled carts, like small cabooses. Oh, to have a personal valet accompany me, that would be glorious.

So many styles, so many fabrics, I can't wait to experience the variety of shopping here! It's as if the magazine photographs I longed to see in person have opened up and swallowed me, and now I can swim in this oasis of fashion. The trouble is, you must have an eye like I do, in order to see it amidst all the interspersing ruffians.

Ugh, and then there's this repugnant smell. It is everywhere. Forget having separate quarters on the ships, they should have separate ships – and perhaps separate cities as well, the stench from the unsavory is so strong. I'm thankful my handkerchief still has the gentle scent of my favorite perfume left on it; I can at least be domesticated among these swine-ish creatures.

Whatever is Mamie doing with that short hairy man? Can't she browse a little, there are plenty of men here. It's like Mamie walked off the ship, closed her eyes, put her hand out like a fishing rod, and reeled in on the first tug. And now she is on his arm like they are courting – all before we leave Ellis Island! Definitely not the girl I left Sicily with.

This is shocking. Our escort is the bear man. I don't believe my eyes. Of all the people in America we find the worst one from Sicily. How long ago was that now? Eight years? He hasn't changed at all; you'd think he would have shaved or washed or something. Ugh. Regardless, I am glad I thought ahead to have someone meet us here in America through our own home church connections, otherwise we would have arrived in America lost and confused, like so many others here appear to be. So far Domenico is doing a fair job, I guess. I can see our new church up ahead – Our Lady of Pompeii.

ം‱‱

"Rose, what wonderful news, congratulations," Her papa said, when she returned to the boarding house on Mulberry Street.

It had been a few weeks in America, and Rose was looking forward to finally getting a job so she could help her family move into a more accommodating, larger lodging room. They will need a bigger space when her siblings Francesco, Concetta, and Grazia come in less than a year.

"Thank you, Papa. I am so glad to be able to help those coming from Sicily and help our family get here too. Working at Our Lady of Pompeii with the immigration mission will be perfect, but I suppose I can start out as a housekeeper's assistant. Have you found a job too, Mamie?"

Papa and Rose looked over at Mamie expectantly, but in return, she lowered her eyes without moving from her chair.

"Ah, well, there is tomorrow to try again." Her papa encouraged and went back to trying to read the newspaper.

Rose looked at her sister to read which mood she was in today. Some days she would act strong and ready to conquer anything and others she still seemed sick, or upset, or tired, or wavering between the three.

Why is everything always about Mamie? I had big news and Mamie and Papa just continued doing whatever they were doing before I got home. I would love to go out to celebrate getting my first job in New York, but certainly not by myself. I guess I'll just praise myself by making a snack and sitting by our only sunny window, alone.

From a shelf in the corner that served as their kitchen, Rose tore off a hunk of day old bread. She adjusted the curtain to soften the direct sunlight and sat on the first object she possessed in America. They were lucky to find a discarded armchair that her papa was able to fix, and Rose sewed a small cushion from a few rags. She was pleased with the find and with the way they remade it to be comfortable, and she settled in, continuing to reflect.

Why do I always seem to miss out on celebrating life events because of Mamie's constitution – just like it would have been nice to be here at the turn of the century. Ah yes, the original plan.

It's unfortunate that we were delayed for three years, or else we would've been here in the year 1900 when there were probably many celebrations and exciting things to do. But whatever happened with Mamie that delayed us is still a mystery to me.

As I recall, she was sick or something, even then. Well, she has always had nightmares and trouble sleeping, and that's been going on for a long while. Everyone thought the fire a few years earlier was still taking a toll on her, even after we moved to Regalbuto.

That's when Papa arranged for her to go away to try to forget and relax. He contacted his sister's husband, Antony Russo, in Trecastagni, where Papa was from. He told me their family had recently lost a child and would love Mamie to come to help his grieving wife with their other children. Papa said the arrangement would allow Mamie to have extra time for herself, and they would pay her wages for watching the other children. I remember telling Papa that I was better suited for the job, why couldn't I be sent to help? Papa looked cross at my suggestion; he was not even open to it. He just put his foot down and said it must be Mamie, for her own good.

Rose adjusted her cushion, but it still felt flat, she took it out from behind her back and punched it to fluff it a little more. She finished her bread.

Mamie didn't have a choice in the matter. She was looking terrible, lacking sleep, and gaining weight, which was odd. She needed a change, he told me. 'Besides, Mother is in the last few weeks of her pregnancy and would need you here with her, Rose.' Papa said. I supposed that was true, but I would have liked to have made the money Mamie did for those weeks. And when she returned, she was still the same: sad or sick. The time away did not remedy her illness. It was a mystery that something was still wrong with her.

When Mamie returned from Trecastagni, it was the same night Mama had baby Mary. So now we had to wait until baby Mary was old enough to travel. That was obviously our setback; but I can't help but think that somehow Mamie feels responsible. We all got over the disappointment of leaving for America later than expected, but she never did. Perhaps she missed those Russo children?

That thought gave Rose an idea as she cleaned up her crumbs and left her perch by the window. "Mamie, maybe there are some women in the boarding house here that would pay you to watch their children so they can work? You have experience doing that, remember, for the Russo children? Have you thought of that?" Rose suggested.

Mamie inhaled sharply and looked like she might cry.

What did I say?

Their papa looked at them both. "Rose why don't you and Mamie take a walk outside to get some fresh air. Domenico will be coming over soon and then perhaps we can all get something to eat, it might be a nice change of pace to try a restaurant. It is good to celebrate our small victories."

Does he think that my new job is the victory, or that Domenico seems to be interested in Mamie?

CHAPTER 25

Rose, 1905

July
New York

Two years passed. Rose continued working at the church along with Domenico, who did maintenance there in the evenings but had started work as a mason elsewhere in the daytime. Mamie had been working odd jobs, her latest one was cooking for the merchants that their papa worked with.

Mamie was doing much better, her moods evened out, and she began making plans for her future again. That morning she announced to Rose that Domenico proposed.

Rose sat at the small desk in Father Domo's office, reflecting on her sister's news.

Of course, I'm happy for my sister, but having the bear man be part of our family will take some getting used to. I really don't know what she sees in him. And he's thirteen years older! He is closer to our father's age than hers! I don't understand it. But she looks happy for a change. Love wants what it wants, I guess. Maybe I am not a good judge of what love should look like.

"Rose, have you checked Father Domo's schedule for the week?" The head housekeeper peeked her head into the office.

"I will, Miss Canali, just as soon as I am done."

I've been doing this job for nearly two years now; I know my tasks. Miss Canali is easy enough to work with, and work for, but she can be redundant in her requests. I suppose it is nice to split my time between helping her with cleaning duties and working here in the office. It's so glorious to spend time in a nice room with a lovely desk and few interruptions.

"You seem distracted today Rose, what is going on?"

"Oh, well, I was just thinking, what will we do after Domenico gets married? I mean here, at the church?"

"Well Rose, he has talked to Father Domo and wants to move out, buy a house; he will probably keep his job as a mason but no longer work here, which is only right. We can house a bachelor but not a married couple."

"So have we put out an advertisement for a new handyman?"

"Oh yes, that is already in progress. Father has a few prospects he will be interviewing. Didn't you see that on the schedule?" Miss Canali looked concerned that Rose didn't seem to remember the conversation about this just last week. She walked into the office to sit down.

"Really Rose, what is going on?"

"Oh, nothing, I'm just excited, I guess, because my family has finally reached the moment we have worked toward for years." Rose didn't sound convincing.

"Rose that is wonderful news! But you don't look happy."

"Yes, we have worked hard, and it will be wonderful to all be together again but…"

"What do you mean, 'but'?" Miss Canali asked, concerned.

Rose confessed, "I can't help but feel something bad is going to happen."

"You can't think that, why would you think that?"

Rose took a deep breath and began. "It's just a feeling. Whenever my family tries to move forward, something happens to set us back. First, we suffered a fire and had to move in 1897, then we were going to come to America in 1900. Then Mamie got sick, and Mama had baby Mary. So, we left in 1903 instead, in shifts. Francesco, Concetta, and Grazia came last year, and now, finally, the rest of the family is due to be here this week, but…"

"Oh Rose, just have faith that God will provide and care for those who love him."

"Yes, I know. Thank you, Miss Canali." Rose sighed; the advice did not help suppress her worry.

੭੭ၛ੪

"Oh Papa, it can't be." Rose attempted to read the telegram, but her papa held it close. Mamie was quiet in the corner.

"I am so sorry Mamie, Rose, we worked so hard, but these things can't be helped. All we can do now is pray everyone is well and begin to chart a new course."

Mamie looked understandably disappointed. The family would not be arriving today, and they would also miss her wedding. Rose moved to hug her sister's shoulders, but Mamie stood up to avoid it, saying, "I'm going to let Domenico know, I will see you later at dinnertime."

"Papa, can I read it?" Rose asked to read the telegram again. *Why won't he let me?*

He gave her a quick pat and left abruptly with the paper close to his pocket.

"Sorry Rose, I will be home later as well. I have some things to take care of."

I did have a feeling something like this would happen. Oh, why did I have to be right?

ᏚᎯᏟᏒ

The wedding day arrived: September tenth, 1905. For Mamie's sake, Rose and their siblings Francesco, Concetta, and Grazia, made a pact to pretend to not be disappointed that the rest of the family was back in Sicily and would miss her big day.

Rose was up early, having barely slept. Mamie wouldn't be waking for another hour, so she quietly made herself some tea, and sat on her armchair by the window not even bothering to fluff her pillow. She couldn't stop thinking all night about the recent events leading up to this day, and what was going to happen next.

They would have been here in plenty of time. I wonder what happened. I can't imagine how Mama managed – alone, with all the little ones. All that time to get them here, to America, only to have to turn around and travel back again to Sicily. Poor Mama.

After Papa received the telegram from Mama, he left the next day without any thought as to the financial hardship it was. It will take some time to recuperate funds, yet again.

Oh, what went wrong? I would be upset if both of my parents weren't at my wedding, I don't know why Mamie insisted on continuing anyway, Father Domo did offer to postpone it as he had a date in November open up just this week. But she didn't want to. Why wouldn't she – so both our parents, and the rest of our siblings could be there? Why rush?

Now the only people attending Mamie's wedding are Father Domo, and our partial family of Francesco, Concetta, and Grazia. Francesco met a nice young girl named Jenny and invited her, and then there are the two distant cousins serving as witnesses to the wedding, and then me. I am Mamie's maid of honor. Of course, Angelo, Domenico's brother, is his best man.

Perhaps Mamie is alright with her wedding day being quieter and less attended; Domenico doesn't seem to like crowds. Plus, his brother is his only family here so he wouldn't have invited many people, regardless. He does have that friend, Cardaci – he's an odd character and doesn't ever visit for too long, thankfully, so hopefully we won't see much of him today. He makes me a little nervous.

I can understand that our side of the family wouldn't have as many guests, but Domenico's? He's worked at the church for all these years, and he's been in America, what, ten years now, I would think he would have more friends to invite. Ah well, it will be a quiet ceremony and an even more quiet reception today.

It will be so wonderful to have everyone together again. We won't have to send our money back to Sicily anymore. We can save and grow our lives here, maybe even buy a house. It will be even more cramped – all of us living here, in these three rooms. Convenient for me since the church is only a few doors down.

Maybe when the rest of the family finally does arrive, we can all celebrate with a nice party. I think I will make that suggestion to Mamie. Well, no, I think I will just plan it. It is just as much a reason for me to celebrate as it would be for the newly married couple.

So, good, the party idea is settled. Now I have something to occupy my thoughts while I wait for this day to start.

Rose peeked at her sleeping sister, and smiled at how peaceful she was. The clock showed just a few more minutes of quiet were left before Mamie would begin her new life. Rose felt restless as the clock ticked.

When will it be my time? What is next for me? Actually, I should probably think about whether I should leave my work here at Our Lady of Pompeii. The reason for working, to bring our family here, is now about done; but I have enjoyed it. I like helping families reunite. It is satisfying work. The only trouble with it has been meeting any eligible men, since the ones that come to my office are ones that need help bringing over wives or fiancés. If I do keep working, I think I could start saving to attend a nursing school and become a nurse, I might like that more. Then maybe I can finally meet someone.

CHAPTER 26

Rose, 1905

December
New York

Last month, the entire family came together for the first time in America, on November 4 – fifty-five days after Mamie's wedding. On the day they arrived, Rose welcomed them with a nice dinner event to celebrate. They even made sure to have a family photograph taken, to commemorate their triumph. Since then, the Priviteras spent whatever free time they had just being a family again, making up for the past two years of separation.

In between the quiet moments that felt like they never even left Sicily and the exciting moments of introducing her family to the novelties America offered, Rose felt unsettled.

When she went to work, she was often distracted, dwelling on what the real reason for her family's failure at the immigration station could have been. The suspicious way her papa kept the telegram from her nagged at her like a fraying hem waiting for her in her sewing basket.

I still don't understand why the family was sent back. It's all so perplexing. And why would Mama, Agatha, and Joseph give different explanations?

Rose greeted Miss Canali when she entered the church and she said she would be working in the office for a few hours. But she didn't feel much like working just yet.

Mama said when they arrived at the Ellis Island port, there were several people sick on the ship who were admitted to the local hospital. Baby Mary had some suspicious symptoms. The authorities thought Mary was too sick to be allowed in the country, so they were all sent back to Sicily.

Agatha told me that Mama had another baby in March of last year in Sicily while we were here in New York, and that she didn't tell Papa yet. The baby must have been conceived right before we left, a goodbye baby. But the baby, who Mama named Giovanna, meaning 'the Lord is gracious,' died in September, at six months old. Agatha thinks Mama hated the idea of leaving her behind, and so she made the family fail at the immigration checkpoint, so they would be sent back to Sicily.

I told Agatha that I didn't think Mama would put everybody through so much trouble, but Agatha seemed sad. I think losing that baby was especially hard on her. All of us older siblings were here, in America, and she had to face the brunt of the sorrow as mother's helper at twelve years old, I remember how that was.

But then it was Joseph who confided something he thought was odd, and I agreed. He said Mama looked worried about a paper, so he paid attention. She was holding Mary's birth certificate, he said. He saw her gathering everyone's, but Mary's was the one the ship inspectors gave back to her. Something about it not being consistent or considered, or something, he didn't understand the word. He said Mama fumbled with it and looked like she was going to cry or scream. He told me he snuck into Mama's bag later that day and compared all the papers. The only thing odd he could see was that Mary had a middle name.

He said the officer from the ship ushered them back to the boarding area, and that's when Mama stopped at a telegraph stand to message Papa, she didn't trust the phone boxes.

Oh, that must be when Papa got the telegram before Mamie's wedding, I remember. So that was July the 25th. Papa kept hiding it so I wouldn't see, and he didn't want me to ask him about it. Why would he do that? Joseph said it read, "Cannot enter America. Mary's birth paper in question. Please help." He is only eleven but seemed sure of what he read.

So why hide this from me? No one would blame Mama if Mary had an illness and that's why they were sent back. And I could understand if she was too sad to leave her recently deceased child Giovanna, or baby Alfia, or even Concetta's twin sister who died years before. But, if there was nothing wrong with the birth certificate, why would she be nervous about it – well according to Joseph.

What could be hidden on a birth certificate? I wonder.

Rose looked at the papers on her desk: the neat piles of sensitive correspondence for Father Domo, the private letters for family members to be delivered.

I suppose a document can have secrets, right? But could someone actually hide some kind of information on a birth certificate?

She remembered the last of Mama's babies she was present for, baby Mary. She didn't remember any midwife being there that night, the baby had come so easily, which was a surprise to everyone after her mother's difficult delivery of Stella three years earlier, days before the fire in Pedara.

What's more, Mama had a difficult time with Alfia's birth the year before Mary was born, when we moved to Regalbuto. So, two difficult pregnancies in a row, then Mary was born easily: healthy, strong. Then, the next baby after Mary, Giovanna, only lived six months; she died before they even left to come to America.

So, in the midst of all of those really difficult pregnancies, there was Mary. As if she just appeared.

Mother even gave her a middle name where none of the rest of us have one.

Joseph told me what it is. Annunziata. Immaculate. Like Mother Mary: an immaculate conception.

Now I don't put it past Mama to name her child with an intended meaning, she did name the baby Alfia when she was mad at Papa. Any of us could have been named Alfia if Mama truly wanted to truly honor Papa; seven others of us girls were born first. And Giovanna means given by God, a gift she didn't expect. But Mary Annunziata? Meaning immaculately conceived? Was she truly that surprised about baby Mary? Or was she named because of something else?

Rose stood to close her office door, so her thoughts wouldn't be interrupted.

Let me go over Mary's birth again. Papa and Mamie arrived back from the Russo's house where Mamie was supposed to rest and relax. She was gone for two months and came back not looking much better. She arrived home the same night that Mama had baby Mary. Mamie spent a lot of time with Mama and baby Mary for the first few months.

Oh, I remember hearing something! Didn't Mama whisper to Mamie about being quiet, that 'no one must ever know'? What secret would they have? She and Mama were never that close. But now, after Mamie came back, they did have moments together. I suppose since she was sick and the trip away didn't seem to do her much good, that Mama began to pay more attention to her. But what was a secret that nobody should know?

Wait, let me run through that again. Mamie and Papa came home after picking her up from her two-month stay with Papa's cousins in Trecastagni the exact night Mama gave birth to baby Mary. Was that just an odd coincidence?

This birth was so easy on Mama, she hardly even broke a sweat. Maybe there was no midwife that night, and I don't even remember seeing any soiled sheets or newspapers now that I think of it. How could Mama not have had help?

Then there was Mamie. She looked terrible. She was heavier in places, and it didn't appear that the time away was restful at all. I asked Papa if she was well, and he said she needed rest from the journey. More rest. She stayed in Mama's room that night. With Mama's new baby, was that the most restful room? And wouldn't Mama need to rest too? I heard them whispering. It sounded like Mama said, 'nurse the baby, but no one must ever know.'

That's ridiculous, why would she tell Mamie to nurse the baby, how would that be possible? No. It wouldn't be possible unless Mamie had a baby.

Wait.

She did look heavier in places.

Wait, no.

Could our sister Mary actually be Mamie's baby? Could Papa have decided they would raise her child as their own? And Mama faked being pregnant? Ah, and Mary is even named for an immaculate conception.

What am I thinking, that is ridiculous.

But it would explain the story Joseph told, that a paper for Mary was questionable and they were sent back to Sicily. Then sure, someone asking to see Mary's birth certificate could make Mama nervous, nervous enough to run back to Sicily if Mary wasn't her child.

I can't believe it. My parents: could they have lied like that?

But. If it was Mamie's baby, how did she get pregnant?

Oh no.

Her nightmares. Of course. I always thought they were because of the fire, but that was too long ago, did something else happen to her? While we were in Regalbuto?

Oh, I do remember her having some mysterious scratches, oh why did I not pay closer attention?

No, not Mamie, oh poor Mamie.

No, stop.

What is the matter with me? No, this is an outrageous story. It cannot be true. I'm so ashamed for even considering this. Of course our sister Mary is Mama's baby, and Mamie was trying to get over a difficult illness. Scratches could have come from berry picking or some other outdoor errand, which wouldn't be so odd, this is Mamie we're talking about.

Right, of course.

Anything else is just absurd.

Rose shook her head and shuffled some papers on the desk.

I need to find something more constructive to do with my time today than imagining ridiculous scenarios.

~ENTRY #9~

2/1/1930

My dear friend,

Mother and Aunt Maria aren't teasing anymore, so that is better now, but now Mother is acting in a new, abnormal way.

This new thing is that she now gets a phone call at least once a week where she hangs up angrily on the person who called, and then picks it up again to call Aunt Maria, all hushed and whispering, but obviously upset.

I wish I could just ask her what is going on, but what if she gets angry with me, like when I asked if she would have a baby sister for me? I don't want to see her like that ever again. Hopefully this will just blow over soon. Maybe she is just worried about some electric bill or something, and I keep thinking it's all about me. What do you think, my dear friend?

On another note, do you remember that I decided to forget Frank and just try to find a boy who embodied some of the things I like about him? Well, such a boy presented himself to me the very next day. I haven't told you much about him yet because, well, all I did was see him that day. But since then, we have now had three short conversations. I think that is

233

something, don't you? From not knowing any boy to meeting one and having a chance to talk to him, that is significant.

So, about this boy. Oh, he is the one who thought my medal was a medal from the War. So, I did mention him. Well, his name is Steven.

Anyway, well, he is fair colored as opposed to Frank's dark black hair and olive skin tone. He seems very tall, compared to Frank's medium stature. He is polite and well mannered, like Frank. And he does have a nice sense of humor like Frank. He tells me jokes about his school. And that's all I know so far, but it feels like that is all there is to know. Does that make sense? I'll try to explain.

When I'm around Frank, he always seems to leave me with something to think about, something that helps to make sense of the world, or my life, or something bigger than we are. I usually miss talking to him when he is not around, and I look forward to talking to him when I can.

This boy does not have that for me. It's not as if I think he is dull, no, he is very smart – he says he wants to study to be a doctor (and we talked about me being a nurse.) And even though it might be interesting to be married to a doctor someday, he just doesn't leave me with that feeling that I want to find out more about him. The conversations just lie there; I leave them when I leave him. I hope that makes sense, I'm just not good at writing it down.

I guess it could be that I just need to give it time. Frank and I have lots of years of history and shared experiences, so I suppose I shouldn't think that a new relationship will be very in-depth right away, right? Right. It will take some time and patience.

I just have to find things we have in common. So far there are a few, but there is also this one big thing we don't agree on. He said he would never have kids. He wants to be married, travel, have a beautiful house and car, maybe two or three – can you imagine – but no kids. It does sound very romantic and carefree, almost like a movie star's life. But I think having children is one absolute for me.

If I can't have a child, I would not feel like life is satisfying. Even if someday my husband and I couldn't have kids; I would still want kids. I think that's why Nan and I thought we'd have a home for kids one day. I think every child should have a home. So, I'd find a way to adopt them if I couldn't have them. That's how important kids are to me.

So, I guess I'll just be friends with this boy; I know it won't amount to more than that. But one good thing that has come from this trial-and-error budding relationship, meeting and talking to Steven gives me hope that I will find someone someday. I just needed to be patient like Aunt Mamie's lasagna.

Until next time, I will keep you posted,

~Zina

CHAPTER 27

Zina

Saturday, February 15, 1930

"Our mothers are going to be consumed with looking at those fabric samples and won't want us to interrupt them for hours, so what do you want to do today, Frank?" Zina asked, still slightly irritated they were told to 'run off now,' like children.

Not having any good ideas at the time, they visited their favorite spot.

"I don't know Zina, the weather is unusually nice for this dreary winter, I like just sitting here at the park. We don't have to actually do something to be doing something." Frank said, contently.

"I agree. But we could go walk along the beach, it's probably not crowded." Zina was slightly preoccupied with another idea.

Just the other day when she was talking with her new friend, Steven, on the train, he asked if she would like to meet him at the beach this weekend. Of course, not to swim, but just walk. Zina was very hesitant about it and told him she was expecting company. That wasn't entirely false, she can expect to see someone from her family every weekend.

But now the idea of walking along Coney Island Beach sounded like a great idea, without Steven. But would she go with Frank? Is that the sort of thing you do when you are courting and not just as a boy and girl who happen to be friends? She wasn't sure.

"Nah, I hardly think it's warm enough for the beach, the water will make the air so much colder. Let's just stay here, Zina. We have all spring and summer to visit Coney Island, especially since subway fares are a nickel, and I am employed now." Frank smiled. He enjoyed his new financial independence resulting from making a few dollars each week at the barbershop. "I can afford to come visit once a week if I can take time away."

He does come often. Is that still okay? Maybe he should be looking for another girl, just like I should be looking for another boy, besides Steven.

"Have you ever thought about who you would marry someday, Frank?" Zina was emboldened and came right out with the question; hoping it sounded like she is in no way considering herself in that picture, once and for all. *We are cousins that should think of each other as cousins.*

"Why do you ask?" He raised his thick black eyebrows at Zina, questioning slyly as if he thought she had a motive.

"Well Nan says she knows. She has it all planned out."

"Really?"

"Well, she says she does. She has big dreams." Zina explained.

"What sort of dreams?"

"Well about the life she will have, where she and her future husband will live, how many children, all that." Zina said.

"Oh. Well, I do know that when I am married, I want my life to be full of children, grandchildren, and lots of space for them to all run around in. But a close family, one where they don't have to drive far to visit when they get older."

"Yes, living far away is a disadvantage. I agree," she said. "And I'd also love to have a place where everyone can come visit, or a vacation home, something on the beach where family can come, play cards, swim-"

"And have a boat!" Frank added enthusiastically, as if they were both painting the same dream.

"Do you like boats, Frank?" Zina hid her giggle; she didn't see the excited little boy side of Frank very often, apparently 'boats' brought that out in him.

"I think so, I've always wanted to try to sail."

"Well then. My summer house will have boats so you can come visit and try them out." Zina looked away shyly and changed the subject, forgetting to not sound encouraging. "Do you think you will be a barber, Frank? I mean, later, when you are an adult?"

"I think so, it's good work for my father, why couldn't I make a living with it too? But I have other ideas as well. I want to find a way to invest so I don't have to work for my entire life."

"Wow, Frank, investments, really? I hear the stock market is terrible now."

"Yes, but I am thinking real estate, it doesn't disappear like paper in a stock market. I might buy some houses."

"That sounds interesting, and what would you do with 'some houses'? You can't live in all of them at once." Zina joked.

"Yes, but maybe I can be the bank. Let people rent their house from me.

Wouldn't that be a way to set yourself up for life? Be a bank?"

"I suppose." Zina thought of the large institutions and couldn't imagine this boy in front of her having a business of such magnitude. She smiled politely anyway, not wanting to be someone who stood in the way of someone else's dreams; she knew how discouraging that felt.

"Frank, I think you will make some young woman very happy someday." Zina said quietly.

Frank looked away. "That is what I was thinking too, Zina." And then looked right back at her. He caught himself meaning something else and stammered- "Right, I mean to say...you would make someone happy someday too, Zina."

⁊ƆɆ

The mothers were done earlier than expected, so Maria met Frank and Zina on the sidewalk as they were heading back.

"Bye Aunt Maria; see you Frank," Zina called to them as they walked to the bus stop in one direction and Zina walked in the other direction home.

She kept thinking of her conversation with Frank. *How does someone make plans for their future like Nan has?* All Zina wanted to do was be a nurse and that got taken from her, and now she wants to have a family and beach house someday. *How does someone get from here to there? I am only nearly twelve, so I guess I have time to figure it out.*

"I'm home, Mother." She walked past her mother sitting at the small desk in the living room where she would occasionally pay a bill or write a letter, but she was spending a lot more time there lately.

Her mother was so engrossed in whatever she was writing, Zina didn't think she heard that she came in. She stepped behind her to say hello but two strongly underlined words on her mother's note caught her eye.

<u>Please stop.</u>

Zina shivered. *What kind of note was Mother writing?* She slipped into the kitchen, still unnoticed, when she heard the front door clatter and swing open.

"Hello, Rose!" a male voice boomed.

Her mother's brother Francesco burst into the house. He and his wife, Jenny, lived on Long Island with their kids, and seldom visited. So whenever he did, he would make a grand entrance.

Zina watched from the cracked open kitchen door to see her mother rush to put all her papers away too quickly, not her typical style of organization at all, and stood awkwardly from her desk to greet him.

"Francesco! My crazy little brother, you have always loved surprising me." Her mother said, with a small amount of annoyance at her brother, and ushered him outside to talk on the porch. Being she was caught off guard, Zina just assumed her mother didn't feel the house was in shape for visitors today.

Zina glanced again at the desk. *It's not intruding if I just walk past and 'notice' the note, right?*

Making sure the adults were settled in their conversation, Zina casually strolled in the living room, lingering ever so slightly by a certain piece of furniture.

> <u>*Please stop.*</u> *You have been through a lot, I know, but this is what you agreed to. You cannot go back on it now, it wouldn't be fair, not to any of us, and not to Vincenza. You will not feel better afterwards, trust me. Please just let it go and stop calling me about reconsidering: because I won't.*

Zina quickly went upstairs to her room and sat on her bed, nervous, her heart racing.

What is going on? Oh, why did I even look at that note. What do I do now, I can't ask about it because then she will know I looked at her private papers. But it has to do with me, right? So, is it still wrong of me to have seen it? And who was she writing the note to, anyway?

"I wish I knew what was going on, Duey. Who is this letter to and why is it about me?"

She thought about posing her questions to her journal but felt so guilty and confused, she curled up with Duey under her blankets instead.

I can fashion the life I desire by applying enough focus and determination.

CHAPTER 28

Rose, 1907

June
New York

Because it was an unseasonably cool and comfortable day, Rose took her time walking to the church for work. She permitted her thoughts to wander to everything else but the daunting mound of paperwork that awaited her.

It feels more like fall than summer – sunny and cool, like September. It reminds me of Mamie's wedding day. I can't believe Mamie has been married almost two years now. So much has happened. She's pregnant with her second baby, due next month. So terrible that their first baby lived only two months, but now Mamie has been having more good days than bad days for a change.

Oh, there's another rooming house with vacancies, but no, it won't be any less crowded than our three rooms on Sullivan Street. I wish Mother liked the city more, but I do think it would be better if Papa started to look outside of Brooklyn to find a house for the family. Maybe Mamie and Domenico could find one too – wouldn't that be nice if they still stayed nearby, especially as our families grow.

Arriving at her desk, she sighed, dreaming of her own future family, but she had to start work. She pulled the first document from her pile. She monotonously completed some tasks, and time was passing slowly.

First, I have to find a man. I can't expect that my future husband will just walk in my office one day. Typically, the ones I meet come in to see me because they are attached – sending money to their wife and family in Sicily or planning their wedding here, at the church. I guess I will just have to wait it out. Someday, maybe I will be helping with the arrival of a wonderful gentleman who is fresh off the boat, and he will decide he has been looking for me all along.

Rose sat, looking out her window with a pencil propped over the calendar to schedule yet another wedding when she heard loud footsteps approaching her office.

At her open doorway, a loud voice shouted, "Hello, Rose!"

"Francesco! My crazy little brother, you startled me!" She set her pencil down and walked over to give her no-so-little-anymore brother a hug. He loved to catch her off guard.

Francesco entered her office with a man she never met and went directly to the window to peer at something going on across the street. The men were continuing their conversation, talking and laughing about something and she wasn't interested in finding out what. *Likely it's some odd male humor,* she thought.

She surveyed them both. Never in a million years would she have thought her little brother, now eighteen, would be such a fine businessman and barber, as he was always a dreamer and a troublemaker. She figured he would be causing trouble until he was old and grey. Now he was so polite, spoke English so nicely, and had wonderful people skills. In just two years, he built a wonderful business in America with a clientele that trusted and liked him. Rose realized it was easier for a man in America, the same as it was in Sicily – unfortunately that fact hadn't changed with the continent.

Her brother laughed at something his friend pointed to out the window.

His friend seems nice, but not my type.

The men turned her attention back to Rose, who was now staring at them expectantly, insinuating they had been rude with her loud 'ahem.'

"Oh Rose, I brought a new friend who can use your help. He too, is named Francesco, Francesco Vincenti. He is also a barber, he works in our shop, and he's eighteen, like me. He's from Caltagirone."

"Oh Caltagirone! How nice. We grew up in Pedara, then we moved to Regalbuto; we could have been neighbors. I just love to hear about where people are from. It's a connection we have here in New York that seems to be a bigger deal than if we met on a street in Sicily. Meeting here, it's almost a celebration of survival – we all know what it took to get here. If you were from Sicily, we were neighbors. It's nice to meet you," She shook off her melancholy for their home country and got down to business. "Well, how can I help you, Francesco Vincenti?"

Her brother interrupted before they began, "if you don't mind, Rose, Frank, I will excuse myself. I'm going to keep looking for that certain someone down on the street, while you talk."

Oh. A young lady, perhaps?

He continued, "I'll leave you to it. Frank, you are in good hands with my sister, she will help you." Her brother said that last bit in English and Rose wasn't sure why. *Perhaps that was what this friend was more fluent in?*

"Ok, So, Francesco, what can we at Our Lady of Pompeii do to help you?" Rose asked in her best rendition of the few English words she learned at this job.

"Please, call me Frank. There are many Francescos in America!" He struggled to find the words. "Yes, I need help. Soon I need you to be my wife."

Rose nearly choked with her sharp inhale. "What?"

"No, no, I am still learning the English. May we speak in Sicilian again?" Frank said, correcting his mistake, and then continued speaking more comfortably. "My apologies. I need you to help me with my soon-to-be wife. I already have a sweetheart; she is still in Caltagirone; my Maria."

"Yes, well, yes, it is Father Domo that will be helping you, I can get your information to share with him. Father Domo has been assisting immigrants with documents and passage cost transfers since well before I started here in 1903. I will check out how to work with her church in Caltagirone. Which one is it?"

"Cattedrale di San Giuliano."

"Ah, yes, in the center of the city, yes, we have worked with them before. Alright, and are you looking to send Maria money, or help with getting her tickets, or are you traveling to meet her, and what is your time frame?" Rose began her typical list of questions.

Frank looked down at his hands. "I just got off the ship myself on June the seventh. For the last two weeks I have been looking for a job, and I have just started at your brother's barber shop. I have a few dollars to send to her now, but I am afraid to since I don't want it to be lost in the mail." He was a little apologetic.

"No problem, I can make sure it is wired to her. Give me all of her information." Rose gave him her best reassuring smile.

He handed her the money, thanked her, and turned to leave, reminding her that he was working in the same barber shop as her brother, so she should know how to get a hold of him if she needed to. He looked back at Rose again, tentatively, a bit shyer than before. "I plan to bring Maria and her mother here in three years. Do you think that is feasible?" He asked quietly, hesitatingly, as if he couldn't bear it if the answer was no.

"Yes, I believe that is feasible. My father, sister, and I raised enough in one year for three siblings to travel here, then the following year five of us raised enough to send our papa back to get the rest of our family – all five kids and my mother. You surely can raise enough in three years for two to travel."

His entire demeanor changed as if the weight of a thousand fears and anxieties lifted. He smiled broadly and sighed. He seemed more comfortable now and so excited, a completely different attitude from when he arrived at the office a few minutes ago. "It's going to be a really hard three years to wait." He looked like a child who couldn't be patient to open a present. "Maria and I have known each other since I was thirteen and she was nine, the year her father died, in 1901. We have seen each other nearly every day for the past five years. We've never been separated like this."

"Oh, I'm sorry about her father. But it's nice that you both have known each other for such a long time." *I can't think of a single person outside of the family that I have known since I was thirteen, oh except for Domenico, but he doesn't count.*

"It's been really hard on her, and her mother. I've tried to help them, but things started to get really bad in Sicily for our families."

Rose motioned for Frank to sit down on the chair by her office door and she sat on the chair opposite. He seemed to need to talk. That's one thing she has learned while working in a church, people always want to talk. Some she would need to allow to, some she would need to cut off.

Frank was brimming with the need to share his feelings for his girl and his plan. "Maria is such a determined girl, she learned a lot from her father in the nine short years she had with him, and she has big dreams. She was the one who put the idea in my head about the possibilities of America." Frank looked at ease while he discussed his sweetheart. He had a glow about him when he spoke of her.

The change in his face. Intriguing. I hope I find this kind of love. Is it only available for those who grow up knowing each other? If that is the case, then I will be an old maid. I'm twenty-one years old now, and I would like to be married soon. When will it be my turn to find real love?

Rose realized she may have missed some of what Frank was saying, but tuned back in.

"So, I developed my trade in barbering in Caltagirone and helped her and her mother as much as I could. People stopped having their hair cut when they couldn't feed their family. Imagine that. So, America was really our only option. I turned eighteen and came here by myself. She will be eighteen in three years and by then I will have the money for them both to come over."

"Certainly." Rose liked this young man, he's three years younger than she, but he had a light and determination in his eyes, and she liked how he was so loving toward his Maria.

I hope I find a man who is devoted to me like that.

Rose thought their business was done, but Frank remained. Rose wondered why, and the reason walked in the door a few awkward moments later.

"Sorry, I think he got lost trying to find the building." Rose's brother said walking back in her office with a man from the street, apparently whom he was looking for.

Frank stood up and hugged the man. Frank turned to Rose to proudly introduce him. "Rose, I'd like you to meet my cousin, Giacomo. He has just arrived from Sicily!"

"Giacomo, this is Rose, we have just met but I already know she is most helpful, and she is a good, sympathetic listener. She's going to help me send money to Maria to bring her here. Perhaps she can help you post your letters back home too?"

All I can do is nod a response. A singore biondo. I know I'm blushing when he takes my hand and kisses my knuckle. I notice his gentle eyes and strong chin. He is gracious and well kept. I admire the stitching on his coat, and he says, 'thank you, I tailor my own.' Impressive. I like the small details and fine lines.

Rose paused to find some words. "So, um, you are from Caltagirone as well?" She returned to the safety of her desk and sat down.

"Yes, Frank's father, also named Francesco, and my mother, Vincenzia, are siblings. So, Frank and I are cousins. We grew up together; Caltagirone is a very large but tight-knit community."

Rose just nodded, pretending to take copious notes while she really was trying to remember to breathe.

How is it that people walk in and out of my office all day but today someone walks in that stops all the traffic in my head? I like this man. I like Frank. Frank and Maria sound like they would make a nice couple and nice friends. I feel like we would all get along so well. But one small detail before determining just how perfect this is. Does this man have a soon-to-be wife in Sicily too?

She finally cleared her throat and started in an official tone, "Giacomo...?"

"Yes, Giacomo Sagone. Frank says I should be called Jack in America." The men looked at each other with smiles and nods.

"Well, my name is Rose Privitera. I can help you post your letters home, surely. Would there be any passage or immigration you also need help with, as in bringing loved ones to America?" *Please, I'm hoping he says no. Please say no.*

"Oh, I have two sisters, Rosina and Teresa, they are very anxious for mail from me."

Frustratingly, he doesn't mention a betrothed. Should I still clarify the question, or will I appear to be affected or prying? I really like the look of this man, his style, his smile.

He caught on and continued. "But I do not have anyone whom I need to help with immigration. I wish to find my bride right here." He paused and Rose perspired a little with anticipation. "Here. In America. Maybe even here, in New York City."

Our eyes connect and I can't pull myself away.

He took a step closer to Rose's desk and said quietly, mesmerizingly, almost breathlessly, "Maybe even here, in this…"

"Giacomo," her brother cut in, seeing the interaction.

Rose gave him a look which she hoped meant she was not happy that he interrupted.

"Let us allow Rose to get back to work today, we will return tomorrow with your letters, shall we? We men must all get a bite to eat."

They left, and Rose finally breathed a full breath. *I am a lovesick girl! Giacomo has made a great first impression on me, he has just the sort of look I like. What if? I have been hoping for a man to just walk in and fit right into my life, and this man looks like he is quite fitting.*

Eventually, Rose remembered she was putting a wedding date on the calendar.

Do I dare be so presumptuous, so bold, so assuming? I only met him minutes ago. I suppose we will have plenty of time, but Father Domo's calendar is filling up fast.

I think I just found my perfect man.

CHAPTER 29

<u>Zina</u>

Monday, February 24, 1930

"Happy Birthday Day, Duey!" Zina looked back at her kitten to share her enthusiasm. "Oh! Nan will be here soon and then Frank will be by around six o'clock."

Duey was apparently more interested in grooming himself than in whatever a 'birthday' might be. Zina smiled at him and quickly got changed out of her school clothes behind her screen and began to fix her hair.

As she smoothed her nearly black shoulder length hair, she struggled with a particularly unruly curl twisting the wrong way. She licked her fingers to try again. Duey copied her with his white tipped paws.

She giggled about how he mimicked her, but she certainly wouldn't use his techniques herself. "I'm not going to care today about this cowlick, Duey. Even if it were called a 'catlick' you aren't going to help me, but thanks anyway." Zina was sure he understood, as he turned his attention to his other paw, nonchalantly.

Satisfied with her appearance, she went downstairs and out to the porch. Nan was already there.

"Hello, fellow twelve-year-old!" Zina greeted Nan; they locked elbows and walked toward the park to wait for Frank by 'Aunt Etna'.

It was a beautiful sunny day for February, and although the air was brisk, it was wonderfully dry and void of snow.

"I know what I wish for you, Zina. That you finally find the perfect boy you are looking for. Oh, it is the most wonderful feeling!" Nan began skipping with happiness.

Zina smiled at her best friend while trying to keep up, metering her breath as best as she could to avoid a coughing fit.

"Oh, and I can't believe I almost forgot to tell you!" Nan came to a sudden halt to face Zina. "I talked with Father Antonio after our church meeting on Friday and he gave me an answer about the cousin question." Nan was more excited now than anyone would normally be after talking with their priest.

"So, Father Antonio said that Michael and I would be allowed to marry!" Nan squealed.

"Nan, wait, you asked Father about Michael?"

"Well, I didn't drop names, but I asked about the rules. I know we share the same uncle on his father's side, and the church has rules about cousins getting married. So, the point is, Father Antonio said its allowable; we are within the rules!" Nan released Zina to spin and twirl with pure happiness.

"But Nan, we are twelve, remember? Well, technically. You'll be thirteen in two months, but right now we are all twelve, you, me, and Frank."

"I know, but that is not the point." Nan brushed the small detail of age away like lint off her skirt. "Of course, we have to wait a few years still — plenty of time for Michael to fall in love with me." She squeezed Zina's hand with confidence.

The girls walked together in awkward silence since Zina's mood shifted. *What are these rules for cousins? Frank and I share an uncle too, and we are closer relatives than Nan and Michael are. We are most likely outside of the rules Nan mentioned, but that really doesn't matter anymore, I can't think of him that way.*

Nan began talking again about all the visions she had for her future. Zina just smiled and was happy in all the right spots for Nan as she went on and on with her dreams of marrying Michael.

Zina wavered in her thoughts of Frank — now she wished Frank weren't a cousin. *Will I ever find someone else?*

"Oh, there he is!" Nan exclaimed and Zina's heart skipped as if Nan produced a boy in answer to her 'find someone' question.

"Oh hi, Frank," said Zina, shaking off her previous train of thought and trying to be as natural as possible.

"Hi Zina, hi Nan. Happy Birthday Zina!"

"Thank you, Frank." Zina regained her composure. "Isn't it the best day today, that we are all twelve! Let's head to the candy store and share a malt to celebrate. You'll be thirteen tomorrow, Frank, so we don't have any time to waste." Zina smiled.

"What are you wishing for your birthday, Frank? It's so funny that you and Zina's birthdays are one year apart, and one day."

"I have a very special wish this year."

"What is that?" Nan asked.

"If I told you, it won't come true."

"I thought that only holds true when you blow out candles." Zina said.

"No, I'm pretty sure it works with any birthday wish."

"Whatever you say Frank." said Nan.

⃀ѓ

On the walk back to Zina's house, Frank purposefully fell behind so he could talk with Zina alone. Nan eventually got the hint and started skipping ahead with the sucker she bought.

Frank took this chance to give Zina something he brought for her. "I know we have our candies, but I have an apple for you, Zina. I saved two from the final harvest last fall, especially for our birthdays."

"Oh Frank, the first of the year for me. Thank you, that's very sweet of you."

"Funny, I'm not so sure how sweet the apple is, but you can try it." Frank smiled.

Zina bit into it and said it was the perfect amount of sweetness.

Frank brought out his pocketknife and proceeded to walk and peel his apple in a long continuous peel, the way he always did. He'd start from the top by the stem and go in a spiral motion, coiling the peel as he slivered it off, creating one long strand that kept going, all the way down to nearly touching the sidewalk. He made sure he stopped before it hit the ground. Next, he grabbed the edge of the peel with the knife hand and brought it to his lips. He started eating the end of the peel, moving and sliding it into his mouth inch by inch, chewing the entire length before he took a bite of the apple that he removed it from. Zina looked at him in disbelief.

"If you were going to still eat the peel, why did you even peel it? I just don't understand you, Frank."

"There's nothing wrong with the peel so why waste it?"

"Well why don't you just eat it with the apple? Why cut it off at all?" Zina asked and took another bite of her apple.

"Oh, that? I think it's fun. Why do you crochet granny circles?"

"What? How is that in any way similar?"

"Well, since you asked Zina, here is what I think. They are both lines and circles. Your crocheting is a line being made into a circle and my apple peel is a circle, or I suppose a sphere, being made into a line. The line becomes a circle in your granny circles, and the circle becomes a line with my apple peel. They were one of the same, and then, they were different."

It was just an apple, wasn't it? Until Frank explained it, it was. Frank always sees things for more than what they are.

"Ok Frank, are you going to do that other thing now?"

"Of course," he said. He had just finished his complete apple. He ate the entire core but saved the seeds in his cheek. He did this with every apple she had ever seen him eat. As they were walking, Frank made sure to go to the edges of the woody areas at the north end of the park. He spit out one seed onto the ground, after making a divot in the dirt, and then covered it over. The ground was hard, but he could scratch some dirt to cover.

"Someday it might be a tree. Perhaps not, but it has a chance now. I can't always see what will happen, but I can set things in motion for them to." He spit the last seed in the last hole.

"Like how the seed can't see the tree it will be someday." Zina handed him her finished core.

He smiled, she remembered.

"The seen and unseen – exactly," he said, as he made an extra-large hole and dropped her entire core into it. Zina looked at him in surprise. "But maybe this will work just as well."

Zina smiled.

"Zina, imagine what the apple might think, if it could think. It has just been devoured, now it is buried in the ground."

"How morbid." Zina shuddered.

"Right, but think of it, now the apple has two choices, to decay and die right there, or to wiggle its seeds deeper in the soil and grow into something new."

"You are a puzzle, Frank. Ah, but there is one more thing that could happen to the seed. It could get scratched and pecked at and eaten by a bird. It has no choices then."

He laughed and she smiled.

"If I plant enough seeds, one will take eventually, right? And can you imagine how many apples we'd have then?"

"From one tree Frank?"

"No, from one tree and the seeds of all those apples. Then the seeds from all those apples that were just seeds, and so on and on."

"Oh," Zina got quiet. Sometimes Frank overwhelmed her with the visions he had. *He can see the entire universe in the blink of an eye*, she thought.

"Happy Birthday Zina, may all of the small seeds in your life grow to bear countless fruit."

"Happy Birthday, tomorrow, to you too Frank. May you always see the universe in every small seed."

They both smiled. A friend that understands you completely. Birthday wishes do come true.

CHAPTER 30

Rose, 1907

July
New York

Giacomo came around, usually with his cousin, Frank, when Frank was sending letters to Maria with some money, which was at least twice a week. When Giacomo posted letters to one of his sisters he would bring Rose a single flower, or a cookie, or a small book. She loved the items and the attention.

One day he brought her a small rectangular box. It was handmade; beautifully stained wood with a painted flower on the carved sliding door on top, perfect to house letter writing implements. Giacomo said his mother gave him the box, that her father made it when he picked up a woodcarving hobby in Sicily after he sold his business. His mother wanted her only son to have it. It was lovely, both in sentiment and in design. Now, he wanted Rose to have it.

"I can't accept this, Giacomo, it is a family heirloom."

"Yes, Rose, it is my family's heirloom and I want you to have it."

Rose looked down at the box, her hand beginning to shake just a little.

"What about your sisters? Shouldn't one of them have it?" This was a special gift, more endearing than any of the tokens he had brought her so far.

I've waited so long for something so romantic, why am I questioning how fast things are progressing?

"My sisters are already married in Sicily and I'm afraid they have no interest in ever leaving or ever visiting America. I wouldn't mail it to them anyway, it's too special. Much too special to chance losing it." He took a step closer to Rose, holding the box, but was really talking about something else.

"Oh, um. I'm sorry. Is it lonely for you here in America without your family?" She stammered, grasping for conversation, but not sure why.

His eyes were fixed on hers. His hand reached out for her elbow. He touched her arm and she felt instantly warm. "Well, no, Rose, I won't be lonely because I intend to start a family of my own." He paused to deeply inhale, then exhaled and said, "If you will have me." He presented the special family heirloom, lowered down on one knee and asked for her hand.

I am floating, weightless, slightly dizzy. Is this real? It is so sweet how he is so humble but refined; strong yet caring.

Inside the box was a beautiful string of pearls. "You can use the pearls on our wedding day, they were my mother's. We can shop together, if you'd like, to pick out a ring. Meanwhile, the box can be used to hold pencils as you continue to do your good work helping others come to America."

We met just a month ago, and here he is! The man of my dreams has realized my dream for us!

She said yes and they both laughed with relief and happiness.

As they waited for Frank to arrive with his letter to mail, they talked nearly nonstop. Rose shared that her dream was to not only help others get to America but to help them in their lives; she wanted to be a nurse. Giacomo said he would support anything she'd like to do in America. "This world is vast and wide, and we can all find our passion in life and pursue our dreams, that's why we are here."

When Frank got there, they told him the news of their engagement, and then they all planned to go somewhere to celebrate. Frank hugged them both and gave an intense look. "Hurry and post my letter to Maria! I need to get her here faster now than ever. It's time for all of us to begin the rest of our lives!"

Exactly what I was thinking.

℀℈

The next week Rose and Giacomo visited Mamie and Domenico to share their happy news, and visit their baby, Josephine, who was born on July 17, 1907. She was the sweetest black haired little girl, with big eyes that seemed to always be questioning everything. She was named for Domenico's mother, Guiseppa; 'Josephine' was the Americanized version.

Mamie said that she remembered Domenico's mother fondly from Regalbuto but felt sad her baby daughter would never meet her namesake. "I suppose family not meeting across the waters will be a new custom we will all have to get used to," she said.

Giacomo and Rose talked about the children they would have together. Giacomo hoped to have a baby girl first, he said, just like Josephine, with dark brown hair and inquisitive eyes. He was so close to his mother and sisters growing up that he would love a daughter. Rose told him that she would love to have a son first. A son would be helpful with chores and helping the family work. They both agreed it wouldn't really matter; they were just excited to start a family together.

℀℈

The next Sunday was Josephine's day of baptism and Mamie had all of the family over to their new house for some rigatoni and meatballs.

Rose watched her getting dishes out from her cupboard. Then, Mamie walked over to stir the sauce on the stove. She seemed so mechanical in her movements: she was not her normal talkative self and looked tired. But this kind of tiredness wasn't typical for her sister. *I can't stand to see Mamie not feel well, it must still be a reflex in me from when we were younger, and I would try to help her cope with all her nightmares.*

"Mamie? Mamie are you alright? Mamie-?" Rose touched her arm. She was so far away in thought, as if in a trance, going through the motions but not really being present, sprinkling crushed herbs into the sauce.

Rose remembered she went through a similar trance-like phase in Regalbuto after she stayed with the Russo family and a few months after baby Mary was born. She was like this again in the first year she and Domenico were married. She was so difficult to talk to then, too.

"Mamie, can I help you with something?" Rose tried again to get through.

Mamie shook her head slightly, perhaps to say no, or perhaps to become more awake. She said sorry and turned her mood around so fast that Rose knew she was hiding something.

"Oh Rose, can you taste the sauce for me? I'm not sure if I put the basil in."

"Sure, of course." Rose knew she put some in, she could smell it.

I had better taste this sauce if she doesn't even remember what she put in it. She turned her attention to the pot but thought about her sister's mood.

Rose watched Mamie more that day: while they were eating and while Josephine was being passed around. When she was asked if Josephine was a good baby, she smiled weakly and said yes. "She is a nice quiet baby that nurses well and is happy."

When their sister Mary held baby Josephine, Mamie looked green and had to excuse herself abruptly. Domenico sent everyone home saying Mamie felt sick, and she needed rest.

☎)☎

Rose visited the next day to help her sister finish cleaning up from the gathering while the baby slept. Mamie appeared to be feeling better.

She told Rose nothing was wrong and that yesterday her sickness was just a small headache, and she was fine now, so Rose didn't have to worry.

Satisfied that the matter was resolved, Rose changed the subject. She told Mamie that she didn't bring a gift for the baby but had an idea for something that she might like.

"Oh Mamie, I saw the sweetest picture frame in a shop window last week. It was a baby's announcement printed and mounted behind glass; it looked so darling." Rose asked if she could see Josephine's baptismal certificate. "Or maybe her birth certificate?"

Mamie threw a look at Rose like she asked the most surprising thing.

"What?" Rose questioned. "Why are you so jumpy? I think it would be nice to put it in a picture frame and hang it in the baby's room."

"Oh. Why not frame something else, Rose." Mamie looked distracted again.

"Can't I see the birth certificate? Maybe it is pretty, like our marriage certificates are, and it would look nice in a frame. Where do you have it, Mamie? You know, you are the first to have a baby in America, and she's your first baby, and I want to see what the certificate looks like."

Oh no. Rose remembered. "Oh, I am sorry. You know what I mean, Mamie, I'm so sorry." She attempted to correct it, but it was too late.

Mamie looked so wretched.

263

Rose felt badly about how callously she mentioned her first baby; she knew Josephine was not her first baby. They lost their first born shortly after they were married, a son.

"Mamie, please talk to me."

"Rose, I can't handle it anymore. Why does everything always happen to me? I can't show you the birth certificate. I'm so ashamed. I can't even tell Domenico."

"Whoa, wait, slow down, Mamie, what are you talking about? Your husband can't see his own daughter's birth certificate? What is going on Mamie, what are you hiding?"

Something hidden on a birth certificate. Rose remembered another time she thought that was possible.

"Oh, Rose," she sobbed and pointed to where the paper was hidden under the clothes on the dresser. Rose got it and Mamie wailed even louder, as if knowing she might be found out any second.

Rose read the certificate. "What is wrong with it? Says here you are the mother, Domenico is the father, the baby's name, Josephine, that's right. What is this? Her last name is spelled Bregas and not Brex? Is that what is bothering you?" *That sloppy-spelling husband of hers.*

She shook her head no.

"What is this column, number of pregnancies? Does that mean before she was born? Ok, there's "one" written here. So, the baby you lost. I don't see what is wrong here, Domenico knows that, so what is the problem?"

"No, Rose." Mamie broke down into a full wail now, tapering to sobs that were so silent but heart wrenching.

"Mamie, I am so sorry. I know the loss of your first baby was hard. I didn't mean to remind you. Why on earth does the birth certificate need to state how many other children you have? Calm down Mamie, it's all okay."

"No, Rose, you don't understand, and I can't tell you. I can't tell Domenico; I can't tell anyone. No one must ever know."

'No one must ever know.'

Wait, I've heard that before – the night that Mamie came home, and baby Mary was born.

Mamie looked like she intended to escape but couldn't find the door. She fell to her knees and sobbed some more. There was no talking to her now.

Rose helped her to her bed and sat while she let her fall asleep, just like all those years ago while calming her nightmares. She wondered what secrets her sister kept locked away, and whether she really wanted them to come to light.

~ENTRY #10~

3/1/1930

My dear friend,

Monday was my birthday, but since then, I've been too upset to write, I know that's not like me. I've been struggling with thinking I might be acting selfish. Please don't think badly of me because of what I'm about to share, my dear friend.

So, Papa is very generous with me sometimes, thinking of things I might like as a gift, trying to consider my feelings. I just don't understand why Mother doesn't approve of that.

Like when Papa first brought home Duey. It was after my first cat, CeeCee, ran away about this time last year. (I still miss her.) Papa got her when I was born, so we grew up together, being the same age. Papa didn't have to get me a new kitten, I think he just felt bad about CeeCee. So, I named my new friend CeeCee Too, or Duey, which is Sicilian for two. I thought it clever of me.

Mother was not happy about that gift. At all. But she didn't make him take him back or anything. That's why Duey is only allowed in my room or outside, not in the rest of the house or Mother gets mad.

So, now this is what happened on Monday for my birthday: Papa surprised me with a beautiful and expensive rabbit coat!

Then, Mother made him take it back!

She said it in front of everyone. Yelled it even. The Bregas family was over for cake. The party atmosphere was most certainly over then. 'She can't have things like this. You shouldn't encourage her to want things she can't have.'

This seemed to strike a chord in everyone. Aunt Mamie started yelling at Mother, essentially saying what a bad mother she thought she was, even saying that Mother was cursing me with her jealousy! She kept throwing salt and saying something about that amulet again. Then Aunt Mamie said, 'why can't Zina have nice things?'

This, of course, confused Gracie because her mother doesn't give gifts like this to them, so why was she saying I should get them? Gracie asked her mother what she meant by getting mad about this, but Aunt Mamie left, crying. Do you believe it?

Mother kept mumbling something to Papa about spoiling me. They continued their semi-loud discussion in their room, and of course, I listened in.

Mother was also mad that Aunt Mamie spoke against her opposition to the gift and said to Papa that "she has no right to say anything, ever." Which I thought was harsh. She yelled something at Papa about how gifts like this can affect me in the future. She told him that if he spoiled me, I would never be satisfied with my husband's attention, because what if my husband couldn't afford to lavish me too?

I didn't want to hear more; I thought it unfair. Maybe someday my husband could lavish me, maybe not. I don't think I would be spoiled. I'm just missing out on a chance for nice things now only because there's a possibility that I still can't have this same treatment in the future. I just don't agree with her logic.

At least Aunt Mamie would agree with me, I don't--

~ I'm sorry, my dear friend, that I never finished that entry. Papa came up to my room to talk to me. He said:

'Many situations we don't always understand, things that we wish would be different, but we have to learn to appreciate what we have and not expect more.' This was his little talk. That's why he has to bring back the coat.

But why did he buy it for me in the first place if having something more is so wrong? Papa got up and left, and I was just feeling empty. Why can't I want more?

It sounds as if my parents want me to just settle for whatever comes and not try to have things I want in my life. They want me to trust them to decide these things for me, like what to do in school, even how some future husband would treat me. But why? Because it is the tradition in Sicily to do that? But we are in America; so, can't they change?

It's so interesting that they came to America to make a change in their lives, but now they just keep changing everything back to the way things were in Sicily. That doesn't make sense to me.

I wish I could have known them in Sicily, what it was like when they were my age. All of them, Mother and Papa, Uncle Domino and Aunt Mamie. They had to have been children once in their lives, with dreams and ambitions, right? They are all so mean and grumpy now, well sometimes anyway. I am in a bad mood so I'm only thinking of how unhappy they seem, like all of their dreams have been shattered so now they think mine should be too.

Well, speaking of dreams, I'm tired and it's late. Good night, my dear friend. I am grateful I don't have to give you back at least. (Duey too)

~Zina

CHAPTER 31

Zina

Monday, March 3, 1930

"I just called to make sure you are okay, Zina, you know, about your papa's birthday gift situation." Frank said.

Zina thought it was nice of him to call on this Monday evening, not a typical time to hear from him.

"I guess I am okay. Thanks for calling, Frank." She was not interested in talking about the returned rabbit coat anymore, she had other things on her mind. Things she hasn't been able to sort out yet.

"Zina, is there something else going on?" He asked, but thought he already knew.

She felt relieved that he picked up on her mood and decided to see what he thought about what she was feeling. She looked around first to make sure her parents couldn't overhear.

"It was more than just the gift, Frank. You know how we joke sometimes that 'at least Mount Etna isn't erupting'? Well, something is going on, I can feel it. Nobody is acting like themselves."

"It could be something in the stars, you know, it seems everyone is stressed out this month." Frank eluded.

"What? What do you mean?" Zina worried, wondering what world situation has happened now.

"Well, you know, March is full of palindromes. It must affect people's moods; like how the moon and the tides can push and pull. For instance, today's date is 03-3-30." Frank stated as if that explained it.

"Whatever, Frank. I don't believe in that sort of thing." Zina just came outright and told him. "I think there are some secrets going on and that is why everyone in my family is on edge. Do you want to hear what I found?"

Frank felt a surge of excitement. He hoped somebody had finally told her.

"Well, I saw a letter my mother was writing." Zina admitted. "I know it's wrong, but it just caught my eye, and I couldn't help myself." She told him about what she saw – that her mother was asking someone to stop doing something. "My name was in it, something about a decision that can't be undone. She was asking for the person to leave her alone. Who do you think it is? What do you think it's about?"

Frank couldn't decide what to say. He realized she still didn't know; her mother still hadn't told her. "I don't know, Zina, maybe it was a letter to your school or something?" He purposefully meant to throw her off, and he hated being in this position.

"If you can't get it off your mind, why don't you just ask your mother? Just come right out and ask if she has something she'd like to tell you? Maybe she wants to, but she doesn't know how." Frank suggested, hoping that might be a good idea. He didn't like tiptoeing through everyone's feelings,

271

he was never quite sure what the right approach might be.

"But what if it's something really bad? What if I make my mother really mad again by asking? I don't like it when she gets mad, she looks like her head will explode like a volcano."

"I'm sure that won't actually happen." Frank said.

"Seriously Frank, something is going on. I feel like there's going to be some huge eruption, something destructive that would hurt my mother, or worse."

Frank didn't like her heading down this path. He knew what the real reason was, but he wasn't permitted to tell her. She was making it really difficult to keep his promise of secrecy. He knew he could fix it and tell her, and it was painful for him to watch her struggle. He changed the subject so she might think of something else. "Zina, remember when we were talking about the apple trees?" Frank asked.

Oh brother. Another mind puzzle, Zina thought.

"Every one of those beautiful, fruit-filled trees started as a seed, right?" Frank started.

"Yes, Frank." Zina threw back, impatiently.

"Think of that seed now. Do you know how much destruction, pain, and suffering it must have gone through?"

"Really Frank? Not this again."

"Will you let me explain? Yes. Think about it. It's hard protective shell had to crack open, split apart, all its insides had to grow and survive before it could take root and thrive. You see, Zina, we can see one thing but, sometimes, something else is happening under the surface."

"Frank, I don't understand what you are trying to tell me. What does this have to do with me, and with the letter I saw? Do you think I am the source of trouble for my mother?" Zina said softly, trying not to cry.

"No, I think you are loved and cared for Zina, more than you probably realize. You mean a lot to everyone who knows you." He blushed and was glad that she couldn't see him. His comment felt a bit too revealing.

Zina was glad that he said that but wondered if it really did apply to her mother.

~ENTRY #11~

03-11-30 (another palindrome for Frank)

My dear friend,

I'm not sure what to do. Last week, Frank suggested talking to Mother, clear the air. He said to just ask her if there's something she wants to tell me about how I'm behaving, that everybody seems to be afraid to say to me.

Do you think I should, my dear friend? The last time I asked her a serious question, about wanting a sibling, she was so mad. Then the "not wanting more" birthday fiasco, I don't think she has even looked at me since then. So, do I dare approach her with this?

I suppose if there was nothing to tell, she wouldn't have anything to be angry about. But if there is something, and she wants to tell me, would it help if I ask her first? I don't know.

Can I ask anyone else? Maybe, but Mother might not like that either. She might think I'm going behind her back and become even more angry. Oh, I wish everyone would just be more open and disclosing!

So, what if there is some secret, right? Like Frank's seeds, if it just lays in the dirt with its hard shell of protection it can never grow into something. I guess a seed that holds a secret could grow into a terrible weed, but what if the seed is meant to be a beautiful tree? I think it would be more terrible if the tree never got to be what it should be because it thought it might turn out to be a weed. That would be a tragedy.

Now I sound like Frank. (And did you notice the palindrome date today? Frank would be proud if he knew I noted it.)

So, thank you, my dear friend, for listening. I don't think I will ask my mother. I will give her a chance to approach me in her own timing.

~Zina

CHAPTER 32

Rose, 1908

May
New York

With one hand, Mamie held her beautiful daughter, Josephine, on her hip, and with the other, she primped the last ribbon in Rose's bouquet. She and Francesco's fiancé, Jenny Dicanzo, did so many of the special touches. Mamie looked pleased with the beautiful silk flowers she made like Giuseppa Timpanaro taught her back in Sicily.

Rose looked over at her older sister while smoothing her handmade lace dress with a mix of satisfaction and anticipation. The sisters exchanged smiles.

I feel like an heiress in the society pages! Everything is going just as I have always dreamed, and Mamie looks happy too. It does me good to see her in a content and peaceful state. If she is behaving this way only for my benefit on my special day, then I am grateful.

But really, Mamie has been better since that day when she was so distraught that I asked about Josephine's birth certificate. It is like those tears cleansed her conscience and she could finally be at peace. I won't ever mention that framing idea again, that's for certain. I still didn't get to the truth, but if she is happy, I won't go looking for trouble.

Maybe she is feeling better since she suspects that she is pregnant again. She does seem to be most at peace as a mother-to-be. So perhaps that, as well as my wedding plans, have been good distractions for her from her moods of the past.

After depositing Josephine with one of their younger sisters, Mamie waited with Rose in the rectory for the cue as part of her matron of honor duties. But Rose would have her with her regardless.

"Mamie, it's happening! All the dreams we've had for our lives to be better in America! Look at me now, getting married." Mamie straightened her sister's pearl necklace. She smoothed Rose's veil and gave her a small smile.

"Look at you and your growing family." Rose touched her sister's belly. Mamie winced a little and gave her a weak smile. Rose stopped reminiscing, not wanting to change her sister's peaceful mood.

The doors opened and Rose took one last look around the rectory. Miss Canali was thoughtful enough to decorate with items that were personal and meaningful to the bride: her favorite flowers budding in a vase, her favorite scent hinted on pew ribbons, and the special heirloom pencil box – shined with not too much lemon polish that it might overpower the flowers.

Leaving her single life behind, Rose looked through the open doors down the aisle. Everything was perfect in the chapel of Our Lady of Pompeii. This church will always be her home and Father Domo will always be her priest no matter where she and Giacomo would decide to live in the future, she thought.

Rose smiled as she passed her brother, Francesco, who was holding the door open for her. He thought he would be the best man since he took the credit for their first introduction, but of course Frank Vincenti, Giacomo's cousin, was the best man.

Oh, is Giacomo as nervous as I am? Will he be a good husband? Will I be a good wife?

She peeked in the sanctuary to count the backs of her family's heads.

They are all here. Perfect. Today cannot be more perfect.

I am about to walk into my destiny with a man who adores me. We will leave this room today, and our future will begin.

We will have children right away; we will buy a house in Brooklyn. Giacomo has a good job as a tailor, and with my sewing jobs on the side, I will help us save, then I will begin to volunteer at the hospital until we save enough money for nursing school. I will continue working at this church until we move, or I am pregnant, whichever comes first.

Oh, all my dreams will come true!

Here I go.

CHAPTER 33

Rose, 1909

July
New York

"**A** toast," Rose raised her teacup. "To happiness and success, friendships and love. *Chin Chin*."

Maria laughed. "Do people toast with their tea in America, Rose?"

"Nevertheless, we are celebrating." Rose smiled. "I'm glad we finally have this time to talk and get to know one another, Maria. Ever since you arrived, Frank has not let you out of his sight."

Maria blushed, reflecting on how attentive Frank had been as she admired her new delicate gold ring.

Maria arrived with her mother, Concetta Arcoleo, a week ago on the 10th. Frank was overwhelmingly excited, he fell on one knee and proposed the minute he saw Maria, before she even had both feet off the ship.

"Yes, and of course I said yes. He wants us to be married in January, on the 23rd. It's only six months to wait to start our family."

"What is special about January 23rd?"

"Frank picked it because it reads one, two, three. He says it mirrors his desire to marry quickly."

Rose thought he may have had too much time to think about this, but she said it was sweet.

Rose liked Maria immensely, just as she thought she might. Maria had a very practical side and another side that was all business. She could be a lawyer, they joked. They talked about what America was like, what Rose had learned so far in her six years of being here, and they talked about their futures. Rose was envious.

"Rose, what is wrong?"

"I'm sorry Maria, I am happy for you, of course, I hope your plans move along as quickly as you want them to. It's just that…my husband and I have been married for over a year now, and still no baby – when it seems others are having no trouble at all."

Maria said, "Oh I'm sorry, but it's like you said, maybe it only seems that way, you know, since you are focused on it."

"I suppose. But, in the past year, there have been four babies born in my family; even my little brother Francesco and his wife Jenny have a sweet baby boy, named Alfio, for Papa."

Maria understood and wanted to support her new friend. "Rose, your time will come. You said it yourself; it's only been one year."

I certainly don't plan to leave my destiny to chance.

CHAPTER 34

Rose, 1911

March
New York

*A*nother baby – the bear man's brother and his wife now have a baby;

they also name her Josephine for Mrs. Timpanaro. It has now been three years since Giacomo and I got married, when will it be our turn to be pregnant? Maria says maybe the third is the charm.

The baby was appropriately blessed; the happy couple gathered with the rest of the family to converse. Domenico handed the baby girl to Miss Canali, who was more than happy to take her to the offices and show her around when she began to fuss.

Rose was also restless during the baptism, not being able to keep her mind from oscillating between both her future and the state of cleanliness at the church. She stood on the outskirts of her family as she noticed the sunlight dimming through the sanctuary's stain glass. Rose assumed that it needed a more thorough cleaning.

But Giacomo noticed it too and looked outside. Darkness that began to block the sun from shining on the city street looked like smoke, he said.

"Did he say smoke?" She wondered aloud.

The gathering scattered. Rose went outside to see flames erupting from the windows of a nearby building. Gasps and screams all around her.

"God help us. Yes, yes, aid will be needed: prayers and provisions for the injured. How else can the church help?"

She headed back inside to find Miss Canali.

ಲಂಡಿ

Domenico

"Here, Miss Canali, yes, please take baby Josephine." He handed the fussy newborn to the housekeeper's wide open arms and turned back to his brother.

"She's a beauty, Angelo, congratulations. Ah my baby brother, you are a father now. You are a lucky man." He slapped his brother's shoulders and gave him a hug.

Somebody screamed after Giacomo opened the church doors. Domenico smelled the smoke. Heading out to the street, he turned the corner and saw the blaze. The building ahead was like a lit candle, wax sliding down its tapered sides. Horrified, he realized what the 'wax' really was. People had no other way to escape the upper floors.

Not thinking, he ran toward the crowds to help someone, but there wasn't anything to be done. There was no connection from the street to the helpless people seven stories up.

He made his way through the chaos: pushing until he got into the lobby, fighting the current of screaming women leaving the building. He reached the elevator and stopped. It was not being run.

"How will people get down? Stairs. Where are the stairs?"

Outside he heard tremendous cracks and groans. The fire escape ladders that were incorrectly built were melting, peeling away from the building, and crashing down to the street.

₧₨

Mamie

"Domenico, wait, where do you think you are going?" Mamie screamed when she looked out the door. "Wait, don't. Rose, stop him, Rose, where are you going? What is happening? Domenico?"

She took a few steps to see where Domenico went and a crowd on the street engulfed her instantly into a whirlpool of panic, and she was being sucked into the center.

Helpless, not being able to tell if she was doing the moving or if those around her were just carrying her, she was too terrified to make sense of anything; she just kept staggering along with the flow.

"Domenico!"

She backed up, fell backwards, or a mix of both, and then she felt the solidity of a brick wall against her. She followed it with her hands, turned the corner from the heat, and found a small solace from the turmoil in an alley. The air was cleaner, cooler, quieter. It was not as populated. She took deep breaths and rested her heartbeat.

She desperately wanted to get back to the church, so she left the alley and returned to the street. The crowd was in front of her. She heard the fire rescue; their sirens and bullhorns announcing some order in the chaos. She realized she was lost.

Looking around, she bumped right into the chest of a man walking quickly toward the scene. She banged her forehead on his chin. "Umph!" they both said, and he didn't stop. He halfway turned his head to throw a comment back to her, "sorry miss-ss." He rubbed his chin and kept walking.

Wait, I have seen that face before.

No.

No. It can't be. He cannot be here. He haunts my nightmares; how can he be real... here...

She panicked and ran back into the alley.

Everything was covered in soot and ash, but she didn't care where she was sitting. She pulled up her knees tightly and hid her face on top, sobbing and shaking.

Can't breathe. Can't move. It was him. The fire. The lava.

ഇൗരു

Domenico

Everyone was pushing to get out of the building. He was going the wrong way.

The door leading to the stairwell in the lobby was impossible to penetrate. Everyone who could access the stairs from above was pouring down it. Some were shouting that the floors above are locked; nobody from the floors that are on fire were able to get out.

Hearing this, Domenico made a decision. He found a man's discarded cane in a miraculously untrampled corner of the lobby and used it to push his way through the crowd to go up. He reached a point where the crowds thinned, and he ascended more quickly.

From the third floor landing, he heard dull thuds from up above. By the fifth floor he also heard screaming, the thuds were louder but becoming less frequent. When he got to the seventh floor the screams formed words: calls for help.

He looked at the cane and the door. Cracking the cane over the locked handle didn't cause it to budge, but instead fractured it into a narrow pry bar. He wedged it next to the door handle, putting all his weight into it to bend the jamb away from the door, kicking and pulling until it gave way. A deluge of maybe a dozen screaming, frightened girls on the other side forced their way through the now open door, coughing and stumbling over each other; pushing him down on the landing.

The last one of them yelled backwards to another who wouldn't follow. Domenico got up and went through the door, yelling for the girl to come. He saw her cowering in a corner, hiding her face, and whimpering.

He looked above her and saw the ceiling beginning to bubble, ready to erupt. He rushed in to grab her, and she started screaming and fighting with him. He pulled her up, and she wriggled so much it threw him off balance. He backed into a red-hot metal pole and screamed. His forearm was seared, blood and black soot replaced the hair. His scream stunned her to her senses, and he was able to get her down the stairs and out the building.

Others ushered her away from the scene and led Domenico to the ambulance after seeing his raw arm. But all he could think about now was Mamie. He headed back to the church.

A young lady in the alley caught his eye, she cowered against the brick wall, much the same way the young girl did moments before.

But realization hit him. "Mamie! What on earth! Why are you out here, are you hurt?"

She lifted her head and cried harder when she noticed his raw arm.

"It will be ok. Just a bad burn. Why didn't you stay in the church with the others?"

He helped her up. Mamie looked terrible. He couldn't figure out if she was hurt or not. She was striped with moistness and soot, sobbing into the shoulder on his uninjured side.

"I saw... I saw…" She tried to explain between sobs.

"It's ok, Mamie, the fire is almost out. Let's get you home."

�����

Everyone found out later that the building owners of the sewing company thought they would prevent smoking breaks in stairwells by locking the doors during work hours. That didn't deter the workers, who found new places for smoking breaks; one such place was tragically too close to the garments being made.

Too many perished; some because they attempted to escape out the windows of a building that didn't have long enough fire escapes; others because the doors to the stairs were locked.

The entire city was united either in their grief or in their fight. Peace and justice were sought but to very little satisfaction. Time was needed for healing. It didn't seem to matter how much time; pain has no schedule.

CHAPTER 35

Rose, 1911

June
New York

Three months passed, and physical wounds were improving. Domenico was just one of the many anonymous heroes that terrible day, he helped many young girls move to safety. His arm would heal, and he was told the ugly scar may fade in time.

The unseen wounds still needed time to mend.

When Rose saw the flames that fateful day, she made her way to the office at Our Lady of Pompeii. She saw the injured on the street but didn't go to help. She was horrified at the scene and appalled at herself. She thought she wanted to be a nurse but at the first sight of real pain and suffering she ran to hide behind administrative tasks.

For the next few weeks, out of guilt or duty, she stayed at the church office every day to aid those searching for loved ones on the lists the coroners put together. Completing paperwork, making calls, and consoling family members consumed her time, but she was deeply disappointed in herself.

Her newly discovered limitations combined with her unmet expectations of starting a family caused Rose to became uncertain about her future for the first time in her life.

Mamie hadn't yet recovered from the incident. The nightmares from events in her past compounded – residual anxieties were now constant and unrelenting on top of processing the recent horror she witnessed. She refused to leave the house, she barely ate anything, and her eyes would become wide and frightened at the slightest startle.

Rose gently coaxed Mamie awake on the morning of their sister Concetta's wedding. "Mamie, let's get ready, it should be a happy day."

Rose instinctively helped her sister, still, even though she was struggling herself. In doing so, she began to soothe and forgive her own shame. She decided she still had the capacity to help someone in their time of need, just not in the way she imagined.

"Mamie, won't you come downstairs with me? Concetta would love to see you this morning, even for a little while before she does some last-minute errands today. She wants you to be part of things and she's worried about you; we all are."

"But what if I see him again?" Mamie mumbled.

Rose sat down next to her sister on the bed. "See who again, Mamie?"

"Why is he here? Is he still looking for me?" Mamie's eyes were wide and apprehensive, peering out from under her quilt. Her voice trembled.

"Mamie, who are you talking about?" Rose wondered as there was nobody else in the room.

"No, this can't be happening, not again. He can't be here in America too." Mamie went on, her panic rising. She sat up, pulling her knees in close, keeping the blanket around her.

Rose moved her hand toward her sister, warily; Mamie hadn't spoken this many words in months. "In America too? Mamie, did you recognize someone from Sicily? Someone you are...afraid to see?"

"Is he here? How can he be? No, Papa told me the man went away to jail in Sicily. But he is here. Is he here? Is he going to find me again? What is real, Rose, was he real?"

"Shh, Mamie, who? Who is this man? And nobody is coming after you, you are safe-"

Mamie cringed at Rose's touch. The terrors from the past that she had locked up in her mind materialized when she bumped into that strange man in the street. His was the same face she saw back in Pedara, when she was knocked unconscious by a man who set fire to their shop. Her mind flashed replays of the scene and she softly tried to explain, "He was after Domenico. I told him that Domenico went to America; don't you remember? That...that blonde...gentleman we saw the day after Domenico came in our shop all those years ago. That...man was trying to track him down for two years and blamed me when he didn't find him, he thought I tricked him. Nobody was around that day, so he, he...it was all my fault."

Rose remembered that day. "No, Mamie, you couldn't have known that man's intentions. You were not at fault."

"No Rose, he was so angry with me, he said everything was my fault." She shuddered, curling her knees tightly back up to her chest, remembering his face years later. He forced her down, held her there, and smiled sickeningly – that man who blamed her and took his revenge. "And he said it again, later," Mamie took a brave breath and admitted, "when he...he found me again in Regalbuto." She hid her face, hoping to block the details from her consciousness, she didn't want to remember more about what he did to her, even now.

Rose was stunned. "Wait, what?"

Mamie answered quietly, "when we moved to Regalbuto, he found me again. He...He..." She gulped, shook the rest of those words away, and continued. "Then all the plans for our futures changed. It was because of something that happened to me. I should have told you years ago, and I should have told Domenico; but I wanted this new life so badly, to leave everything behind, but..." This admittance opened the door for her nightmares to be present: meeting her face to face. She shivered.

"Mamie, I am so sorry. But none of this has been your fault. You were not the cause, and we don't blame you. You have to find a way to move on and live your life now; leave those memories behind. You are stronger than this. He can't hurt you anymore."

Mamie snapped. "Oh, is it that easy, Rose? I have tried, you know, and I thought I was finally succeeding, but then I saw him again. Will he ever leave me alone? How can you be sure he won't come after me again? Wait, don't tell me. I know what you're going to say, Rose, please don't say it."

"What? What am I going to say, Mamie?"

"That I can '*be* sure because I can *make* sure it happens that way.' You've always been so sure things will happen the way you want them to. But sometimes you are not in control; do you know that? Someday you will find that out and it will be painful for you too, Rose." Mamie spat.

Rose blinked, this truth striking her unexpectantly. She quickly regained her composure, falling back into the role of helping Mamie, ignoring how her sister's words affected her. "I don't mean to diminish your pain, Mamie. And you might not have been in control of those situations, but you can control every thought you think since those events happened. You can stop allowing the pain to surface and get the best of you. When you stop letting him win; you will win."

"No Rose, you don't understand! No amount of 'thinking' is ever going to change what happened, or what happened *next*." She paused, took a breath and admitted, quietly, "it's not only about what he did to me, but also about what I had to do *after*. And something Mother told me that no one must ever know."

291

No one must ever know. Rose remembered that day when it seemed like her mother and Mamie were hiding something. She asked quietly, carefully, "Mamie. What happened? You can tell me."

Her sister hid her face, now twisted in anguish. Rose looked away, regretting pushing her to talk about it. Mamie was quiet for a few long minutes.

When Mamie finally looked up, her eyes emitted defiance, determination. "I am sick of this pain, this feeling that I've been helpless. I've kept it quiet, but why? Who was I protecting? You are right, I have to stop letting him win. So yes, Rose, do you want the truth?" She took a deep breath and wailed, "I had a baby in Regalbuto. I was..." Mamie choked, her hand sprang to her mouth to snap it closed, she couldn't say the word out loud.

Rose froze in disbelief. She slowly moved to sit next to her sister, cautiously. "It's okay, you don't have to say it, Mamie."

Mamie took a breath, her voice started to break. "Do you have...have any idea what I went through eleven years ago, when I was seventeen, on the road in Reg...Regalbuto? The fear, the pain..." She whimpered. "Then the loss, the idea that I would ruin our family a second time; first the fire in Pedara, and then that...that...scandal?" She paused, sobbing. She couldn't say the words she wanted to say. She shook her head and squeezed her eyes closed, attempting to stop her tears.

"Mamie, I am so sorry, this explains...all those nightmares you had. I'm so sorry. Please, if you don't want to talk anymore, it is okay."

Her sobs began to quiet but she continued shaking her head. "Nobody knows except Mother and Papa. Domenico does not know. Please Rose, don't tell anyone."

"But Mamie..." *Her husband doesn't even know.* Rose thought. *How can she keep such a secret from her own husband?* "I'm sorry I was frustrated with you all those nights with your nightmares. I didn't understand."

"The nightmares – do you think they will finally stop if I tell you everything? There are some things I probably will never be able to talk about, but maybe..."

"Mamie, yes, I think it could help to talk. Father Domo helps people all the time by talking. But first, you have to realize that you are safe now, the man you fear is part of that terrible memory, he is not part of your reality. Now, do you believe me? You can tell me more if you want to."

"Rose, I think I have to." Mamie repeated, desperate now to be done with the secret. She took a brave breath and began. "When my pregnancy was close to the end and I could no longer hide it, Papa had to act. He had to do it. There was no way I could have hidden what happened so Papa sent me away to the Russos' house. Do you remember that Rose?"

"Oh. Right, to watch their children and recuperate from your '*illness.*' I remember the night you got home."

"Wait, why did you say it like that?"

"Like what?"

"You said, '*illness,*' like you didn't believe that's why I was sent away back then. Rose, did you know? All this time I struggled with this, and you knew it all along? Rose, how could you? All this time..."

"No, I didn't know, Mamie, I mean, I was suspicious – but only much later – it was just a scenario that popped into my mind when the family was sent back to Sicily because of Mary's birth certificate. As if there was some secret hidden on the document. But I dismissed it, I didn't think it really could be true, I didn't want to believe it, I'm so sorry Mamie." Rose explained how guilty she felt about suspecting it in the first place. *But it is true. Mamie just admitted it, I can't believe it, my poor sister*, she thought, *both my sisters. Oh, how would Mary take this news about who she really is? I know I won't be the one to tell her, that is for sure.*

Mamie was so surprised by Rose's revelation; she lost her train of thought in the final part of her confession.

After a few moment of silence, Rose spoke first. "It's okay Mamie, you don't have to explain more. Family is family, and I never said anything or treated Mary any differently."

"Wait, what are you talking about Rose?"

"It's okay, I won't tell anyone. I remember Mama was so nervous about her own pregnancy, which is why she spent most of her time in bed when you were gone. I waited on her constantly. Then you came home that night. When I saw you both, Mama was lying in her bed, looking as happy and healthy as ever, holding a clean, beautiful, newborn girl. You, on the other hand, looked terrible. You went away to feel better, and I thought you came home looking worse. Then Papa told me to go back to sleep. I walked out to the hall, but I overheard you and Mama talking."

Mamie looked away, and Rose put her hand on her sister's. "Mamie, I am so sorry. I can't believe my worst thought is actually true." She explained. "I heard Mama say something that created my suspicion that she did not just have that baby. She said, '*now nurse the baby but no one must ever know*.' Mama faked her pregnancy and pretended your baby was our sister, Mary. Right?"

"Wait, what Rose?" Mamie gasped, confused. She exhaled a slow, "nooo," while shaking her head. She stared at her sister like a reprimanded child, frightened after being caught doing something wrong.

Rose interpreted it as admittance.

Concetta softly knocked at the door to ask if Rose and Mamie were going to be ready. Rose replied they would need a few more minutes.

Rose handed Mamie a handkerchief to wipe her face and gave her a smile of support. She was proud of her sister for facing her fears, and to a small degree, pleased with herself for her role in helping her sister face her past.

CHAPTER 36

Rose, 1912

July
New York

A year later the families found a way to move on – in a literal sense.

They moved out of the city. Giacomo and Rose found their perfect home in Brooklyn on Lloyd Court. Their sister, Concetta, and her new husband bought the house next door. Mamie and Domenico's new house was only about a block away.

There was a beautiful park and schools nearby. The bus to the train station was close, so Rose could visit the church easily, and Coney Island was also accessible so they could spend weekends at the beach. It was a perfect location. She hoped getting out of the city would improve her chances of becoming pregnant soon.

Rose stopped her work officially at Our Lady of Pompeii, but she planned to visit once a month to help Miss Canali with the heavy cleaning. Much of the immigration had slowed significantly, so Father Domo didn't need her help as much. Since Rose realized that becoming a nurse wasn't her calling, she decided she could help her husband by taking on some of his tailoring jobs. She began to sew dresses and collars for some of his customers, and she enjoyed the change. She thought that the change in workload might also help her chances of a baby.

But just as the excitement of the move reduced, and Rose felt like life was settling back down and she looked forward to the future again, Giacomo received a troubling letter from Sicily.

"What is it? Rose asked, seeing the concern on her husband's face.

"My sister writes that my father is not well. Rose, she is begging me to come to visit, it might be my last chance."

Rose shook her head, thinking, *why is it that whenever my family tries to move forward, something happens to set us back?*

"Then you should go, Giacomo."

"I would not go without you, Rose. But this house, how can we afford it right now?"

"We can borrow the passage money if we need to, this is important, we will figure it out."

In the next few weeks, Rose looked forward to the trip. She was sad about Giacomo's father being sick of course, but she was happy that she would have the chance to meet Giacomo's family for the first time. She was also excited to step on Sicilian soil again. It would be ten years since she left, so it will be sort of an anniversary – maybe she and her husband can rekindle their relationship, she thought.

Perhaps the trip will be fruitful; I am finally feeling hopeful again that our time will come.

Concetta is due in July, and Maria is due in October. Maybe I will be next.

CHAPTER 37

Rose, 1913

February
Caltagirone, Sicily

During their first month in Caltagirone, Rose and Giacomo spent as much time as possible with Giacomo's father and family. After he passed and the mourning period was over, they spent a few weeks rejuvenating their souls before they would head back to New York.

Rose enjoyed herself considerably in those weeks. She often remarked to Giacomo how different it was there than Pedara or Regalbuto. She loved how the streets were brimming with colorful ceramics everywhere she looked, it reminded her of arriving in New York for the first time and seeing all of the styles and fineries. She loved the art and felt immersed in pattern and beauty.

Giacomo's sisters, who had been sending letters to Giacomo so often, were wonderfully warm, welcoming Rose into their family officially, since they had not had the opportunity to meet in person before. Giacomo's mother, on the other hand, seemed quiet and reserved, watching Rose intently whenever Rose happened to glance in her direction.

It was the Sunday before they were to travel to visit Pedara again before they returned back to New York and the Sagone family had a large gathering in their honor, to wish them safe travels.

Rose couldn't believe the trip was coming to an end. She mentioned to one of Giacomo's sisters that she had one more thing she'd like to do before they left; she wanted to visit their church, Cattedrale di San Giuliano.

"Oh that would be a worthwhile stop, how nice."

"Well, yes, and I brought a copy of our marriage certificate. I would like for it to reside in the record books there, among the many other marriages in this family. Someday, someone will know we left for America, and we continued our lives there." Rose looked at Giacomo, but he was occupied, talking with his mother.

"That is a beautiful idea, Rose." Giacomo's sister replied. "How long has it been now that you and Giacomo have been married?"

Rose didn't have a chance to answer. Giacomo came over to tell her that his mother wished to speak with her. Rose was apprehensive. His mother hasn't said more than "*ciao*" to her for the entire time they've been visiting. Rose didn't think much of it before, she respected the grieving widow's space. But as the trip continued on, she still hadn't spoken with her – and now, Rose felt very awkward.

"Rose, please sit with me awhile. Let Giacomo visit with his sisters and let us talk."

Rose gave a strained smile. She wasn't sure how to interpret Giacomo's mother's demeanor.

"Rose, I would like to tell you something, it has to do with Giacomo. It has to do with when he was a child, and he doesn't know about it."

"Why tell me, then?" Rose asked her.

"You have a right to know. I never agreed with my husband's wishes to not tell our son the truth. But now that my husband is gone, God rest his soul..." she began, but Rose interjected.

"The truth? About what?" Rose was uneasy about the how the older woman's eyes kept drifting down to Rose's midsection.

"You are a beautiful girl; so wonderful to marry my son." His mother mumbled. "I am just sorry you won't have a family."

"Right, I know, not yet. It's been some time, but it will happen for us, I know it will. I haven't given up yet."

"No, my dear Rose." The older woman leaned in to whisper. "Giacomo had the mumps as a child. That takes all fertility away from a young boy."

"What?" Rose processed this, shocked.

Giacomo's mother looked displeased. "Please lower your voice, Rose."

She tried to compose herself. "Wait, so you are telling me he *cannot* have children? Does he know this? Why didn't he tell me?" She was confused.

"I am sorry. I do not know why his father wanted this kept from him. I suppose he wanted our son to still have a chance to find a wife and to be married. Maybe he didn't believe the doctors and still had hope. I don't know. We can't ever know."

Rose sat, stunned. Her eyes and her hands now on her own stomach.

"But you cannot tell him, Rose. He must never know. We must honor my dear husband's wishes that I would never tell him." Giacomo's mother reached for Rose's hand, apologetically.

Rose noticed her gesture but didn't react.

The older woman pulled her hand back again and muttered, "But my husband, God rest his soul, never asked me to promise that I wouldn't tell his wife."

ഇൗന

During the rest of our trip, I try to understand.

Giacomo is confused by my mood now, but I can't help it. It is so unfair. Unfair that Giacomo wasn't told the truth. I might have married someone else. Could I have? No, I was so in love. Or was I in love with the idea of love? It was all a lie. I can't ever create the life I want; I can't ever create a life. I will never be a mother.

We ride for hours to visit Pedara next. In complete silence. I can see Mount Etna now on the horizon.

The volcano and I are the same, heat and fury beneath a supposedly calm and cool mountaintop.

CHAPTER 38

Rose, 1916

April
New York

*T*here have now been nine babies in the last seven years in my family.

I am stuck. I am stuck in a life I did not plan to have.

We fight now. He knows I am disappointed.

I keep my promise to his mother, and I don't tell him what she told me. I don't know what good that does.

He tries to give me nice things, coats, dresses; I feel like they are pity gifts. I return them to the store.

We drift apart. Why shouldn't I tell him what his mother told me not to? She would never know I did. Why should I conspire to keep his hope alive, when mine has been destroyed? Why should I feed the delusion that the doctors could be wrong, and we could have a child? I doubt it will happen now, as we hardly spend any time together.

Oh, who cares anymore? Why does it matter? Dreams don't come true, what was I even thinking?

Maybe I should go back to Sicily, by myself, and start all over again. Why'd I even come to America? The language is clumsy; the volume of people here is overpowering. I am lost.

I regret these choices. This is not the destiny I had in mind.

CHAPTER 39

Rose, 1916

August
New York

S he shivered as a warm gust of wind hit her.

Mamie had a baby three months ago, six years after her last baby. She named her Mary, for Mama, but she said they would call her May. I guess time is healing her wounds; it is nice that she is moving on and forgetting her pain.

But when you're the one that has been forgotten, a day feels like a year, and nine years of an unfruitful marriage is an eternity.

It was a warm August morning and Rose went to the church to help Miss Canali with the monthly cleaning. She expected that the sights and sounds of the city would be a shock to visit again after living in a quiet neighborhood for the last five years, but she didn't even remember the walk there or the train ride, her mind was so clouded – it's like she drifted with the breeze.

At the doorway of the church, she took a deep breath before entering. "Oh.

Good morning, Miss Canali." Rose forced a small smile.

She greeted her old coworker and exchanged niceties. Miss Canali doesn't ask Rose what is wrong anymore. They began polishing in the sanctuary in silence.

Frank and Maria have two little girls and Maria is about to have another child. Long ago, Maria and I promised each other that we would have our babies at the same time so they would be the same ages. Maria held her end of the bargain; I don't know what I am going to do. I can't tell her the truth about Giacomo; I'm still so angry.

Miss Canali handed Rose a new rag since she didn't notice it was time to change it.

Maria is beginning to be impatient with me. She doesn't come right out and say that she can't understand why I am not conceiving, and she doesn't put pressure on me, but I feel it daily. A weight. A noose. She says 'perhaps you will get pregnant with this third baby match up. Third one's the charm.' All I can do is nod; I'm so sick of the charms.

"Mrs. Sagone, perhaps I should make us some tea." Miss Canali suggested, not waiting for an answer.

Rose noticed she was alone and stood to clean herself up.

Conception is happening all around me, not only to Frank and Maria, but my brothers and sisters have all started families too. In the nine years since Giacomo and I were married there have been fourteen children born.

Fourteen.

Domenico and Mamie have four now. Four. How is that fair? It's not. And I'm not even counting baby Vito that they lost, or 'our sister' Mary, who Mamie gave to Mama.

"Come, Rose, let's sit." Miss Canali guided, and Rose joined her.

"Ah, Rose, this windy weather of August; I feel it is a good trend arriving. We may be walking a path, and the gentle winds go unnoticed. The heavy winds get our attention, can blow things off course, or possibly push us in the direction we need to go. Do you feel it too, Rose?"

Rose nodded absentmindedly and sipped her tea. *Yes, I've been blown off course. Yes, my life is not going as I planned. But what does she mean that 'the wind can push me?'*

Miss Canali might have said more, but Rose was still processing.

I have tried to control my life direction for so long, is the wind like God speaking to me to let Him *do the controlling? Is that what she means?*

Miss Canali removed the tea set, and the women left the small kitchen.

"Rose, sometimes we cannot create the path we desire, we are just led to it. God uses all things, no one can ever know His plan." She said, as they resumed their polishing chores.

'No one can ever know.' The words rattled in the back of her mind like a stubborn spot that wouldn't buff out. She moved to a new area, left that one alone.

I guess there is one path to being a mother I have not allowed myself to explore yet. Perhaps I should. Adoption. Even at Our Lady of Pompeii there are many connections to orphanages.

We could adopt a child, there are so many that need a good home. I suppose it's still an option, but am I strong enough to love someone else's child as I should? That's a humiliating thought. It wouldn't be fair to the child if I can't be honest about that.

I have to figure something out. I want a baby. There's got to be a way. If I have to, I will make a way. Whatever the wind is doing, I am tired of waiting.

Something must happen soon.

CHAPTER 40

Rose, 1917

March
New York

Maria has her third baby. It's a boy. Born February 25, 1917. After two girls she now has a son. She names him Francesco Junior after his father. They call him Frank. He is dark haired, with dark lashes accentuating already inquisitive eyes.

Giacomo and I go to visit the baby. Maria whispers to me, 'it's your turn now, Rose, I just know it,' and I can't stand it anymore. The weight of keeping up a happy face for everyone is taking a toll. I can't go on like this. I am tired of waiting. There has to be a way.

I must make a way.

CHAPTER 41

Rose, 1917

April
New York

My sister Concetta has her second child. It is April 24, 1917. A beautiful dark-haired girl named Antoinette; they call her Nan. It is time to do something, but what?

It is now May.

Mamie is pregnant again.

Again.

I have waited long enough.

Today, it begins.

Tonight, I will cook a nice dinner and spend the evening with my husband.

Time to make amends.

ഇ)രു

It's just a week later, but I tell Giacomo that I have been feeling sick.

Nauseous. Morning sickness.

We are overjoyed.

'It is a miracle,' he says.

I say, 'where there is a will, there is a way.'

I'm just not sure what that way is quite yet.

ഇ)രു

A few months pass and it appears that I am growing more and more pregnant. It looks to everyone as though Mamie and I will be having our babies at the same time.

'Rose, how wonderful!' everyone says.

I say, 'yes, it is.' The flatness of my tone they attribute to pregnancy tiredness.

Mamie is my guide; I am her mirror.

When I notice that she is letting out her dresses, I fix mine.

When she is eating more for her baby, I do too.

PART 4

A seed doesn't grow in a day, it takes years. Would a seed have patience while it waits for its life to start? Then, once it becomes a fully grown tree, would it ever look back and remember what happened in those days, under the surface?

~ Zina

CHAPTER 42

Zina

Sunday, March 16, 1930

"Vincenza? Are you off the telephone yet? Gracie is here and she needs to see you." Her mother called for her as she was hanging up the phone after talking with Frank.

Zina walked into the living room where a worried Gracie stood, wringing her hands.

"What's wrong, Gracie?"

"I don't know Zina; she won't even get out of bed." She whispered, looking down.

"Who, Gracie?"

"Mother. There was a letter in the mail today. She took it with her into her room and she hasn't come out again."

"Is she sick? Or maybe it was some bad news?" Zina offered, unsure why

Gracie had to come tell her this.

"I don't know, Zina. This has been going on for some time. I don't think she is sick because sometimes she seems just like herself. Maybe the letter she got had some bad news, but how does that explain her crying all the time, even before today?" Gracie looked so worried now, so Zina led her to sit on the couch.

"She stops crying for a little bit and then starts up all over again, like in waves. Sometimes she sounds like she calls for my papa, and sometimes she yells your mother's name very angrily. Sometimes she tries to call for her parents. She pleads, 'let me keep him', or 'let me keep her.' Zina, she is not making any sense."

A tear slid down Gracie's face and Zina put her arm around her.

"Maybe my mother can come help her; talk to her?" Zina suggested.

"Josephine had that idea too, but it won't work. Mother won't see her. She doesn't want anyone, Zina." Gracie looked up at her cousin with a questioning glance from her red, wet eyes. "But she does call for you."

Zina was confused. "Me? Why would she call for me?" she asked with a shrug.

"Oh Zina, would you come with me? Maybe Mother will talk to you and then she can feel better and be herself again." Gracie looked so hopeful; Zina couldn't refuse.

Zina left quickly with Gracie for her house. Gracie told Zina just to head up the stairs to her mother's bedroom. Zina stood by the open door as Josephine, who was already at her mother's bedside, whispered to her that Zina had come. Zina looked everywhere but at her aunt Mamie. Seeing her in her bed was too uncomfortable and private. Zina's eyes wandered to a letter on Aunt Mamie's dresser next to the door.

It was in her mother's handwriting: on her mother's stationery.

Please stop.

Zina's heartbeat ramped up and she backed out into the hall.

The letter my mother wrote.

It was to Aunt Mamie? Aunt Mamie has been making my mother's life miserable? Aunt Mamie wants to undo something my mother has done? And this has to do with me? I don't understand, Aunt Mamie has never been anything but nice to me.

Zina was flustered, realizing that her mother was having a problem with her aunt Mamie and here she was, coming to her aunt Mamie's aid. She didn't even tell her mother she was going there. *What if they fight more now because I came? What if my mother gets mad at me because I am here?*

Josephine saw Zina at the door, and apologized on behalf of her mother, "Zina, maybe you can come back later. Mama is just going to rest now."

But Zina was already down the stairs, hand over her mouth, trying to hold in her emotions.

"Zina, what happened, are you okay?" Gracie called after her, but Zina didn't hear.

She ran most of the way home, her eyes blurred with tears.

A seed doesn't grow in a day, it takes years.

~ENTRY #12~

Today is 03-22-30 and the time is 3:23 (I did that on purpose)

My dear friend,

I gave it a week and now the air feels calmer. Last week I was upset about there being so many confusing secrets. But since then, Mother and Aunt Mamie haven't been around each other so maybe they forgave whatever happened and worked things out. I hope so. I still don't know what the note was all about, but maybe that's best. Sort of like when I find a loose yarn end in my granny circles. Everything can unravel easily so it's better to tuck it in than it is to pull on it. Maybe it's all over now.

I'm hoping winter is over too, it is especially nice outside today for the end of March. The crocuses are sprouting, the air holds just a hint of spring. I should take you outside soon, my dear friend.

Frank told me on the phone the other night that today is the last true palindrome of the year, 03-22-30, and I should expect something special to happen. What do you think it will be?

So, Frank came over early this morning, he had the day off from the barber shop, and he brought his little brother Vinny.

Nan, Frank, and I took Baby Vinny to the swings at the park around the corner. Nan brought her roller skates and went in circles around us on the pavement while Frank and I took turns pushing while talking. Vinny just pumped, soared, and giggled.

Frank asked me how school was, and I told him fine, and then I asked him how the barber shop was going, and he said fine. He doesn't much like having to sweep after the barbers on weekends, but he is learning more things about shaving and cleaning the instruments.

I've been doing a good job at keeping my thoughts at bay about sharing a future with him, but today I had a sense from him that he wanted to talk about something.

What do you think was really on his mind? Is he planning some sort of surprise for this 'Palindrome Day'? I didn't get to find out since he, his brother, and Nan all had to go back home after lunch. Now, the Bregas family is coming over tonight and Mother is probably going to need me in the kitchen.

So, I had to come and tell you, my dear friend, about the morning at the park before everyone comes over. Gracie might sleep over tonight so I won't have you to myself later. So, until next time,

~Zina

Sorry for this late post script, but I don't know what to do.

Oh, my dear friend, something is really wrong. I wish you could help. I need to talk to someone. Everyone around me has definitely been hiding something, just as I suspected.

In the after-dinner conversation, Josephine said something by mistake; angrily, accusingly. Nobody knew I could hear them. It had to do with something Mother wanted to keep a secret – from me, apparently. And when she realized I heard, oh, I've never seen Mother's face look that angry – not even when I asked her about a baby sister, this was way worse.

I will never joke again that "at least Mount Etna isn't erupting," because this felt <u>that</u> serious.

I don't know what to do. What should I do? I wish you could actually answer me.

Maybe I will just head downstairs and come right out and ask. They can't close me out of this conversation. They are all upset about something that involves me so don't I have a right to know what it is?

I'll let you know what I find out,

~Zina

CHAPTER 43

<u>Zina</u>

Saturday, March 22, 1930

Zina left her room and went downstairs about fifteen minutes after the commotion, squeezing Duey for moral support.

"Where is everyone, Duey?" She whispered.

She carried him outside to the front porch and looked around; it was deserted.

"Duey, what is going on? I go upstairs, come down again, and now everyone is gone."

She turned when she heard someone shout. "Zina, what in the world happened?"

Nan ran over.

"Oh, Nan, it's you. Did you see where everyone went?"

"Maybe to the Bregas' house? Zina, what happened? Everybody was yelling and running out of your house. I heard them and looked out my window – first Josephine, then Aunt Mamie, then your mother. Zina, your mother was crying and screaming, running after Aunt Mamie with a broom! Oh Zina, it had to be something awful."

Zina gasped, not realizing what went on after she retreated to her room. She didn't hear any of it; her blankets must've blocked the sound when she dove under them.

"Nan, something they said...and Mother," she cleared her throat, a lump rising. "She...so angry...then, everybody was yelling."

"It's okay Zina, take your time, breathe. Start again, what did they say?"

"The most peculiar thing after dinner...then Mother looked at me with such shock and anger. Then everyone was yelling. I ran up to my room and hid, I was so scared...not sure what was going on." She gulped and cleared her throat again. "Now I come down here and everyone is gone. What is happening Nan, what is going on?"

"Shh, my dear you are shaking. Calm down and tell me what you heard. Come on, sit down." Nan put her arm around Zina. They sat on the front porch with Duey curled up on Zina's lap: comfortable, yet clueless.

"Well," Zina took a breath and started, slowly. "I was cleaning in the kitchen after we finished eating, and Mother, Aunt Mamie, and Josephine were sitting at the dining table. The door between the rooms was closed while I stood at the sink drying the pans and spoons, just listening to their gossip, trying to be quiet. They typically get very involved in their conversations and don't pay attention to who is listening; it's all very interesting what I hear sometimes."

"Yeah, I know, I do that too. But then what happened? Must've been some good gossip?"

"Not gossip, I heard about a letter. Our Great Aunt Antonia Zappala died in Sicily, did you know about that, Nan?"

Nan shook her head. The girls made the sign of the cross which disrupted a snoozing Duey. They both reached out to quiet him, and Zina continued.

"So, they were talking about how she never had children. So, in her will, she left money to each of her nieces and nephews, like to my mom and to your mom, Aunt Mamie and all their other brothers and sisters. They are to divide the money amongst their children, like me and you. This is exciting news, to come into money; but sad too, yes, may she rest in peace."

The girls paused appropriately.

Zina started again, a little more calmly. "So, today when the Bregas family came to our house for dinner, I guess they decided to discuss that letter. I was excited to hear about the money, and I wasn't sure why they sounded mad. Nan, we are talking about three thousand dollars apiece! I was listening and dreaming about how I can use the money for my future life while I was drying the dishes. I heard Josephine say that the money would be a big help with her marriage plans."

"Okay, then what?"

"So, the door between the kitchen and dining room is closed, and they don't know I'm listening, right, and Josephine began talking more quietly about how it's not fair how much of the money *I* got. Why that mattered to her I couldn't figure out, so I started to pay closer attention. The kitchen door is pretty thin."

Nan nodded, agreeing.

"So did you realize, Nan, that the three thousand dollars each family is to get is for the entire family of children, not for each child. And I'm an only child."

Nan stared at Zina, understanding the issue of the math.

"Josephine spoke in a whisper, but I heard her loud and clear. She said, 'it's not fair. Just because she is *technically Rose's daughter*, she doesn't have to split her amount? There are seven of us and WE have to split it seven ways?'"

"Wait, what? What does that mean?" Nan was as confused as Zina.

"I don't know. I was looking straight at the door between us when Josephine burst through it, coming right toward me, saying 'Mother, she's one of US.' She stopped, held the door open, and they all saw me and knew that I had heard them. I felt caught, like *I* had done something wrong.

"Josephine immediately covered her mouth in horror, looked at me like I just appeared out of thin air, and then ran past me through the other door into the living room. Aunt Mamie got up and pulled the kitchen door closed again, as if nothing happened, as if someone was letting a draft into the dining room. She ignored me standing there staring at her while I was still holding the damp kitchen towel."

Zina began to sob quietly again. "I can still see my mother in my mind. She was facing the door, and facing me, her eyes wide and frozen in shock, staring right through me, like I was a ghost or something. Nan, her image remains burned in my mind even when the door separated us. I never saw that look on Mother's face before." Zina shuddered, choking back her tears.

"What did you do?"

"I felt like...I couldn't move. I stood at the kitchen sink and listened to them whispering, loudly, again. Aunt Mamie and Mother were obviously mad because they started using some Sicilian words we are not allowed to say and I couldn't understand any of it, it was so fast and overlapping, so it didn't matter that I could still hear them.

"Then they got much louder, and I heard things crashing around. That's when I left and went into my room." Zina began to shake again.

Nan patted and rubbed Zina's back.

"So, Zina, what I can understand from what Josephine said is that she doesn't think you should get the full amount when her family has to split it seven ways. Sure, that doesn't seem fair to me either. But I don't understand why she said you were 'one of them.' What did she mean? We are all cousins, yes, but why would that comment cause your mother and Aunt Mamie to fight like that?"

"Right, otherwise, everything else makes sense – your family will get three thousand dollars also, and you will divide it by three children. Josephine should be mad at you too, since you would also get more money than she would."

Nan shrugged.

Zina went back to the other part. "But then she said I was 'technically' Rose's daughter? Now what did *that* mean? Can I help that I am an only child? Goodness knows I have tried to ask for a sibling. After all these years of being lonely it actually seems like a nice gift to not have to share the money since I have not had anyone to share all the loneliness with."

Nan considered this.

Zina thought it all over some more. "Nan, I'm scared about why they were all so mad. I don't understand, but now I feel like everything has changed. Nothing can be undone or unsaid. What did I do to cause this?"

"Zina, you didn't do anything at all. We don't even really know what all this is about, let's go to Aunt Mamie's house and see if we can talk to someone."

Zina agreed and went upstairs to first put Duey back safely in her room.

 හ)ଓଃ

The girls heard arguing from their aunt Mamie's kitchen before they reached the front of her house. "How could you, Josephine? It was not for you to tell." Something made a thud noise. Rose scolded, then asked, "how did you even know?"

Josephine yelled back at the women. "Remember, I was eleven. I was there, on the other side of the door when the midwife was in Mama's room. Nothing happened the way it did when May was born two years before. I was confused, then I became suspicious. Then I figured it out. I'm not sorry Zina knows now; you should not have kept it from her." Josephine stormed out the front door, past the girls on the porch, without even noticing them.

The ladies continued. "She is mine, Mamie. I raised her for twelve years; you can't think that will change just because the secret is out?"

The girls heard Mamie sobbing. "I have always loved her, Rose. My heart has been empty for my baby."

Zina gasped, realizing now what they were saying. Nan put her arm around her cousin and Zina began to cry.

"Yes, well it is wrong of you to think that this means you have a claim on her now, Mamie." Rose said quietly.

The girls did not hear the rest of the ladies' conversation.

Zina sobbed and her shoulders shook so much that Nan couldn't keep her arm around her.

"How? How could they do this to you? This is insane. Zina, you should go in and talk to them, maybe it's all some crazy misunderstanding?"

"No, Nan, would you walk home with me? I...I have to go...I can't hear any more about this right now, please. Please."

"Sure, let's go."

CHAPTER 44

Mamie

Mamie slumped in her chair, defeated. All she could do now was to finally let her past catch up to her.

"She is not yours, Mamie. You should have moved on after Zina was born, like you did with your other baby." Rose whispered spitefully.

"What? How can you say that? How can you be so cruel? There was nothing we could do about that tiny boy. Nothing. Domenico and I still think about him-"

"No, that's not who I'm talking about, Mamie, I would never say that about little Vito, God rest his soul." Rose dismissed that line of thinking. "No. No more pretending Mamie."

Mamie looked questioningly at her sister, then relented. She stared out the window, motionless. "The other baby..." she barely whispered. "I wish I could have kept them both, Rose." She finally admitted, shrinking a little, like a deflated balloon.

Rose heard her sister's desperation, her pain. She felt bad for her, but she was in pain too. Josephine just ripped apart all the seams in Rose's hidden past. "But your other baby is always around, just like Zina, and you moved on and haven't tried to take *her* back from *Mama*."

"Oh Rose, I let you believe that for so long. It isn't true. I was scared to tell you the real truth, the pain and regret I have is so overwhelming, and I didn't want to think of it ever again. My other baby isn't around like Zina, and seeing Zina all the time – well, it makes me ache for my other baby too."

"So, wait. Your other baby isn't our sister, Mary?"

"No Rose, I had a baby boy. I had to leave him with the Russo family back in Sicily. Papa arranged the whole thing." Mamie finally admitted.

"What?" Rose, surprised and confused, muttered a mix of disjointed thoughts, "but...but that's how I had the idea to...and it wasn't even true? I believed that if Mama could fake...then so could I, and it's not even true?"

Mamie didn't hear her and continued quickly, like a dam bursting, finally getting out what she held back for so long. "When I had my baby and left him there with that family, they were overjoyed. They were very loving and so very happy. My head was glad, but my heart was broken. I went home with Papa only two days after his birth, they didn't even let me hold him." She sharply inhaled but continued, exhaling slowly as she released more of the story.

"And yes, of course Mother gave birth that night, it was all a coincidence." Mamie said. "I suppose I can see how you would think that Mother didn't have a baby at all. The midwife said it was the easiest birth she had ever seen."

"Right, right," Rose remembered. "I didn't even realize the midwife came over that night. I woke up because I heard the front door open and close when you and Papa got home. I went to Mama's room and saw..." Rose stopped there and thought for a second that maybe she should not ask her next question at all, but she had to know. "Mamie, did Mama say, '*now nurse the baby but no one must ever know*'? Why would she say that?"

Mamie took a deep breath and explained. "Mother was so happy because the midwife warned her that the birth may be difficult because of what she went through with Stella, or that the baby wouldn't survive. Did you know she lost a baby? Her name was Alfia. I overheard her talking one day about her." Mamie remembered the conversation in Regalbuto.

"Yes Mamie, I knew about Alfia and about Giovanna too. I remember all of the births, Mamie. I remember the conversation after Stella was born when Aunt Agatha said if Mother could no longer have children, she would no longer be important." Rose felt a sharp pain, that comment cut too close to her own worst fear.

Mamie remembered Rose's role of 'Nurse and Deputized Mother' and shook her head to not think about that now. "So, when Mother's baby was born the night I returned, she was very healthy and robust and Mother wanted her to stay that way. It hurt me so much to see her pretty baby girl when I knew my baby boy was far away and that I would never see him again.

"So, Mother asked me to be her wet nurse, Rose. That is what we had to keep quiet. I nursed the baby since Mother thought my milk would be healthier than hers. At first it was terrible, this substitute arrangement for the baby I couldn't keep. Then, I was happy for the time I got to spend with Mother's baby – until she thought I was getting too attached. Then, she made me stop; it was painful and difficult. I laid in bed, I had nightmares, my body tried to shake all the memories – all of them – for so many months after. Then came the day that Papa said we were leaving for America."

Rose just stared at her sister and thought about how Mamie had to leave that baby behind in Sicily. It made sense now that Josephine's birth certificate upset her, it was a record that she had only one other baby before, not two. This baby she had to give up wasn't counted. There was no corroborative evidence tying Mamie's life to her son's except for what she knew in her heart; that was the only place he was hers.

"I'm so sorry Mamie, I thought that our sister, Mary, was actually your baby. That you gave her to Mama, who pretended she just gave birth." Rose paused, gathering strength for her own confession. "That is how I got the idea to fake my own pregnancy when you had Vincenza. Mamie, I am so sorry, I'm sorry for what you went through and, well, for not being more sensitive in realizing how difficult this has all been for you. You've carried around such a weight."

"Yes, yes, Rose, so now do you see now how hard it is for me to let Zina go? And I see her every day, knowing she is mine, but I cannot be her mother."

"Wait, Mamie. Don't take that the wrong way, I am not reconsidering. You cannot think that." Rose's sympathy reversed back to anger again: anger that she let her guard down.

"I suppose I know that in my head, but my heart is stubborn, hopeful." Mamie was dejected.

"And selfish. Mamie, you are being selfish. You made some decisions that were selfless, yes, you gave away two of your children. But now that Vincenza is established in our home, in our family, as our child, you must think of her, what is right for her, and all who would be affected if you go back on this now. Selfish!"

Rose began to pound and throw things around the room, Mamie backed away and mumbled under her breath, *"I am selfish?* What about you, Rose? You couldn't have a child, so you schemed to take mine?" Mamie covered her mouth, holding back any other words from escaping, wishing those didn't.

Rose, in her ruckus, didn't hear the comment.

Mamie realized driving Rose away right now would damage what little relationship she does have with Zina. "Wait, Rose, I am sorry. I know what it is like to have a child taken from me, I realize that might be how you feel now. But no, I don't have to take her from you for me to be in her life. I can still be in her life, right Rose?"

"Mamie, you have been, and will always be in her life – you are *her aunt*. If that is what you mean then yes, that will not change. Anything more is not appropriate, and I won't allow it." Rose turned to leave, the words "you are her aunt" still echoing in her head.

She was partway home when she realized the full extent of that statement, how it was true and untrue at the same time, and she hoped she'd still be able to tell the difference.

CHAPTER 45

Zina

Sunday, March 23, 1930

Early the next morning, Zina's mother went outside to sit down with Zina on the front porch of their house, both of them looked like they were crying all night. "Vincenza, this does not change anything. You are my daughter, your Papa's daughter, we have always loved you, wanted you.."

"But I don't understand. How? Why? Why the lies?" Zina said, flustered.

"Would you have stayed with me?" her mother asked, quietly.

"What?"

"You were always hinting at how lonely you were, even asking me to have a brother or sister for you. I thought that if you had the chance to live with all of your siblings you would take it and leave us. I didn't want to lose you, and I don't want to lose you now."

"But you could've given me a choice and told me the truth, now I don't know what the truth is, you manipulated everyone. How do I know you are

329

not still lying? How many other times have you lied to me?"

"No, Vincenza, never. I am so sorry. I never actually thought of it as a lie, only a choice. Your papa and I tried for ten years to have a baby; we tried so desperately. The arrangement with your aunt Mamie was a choice we agreed to, and we just picked up with life like it was completely natural. Everyone was willing. Until recently when Mamie started to change her mind. But you see, we all chose it, it wasn't really a lie, just a little adjustment."

"Just a little adjustment? You are talking about me, a person, not a dress you pull apart to fit somebody else." Zina started to cry.

"Vincenza, I understand how you see this. I am so sorry to hurt you. We just wanted a baby so badly, we wanted YOU so badly, we couldn't see twelve years down the road to now – to how you would take it when you would find out. If I had my way, you would have never found out. But if I had to do it all over again, when you were born, I would do it all again to have you."

Zina got quiet and thought about the boy on the train who would choose to be a doctor but not a father – it felt like an empty future. She thought she, too, might be upset, maybe desperate, if she couldn't have a baby.

Her mother saw Zina's quietness as distance, and she began to sob. She hurried inside, leaving Zina before she really started to cry.

"Mother, wait." Zina yelled after her, but Gracie caught her attention.

Gracie stood on the sidewalk, looking at Zina, tears in her wide eyes but a big smile on her face. Zina forgot all about the sleepover they were supposed to have, and Zina was perplexed that Gracie looked more happy than disappointed. Her cousin ran up the porch steps, threw her arms around Zina, and squeezed.

"What Gracie? What? Is everything okay?"

"Oh, it's good! Oh, Zina!" She beamed with happiness. "Come home with me, Mama wants to talk to you."

Zina winced. Gracie gave Zina a small kiss on the cheek and took her hand. They walked in silence; Zina's heavy steps contrasted Gracie's skipping.

Gracie led her to their front porch, sat her down, and went inside to announce to her mother that her assignment was complete.

Mamie came out, took one look at Zina, fell to her knees and sobbed. "I need you to understand, I never meant to hurt you, Zina. It sounded so easy in the beginning, the whole arrangement, we'd all get what we wanted, and we'd still stay close, nothing would really be different.

"I always wanted you, missed you, cried for you. My family never felt complete because you weren't in the room with us; with all of my children. It is different to see you every day and not be able to tell you something as a mother; not treat you as a daughter, a sister to my children. It's been dreadful. And you are growing up to be such a beautiful young woman. I want to be in your life, hear your dreams and wishes, be with you every step of the way."

Zina didn't know how to respond. She couldn't bring herself to call her mother. "But how could you do it? Why me? How did you all keep this a secret?" Zina asked.

"Rose, um, your mother...um, it was shortly after your Aunt Concetta had Nan, and your Aunt Maria had Frank. I was pregnant, with you, at the time, and I thought it was wonderful that we were both pregnant at the same time, I didn't know she was faking it."

Zina listened intently.

"Then, it was one day in July of 1917, I remember the month since everything always seems to happen to me in July, Rose came over and our papa and mama were here. That's when the decision came to be." She explained. "I had just finished telling them that your uncle Domenico lost his job with the masons. America had entered the War in April and we had no income and a baby – you – on the way. We had a hard enough time feeding all six of us to begin with, and I was overwhelmed.

"I don't remember exactly what I said but she twisted my words to mean that I considered a baby to be a hardship and an inconvenience. She said I was being selfish, and she started to cry.

"I asked her what was wrong, I thought she was nervous about the War and the future of her baby too. But then she started crying uncontrollably. I stood behind her and put my hand on her shoulder as she sat in the chair, the closest I could get to hug her and reassure her that we would all be okay and help each other through with our new babies.

"That's when she admitted she was pretending. She wasn't sure why. She was not really pregnant. She was so desperate, so confused, that she somehow thought she could make it happen just by wanting it badly enough."

Zina blinked and looked away, not knowing about that side of her mother. She was sad to hear that she went through so much pain and anguish over wanting a child.

"I didn't know what to do so I prayed out loud, 'Dear God, my sister would like to be a mother, please, bless her. Bless my sister, Rose, with a child.'

"Our papa misunderstood my plea to God and saw a solution. He said, 'what a blessing I have in both my daughters! Praise God, my Mamie wishes to be an angel to my Rose.' He got up, squeezed my cheeks, and gave me a big kiss on the face. I was confused. Rose's sobs stopped. He said to me, 'you will have some freedom in-between children, and Rose will have one to raise. Beautiful.' Our mama stood to say something but sat back down again after a glance from our papa. Then he said, 'Mamie, if your child is a girl, she shall be Rose's daughter.'"

Zina looked up, trying to keep the tears in. She was shocked to hear how the decision was made. "Just like that? He told you to give me away and you just went along with it? How could you? You didn't fight to keep me? You didn't want me?"

Mamie stood and sat next to Zina. "Things were different then; I have always obeyed my papa. It wasn't something I questioned. And you should have seen Rose's eyes, full of hope. I hadn't seen my sister that happy since her wedding day. It was impossible for me to say no."

Zina shook her head. "I don't know what to think yet. But tell me the rest, you both appeared to be pregnant at the same time, what did you do? You couldn't both give birth."

"I asked the same thing to my papa since now we both were 'showing' in our 'pregnancies.' I asked him, 'what will people say?' and 'what if my husband doesn't agree?' That's when we talked about keeping this a secret, but your uncle Domenico had to know since you were his baby too."

Zina hadn't thought that far. Uncle Domino and...her Papa.

"Rose said she would tell Giacomo when she was ready, she wanted him to believe you were his. We had to say that our babies were born on the same day, but mine died in childbirth. I cried and shook my head no; I wasn't going to go through with it. I couldn't do that again."

"Again?" Zina asked.

Mamie covered up that slip, and corrected, "I couldn't do that, but Rose began to beg me. This solved everything for her. Our papa kept telling me to not think of this plan as a punishment, but as a loving act for my sister. He said, 'you love your sister, which is why you can let her know the joy and love of being a mother.'

"I asked if I would still get to see you, be a part of your life, and our papa promised for Rose, 'yes, we are family, Mamie, you will see her at all of the family gatherings, she will grow up alongside many, many cousins. But she will be Rose's child to raise the way she wishes to raise her.'

"Rose looked up at me with her teary eyes, so hopeful, so expectant, so desperate. I love my sister, Zina. So, I had to do this for her."

Zina's face was wet with tears, her mind was still brimming with questions. "But you didn't just do it for her, you gave me up because you couldn't afford me." Zina choked out the words.

"But that doesn't mean I didn't want you; I did. How would I know that the war would end nine months after you were born? It had already been going on in Europe for a few years. When the war was over, I did ask to have you back. I wished I could undo it, I cried so much, I begged her. But, oh Rose – she was so happy to have you. She wanted to erase the fact that I was your real mother, pretend that it never happened, make sure I could never get you back. So, she went to get your records fixed and legal, so I had no ties to you."

"What do you mean, fixed?"

Mamie considered downplaying it, realizing it was a detail that could go unmentioned, but she was tired of the secrets. "Oh, well, she found someone who could change the names. Have you ever seen it? Haven't you wondered why your baptism is dated a year later than your actual birth? Rose met with some man Maria knew from their barbershop connections. His daughter had a clerical job at an educational institute, their neighbor's son was an apprentice at a printing shop. Together they created a convincing document. She did everything she could to erase the fact that I ever had ties to you in the first place. If you ever do a paper trail it will always lead to her, no one will ever know I am your real mother."

"It's a fake?"

"Well, it's not fake now, it's filed legally, according to your aunt Maria. It just wasn't drawn up by the original midwife. Zina, the midwife had her reputation to protect, you know, she had to protect her job. Rose asked her to put 'Sagone' down when you were born but she knew me, delivered my other babies, so she wouldn't do that."

Other babies. Zina realized now she was one of many others – siblings. But the thought made her cry. "The others...and you didn't want ME. What was wrong with *me*? You kept all of your other children except for me."

Mamie gulped.

Zina struggled to get the words out, "Do you have any idea how often I cried and felt left out; how bored and lonely I've been? When all this time I had an entire family of siblings that belonged to me. But you didn't want me. You made it so *I* didn't belong. And you all lied about it too! Made my life a big secret, a big joke, and you were all in on it!" Zina couldn't stay any longer, she left the Bregas' house, crying uncontrollably now.

"Wait, Zina, please, wait!" Mamie shouted after her. Domenico was listening from inside the front door the entire time. He stepped out to grab his wife's arm to hold her back from running after the girl. She sobbed in his arms, "My Zina, my baby."

"Mamie, she'll need time. She has a new life; we have discussed this many times. We can know her, we can love her, but she is no longer ours. She is not your baby. When she is ready, she will be a part of our lives again. And with this new understanding, the secret now in the open, our relationship with her will be whatever she is ready for. You must be patient."

Gracie raced after Zina when she saw her leave. "Zina, but don't you see." Gracie caught up and turned her around to face her, smiling again.

"Did you know about this too, Gracie?" Zina spat.

"What? No, I just found out, like you. But isn't it wonderful news?" Gracie was still so happy.

"Gracie, everybody lied to me about who I am, how is that wonderful?"

"But, but, we are really sisters, Zina. I think that is wonderful." Gracie said with her head low, in a hurt and small voice that Zina didn't hear.

"I'm sorry, Gracie, I need to think. I can't feel happy that everyone lied about this. Don't you see? It's like getting a gift; and worse than having to give it back, it's like finding out it was stolen."

CHAPTER 46

Zina

Later, That Same Day

In response a frantic phone call from Rose, Maria traveled on the next subway to Brooklyn with Frank. They heard that Zina found out and how she found out.

On Zina's porch, they were surprised to find Gracie, who had been patiently waiting for Zina to be ready to talk with her.

"Hi Gracie, is your Aunt Rose inside? Where's Zina?" Maria asked.

Rose heard Maria's voice and came outside. She noticed Gracie and Frank and tried to remain composed in front of them while whispering to Maria. "Maria, it's a nightmare. What have I done? I didn't want her to ever know, but I also didn't want her to know like this. I've lost her, I've lost my baby."

Maria looked at Gracie again, more seriously. "Do you know where Zina is?"

Gracie hung her head. "I...I don't know. She was at my house a little while ago and left, she said she had to think. I don't know where she went, she didn't come back here yet."

"So where is she? Did she run away?" Maria continued to hide her worry while holding Rose upright.

Gracie just shrugged.

Frank said, "Wait, I think I know where Zina could have gone. I'll take you there."

Maria reassured Rose that Zina would be found and advised her to wait in case Zina returned home. "You too, Gracie." Gracie nodded, planning on waiting anyway.

Frank led his mother to the park and 'Aunt Etna.' Zina was there, as he suspected.

She looked at Maria with suspicion. She looked at Frank like he blasphemed their rock.

He left them to talk and went to the swings.

"Please go talk to your mother again, Zina." Maria said. "I understand that you may feel betrayed by this...situation, but she wanted it to be the truth so badly that now that the real truth has been told she, too, feels betrayed. She never wanted you to know. She feels guilty and embarrassed, and wants you to understand, wants to be close to you."

"I have never felt close to her." Zina admitted, sadly.

"Well, maybe now there is a chance for that to change. She always had the weight of guilt and feeling like she stole something – you, maybe she didn't get too close to you in case you'd be taken away, or that you would hate her when this day came. Maybe now, you can have a new relationship, a new bond, or at least a friendship?"

The word 'friendship' caused Zina to look over at Frank, swinging in circles. She was not ready to talk to him yet.

"Okay, I will talk to her." Zina conceded. She did always wish she could feel closer to her mother.

ℰᗡᑕᘔ

Zina headed home from the park, then walked in the backyard kitchen door.

Her mother sat at the same table, in the same chair, where all of this started just yesterday.

"Hello Mother. Aunt Maria said you'd want to talk." Zina said, coolly.

"Oh Vincenza." Rose stared out the window, eyes red and puffy, thoughts brimming over now that the tears had dried. "A lie is a terrible thing. To protect it, it has to be fed and watered. Then when it does grow it becomes such a burden, so enormous, like a tree, a terrible tree. One that sends its roots to destroy nearby foundations. One where the inside becomes hollow, the branches rip and grab everything in its way, pulling a nearby house down as it dies and falls. I don't know if you'll ever forgive me, but I suppose I am relieved you finally know. I feel free of such a terrible burden."

Zina considered this new tree, the burden. It was quite different from the growing and planting discussions she had with Frank. *Can a lie be like a tree? Like Frank's philosophies, a seed is the unseen part of the tree. I suppose the results of a lie can be unseen too, hidden. Then it can grow, like a tree, and become a burden instead of beautiful. The seed didn't know it would turn out like this, it just happened.* "You are talking like Frank now, with your trees." Zina mumbled under her breath.

"What did you say about Frank?" Rose looked at Zina with a twinkle in her

339

eye and a slight smile.

"Wait, did Frank know about this...all along? Did Aunt Maria? Has everyone been keeping this from me all this time?"

"Oh Zina, I don't want you to be upset. Of course, your aunt Mamie and uncle Domenico knew, and I guess Josephine somehow, but not everyone knew-"

Zina interrupted, not really hearing her answer. "Wait, so is this what all the phone calls were about?" Zina admitted to overhearing.

"You know about those? Yes, Mamie was calling me asking me to change my mind. She has mentioned it here and there over the years but for some reason, this year she has been more persistent. She's called me once each month after you started school in September, and then after New Years she would call weekly, sometimes daily. I had to talk to someone, and so I would call Maria."

"So Aunt Maria knew? What about Frank?" Zina braced herself.

"Yes, your aunt Maria knew from the beginning, I confided in her. So, when your aunt Mamie would call, it would upset me so much that I needed someone to talk to about it, so I would call your aunt Maria. That is how Frank found out – only recently; he overheard her talking to me, trying to calm me down. Maria said he confronted her about our calls, he was afraid for your safety, Vincenza. He didn't know what we were keeping from you. She had to tell him what it was about."

Zina recalled her recent conversations with Frank and saw them in the light that he knew this secret all along.

"Vincenza, I want you to know that he begged us to tell you. He wanted us to be considerate of your feelings, I just didn't know how to do it."

Zina couldn't hold back a dam of frustration. "I know that Mother, too well.

This has been the pattern of everything in my life. You and Papa haven't considered how I feel about anything; being an interpreter, taking the train to a school that I don't want to go to, and even teasing me about Frank. And now this — the biggest lie you can ever tell. You just keep making decisions you think are good for me, but they turn out to not be good at all. Can I please have a say about something in my life?"

"We can all talk about this tonight, when your papa-" Rose stopped suddenly when she saw him out the window. He was sitting under the tree in the backyard.

Zina noticed the change in her mother's face. "Wait. You didn't say if Papa knew about any of this." Zina said softly.

"He didn't. But he does now."

CHAPTER 47

Giacomo

Moments Later

Rose ducked under the low-lying branches and tentatively approached her husband. He sat on the ground with his back against the trunk. Dropping to her knees next to him, she mentally prepared herself to plead for his forgiveness.

She met his eyes for the first time in what could actually be years. The lines on his face were deeper, his eyes were red and wet.

"Oh Giacomo. I never wanted you to be hurt. I only wanted to have a child for us to love. I never meant for you to hear this, not this way. I was going to tell you when I thought the time was right, just not now. I wasn't ready to face all of this yet."

Giacomo looked at this stranger of a wife. "When would it have been the right time? You lied to me. To her. Am I a father? Who am I anymore?"

Rose gasped, covering her mouth. She realized she hadn't considered his feelings all this time. She stood and left quickly, sobbing; she was not ready.

Zina watched her mother leave, went to her papa, and sat down. "Papa?" She said, in a broken whisper.

He beheld his daughter with a wounded expression, as if he could crumble into dust at any moment. He reached for her hand, and she gave it, her touch was like glue that held him together. Fat tears escaped both their eyes.

"Shh, Zina, hearing you call me Papa has always been the reason I smile every day. Now, it lets me know maybe things don't have to change."

"No, they don't Papa, you're still my papa. How could Mother have kept this from you? I can't believe…"

"Oh, Zina my dear," he patted her hand and held it reassuringly before Zina's emotion could escalate. They sat together, deep in thought, until Giacomo came to a realization.

"I have been thinking, Zina. It was a shock for me to overhear this…this information yesterday, and all I have done is think about how I was betrayed. But I don't see it that way now."

Zina wiped her eyes with her free hand and listened.

"You have been my gift. Your mother has given me so much, even if I wasn't aware of the truth behind it. She has given me the chance to be your father. When she first told me she was pregnant I had no reason to disbelieve; you were the dream we've waited so long for, you were our miracle. Overhearing the truth yesterday doesn't change that."

He brought the back of Zina's hand to his lips for a small kiss. "Don't you see, my dear? You made us so happy just by being you. However you were brought in the world, you have given me the best twelve years; and I hope many, many more, of being your papa."

She leaned in, and they hugged.

"I was just thinking that I am actually glad I didn't know." He held his daughter at arm's length, to say it to her face, "Now I won't ever have to wonder if I'd love you as much if you were my own. I know. I would. Nothing could ever change that."

CHAPTER 48

Domenico

Domenico continued his attempts to console Mamie, talking privately in their room that evening. "We had to give up Zina. Remember? It was wartime and I did not have a job then."

"Domenico, there is something else. All of these emotions have stirred up more in my past that I have never told you. I need to tell you, and I might as well say it now. I am upset about Zina, so this won't be much more painful for me if you hate me about this too."

"I don't hate you about Zina, like I said, we had to do it."

"Well, Domenico, I had to do something else that I never told you about."

Domenico froze. Her tone in saying 'something else' made him think of a similar situation. The other baby. He had known this secret all along. He didn't really want her to tell him.

He knew it when she wasn't so shocked about the symptoms of first being pregnant. He knew it on their wedding night but didn't say anything. She seemed changed when he saw her at Ellis Island for the first time as a young woman, and he knew he still loved everything about her; her quiet strength, her determination to have a good and happy life in spite of what happened to her. He knew he still didn't deserve her.

Despite their age difference, no other woman had ever given him a second glance and he never had eyes for anyone else. She never questioned his past, what he was running from in Sicily, or his need to protect the identity of his sons. They grew together in trust with kindness, and that meant more than anything else.

He wouldn't go back on the promise his mother asked him to make in a letter she sent years ago — to never tell her. So, he told Mamie that he thought he knew what she wanted to say, and she didn't have to say it. To say it and hear it would devastate the both of them. Best to have a quiet understanding.

He told her it didn't matter what she had to do. They were married now for twenty-five years. She gave him a wonderful family and a beautiful life. Seven children. A life, a home. Nothing in the past would still harm them.

He gave her a hug and they stayed like that for a while until he felt her heartbeat slow, and she relaxed.

CHAPTER 49

Domenico, 1903

August 12
Mamie's Arrival Day in New York

H e reviewed his manifest for the day, there was only one family to escort from the immigration station. He stared at the name in disbelief.

I must tell Cardaci. Oh, where did I put that letter? The last letter Mother wrote me, the one where she told me about Domenica. I must read it again.

He snatched the letter from his desk drawer and ran out of his room, down the stairs, into Father Domo's office. Cardaci returned from Sicily again and was meeting this morning with Father Domo about more funding for the mission.

"Cardaci! It's Mamie!" He checked himself and toned down his enthusiasm. "Ahem, um, Domenica is arriving, here, in America. I am to escort her and her family from the docks, they are my assignment, she arrives today. Can you believe it?"

Cardaci and Father Domo looked at him, surprised that the calm, cool Domenico was so excited and almost giddy about a girl.

He looked back at the men with a new resolve, switching from elated to serious. There was more to tell. "Father, Cardaci, I have decided I will marry her, well, that is if she will have me."

"Domenico, really? How well do you really know this girl?" Cardaci cautioned.

"I know what I need to know." He held out the letter he received from his mother years back and let the men read it.

Regalbuto, Sicily, 1901

My son,

I hope in your heart you will forgive your childhood. I hope you will forgive your father for leaving us so soon, some days I still struggle with it. I hope you will forgive that I re-married. I pray that your life in America is as happy and free as your father and I have always wanted for you and for Angelo. I know that you will look after your little brother as you always have.

There is something I must tell you. There is one consolation to all of the pain that 'That Man,' as you call him, brought upon us, and I wish to tell you this secret. I do not know if you will happen to learn of it before this letter, but it will do me good to have this confession before I meet God. I do feel guilty in having a small amount of satisfaction for what this information could mean to Vince, although I believe it came with a great price to a young girl. A girl you know: Domenica Privitera.

After you left home for America in 1895, Vince went after you.

He must've been so frustrated that he could not find you after two years, so he returned to Sicily and lashed out violently in the last place he knew you were, the Privitera's store, in 1897. He was then sent to prison for the robbery, fire, and assault on the girl.

That family needed a fresh start, so through connections with Cousin Cardaci, in 1897 the Priviteras came to Regalbuto to help me and Angelo, and they became our good friends. Angelo left for America in 1898 and I know you both found each other because I was told by Domenica that she got a letter from you.

In 1900, Vince was released from prison. Here's where this story becomes hard to write to you about. Domenico, Vince met Domenica for the second time while she was on an errand that I requested. He was drunk. He was violent again, and this time with an even more terrible outcome.

A few months later we suspected Domenica was pregnant. The poor girl. That poor family, having to delay their trip to America, since originally, they planned to leave right about the time it happened. Even as I write this, they are trying to uphold their reputation, protect their daughter, and be discreet about the baby boy – born just a few months ago. The family sent Domenica away to live with relatives for the birth. I know all this because I had to help Cardaci and Domenica's father with the details. Domenica to left the baby with the relatives for them to raise as their own.

Domenico, these are good people. I regret that my decision to marry 'That Man,' has brought pain and suffering not only to *our family, but to theirs. I have wished and prayed that there would be a way I could right the wrongs he caused.*

And now, I have thought of a way, but it would involve you. My fear for Domenica is: what if he ruined her future? So, my son, if you could find it in your heart to marry this poor sweet girl, I know it will make the wrongs right. I am ashamed to admit that it is satisfying to know that Vince actually has a child in the world. His own flesh and blood, the baby Domenica had to give away is being raised without his knowledge of its existence. It may be cruel for me to have peace in that fact, but that is my own burden to face on judgement day. Let me be the one who carries the weight of those vengeful feelings.

I hope that you can see that what I am suggesting is a way to set things right again. You have my blessing to marry Domenica. It is my hope that you will consider this. I hope that you will be very happy and have many, many children together.

Your mother who has always loved you,

Guiseppa Timpanaro

The men were astonished. Domenico waited patiently for them to finish reading, remembering every word. *Every time I read Mother's letter,* he said to himself, *my heart aches. Domenica. 'That Man.' A child.*

"Cardaci, I decided a while ago that if I ever come face to face with Domenica again, I would look for a sign in her eyes. A sign that she doesn't blame me for what happened. I won't hesitate to tell her how I feel; and no, those feelings aren't there because I am being a dutiful son. No. I have not forgotten this young girl in all these years. She has left an impression on me that pulls at my heart. If I see that she remembers me fondly, well, I want to protect her, shield her, make her happy."

"Well, you will meet her again in a few hours and perhaps have your answer." Father Domo sensibly replied. He shook Domenico's hand, nodded to Cardaci, then left the room.

ଈୠଔ

Is this really happening?

I spot Mamie standing on the gangplank, waiting to disembark. My voice hoarse, trying to yell their last name over the crowds; I want her to see me.

I wait for the crowds to thin so I can make my way over to her. But what will she think of me?

Ah, finally. The crowds clear enough, and I can no longer wait. The father: we shake hands. Mamie: the shy glances. She remembers me. She smiles sweetly at her shoes.

She looks at me.

Oh, her eyes! Her soul is deep and sad, but she is trying to push through her pain. I know that look. I offer and she takes my arm.

Chills. Comfort, familiarity. Connectedness.

This is the moment. Life is going to be different now.

Would a seed have patience while it waits for its life to start?

~ENTRY 13~

3/29/30

My dear friend,

I've been a little distant lately and I'm sorry. I am still processing what all of this means and how my life is going to be different. I know who I really am now, but who am I supposed to be?

I am not Zina Sagone, I was given to the Sagones. Rose is not my mother, but my aunt, and my real mother is my aunt Mamie. My papa is not my father at all, yet he is the only one who has truly made me feel loved my whole life. He is hurting too.

I suppose I should be happy that I have the best of two different worlds. I have quiet solitude, and I have siblings. But having both doesn't seem as easy as it sounds. When do I do sibling things? When do I keep to myself? Who decides which occurs when? Do I just make it up as I go along?

My Bregas cousins are all my sisters and brothers. No wonder Josephine was angry about the money, I am one of them. I

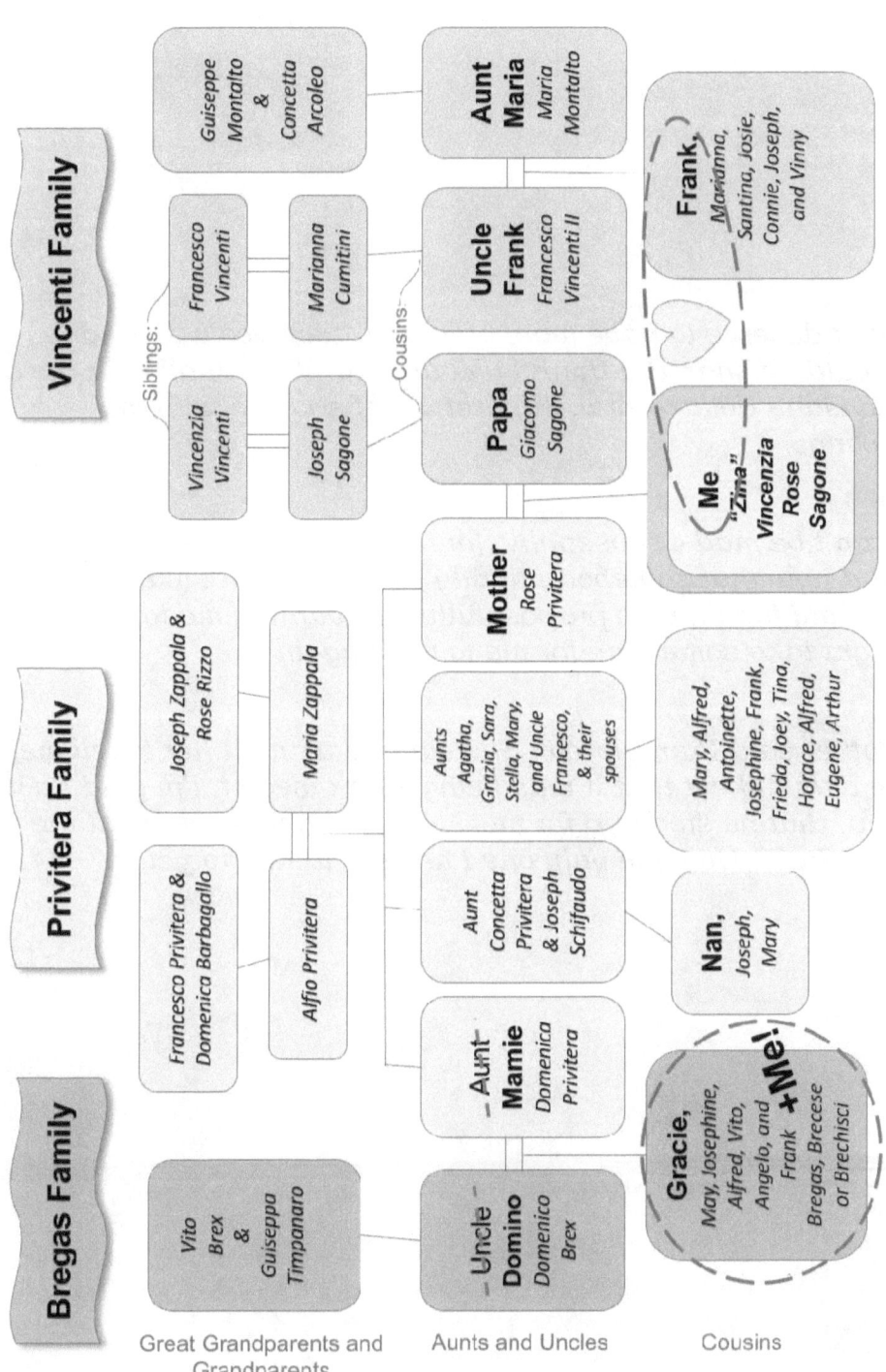

Vincenti Family

Guiseppe Montalto & Concetta Arcoleo

Francesco Vincenti

Marianna Cumitini

Vincenzia Vincenti

Joseph Sagone

Siblings:

Cousins:

Aunt Maria Maria Montalto

Uncle Frank Francesco Vincenti II

Papa Giacomo Sagone

Frank, Marianna, Santina, Josie, Connie, Joseph, and Vinny

Me "Zina" Vincenzia Rose Sagone

Privitera Family

Joseph Zappala & Rose Rizzo

Maria Zappala

Francesco Privitera & Domenica Barbagallo

Alfio Privitera

Mother Rose Privitera

Aunts Agatha, Grazia, Sara, Stella, Mary, and Uncle Francesco, & their spouses

Mary, Alfred, Antoinette, Josephine, Frank, Frieda, Joey, Tina, Horace, Alfred, Eugene, Arthur

Aunt Concetta Privitera & Joseph Schifaudo

Nan, Joseph, Mary

Aunt Mamie Domenica Privitera

Bregas Family

Vito Brex & Guiseppa Timpanaro

Uncle Domino Domenico Brex

Gracie, May, Josephine, Alfred, Vito, Angelo, and Frank **+Me!** Bregas, Brecese or Brechisci

Great Grandparents and Grandparents

Aunts and Uncles

Cousins

355

don't deserve to have more of it on a "technicality," and it should be shared. I think I will do that. We can all split the six thousand dollars total. My first act of sharing with my siblings.

I can't be mad at Josephine for disclosing this secret, I am glad now that somebody finally told me. I don't like the idea that my family was purposefully not wanting me to know, it might take some time for me to trust again.

Mother said Frank knew. She said he wanted her to tell me, he didn't like it that it was being kept a secret. I'm glad about that, that he stood up for me. He is going to meet me at the park later. He's the only one I haven't talked to yet.

~Zina

CHAPTER 50

Zina

Saturday, March 29, 1930

Zina found Frank sitting on their rock, walked over, and sat next to him.

He put his hand by his mouth, nervously trying to hide his smile to see her. "Ahem, well, I've been thinking. Zina, I know you are mad. I wanted our mothers to tell you. I'm sorry you found out the way you did, that was too abrupt, too sudden."

"They were all so angry, Frank. They were all wrapped up in their own feelings, nobody considered mine." Zina realized that wasn't completely true. "Well, except for you, thank you for that."

Frank cleared his throat and looked away. He looked at the tree above them, the swing set, and pretended to inspect the rock behind his legs more closely. He couldn't look directly at her; he was afraid of what his face would show. "So, um, will you be forgiving them soon?"

"Well Frank, it still hurts. How could they play with my life like this?" Disbelief washed over her again as her eyes dampened. She blinked to focus on his profile, his long dark lashes veiling his shy glances.

"Just think about it, Zina. Regardless of the choices they made, you still have the best of both worlds."

"What good is having the best of both worlds when it's all because of lies? It's like a stolen gift. You wouldn't call them generous, right?"

"But Zina..."

"Frank, they lied to me about who I am. My whole life. Twelve years. Did they ever think about me, about what *I* would want? I was never given a choice, they just did it." She couldn't help but spill all of her frustrations now; he did ask.

"They didn't know it would all lead to this, they had their reasons." Frank fidgeted; this conversation wasn't going the way that he had hoped.

"Yes, selfish reasons and not for my benefit. Maybe I'd understand if it was for my own good or something, but no, it was all about them, what they wanted." She stopped to clear her throat. "And now, where does this leave me? Where do I belong?" Her rant wound down and she was breathless, feeling exhausted. "Who am I, really?"

"Do you want to know?" Frank asked.

"Yes, please tell me." She pleaded, hoping for some revelation, some deeper explanation that would make sense of all the emotions she had been experiencing. The sun peeked out from behind the clouds and created a sort of halo around his head, she waited for it and...

"You are who you are, Zina."

She exhaled loudly, exasperated. "What?"

Abruptly he tapped the tip of her nose and hopped down off their rock like a gymnast off the pommel horse. He waved goodbye as he jogged to the sidewalk leading him back toward the bus stop as if they just had a conversation about the weather.

The sun retreated behind the clouds.

⅜⅛

"Can you believe him, Nan? 'I am who I am'?" Zina was pacing and breathing heavily, not a good thing for her easily irritated lungs.

Nan shook her head in solidarity. She sat on Zina's bed and pet Duey while Zina talked. She had been doing that a lot these last few days.

"So, he just touched my nose and left. What was that about? He has never done that to me, I've seen him do that with his younger sisters – did he mean to treat me like a kid?" Zina's throat tickle began to act up.

"Zina honey, you know I am on your side." Nan handed her a lemon drop from the nearby nightstand. "You are my favorite cousin and my best friend. I can't believe our family did this and I will help you to work it out. But I don't think Frank is the enemy here."

"I know, you're right, he's not. I'm just so frustrated and confused. I thought Frank might help me sort things out. He is usually good about seeing the bigger picture."

"So that was it? He didn't say anything more after your stolen present analogy?" Nan asked, surprised that Frank had so little to say.

"No. Then he said, 'maybe there was a good reason' and I started again, almost yelling. How could there be a good reason?"

Nan stared, not even blinking. "Oh, Zina. I'm so sorry." Nan was deflated too.

"I feel so betrayed. I don't know if I should feel happy about the news, after all, I have brothers and sisters now. Or am I supposed to feel sad about all those years of missing out. Why did Aunt Mamie not want me out of all the other kids? Why was *I* the one to be given away, she had May before me, she could've given her up, so why *me*?"

Nan consoled her. "Zina, you were given before anyone knew you. It's not anything you did or because of who you are at all, you have to know that."

"I'm not sure what I know anymore."

CHAPTER 51

Zina

Sunday, March 30, 1930, The Next Day

Zina couldn't stay in her room, or in her house for that matter. The quietness made it impossible for her to think and being reminded of all her lonely moments there made things worse. She thought the boulder at the park was a better alternative. Apparently, Gracie had the same idea.

"Hi Zina." Gracie saw Zina with 'Aunt Etna' and tentatively approached.

"Hi Gracie. I'm sorry for not wanting to talk much lately. Can we be friends again now?" Zina asked, sliding down from the rock and standing in front of her.

"No, Zina. Let's be sisters!" Gracie jumped up and gave her a big hug. She made Zina laugh for the first time in what felt like forever.

"You know, Zina, I've been thinking. All of my siblings have different last names. Some are spelled Bregas, some are Brechisci, or Brecese. We don't really know why that is, Mama says it's because the midwife spelled them wrong, but why only the boys names are different nobody can figure out, all the girls are spelled Bregas."

Zina looked at Gracie, trying to understand where she was going with this.

"So, the way I figure it," Gracie continued excitedly, "is that Sagone is just another way to spell Bregas. It's just what we do in our family."

Zina started to cry. "Thank you, Gracie."

"Ahem." Frank cleared his throat, embarrassed to witness all the hugging.

"Oh, I have to go!" Gracie let go of Zina and left quickly.

"Hi Zina." Frank said, shyly. He had so much he wanted to say to Zina now that she knew the truth, he didn't know where to start. Yesterday when he saw her, he lost his nerve. This time, he planned to stay until everything was said that needed to be said, finally.

"Hi Frank. Wait, before you say anything, I want you to know that I realize what you meant yesterday by 'I am who I am.' What my parents did doesn't change the person I am. Who calls me daughter doesn't mean I am different." Zina took a breath, gathering her composure.

Frank motioned for her to sit up on the rock, and then he joined her. He listened as she continued.

"I realize now they all made mistakes, but they are human. The decisions were for love, love for my mother and Papa to have a daughter of their own, love from Aunt Mamie and Uncle Domino because they thought I could be raised in a special way since I would be doted on singularly and lovingly, but never too far away. Aunt Mamie loves her sister, my mother. She wanted her to be a mother too; she made a beautiful sacrifice. It might take me a little time to mend relationships and know exactly how to behave with everyone now, we will all heal. But-" Zina paused.

"But what, Zina?"

"I can't just forgive what they did."

"Wait, what? Why not?"

"Well, what I mean to say is, I can't *just* forgive it." Zina gave him a slight smile. "You know how you tell me about the seed not knowing the tree it will be? It is like that. My mothers didn't know how their choices would work out, and we still don't know what the long-term effects will be on my life. But I think this moment in my life is like your crushed apple seed story, and I have two choices: to forgive or not forgive."

Frank smiled that she recalled the apples from her birthday.

"Also, I can work this situation into a new creation, right? Like how crocheting turns yarn into something beautiful."

Frank jumped off the rock, too excited to sit. "You are understanding the seen and unseen now, Zina!"

Zina was stunned by his outburst.

"Yes, you see one thing – like how you felt when you found out, but what is unseen is happening too – like how your mothers felt. And yes, you can choose how to move on with this knowledge."

Zina nodded.

"Here, I have a new one for you." Frank took a dime out of his pocket, with a flourish, like a magician would. "Look at this coin. It has two sides, right? A back and front. Just like there are two sides to the story, your mothers' side and your side, right? But there is another side."

"Um…" Zina paused, confused.

"The edge. The edge of the coin connects both sides together. The sides have to be held together by this edge. The edge is what you are understanding now. You can pick a side when you toss the coin in the air, and you always see the edge with either side you pick. One side is seen, and the other is unseen. You can't see both sides at the same time. Do you know what the edge is like in your situation, Zina?"

"Is the edge forgiveness?"

"Well, yes! The edge, or forgiveness, it is the connection between both sides."

"But why a coin, Frank? Doesn't everything have sides and an edge?"

He stood with his back to the boulder. "I chose a coin because its round, like a circle, and the edge is a line. And because it's a dime – the number ten is a line and circle too." Frank smiled with satisfaction.

"Oh right, the line and circle again." Zina chuckled. "Of course, like my ball of yarn and your apple peel."

"There is something to this, Zina. I will unlock it someday, it's like the secret of the universe."

"Ok, let's not go crazy. I understood the coin, let's not head off into outer space now."

"So, you're willing to forgive and forget?" Frank turned and shot a hopeful glance at Zina, sitting so prettily on the giant rock. He really wanted to steer the conversation to something else he had on his mind.

"Yes, I suppose I can eventually forget what they did. I can live now in the new knowledge. I have sisters and brothers. I have two sets of parents. I can be an only child whenever I want to be alone, although I think I will be having some swapping time with Gracie and May, let them have my bed a few nights and I'll sleep in their room some nights. Oh sisters, what a wonderful word!" She smiled widely for a brief second, then frowned, remembering when she asked her mother for a sibling, realizing now that the reaction she gave Zina could have been more about pain than anger.

"Is that all? Is there something still bothering you?"

Zina got quiet, slowly sliding down off the rock. "If my mother, Rose, wanted me so badly why doesn't she love me, Frank?"

"I don't know that she doesn't love you, I can't imagine anyone not loving you, Zina."

She looked down to smooth her dress and to hide the redness rising in her cheeks.

Frank decided it was finally time to tell her everything. "You know Zina, I've known you your entire life. You are special to me; it doesn't matter who your parents are or which house you grow up in. As far as I can see you are lucky to have siblings yet be an only child too. You can choose what you want to make of it."

Zina looked up at him, mesmerized by Frank's serious side.

"And you know, when we first met, my mother told me I was going to meet my baby cousin." Frank reminded Zina of the story they overheard. "I guess all of this means we aren't cousins anymore, huh. My father and your father are cousins, but if your father is not your real father, we aren't cousins."

She was quiet. Their mother's teasing made sense now.

"Do you realize then Zina, we only met *because* we were cousins? Or technically cousins? You see, this adoption arrangement brought us together. We would have never met otherwise. So, what you see now as having the best of both worlds has created the entire universe for us..." He paused to gather the nerve to finally say it, "...one where we might have a future together."

He turned to face her, and she looked up at him expectantly, yet again, but with a renewed hope as the realization was hitting them both. He held his hands out for hers and she gave them freely.

They stood staring into each other's eyes for what could have been a second, and perhaps that's all the time they needed to see a lifetime reveal itself. Their fates were set in motion by people and events well beyond what they could ever really know, like when a seed is planted. Now they have the opportunity to grow a future together. The twist that had always been a snag for them both, became untangled, loosened, and was now set straight to be worked into a beautiful new creation.

"I can tell you one thing about who you are, Zina."

"Yeah? Who is that Frank?"

"You are Zina. Because Vincenza Vincenti was too sing-songy and I didn't think you would like it; so, I renamed you early in life."

Zina inhaled sharply, surprisingly without coughing.

Then Frank, ever so sweetly, shifted his weight toward her, closer. She held her breath, expectantly.

The sun peeked out from behind the clouds and created a sort of halo around his head, illuminating his always perfectly trimmed and styled hair as if he was radiating enlightenment while the heavens hushed to hear.

What did he say? Did he kiss her? Was this a beautiful moment she would later capture in her journal? Did she tell Nan and Gracie about it? Did she tell her kids and grandkids about this moment and this day?

The day Frank declared that she was his and that's all that mattered.

Possibly.

We can't always see the tree the seed will be.

But...

...perhaps in a hundred years we can.

Zina with Giacomo and Rose Sagone about 1934

~ENTRY #14~

February 24, 1934, My 16th Birthday

My dear friend,

Things are better now; I am happy to say. My relationship with my family – all of my family – is much improved, and I have a really nice romance brewing with Frank! School stress is gone, since I am no longer in school, but I am working at the Peter and Polly Children's clothes factory. Frank and I are saving for our future. A tree doesn't grow in a day, remember?

I'd like to continue telling you about our life together in the days to come but being I'm now on the last of your pages, I will just record some important dates as they come up.

In case I never said it, <u>thank you,</u> my dear friend, for being such a good listener during those difficult and confusing moments in my life. You've helped me see the good come from the situation – like the seeds and trees. The seed was what I didn't know, that grew to be a tree. That tree produced fruit, and now Frank and I are planting countless new seeds together. For that, I am forever grateful,

~Zina

June 1935: Frank graduated as Valedictorian of Mineola High!

April 28, 1940: I am now Mrs. Frank Vincenti

August 1941: We are expecting our first child in a few weeks! Lots to prepare, no more time to write!

∞⁂

(P.S. I guess this would qualify as a PS, it is a very, very post script: 56 years later!)

May 19, 1990

My dear granddaughter,

This book really brings back memories – the days before and after I discovered the truth my entire family kept from me.

Sure, I have been able to forgive over the years, and most of the time I have forgotten it all together; because what does it matter anymore? What is done is done, right? I am who I am. And it all turned out for the best so why delve into this?

For understanding. That's why I'm giving this journal to you, Lee. You visited home from college with an assignment to write a memoir for a family member. You know that I only gave you the highlights when we talked, right? My life wasn't as rosy as I said it was. I'm sorry that I refused to show you my birth certificate, when you read this you will know why. I couldn't let you believe the lie.

The actual truth would never be found in any document, and it could never tell how I felt. It will never explain the circumstances around the decisions that shaped me – and your grandfather – into who we have become.

So here you have it. I am hoping that by reading what I wrote when I was eleven and twelve, you can see beyond the words – into the lives of all my parents. Maybe this way my future family can know them and know me a little better, even after we are gone.

So here you go, Lee. I will share the truth with you. Please tell everyone.

With love from your grandma,

~Zina

Author's Notes

About Zina

My grandma first told me her story when I was in college, and I had an assignment to write a biography for a family studies class. She told me about the adoption and how she felt "jipped" out of having a typical childhood with her brothers and sisters.

Years later, when my mother, Rose Lynn, and I started doing genealogy research, we realized that the entire story of the adoption would never be evident in the historical records since there was no paper trail that led Zina to Domenica, her birth mother. We knew the truth because we knew Zina and heard it directly from her. I found that to be a fascinating point and wanted her story to be told for her future family whom she will never meet. She died on December 9, 2008.

So, I began a journal myself. During the past fifteen years or so, I wrote bits and pieces, on a casual basis, of what I imagined Zina might have thought and felt when finding out such a secret was kept from her.

The real-life Zina I knew as grandma wasn't as expressive as I showed her as a 12-year-old, so through her journal entries I felt I was giving her permission to think all the things she might have but didn't relate to others – or have the words for. I think she has been smiling and laughing in heaven that I would spend so much time trying to figure her out and giving a loud "ha!" at all the details I imagined for her.

In my attempt to put all my journal thoughts together cohesively, I felt the need to explain the choices that led up to Zina's story – and that went back to her parents. All their stories started with a few facts from my mother's genealogy research. From birth, death, and marriage records I knew names, dates, and places from different points in time, I just needed to connect the dots. Of course, I've never met that generation, but with the help of some memories from my mother's older sister, Marietta, I formed some impressions of their personalities and imagined where, when, and how their perspective of the world may have been shaped.

About Frank

My grandpa once told me he always loved grandma, his whole life. Since they were babies, he thought she was the most beautiful girl in the world. He adored her for all the 90+ years they were alive together on this earth.

Frank was a barber and a hobby philosopher; he had grand ideas of how to explain the universe, breaking everything down to the elemental components of a line and circle. This was way before a binary code for a computer was conceived. He was a thinker, a noticer, a dreamer, and a believer in some cosmic power. He died on January 11, 2010. That is 01-11-10. I don't think it was a coincidence. The palindromes in this story were for you, Grandpa.

I hope that I have done his philosophies some justice in this story. Many of them I remember him trying to share with me in my young years as I would only half listen and think, "there grandpa goes again." He began to write philosophical essays about the origin of the universe and send them to me, hoping I would write his research into a new book, one that was relevant to a new generation.

He clipped a note to one draft which read, "Lee, someday you will write your own book." Grandpa, I'm not sure if you meant one "based on a true story" of your life and Grandma's, but you inspired me so many years ago to write – something. I'm grateful this little book has given me time with you and Grandma every day while writing it: to feel your love for each other and for all of us who knew you both.

I am proud to have finished the first draft in 2018. Achieving that goal meant a lot to me – a tribute one hundred years after Zina was born and one hundred years after Frank would have met her; it was my personal Vincent-ennial celebration of their lives.

The entire process of writing this book revolved around noticing details in my own memories of my grandparents that were most likely the most insignificant-seeming parts of life. Conversations, relationships, and choices are never insignificant. I hope everyone cherishes all the moments with those they love. You can't see the trees the seeds will be.

~Leslee Sambor

Acknowledgments

First, my grateful praise goes to God.

I would also like to thank my husband, Dave, who knew that I desperately needed to complete this book. He encouraged me to see it through, even to the point of taking me to Sicily so I could experience the towns and churches my great grandparents grew up in, touch their church doors, and feel a connection.

To my three (now adult) children, Jonathan, Jessica, and Jason, thank you for your patience all these years in listening to how my writing and editing process was going, and to Jessica, for reading the manuscript, suggesting edits, and helping me with the final cover touches.

A big thank you to my mom for listening to all my connecting-the-dot scenarios and telling me they were making a great story even when they didn't make sense yet. You allowed me to think I had a knack for seeing the life behind the dates and research we did and that gave me the desire to keep imagining this book.

Thank you to my sisters, cousins, and aunts who read through an early draft. The entire book has undergone a complete reorganization since then (many, many times), I hope you like it now, and I hope you feel the smiles from Grandma and Grandpa like I did while writing.

Thank you and *grazie* to my new friends and family in Sicily, especially to cousins Enza and Cristina – I was so happy to meet you over Facebook and elated to meet you both in person, along with your families – my new extended families. You all welcomed us with open arms, it was so magical and beautiful, an experience I never imagined could happen and will never forget. I can't wait to see you all again! Thank you also to Eszter and Alfred of *You, Me, and Sicily* for an amazing itinerary introducing us to the food, wine, towns, and especially Mount Etna. Your love of Sicily is contagious!

A special thank you to cousin, Sonia Alario who gifted me the beautiful art by her father-in-law and her husband. I can't explain how I felt when I saw these drawings for the first time, it was like the artists knew my heart and the story I wanted to tell. I knew I found the perfect artwork for this book. *Grazie mille!*

About the Artist

CALTAGIRONE 20 NOVEMBRE 2018

A Leslee,

My husband is an artist, like his father, I have the pleasure of giving you these works of art to leave you e memory of us.
With love
Sonia Alonis

Artist:
Giovanni Pitrolo Gentile
Cover art:
Exerpted from "Il guerriero" Olio su tela, 1993
Book plates:
"Le mele nerene"
"Citte` con budimo"
"Tulto il sopere per andora in cielo"
"L' arancia genitrice"
Chalcographic engravings, Caltagirone

Photo Gallery

Mamie about 1903

Domenico and Mamie on their wedding day, September 10, 1905

The entire Privitera family reunited in New York, December 1905

(Back L to R) Agatha, Concetta, Francesco, Rose, Mamie, Grazia
(Front L to R) Sarah, Maria Zappala, Mary (Baby Mary), Alfio Privitera,
Joseph,
Stella (sitting)

Giacomo and Rose Sagone around 1907

Rose and Giacomo Sagone on their wedding day, May 10, 1908

Zina in 1919

Zina and Giacomo, Lloyd Court, Brooklyn 1921

Nan and Zina in 1923

Zina in 1924

Frank's family around 1925

*(L to R) Maria Montalto, Josephine (Josie), Frank, Concettina (Connie),
Franceso Vincenti Sr, Marion (Marianna), Santa (Santina)*

Not pictured because they were born after the photo: Joseph and Vinny

Zina and Nan in 1935

Zina and her friends at a break from work at the Peter Polly Children's Clothing Factory (Zina is second from the left)

Frank at work at Frank's Barber Shop on Willis Avenue, Mineola NY, around 1937

(The door to the staircase leading to the apartments is in the right corner.)

Zina as a bridesmaid in 1937

Zina 1938

Middle row: Nan and Zina
Front row: Gracie and Mary (May)
Mardi Gras at Coney Island, 1939

Zina and Frank Vincenti on their wedding day, April 28, 1940

Zina on her honeymoon in Florida

Zina and her brothers (minus Alfred) and sisters in 1947

(L to R) Frank Brechisci, Zina, Gracie Bregas, Mary (May) Bregas, Joan-wife of Angelo, Angelo Brecese, Josephine Bregas, and Vito Bregas

Frank and Zina's children around 1949

(L to R) Cynthia, Rose Lynn, Marietta, Jimmy, Frankie